ABIR MUKHERJEE

PEGASUS CRIME
NEW YORK LONDON

A Rising Man

Pegasus Books Ltd
148 West 37th Street, 13th Floor
New York, NY 10018

ISBN: 978-1-68177-670-5

10 9 8 7 6 5 4

Printed in the United States of America
Distributed by Simon & Schuster

In loving memory of my father,
Satyendra Mohan Mukherjee

Calcutta seems full of 'rising men'.

RUDYARD KIPLING,
'CITY OF DREADFUL NIGHT'

ONE

Wednesday, 9 April 1919

At least he was well dressed. Black tie, tux, the works. If you're going to get yourself killed, you may as well look your best.

I coughed as the stench clawed at my throat. In a few hours the smell would be unbearable; strong enough to turn the stomach of a Calcutta fishmonger. I pulled out a packet of Capstans, tapped out a cigarette, lit it and inhaled, letting the sweet smoke purge my lungs. Death smells worse in the tropics. Most things do.

He'd been discovered by a skinny little *peon* out on his rounds. Almost scared the life out of the poor bugger. An hour later and he was still shaking. He'd found him lying in a dark dead-end alley, what the natives call a *gullee*: hemmed in on three sides by ramshackle buildings with the sky only visible if you craned your neck and looked straight up. The boy must have had good eyes to spot him in the gloom. Then again, he'd probably just followed his nose.

The body lay twisted, face up and half submerged in an open sewer. Throat cut, limbs at unnatural angles, and a large brown bloodstain on a starched white dress shirt. Some fingers were missing from one mangled hand and an eye had been pecked out of its socket – this final indignity the work of the hulking black crows who even now kept angry vigil from the rooftops above. All in all, not a very dignified end for a *burra sahib*.

Still, I'd seen worse.

Finally there was the note. A bloodstained scrap of paper, balled up and forced into his mouth like a cork in a bottle. That was an interesting touch, and a new one to me. When you think you've seen it all, it's nice to find that a killer can still surprise you.

A crowd of natives had gathered. A motley collection of gawkers, hawkers and housewives. They jostled and pushed ever closer, eager to catch a glimpse of the corpse. Word had spread quickly. It always does. Murder is good entertainment the world over, and here in Black Town you could sell tickets to see a dead *sahib*. I looked on as Digby barked at some native constables to set up a cordon. They in turn shouted at the crowd and foreign voices jeered and hurled insults back. The constables cursed, raised their bamboo *lathis* and struck out left and right, gradually forcing back the rabble.

The shirt clung to my back. Not yet nine o'clock but the heat was already oppressive, even in the shade of the alley. I knelt beside the body and patted it down. The inside breast pocket of the dinner jacket bulged and I reached in and pulled out the contents: a black leather wallet, some keys and loose change. I placed the keys and coins in an evidence bag and turned my attention to the wallet. It was old and soft and worn and had probably cost a fair amount when new. Inside, creased and dog eared from years of handling, a photograph of a woman. She looked young, in her twenties probably, wearing clothes whose style suggested the picture had been taken a while back. I turned it over. The words *Ferries & Sons, Sauchiehall St., Glasgow* were stamped on the reverse. I slipped it into my pocket. Otherwise the wallet was pretty much empty. No cash, no business cards, just a few receipts. Nothing to point to the man's identity. Closing it, I put it with the other items in the bag and then moved on to the ball of paper in the victim's mouth. I pulled at it gently, so as not to disturb the body any more than necessary. It came out easily. Good quality paper. Heavy, like the sort you find in an up-market hotel. I flattened it out. Three lines were scrawled on one side. Black ink. Eastern script.

I called to Digby. He was a lean, blond son of the empire; all military moustache and the air of one born to rule. He was also my subordinate, not that you could always tell. A ten-year veteran of the Imperial Police Force and, by his own reckoning at least, well versed in dealing with the natives. He came over, wiping the sweat from his palms on his tunic.

'Unusual for a *sahib* to be found murdered in this part of town,' he said.

'I'd have thought it unusual for a *sahib* to be found murdered *anywhere* in Calcutta.'

He shrugged. 'You'd be surprised, old boy.'

I handed him the scrap of paper. 'What do you make of this?'

He made a show of examining both sides before answering. 'Looks like Bengali to me . . . *sir.*'

He spat out the final word. It was understandable. Being passed over for promotion is never easy. Having that promotion taken by an outsider, fresh off the boat from London, probably made it worse. But that was his problem. Not mine.

'Can you read it?' I asked.

'Of course I can read it. It says: **"No more warnings. English blood will run in the streets. Quit India!"** '

He handed back the note. 'Looks like the work of terrorists,' he said. 'But this is bold, even for them.'

He was probably right, for all I knew, but I wanted facts before jumping to conclusions. And more importantly I didn't like his tone.

'I want a full search of the area,' I said. 'And I want to know who this is.'

'Oh, I know who this is,' he replied. 'His name's MacAuley. Alexander MacAuley. He's a big noise over at Writers'.'

'Where?'

Digby looked like he'd just swallowed something unpleasant. 'Writers' Building, *sir*, is the administrative seat of government for Bengal and a good part of the rest of India. MacAuley is, or rather was, one of the top men there. An aide to the Lieutenant Governor, no less. Makes it look even more like a political killing, doesn't it, old boy?'

'Just get on with the search,' I sighed.

'Yes, sir,' he replied, saluting. He surveyed the scene, and sought out a young native sergeant. The Indian was staring intently up at a window overlooking the alley. 'Sergeant Banerjee!' Digby shouted. 'Over here please.'

The Indian turned and snapped to attention, then hurried over and saluted.

'Captain Wyndham,' said Digby, 'may I present Sergeant Surrender-not Banerjee. He is, apparently, one of the finest new additions to His Majesty's Imperial Police Force and the first Indian to post in the top three in the entrance examinations.'

'Impressive,' I said, partly because it was, and partly because Digby's tone suggested he thought otherwise. The sergeant just looked embarrassed.

'He and his ilk,' continued Digby, 'are the fruits of this government's policy of increasing the number of natives in every branch of the administration, God help us.'

I turned to Banerjee. He was a thin, fine-featured little chap, with the sort of face that would look adolescent even in his forties. Not at all the mug you'd expect on a copper. He looked at once both

4

earnest and full of nerves, and his slick, black hair parted neatly on one side and round, steel-framed spectacles gave him a bookish air, more poet than policeman.

'Sergeant,' I said, 'I want a fingertip search implemented.'

'Of course, sir,' he replied in an accent straight off a Surrey golf course. He sounded more English than I did. 'Will there be anything else, sir?'

'Just one thing,' I said. 'What were you staring at up there?'

'I saw a woman, sir.' He blinked. 'She was watching us.'

'Banerjee,' said Digby, stabbing a thumb in the direction of the crowd, 'there are a hundred bloody people watching us.'

'Yes, sir, but this lady was scared. She froze when she saw me, then disappeared inside.'

'Okay,' I said. 'Once you've got the search underway, you and I will go over there and see if we can't have a chat with your lady friend.'

'I'm not sure that would be such a good idea, old boy,' said Digby. 'There are some things you should know about the natives and their customs. They can be very funny about us questioning their ladyfolk. You go barging over there to interrogate some woman and before you know it you'll have a riot on your hands. It might be better if I handled it.'

Banerjee squirmed.

Digby's face darkened. 'Is there something you wish to say, Sergeant?'

'No, sir,' said Banerjee apologetically. 'It's just that I don't think anyone will start a riot if we go in there.'

Digby's voice quivered. 'And what makes you so certain of that?'

'Well, sir,' said Banerjee, 'I'm fairly sure that house is a brothel.'

———

An hour later, Banerjee and I stood outside the entrance to number 47 Maniktollah Lane. It was a dilapidated two-storey building. If there was one thing Black Town wasn't short of it was dilapidated buildings. The whole place seemed to consist of these decaying, overcrowded dwellings, which crawled with humanity. Digby had made some remark about native squalor but the truth was they possessed a vibrant, wretched beauty not dissimilar to Whitechapel or Stepney.

The house had, at one time, been painted a cheerful bright blue, but the paint had long ago lost the battle against unrelenting sun and monsoon rain. Now only a few pale traces lingered, streaks of watery blue on mould-covered grey-green plaster a fading testimony to more prosperous times. In places the plaster had fallen away, exposing crumbling orange brickwork and weeds sprouted from cracks. Above, the remains of a balcony jutted out like broken teeth, its iron railings strangled by foliage.

The front door was little more than a few gnarled, ill-fitting planks. Here too the paint had faded, revealing dark, worm-eaten wood beneath.

Banerjee raised his *lathi* and rapped loudly.

No sound came from inside.

He looked at me.

I nodded.

He rapped on the door again. 'Police! Open up!'

Finally a muffled voice came from inside.

'*Aschee, aschee!* Wait!'

Sounds. Feet shuffling towards us; then someone fiddling with a padlock. The thin wooden door rattled and finally opened a crack. A shrivelled old native with a shock of untidy silver hair stood stooped like a question mark in front of us. Tanned skin, parchment thin, hung off his stick-like frame, so that he looked like some fragile

6

caged bird. The old man looked up at Banerjee and smiled a toothless grin.

'Ha, *Baba*, what do you want?'

Banerjee looked to me. 'Sir, it may be easier if I explain to him
in Bengali.'

I nodded.

Banerjee spoke but the old man appeared not to hear. The sergeant repeated himself, this time louder. The old man's thin brows
knit tightly together in confusion. Gradually his expression changed
and the smile returned. He disappeared and moments later the door
opened fully. '*Ashoon!*' he said to Banerjee and then, turning to me,
'Come, *sahib*. Come. Come!'

He led the way, shuffling down a long, darkened hallway, the
air cool and heavy with the scent of incense. We followed, our
boots echoing on polished marble. The interior was tasteful, almost
opulent, and a stark contrast to the building's shabby exterior. Like
walking through a Mile End doorway and finding yourself in a
Mayfair townhouse.

The old man stopped at the end of the corridor and ushered us
into a large, well-appointed drawing room. Elegant rococo sofas
were interspersed with oriental silk reclining cushions. On the far
wall, above a chaise longue upholstered in red velvet, a bejewel-
led Indian prince on a white charger stared out stoically from a
framed painting. A large green *punkah*, the size of a dining table,
hung stiffly from the ceiling and light streamed in from a courtyard
outside.

The old man gestured for us to wait, then quietly disappeared.

A clock ticked in another room. I was glad for the respite.
It had been over a week, but it still felt like I was acclimatising.
It wasn't just the heat. There was something more. Something
amorphous and indefinable. A nervousness that manifested itself

as an ache at the back of my head and a queasiness in the pit of my stomach. Calcutta itself seemed to be taking its toll on me.

A few minutes later, the door opened and a middle-aged Indian woman entered, the old man following behind her like a faithful pet. Banerjee and I stood up. The woman was handsome for her age. Twenty years ago she'd have been considered a beauty. A full figure, coffee-coloured skin and brown eyes tinged with *kohl*. Her hair was parted in the middle and tied tightly in a bun. On her forehead a smudge of vermillion. She wore a bright green silk sari, its border embroidered with golden birds. Beneath it a blouse of green silk above a bare midriff. Her arms were adorned with several golden bangles and from her neck hung an ornate gold necklace, studded with small green stones.

'*Namaskar*, gentlemen,' she said, pressing her hands together in greeting. Her bangles clinked softly. 'Please sit.'

I shot Banerjee an enquiring look. Was this the woman he'd seen at the window? He shook his head.

She introduced herself as Mrs Bose, the owner of the house.

'My manservant tells me you have some questions?'

She walked over and reclined elegantly on the chaise longue. As if on cue, the *punkah* on the ceiling started swaying, delivering a welcome staccato breeze. Mrs Bose pressed a small brass button on the wall next to her. A maid appeared silently at the door.

'You will have some tea, yes?' Mrs Bose enquired. Without waiting for a reply, she turned to the maid and ordered.

'*Meena, cha.*'

The maid left as silently as she'd arrived.

'Now,' continued Mrs Bose, 'how can I help you, gentlemen?'

'My name is Captain Wyndham,' I said, 'and this is Sergeant Banerjee. I take it you're aware that there has been an incident in the alley next door?'

She smiled politely. 'From the noise your constables are making, I should think the whole *para* is aware that there has been "an incident", as you call it. Perhaps you could enlighten me as to what's actually happened?'

'A man has been murdered.'

'Murdered?' she said, deadpan. 'How very shocking.'

I'd seen English women need a dose of smelling salts at the mere mention of murder, but Mrs Bose seemed made of stronger stuff.

'Forgive me, gentlemen,' she went on, 'but people are killed in this part of the city every day. I don't remember ever seeing half the Calcutta police force turn up and close down a street before, let alone an English officer take an interest. Normally, the unfortunate wretch is simply carted off to the morgue and that's the end of it. Why all the fuss this time?'

The *fuss* was because it was an Englishman who'd been murdered. But I got the sense she already knew that.

'I need to ask you, madam, did you see or hear anything untoward in the alley last night?'

She shook her head. 'I hear untoward noises coming from that alley every night. Drunkards fighting, dogs howling, but if you're asking if I heard a man being murdered, then the answer is *no*.'

Her answer was emphatic, which struck me as odd. In my experience, middle-class, middle-aged women were generally all too keen to help in a murder investigation. It added excitement to their lives. Some were so zealous in their wish to be of assistance that they'd happily recount gossip and hearsay as if it were the Gospel of St John. Her behaviour didn't seem normal for a woman who'd just been informed of a murder ten feet from her home. I suspected she was hiding something. But that didn't necessarily mean it was related to the murder. The authorities had banned so many things

recently that it was perfectly possible she was covering up something completely different.

'Have there been any gatherings in the neighbourhood that may
have been of a seditious nature?' I asked.

She looked at me like I was a particularly slow child. 'Quite possibly, Captain. This is Calcutta, after all. A city of a million Bengalis
with nothing better to do than talk revolution. Isn't that why you
moved the capital to Delhi? Better to roast up there in a desert
backwater surrounded by pliant Punjabis than put up with such
dangerous Bengali rabble rousers. Not that they actually do much
other than *talk*. But to answer your question, *no*, I am not aware of
any gatherings of a seditious nature. Nothing that would contravene
the articles of your precious Rowlatt Acts.'

The Rowlatt Acts. They'd been passed the previous month
and allowed us to lock up anyone we suspected of terrorism or
revolutionary activities. We could hold them for up to two years
without trial. From a copper's perspective, it made things nice and
simple. The Indians, of course, had reacted with fury, and I can't
say I blamed them. After all, we'd just fought a war in the name
of liberty, and yet here we were, arresting people without war-
rants, and locking them up for anything we considered seditious,
from gathering without a permit to staring at an Englishman the
wrong way.

Mrs Bose rose. 'I'm sorry, gentlemen, I really can't help you.'

It was time to try a different approach.

'You might wish to reconsider, Mrs Bose,' I said. 'The sergeant
here has voiced a suspicion as to exactly what sort of an establishment you may be running here. Obviously I think he's mistaken, but
I can have a team of ten officers from the vice division down here
in less than thirty minutes to find out which of us is right. I expect
they'd tear this place apart and maybe haul you over to Lal Bazar

for questioning. They might even suggest you spend a night or two in the cells, at the Viceroy's pleasure, so to speak . . . Or you could afford us some cooperation.'

She looked at me and smiled. She didn't seem intimidated, which was surprising. However, she chose her next words carefully. 'Captain Wyndham, I think there has been some . . . misunderstanding. I am perfectly happy to help you in any way I can. But I honestly didn't see or hear anything untoward last night.'

'In that case,' I said, 'you won't mind us questioning anyone else who was in the house at the time?'

The door opened and the maid entered with a silver tray upon which sat all the paraphernalia associated with middle-class tea making. She set it down on a small mahogany table beside her mistress and left the room.

Mrs Bose lifted the teapot and an elegant silver tea strainer and poured the tea into three cups. 'Of course, Captain,' she said finally, 'you may speak to whomever you wish.'

Once more she pressed the brass button on the wall and the maid returned. Foreign words were exchanged and she disappeared again.

Mrs Bose turned to me. 'So tell me, Captain, you're clearly new to India. How long have you been here?'

'I hadn't realised it was quite that obvious.'

Mrs Bose smiled. 'Oh, but it is. Firstly, your face is that interesting shade of pink, which suggests you haven't yet learned that most important lesson of life here: that you should stay indoors between the hours of noon and four. Secondly, you haven't yet acquired the swagger that your kinsmen tend to display in this country when dealing with Indians.'

'I'm sorry to disappoint you,' I said

'Don't be,' she replied casually. 'I am sure it is only a matter of time.'

Before I could respond, the door opened and four slim young girls entered the room, followed by the maid and the old man who had shown us in. The girls looked dishevelled, as though they'd been roused from sleep. In contrast to Mrs Bose, none of them wore make-up, but all possessed a natural beauty. Each wore a simple cotton sari, in various pastel colours.

'Captain Wyndham,' said Mrs Bose, 'allow me to introduce my household to you.' She gestured towards the old man. 'Ratan, you have already met. And of course Meena, my maid. These others are Saraswati, Lakshmi, Devi and Sita.' At the mention of her name, each girl steepled her hands together in greeting. They appeared nervous. That was to be expected. Most young prostitutes in London were also nervous when questioned by an officer of the law. Most, but by no means all.

'Not everyone in my household speaks English,' Mrs Bose continued. 'You don't mind if I translate your questions into Hindi?'

'Why Hindi and not Bengali?' I asked.

'Because, Captain, while Calcutta is the capital of Bengal, a great many people here are not Bengali. Sita here is from Orissa and Lakshmi is from Bihar. Hindi is, shall we say, the lingua franca.' She smiled, amused by her own turn of phrase, and gestured towards Banerjee. 'I take it your sergeant here speaks Hindi?'

I looked at him.

'My Hindi is fairly rusty, sir,' he replied, 'but passable.'

'Very well then, Mrs Bose,' I said, 'please ask them if they saw or heard any disturbance in the alley last night.'

Mrs Bose put the question to them. The old man appeared not to hear and so she repeated her words more loudly. I looked at Banerjee. He was staring fixedly at Devi.

One by one, each of them replied '*Nahin*'.

I wasn't convinced. 'Seven people in the house last night and none of you saw or heard anything?'

'Apparently not,' said Mrs Bose.

I considered them in turn. Ratan, the old man, was probably too deaf to have heard a thing. The maid, Meena, might have, but her body language didn't suggest she was hiding anything. Mrs Bose was too smart to let anything slip. A woman in her line of work quickly learns how to deal with inconvenient enquiries from the police. The four girls, though. They would have been up most of the night with clients. One of them may have seen something. If so, they'd probably be less adept than Mrs Bose at concealing it from me.

I turned to Banerjee. 'Sergeant, please repeat the question to each of the four girls in turn.'

He did as I asked. I watched the girls as they replied. Saraswati and Lakshmi both answered '*Nahin*'. Devi hesitated for a second, averted her gaze, but then also answered '*Nahin*'. The hesitation was all I needed.

Banerjee proceeded to ask the final girl the same question. She gave the same reply, but I detected no signs of subterfuge. Devi was the one we needed to talk to. But not now, and not here. We'd have to speak to her alone.

'Unfortunately, it seems we cannot help you, Captain,' said Mrs Bose.

'It would appear so,' I replied, rising from the sofa. Banerjee followed my lead. If Mrs Bose was relieved, she hid it well. Calm as a lotus on a lake. I made a final attempt to unsettle her. 'Just one last question, if I may?'

'Of course, Captain.'

'Where is Mr Bose?'

She smiled playfully. 'Come now, Captain. You must realise that in my profession it is sometimes necessary to cultivate
a certain image of respectability. I find that having a husband,
though he is never present, helps to smooth out some of life's
little problems.'

———

We left the house and returned to the blazing heat. The body was
still there, covered by a dirty tarpaulin. It should have been moved
by now. I searched for Digby but couldn't see him.

The alley was a furnace, not that it had much effect on the crowd,
which if anything had grown larger. They packed themselves together,
tight under large black umbrellas. Everyone in Calcutta seems to
carry an umbrella, though more for shade than shelter. I made a
mental note to follow Mrs Bose's advice and be indoors by noon.

From a distance came the sound of a horn and through the
narrow, crowded street an olive-green ambulance truck threaded its
way towards us. In front of it, a constable on a bicycle was shouting
for the crowd to clear the way. On reaching the cordon, he dis-
mounted, leaned his bicycle against a wall and briskly made his way
over to me.

He saluted. 'Captain Wyndham, sir?'

I nodded.

'I have a message for you, sir. Your presence is requested immediately by Commissioner Taggart.'

Lord Charles Taggart, Commissioner of Police. He was the
reason I was in Bengal.

I thanked the constable, who headed back towards his bicycle.
By now, the ambulance had stopped at the cordon and two Indian
orderlies had got out. They spoke to Banerjee, then lifted the body
onto a stretcher and loaded it into the ambulance.

I again searched for Digby but couldn't see him anywhere, so instead I asked Banerjee to join me as I headed back to the car parked at the entrance to the alley. The driver, a large turbaned Sikh, saluted, then opened the rear door.

We negotiated the narrow, congested streets of Black Town, the driver leaning on his horn and shouting threats at the pedestrians, rickshaws and bullock carts in our path. I turned to Banerjee. 'How'd you know that house was a brothel, Sergeant?'

He smiled shyly. 'I asked a few of the locals in the crowd about the surrounding buildings. One woman was more than happy to tell me about the goings-on at number 47.'

'And our Mrs Bose? What did you make of her?'

'Interesting, sir. She's certainly no admirer of the British.'

He was right. But that didn't mean she was involved. She was a businesswoman, after all, and in my experience people like her had little time for politics. Unless it boosted profits, of course.

'And the woman you saw at the window?'

'It was the one she called Devi.'

'You don't think it was her real name?'

'It's possible sir, but *Devi* means *goddess*, and the other three all had the names of Hindu goddesses. I think that's too much of a coincidence. And I understand it's not unusual for such girls to work under aliases.'

'True enough, Sergeant,' I said, adding drily, 'I congratulate you on your knowledge of whores.'

The young man's ears reddened.

'So,' I continued, 'do you think she saw something?'

'She denied it, sir.'

'Yes, but what do *you* think?'

'I think she's lying and, if I may venture an opinion, sir, I think you do too. What I don't understand is why you didn't question her further?'

'Patience, Sergeant,' I said. 'There's a time and a place for everything.'

———

By now we were on the Chitpore road, on the outskirts of White Town. Wide avenues bordered by imposing mansions: the homes of merchant princes made rich from trade in everything from cotton to opium.

'Unusual name, "Surrender-not",' I said.

'It's not actually my name, sir,' replied Banerjee. 'My real name is "Surendranath". It's one of the names of Lord Indra, the king of the gods. Unfortunately Sub-inspector Digby found the pronunciation beyond him, so he christened me "Surrender-not".'

'And what do you think of that, Sergeant?'

Banerjee fidgeted in his seat. 'I've been called worse things, sir. Given the natural inability of many of your countrymen to pronounce any foreign name with more than one syllable, "Surrender-not" isn't too bad.'

We travelled in silence for a while, but that soon became uncomfortable. Besides, I wanted to get to know this young man better, as, other than servants and petty officials, he was pretty much the first *real* Indian I'd met since arriving here. So I asked him about himself.

'I spent my childhood in Shyambazar,' he told me. 'Then boarding school and university in England.'

His father was a Calcutta barrister who'd sent each of his three sons to England to be educated: Harrow, then Oxbridge. Banerjee was the youngest. Of his elder brothers, one had followed his father into the law and been called to the Bar at Lincoln's Inn. The other was a physician of some renown. As for Banerjee, his father had wanted him to pursue a career in the Indian Civil Service, the legendary ICS, but despite the prestige, the young man didn't fancy spending his days as a pen-pusher. He decided to join the police force instead.

'What did your father make of that?' I asked.

'He's not too happy about it,' he replied. 'He's a supporter of the struggle for Home Rule. He thinks by joining the Imperial Police Force, I'm assisting the British in the abasement of my own people.'

'And what do you think?'

Banerjee reflected for a moment before replying. 'I think, sir, that one day we may indeed have Home Rule. Or the British may leave completely. Either way, I'm quite sure that such an event won't herald the outbreak of universal peace and goodwill among my countrymen, despite what Mr Gandhi may think. There will still be murders in India. If and when you depart, sir, we Indians will need the skills to manage the posts you'll be vacating. That goes for law enforcement as much as anything else.'

It wasn't exactly the ringing endorsement of empire I'd expected from a policeman. As an Englishman, one rather assumes that the natives are either for you or against you, and that the ones employed by the Imperial Police Force must be amongst the most loyal. After all, they uphold the system. That at least one of them might be somewhat ambivalent came as a shock.

I confess, my first week in Calcutta had brought with it more than a degree of unease. I'd met Indians before, I'd even fought alongside some of them during the war. I remembered Ypres in 1915, the suicidal counter-attack ordered by our generals at some lamentable little village called Langemarck. The sepoys of the 3rd Lahore Division, Sikhs and Pathans mainly, had charged on without hope of success and were mown down before ever catching sight of the Boche positions. They'd died bravely. Now, here in Calcutta, it was disturbing to see the way we treated their kinsfolk in their own land.

'And you, sir?' asked Banerjee. 'What brings you to Calcutta?'

I was silent.

What could I tell him?

That I'd survived a war that had killed my brother and my friends? That I'd been wounded and shipped home, only to find that as I recuperated in hospital, my wife had died of influenza? That I was tired of an England I no longer believed in? It would be considered bad form to tell a native any of that. So I told him what I told everyone.

'I grew sick of the rain, Sergeant.'

TWO

I was six when my mother died. My father was headmaster of the local school, a man of some importance in the parish and of absolutely none outside it. He soon remarried and I, being considered surplus to requirements, was packed off to Haderley, an unremarkable little boarding school in a forgotten part of the West Country, as far from anywhere of any consequence as it's possible to be in England.

Haderley was no different from the myriad of other minor public schools that dot the shires. Provincial in location and parochial in attitude, it provided a passable education, a veneer of respectability and, most importantly, a convenient holding pen for middle-class children who, for one reason or another, required to be dumped somewhere unobtrusive. That was fine with me. I was happy at Haderley, happier than I'd been at home, at any rate. If anything I'd have stayed longer if I could. I envied the boys who were forced to remain there during holidays on account of their parents being posted to some far-flung corner of the globe, bearing the white man's burden and supporting the enterprise of empire.

The empire – it truly was a middle-class enterprise, built squarely on the shoulders of schools like Haderley. They were the institutions that churned out the fresh-faced, diligent young men who were the grease that kept the wheels of empire spinning; the boys who became its civil servants and its policemen, its clerics and its tax collectors. In turn, those boys would marry and have children of their own, children they would send back to England to receive the same education they themselves had received. To the same schools, to be moulded into the next generation of colonial administrators. And so the wheel turned full circle.

I left Haderley at seventeen when the money ran out. My father had taken ill the year before, and in light of his straitened financial circumstances, the school fees became an unaffordable luxury. I didn't bear him any ill will because of it. It was just one of those things. Nevertheless, it did present me with a problem, which was what to do with myself. University, if ever I had entertained hopes of going, was out of the question now. Instead, I did what energetic young men short on prospects and even shorter on resources have done for centuries. I set off for London.

I was lucky. I'd an uncle who lived in the East End, just off the Mile End Road. A local magistrate with some connections, it was he who first suggested I consider the police force. It seemed a good idea, especially as I had nothing else lined up. So I applied and was offered a position as a constable in the Metropolitan Police's H Division, headquartered in Stepney. People think the Met is the oldest police force in the world. It's not. It's true we had the Bow Street runners, but Paris was the first city with a real police force. The Met's not even the oldest in Britain. That particular honour goes to Glasgow, which had a police force a good thirty-odd years before Robert Peel suggested one for London. Still, if there was one city that needed police more than London, it was probably Glasgow.

That's not to say London was safe. Stepney and the East End certainly weren't, and we saw more than our fair share of murders, though the victims were never found wearing black tie. It just wasn't that sort of place. Still, the boys of H Division were thankful for our trusty old Bulldog revolvers, though I never needed to use mine in anger, the act of aiming it at a miscreant generally having the desired effect.

My break came two years later, at the scene of a particularly nasty double murder on the Westferry Road. The bodies of a shop-keeper called Furlow and his wife were discovered early one morning by their assistant, a girl named Rosie, who, confronted by a scene straight out of a penny dreadful, did the sensible thing and screamed her head off. By chance I was on my beat, and hearing her cries, was the first constable on the scene. There were no signs of a break-in. In fact, there was little sign of anything untoward, except of course for the two bodies in the flat above the shop, dressed in their night clothes and with their throats cut. Other officers soon arrived and the place was cordoned off. A search was conducted and a cash box found, open and empty, under the Furlows' bed.

The press got hold of the story, whipped the locals into a frenzy, and soon CID took over the case. After some persuasion, they let me stay on the case. I convinced them I could be useful – I was, after all, the first copper on the scene and I knew the territory.

We appealed for eye-witnesses and several came forward. They spoke of two shifty-looking men seen leaving the premises that morning. A couple even identified the two as brothers, Alfred and Albert Stratford, toughs with a reputation for violence considered excessive, even for that part of town. We hauled them in for ques-tioning and of course they denied everything. To listen to them, you'd have thought they'd been in church at the time of the murders.

Then witnesses started backtracking. Stories changed – it was dark, they couldn't be certain, weren't even sure if it was the same day – and suddenly we had nothing and the Stratford brothers were going to walk. In a last throw of the dice, the CID officers returned to the crime scene in the vain hope of turning up some evidence that might have been missed. I was left at the station and to my own devices. On a whim, I went down to the evidence locker. With the case slipping away, my stint in CID seemed almost over and I wanted to take one last look at what we had, for old times' sake. I examined the meagre contents: the blood-soaked night clothes, a cracked pocket watch, the empty cash box. It was then that I noticed the reddish smudge hidden on the inside lip of the cash-box lid. In all the commotion it must have been missed when the box was originally discovered. Instantly I knew what it was, and, more importantly, what it might mean. I vaulted back up the stairs, my hands shaking as I held out the box and showed it to the senior officer. Soon Scotland Yard's nascent Fingerprinting Bureau had been summoned. They managed to lift a print, which turned out to be an exact match for Alfred Stratford's thumb. We'd caught him red-handed. I applied for a transfer to CID and was accepted.

As for the Stratford brothers, they were both hanged.

I spent the next seven years in CID, dealing with crimes that would put most men off their dinners. It gets tiring after a while and in late 1912 I transferred to Special Branch, whose primary role at the time was to keep an eye on Fenians and their sympathisers in the capital. Not many people remember that the Special Branch started life as the Special Irish Branch. The name may have changed, but the mission hadn't.

The war came in the summer of '14. I wasn't one of those who welcomed its arrival like so many turkeys cheering for Christmas, maybe because I'd already seen enough death to know it was often gruesome, generally pointless and rarely honourable. I certainly didn't get caught up in the fever that saw countless young men head gleefully to the recruiting office in those early days, thinking it would all be over by the New Year. So many people thought it would be a short affair; that we'd go over there, give the Kaiser a thrashing and that would be that. As though dispatching the industrialised might of the Imperial German Army would be no more arduous than beating the spear-chuckers we liked to fight in our colonial campaigns.

In the end, though, I did volunteer. Not for love of king and country, which is considered noble, but for the love of a woman, which is something altogether more complicated.

I first saw Sarah on the Mile End omnibus one morning in the autumn of 1913. People talk of love at first sight, of violins and fireworks. For me the experience was more akin to a mild heart attack. She was beautiful, in the way one always imagines an English girl should be, and far too pretty to be on an omnibus on the Whitechapel Road – or within a five-mile radius of the place for that matter. Before I could regain my wits, she had alighted and I lost her in the crowds. That might have been the end of it had I not spotted her again on the same bus a few days later. Soon I'd planned my journey with precision, fine-tuning it to coincide with hers. It was nice to have a use for the old Special Branch surveillance techniques that for once didn't involve trailing Irishmen all over town.

For the next few weeks, that morning journey coloured my life; there was joy at the sight of her, and a hollowness when she wasn't there. One day, when the bus was particularly packed, I offered her my seat. She took it as an act of kindness. I took it as an opportunity to start a conversation.

Over time, I got to know her. She was a school mistress, a few years older than me, and smart too. If it was her beauty that first attracted me, then it was her intellect that made me fall in love with her. Hers was a open mind, espousing ideas liberal and radical.

Some men are put off by intelligence in a woman. I find it intoxicating. Those days were the happiest of my life. She had a fondness for nature and we spent many a freezing Sunday afternoon walking in the royal gardens. Nowadays I can't see a park without thinking of her.

But the course of true love never did run smooth, and in our case, it meandered all over the place. The trouble was, I wasn't the only one captivated by her. She had more than her fair share of admirers: intellectuals and radicals mainly, even the odd foreigner. She introduced me to her circle: long-faced, sincere men with shiny new ideas and old threadbare coats, who'd gather in coffee shops and talk heatedly about the fraternal solidarity of the working classes and the dictatorship of the proletariat. It was all nonsense, of course. They were there for the same reason I was – moths around the same flame. If they thought it would help win her affection, each one of them would have happily knifed the others in the back with fraternal solidarity having gone out the nearest window. There was one thing that united them, though – their suspicion of me, a mistrust that didn't exactly diminish when they learned I was a policeman.

Of course, there were other women in the group, but Sarah's light was always the brightest. And she, aware of her position, made sure to distribute her favours evenly: a kind word here, a glance there, just enough so that no one suitor ever seemed to be preferred or any other ever lost heart.

It was in order to set myself apart from these men that I enlisted. Like most radicals, they talked a lot but did nothing, and it didn't take an intellectual to see that she was tiring of the endless discourse. I enlisted because I sensed that, despite her liberated views, what she really wanted was for a man to be a man. I enlisted because I loved her. And then I asked her to marry me.

24

I joined up in January 1915 and received three weeks of the most basic of basic training alongside two dozen other men. Sarah and I were married in late February and two days later, I shipped out to France.

We saw action almost immediately, thrown into the attack at Neuve Chapelle. A number of my comrades died in that battle; just the first of many. There were a lot of dead men's shoes to fill in those days and field promotions became common place. As a detective inspector, I was considered officer material and quickly made a second lieutenant. After that came further promotions, all by dint of me still being alive. One by one, my friends were killed. Family too. My half brother, Charlie, died at Cambrai in '17: *missing, presumed killed in action*. He'd been at my wedding two years before and his funeral was the last time I saw my father, who'd died shortly after. In the end, out of the twenty or so of us who signed up together, only two of us survived, and only me with my wits intact. Though that's debatable.

It was during the war that I first met Lord Taggart. I was pulled out of the line and ordered to report to him in St Omer. He wore the insignia of a major of the 10th Fusiliers, but it quickly became apparent that his real role was military intelligence. He'd read my file, noted my time in Special Branch, and had a job for me. I was ordered to Calais, to track a Dutch national whom military intelligence suspected of abetting the enemy. I tailed the man for several weeks, noting his contacts and meetings, and soon we'd uncovered a ring of spies working at the docks and passing information on our logistics to the Germans.

Taggart asked if I wished to continue working for him. It wasn't a difficult decision: I'd done more for the war effort in a month in intelligence than I had in almost two years of sitting in a trench. The work was for the most part enjoyable, and I proved to be good at it. Compared to the Irish, the Germans were amateurs. They tended to view espionage much as we British view haggling: a slightly seedy business, best left to other races.

My war came to an end in the summer of 1918 at the second Battle of the Marne. It was to be the Hun's last throw of the dice. They let loose with everything they had; a barrage of shells that seemed to last a couple of weeks. I was on a reconnaissance mission in the forward trenches when we took a direct hit. I was lucky. A medical orderly found me and dragged me to a field hospital and a week later I was transferred to a facility back in England. It was touch and go for a while. They gave me morphine for the pain and I spent many days in a drug-induced fog. It was only much later, when they considered my mental state sufficiently robust, that they told me of Sarah's death. They said it was influenza, that there had been an epidemic, that a lot of people had died from it. As if that made it somehow easier to accept.

———

They didn't send me back to France. There was no point. By October it was clear the war was over. Instead, I was demobilised, allowed to return to civilian life. But it's not much of a life when everyone you cared about is lying in a cemetery or scattered over a French field; when all you have left are memories and guilt. I rejoined the police force in the hope of regaining some purpose, as though returning to the familiar might somehow reanimate what was now a hollowed-out husk. It didn't help. Sarah's passing had taken the best part of me with it, and now the days were empty and the nights populated by the cries of the dead, which nothing could extinguish. Nothing except the morphine. When that ran out, I took to opium. Not as effective, but easy enough to get a hold of, especially for a copper who'd cut his teeth in the East End. I knew of several dens in Limehouse alone, and it was while staggering along Narrow Street one freezing December night, past where the Cut flows into the Thames, that I considered ending it all. It would be easy. Just a short walk into the blackness. The cold would numb the pain and it would all soon be over . . .

Then I remembered an argument I'd once had with a sergeant from the River Police at Wapping. It was only the thought of the satisfaction he'd get from fishing my bloated corpse out of the water that kept me from doing it.

I can be petty like that.

———

It was soon after that I received the telegram from Lord Taggart offering me a job. He'd been appointed Commissioner of the Imperial Police Force in Bengal, had need of good detectives and requested that I join him in Calcutta. There was precious little left for me in England, and so in early March, after bidding farewell to Sarah's father on the quayside, I boarded a P&O steamer bound for Bengal. I'd managed to pilfer a stash of morphine tablets from an evidence locker in Bethnal Green before leaving. It was easy enough to do: evidence went astray all the time. There were rumours that certain officers in Wapping earned more on the side from the sale of contraband than they ever did pounding the beat. What concerned me, though, was whether I'd managed to purloin enough tablets for the three-week journey. It would be touch and go. I'd have to ration myself, but hoped that it would be enough to see me through to Calcutta.

Unfortunately, Lady Luck can be fickle sometimes. Bad weather in the Mediterranean added almost a week to the journey and I'd run out of tablets several days before the coast of Bengal finally came into view.

Bengal: verdant, bountiful and benighted. It seemed a country of steaming jungle and sodden mangrove, more water than land. Its climate was as hostile as almost anywhere in the world, in turn parched by baking sun and drenched by monsoon rains, as though God himself, in a fit of petulance, had chosen everything in nature most abominable to an Englishman and set it down in this one cursed place. So it stood to reason that it was here, eighty miles inland, in a malarial swamp on the east bank of the muddy Hooghly river, that we should see fit to build Calcutta, our Indian capital. I guess we like a challenge.

I set foot on the soil of India on the first of April, 1919. *All Fools' Day.* It seemed appropriate. The steamer had made its way up river. Jungle had given way to fields and mud villages, and then finally, around a dog-leg bend in the river, the great city appeared under a crown of black haze from a hundred industrial smokestacks.

Pitching up in Calcutta for the first time without the assistance of drugs is not a pleasant experience. Of course there's the heat, the broiling, suffocating, relentless heat. But the heat's not the problem. It's the humidity that drives men mad.

The river was choked with vessels. Vast ocean-going merchantmen jostled for position at the dockside. If the river was the city's artery, these vessels were its lifeblood, carrying its exports to the world.

To look at it, you might think Calcutta some ancient metropolis. The truth is it's younger than New York or Boston or half a dozen other cities of the Americas. Unlike them, though, it was never conceived out of aspirations of a new beginning in a New World. This place was born of more base a reason. This place existed for trade.

Calcutta – we called it the *City of Palaces*. Our Star in the East. We'd built this city, erected mansions and monuments where previously had stood only jungle and thatch. We'd paid our price in blood and now, we proclaimed, Calcutta was a *British* city. Five minutes here would tell you it was no such thing. But that didn't mean it was Indian.

The truth was, Calcutta was unique.

THREE

At 18 Lal Bazar Street sits a solid-looking mansion that dates back to the glory days of the East India Company, a time when any old Englishman armed with enough brains and an eye for opportunity could turn up penniless in Bengal and, if he played his cards right, end up as rich as a prince. Of course, it also helped if he wasn't too fussy about how he did it. They say it was built by just such a fellow who'd come here with nothing, made a fortune but then lost it all. He'd sold it to someone, who'd sold it someone, who'd sold it to the government and now it's the headquarters of the Imperial Police Force (Bengal Division).

It was built in the style we like to call *colonial neo-classic* – all columns and cornices and shuttered windows. And it was painted maroon. If the Raj has a colour, it's maroon. Most government buildings, from police stations to post offices, are painted maroon. I expect there's a fat industrialist somewhere, Manchester or Birmingham probably, who got rich off the contract to produce a sea of maroon paint for all the buildings of the Raj.

Surrender-not and I passed between two saluting sentries, into a bustling foyer and made for the stairs, past walls covered in the plaques, photographs and other assorted memorabilia of a hundred years of colonial law enforcement.

Lord Taggart's office was on the third floor and accessed by a small anteroom. There sat his personal secretary, a diminutive fellow by the name of Daniels, whose sole purpose in life seemed to be to serve his master, a task he performed with the dedication of a besotted cocker spaniel. I knocked and entered, with Surrender-not trailing two paces behind. Daniels rose from behind his desk. He looked like secretaries to important men always do: pale, unthreatening and several inches shorter than his boss.

'This way please, Captain Wyndham,' he said, leading me towards a set of double doors. 'The Commissioner's expecting you.'

I walked in. Surrender-not stopped at the threshold.

'Come on, Sergeant,' I said, 'let's not keep the Commissioner waiting.'

He took a deep breath and followed me into a room the size of a small Zeppelin hangar. Light streamed in through French windows and reflected off chandeliers hanging from a high ceiling. It was an impressive office for a policeman. Still, I guessed the chief guardian of law and order in such a prominent, yet problematic outpost of empire probably deserved such an office. At the far end of the room, behind a desk the size of a rowing boat and under a life-size portrait of George V, sat the Commissioner. Digby was sat opposite him. I made my way over to join the three of them, Surrender-not a half-step behind me, doing my best to hide my surprise.

'Take a seat, Sam,' said the Commissioner without rising from his chair.

I did as ordered and took the chair next to Digby. There were only two, which just served to exacerbate Surrender-not's nerves. He frantically scanned the room. It was a look I'd seen before on the faces of men stranded under fire in no man's land.

Digby turned crimson. 'Where do you think you are, Sergeant, Howrah station? This is no place for the likes of—'

31

'Wait,' said Taggart, raising a hand, 'the sergeant should stay. I think it appropriate that at least one Indian be present.' He turned towards the door and called out.

'Daniels! Fetch a chair for the sergeant.'

The secretary stood and stared like a startled rabbit. Then without a word, he nodded and left the room, returning with a chair which he placed next to mine, before exiting once again, barely acknowledging the sergeant's words of thanks. Surrender-not sat down and concentrated on staring at the floor. Digby looked like he might be having a seizure.

I turned my attention to Lord Taggart. He was a tall man in his fifties, with the benevolent face of a priest and the devil's charm.

'Now, Sam,' he said, rising from his chair and pacing, 'this MacAuley business. I've already had the Lieutenant Governor on the telephone. He wants to know what we're doing about it.'

'News travels fast,' I said, glancing at Digby whose face was set in a rictus stare. 'We only found the body a few hours ago.'

Digby shrugged.

'Something you should know about Calcutta, Sam,' the Commissioner continued, 'we aren't the only force of law and order.' He lowered his voice and continued, 'The L-G has his own *sources*, shall we say.'

'You mean a secret police?'

The Commissioner winced. Returning to his seat, he picked up a lacquered fountain pen and tapped it distractedly on the desk. 'Let's just call them *alternative channels.*'

I couldn't help smiling. A *secret police* was something only other nations employed. We British used *alternative channels.*

'Whatever they've told him has got him extremely worried,' Taggart went on. 'When news gets out that a senior British civil servant – one of his closest aides, no less – has been murdered, the situation is likely to be explosive. The revolutionaries will have a field day. Who knows what they'll be emboldened to do next? I've had the background from Digby, but I want your assessment.'

There wasn't much to tell him. 'The investigation is at an early stage, sir,' I said, 'but I concur with Sub-inspector Digby. It looks like a political act.'

The Commissioner rubbed a hand across his chin. 'Any witnesses?'

'None as yet, but we're following up certain leads.'

'And how do you propose to proceed?'

'The usual,' I said. 'We'll start with a fingertip search of the locus, talk to witnesses, then to people who knew him. I want to find out more about MacAuley: when he was last seen, and what he was doing up in Black Town last night dressed like he was off to the opera. I'd also like to talk to his boss, the Lieutenant Governor.'

Digby snorted.

'That might be difficult, Sam.' The Commissioner sighed. 'The L-G and his staff are preparing to ship out to Darjeeling in less than a fortnight. We may struggle to fit you into his schedule. Leave it with me, though. Given the delicate nature of the situation, he might spare you fifteen minutes. In the meantime, you should pursue other avenues.'

'In that case, we'll start with MacAuley's secretary, assuming he had one.'

'No doubt,' said Digby. 'Probably some pen-pusher over at Writers'.'

'Very good,' said the Commissioner. 'Carry on, and keep me posted, Sam. Digby, speak to your people in Black Town. See if they've heard anything. I want all the stops pulled out on this one, gentlemen.'

'Very good, sir,' I replied.

'One last thing,' said the Commissioner. He turned towards Surrender-not. 'What's your name, Sergeant?'

'Banerjee, sir,' replied the sergeant. He looked at me. 'Surrender-not Banerjee.'

———

I left the office with Digby and Surrender-not in tow, all the while ruminating on the conversation with the Commissioner. Something didn't sit right.

'What do you think?' I asked Digby.

'Looks like we've landed ourselves a real hot potato, old boy.'

In terms of analysis, it was hardly piercing.

'Start talking to your informants. See if any of them have heard anything.'

He opened his mouth as if to speak, then thought better of it.

'You've a better idea?' I asked.

'Not at all, old boy.' He smiled. 'You're the ex-Scotland Yard man. Let's do it your way.'

I dismissed him and watched as he strode off towards his office, then ordered Banerjee to get an update from the crime scene. The sergeant saluted and set off in the direction of the 'pit' where he and the other native officers sat. In the meantime, I needed space to think.

I walked out of the building and made for the courtyard between the main block and an annexe that held the stables, garage and some of the administrative departments. Here stood the Imperial Police Garden, a patch of grass and a few wooden benches surrounded by flower beds and a handful of scrawny trees. It was a grand title for such a small patch of scrub, but it was still a garden, and that was good enough for me.

For me, gardens recalled memories of happier times. For three years I'd sat in the trenches and remembered the days I'd spent wandering the parks of London with Sarah. I dreamed of being with her again, just looking out over grass and flowers. That dream was dead, but gardens still brought me joy. I am an Englishman, after all.

I sat on a bench and ordered my thoughts. The Commissioner had dragged us back from a crime scene only to impress upon us the importance of the case. That in itself was odd. It was like interrupting a surgeon in the middle of an operation, simply to stress how vital it was that he save the patient.

Something else bothered me. How had the Lieutenant Governor's people got wind of the murder so soon? The *peon* had only found the body at around seven o'clock. It would have taken him about fifteen minutes to make it to the nearest *thana* and raise the alarm. By the time the local constables had arrived on the scene, realised that the *peon* wasn't mad and that there really was a dead *sahib* in dress shirt and dickie bow lying in a gutter with his eye pecked out, it would have been at least seven thirty. It was almost eight thirty by the time we arrived, and Digby didn't even identify the body as MacAuley's for another fifteen minutes after that. And yet, only an hour later, a constable arrives and summons us back to Lal Bazar. Assuming it took him the best part of fifteen minutes to cycle over from the local *thana*, that would mean that within forty-five minutes of us identifying the body, the L-G's office knew about it, had contacted the Commissioner and told him something that spooked him so much that he immediately called the investigating officers back from the crime scene. Like West Ham winning the league, it was possible . . . just not particularly plausible.

I considered the options: one of the constables on the investigating team was working for the L-G's secret police and had got a message to them while Banerjee and I were at the brothel questioning Mrs Bose and her staff. That was conceivable. Even in the short

35

time I'd been here, it was clear that in terms of corruption at least, the men of the Imperial Police Force could give the boys of the Met a good run for their money.

There was, though, another possibility: that the L-G's operatives had known about the murder *before* the *peon* had even found the body. That would explain how the L-G came to know so quickly. But it too raised questions. Were the operatives tailing MacAuley? If so, why didn't they intervene when they saw he was in trouble? He was a senior British administrator, after all. If they weren't going to intervene when a *burra sahib* was attacked, then we might all as well just pack our bags, shut up shop and hand the keys back to the Indians.

On the other hand, the L-G's men may have simply found MacAuley's body after he'd been murdered. That seemed more likely, but if so, why leave it and wait for someone else to find the body? Why not raise the alarm themselves? Better still, why not just tidy up the mess without anyone knowing? It wouldn't be the first time a high-profile death had been hushed up. I remembered the case of a South American ambassador to the Court of St James we'd found asphyxiated in a room above a pub in the Shepherd Market wearing nothing but a noose round his neck and a smile on his face. It was later reported that his Excellency had passed away peacefully, asleep in his own bed.

I was going round in circles. None of the possibilities made much sense. It wasn't an especially auspicious start to my first case in Calcutta, a case which, I was beginning to realise, was as unique as any I'd dealt with before. It wasn't just the murder of a white man in a black suburb. This appeared to be the assassination of a senior British official by native terrorists. The stakes didn't come much higher.

My mind wandered to thoughts of Sarah. What would she have made of me sitting here, thousands of miles from home, leading such an investigation? I hoped she'd be proud of me. God, I missed her.

I must have sat there for some time for the next thing I knew, the sun had shifted, my shade had disappeared and I was sweating. Focusing on the task in hand was becoming increasingly difficult. At that moment I'd gladly have given a month's pay for a shot of morphine or a hit of 'O', but I had a murder to solve. And I didn't yet have a month's pay.

I stalked back up to my office. Surrender-not was sat on a chair in the corridor outside, lost in his own thoughts.

'I hope I'm not disturbing you, Sergeant?'

Startled, he jumped up and saluted, knocking his chair over in the process. He didn't seem to have much luck with chairs.

'No, sir. Sorry, sir,' he said, before trailing after me into my office. The look on his face suggested he had bad news and wasn't sure if I was the type to shoot the messenger. I could have assured him I wasn't, mainly because the alternative would have left me well short of subordinates by now.

'Out with it, Sergeant,' I said.

Surrender-not looked at his feet. 'We've had a call from Cossipore *thana*. It's the crime scene, sir. It's been taken over by the military.'

'What?' I asked. 'This is a civilian matter. What's it got to do with the military?'

'It's military *intelligence*, sir, not military police,' he said, wringing his hands. 'I've seen it happen before, sir. Last year, we were in attendance at the scene of an explosive detonation. Nationalists had blown up the railway lines north of Howrah. A truck load of military personnel turned up and the whole investigation was taken out of our hands within a few hours. We were ordered not to mention a word to anyone, on pain of disciplinary action.'

'Well, I'm glad you told me,' I said sincerely. 'What else do you know about them?'

'Not much, I'm afraid. Those sorts of things are not really shared with people of my . . . *rank*, but it's common knowledge, inside Lal Bazar at least, that there's a unit within military intelligence – "Section H", I believe it's called – which reports directly to the L-G. Anything he considers a political crime falls under their jurisdiction.'

'And there's a law to that effect?'

Banerjee smiled ruefully. 'I doubt very much that there is, sir, but that is irrelevant. One might say that the Lieutenant Governor has certain broad, discretionary powers that he is free to exercise in furtherance of the good governance of His Majesty's colonial territories of the Bengal Presidency.'

'You mean he can do whatever the hell he likes?'

He gave an embarrassed smile. 'I suppose so, sir.'

I was unsure where that left my investigation. But there was one way to find out. Sometimes, in a new job, it's important to set out the ground rules early. What you will put up with and what you won't. What people call 'Red Lines'. I've found that in the early days, at least, your superior is as likely to cut you some slack as reprimand you, especially if he's the man who hired you.

Leaving the sergeant standing where he was, I calmly rose, walked out the door and back up the stairs. Ignoring the protestations of a startled Daniels, I barged straight into Taggart's office.

The Commissioner looked up from his desk. He didn't seem surprised.

'I know what you're going to say, Sam.'

'Am I off the MacAuley case?'

Taggart calmly beckoned me over to a chair while the stricken Daniels looked on.

'With the greatest respect,' I said, 'what the hell's going on, sir? An hour ago you tell me to pull out all the stops and now I find out it's someone else's case.'

Taggart removed his spectacles and cleaned them with a small handkerchief. 'Calm down, Sam.' He sighed. 'I've just found out myself. Look, it's still your case. The L-G simply felt that the crime scene itself should be secured by the military. The last thing we need is the terrorists exploiting the situation any further. The whole area is under curfew. I'll do what I can to ensure the military don't get in the way of your investigation.'

'I need access to the crime scene,' I said. 'We haven't found a murder weapon yet.'

'I'll see what I can do,' said Taggart, 'but it might take a day or so.'

In a day or so, my crime scene wouldn't be worth a tin rupee. Anything of interest would be in the hands of military intelligence, and if they were anything like their counterparts in wartime France, they were unlikely to share. The bile was rising in my throat. I tried to swallow it down. There wasn't much else to say, so I took my leave and headed back down the stairs. At least for now, it was still my case.

Surrender-not was waiting in my office. In my haste to confront Taggart, I'd forgotten to dismiss him. I wondered just how long he would have stayed there had I not returned. Hours possibly.

Now, though, I had work for him to do. The priority was to secure MacAuley's body. Assuming we still had it.

FOUR

It took a few telephone calls to find the name of MacAuley's secretary, and it turned out *he* was a *she*, a Miss Grant. It was surprising that a man as senior as MacAuley should have a woman for a secretary. Then again, times were changing. In England, too, there seemed to be a hell of a lot more women about, doing the jobs of men sent to the trenches. With the war over, they didn't seem in any hurry to return to the kitchen. That was just fine with me. Any man who's spent time in a field hospital being ministered to by female nurses would happily tell you that more women in the workplace was something to be wholeheartedly supported.

My appointment with Miss Grant was at Writers' Building at four p.m. It was a five-minute walk from Lal Bazar so I made the journey on foot, which was a mistake. Even in the late afternoon, the heat was like a lead weight on my shoulders and I was sweating like a Spaniard by the time I turned into Dalhousie Square. If Calcutta has a heart, it's Dalhousie. Like Trafalgar in London, Dalhousie was too big to be elegant. No public space needs to be quite so huge. At its centre sat a large, rectangular pool of water the colour of banana leaves. Digby had mentioned that in the old days, the natives would use it for washing, swimming and religious pursuits. All that stopped after the mutiny of '57. Such things were no longer to be tolerated. Now the pool stood empty, its bottle-green waters shimmering in the afternoon sun. The natives – the ones we approved of, at any rate – now suited and booted in frock coats and buttoned-down collars, hurried around it, heads down, on their way to meetings and appointments, kept at a safe distance from the water by iron railings and signs in English and Bengali warning of stiff penalties should they be tempted to revert to their base natures and go for a dip.

Around the flanks of the square sat the key buildings of British administration: the General Post Office, the telephone exchange and, of course, the massive stone bulk of the Writers' Building. The lives of over a hundred million Indians, from Bihar to the borders of Burma, were administered from Writers', so it was apt that it was as large a building as probably existed anywhere in the empire. But *large* hardly did it justice. The word that best described it was *awesome*. For that was its purpose: to inspire awe in all who saw it, but mainly in the natives. It was certainly formidable. Four storeys high and about two hundred yards long, with massive plinths and huge columns topped off with statues of the gods. Not Indian gods, of course. These ones were Greek, or possibly Roman. I never could tell the difference.

That was the thing about Calcutta. Everything we'd built here was in the classical style. And everything was larger than necessary. Our offices, mansions and monuments all shouted, *Look at our works! Truly we are the inheritors of Rome.*

It was the architecture of domination and it all seemed faintly absurd. The Palladian buildings with their columns and pediments, the toga-clad statues of Englishmen long deceased, and the Latin inscriptions on everything from palaces to public lavatories. Looking at it all, a stranger could be forgiven for thinking that Calcutta had been colonised by Italians rather than Englishmen.

The square buzzed with activity. Trams and motor cars disgorged a steady stream of white and native civil servants in suits and ties despite the heat, who joined the throng of others rushing in and out of the building's wide portico.

I asked at the front desk for Miss Grant and the clerk searched through a directory before ringing a brass bell on the marble counter top. A turbaned flunky appeared and the clerk addressed him in the brusque tone that minor bureaucrats generally use with their underlings. The flunky smiled obsequiously and beckoned me to follow. We crossed to the far side of the lobby to an elevator marked, RESERVED. He opened the grille door and ushered me in. There were no buttons. Instead, he removed a key from his pocket, inserted it into a brass slot and turned it. The lift gave a jolt, then smoothly began its ascent. The flunky smiled. 'Express elevator, *sahib*.'

The lift lurched to a halt at the fourth floor and the flunky led the way down an oak-panelled corridor with a blue carpet thick enough to suffocate a small dog. He stopped outside one of the many identical, unnumbered doors and smiled. The clacking of a typewriter could be heard emanating from the other side. I thanked him and he pressed his palms together in the Indian gesture of *pranaam*, then retreated down the corridor.

I knocked and entered. A young woman was seated behind a desk too small for the oversized typewriter, telephone and stacks of papers that sat upon it. She seemed preoccupied with her typing.

'Miss Grant?'

She looked up, flustered, her eyes red-rimmed.

'I'm Captain Wyndham.'

'Captain,' she said, pushing a strand of brown hair from her face, 'please do come in.' She rose from her chair and in the process knocked over a stack of papers, which scattered on the floor.

'I'm sorry,' she said, quickly bending down to gather them up. I tried not to stare at her legs, which was difficult because they were fine legs and I appreciate these things. She caught me nevertheless, and to hide my embarrassment, I knelt down, picked up a few stray sheets that had landed at my feet and handed them to her. Her fingers brushed against mine and I caught the scent of her perfume. Not floral – something more earthy. She smiled her thanks. A nice smile. The nicest thing I'd seen since arriving in Calcutta, at any rate. A few buttons, open at the neck of her blouse, revealed smooth, tanned skin. Too tanned to be English; not enough to be Indian.

I guessed she was of mixed ancestry. What they called *Anglo-Indian*. Somewhere along the line, there would have been some native blood in her family. It was enough to condemn her, and those like her, to a strange kind of limbo. Not Indian, but not British either.

'Please take a seat,' she said, ushering me to a chair. 'Would you like something to drink? Some tea, perhaps?'

I asked for water.

'Are you sure, Captain? You know what they say about the water here. Maybe you'd prefer a gin and tonic? It's safer, after all.'

The idea of a gin and tonic with her didn't sound too bad, even if we were stuck in an office and about to discuss the murder of her employer. But I was on duty.

'Water is fine, thank you.'

A decanter and some bottles sat on a sideboard. She filled two glasses with water and handed me one.

'I heard the news this morning,' she said, taking a sip. 'A friend at the L-G's office called me. She said they'd found Mr MacAuley's body. Is it true?'

'I'm afraid so.'

Tears welled in her eyes. I didn't want her to cry as I never know quite what to say when a woman gets emotional. In the end, I did what I always do in such situations and offered her a cigarette. She accepted and I took out one for myself and lit both.

She inhaled deeply and composed herself. 'How can I help?'

'I need you to answer a few questions, Miss Grant.'

She nodded. 'Please, call me Annie.'

It suited her.

'Maybe you could start by telling me about Mr MacAuley. How long you've known him, what his role was here, who his friends were, that sort of thing.'

She thought for a moment, taking another drag on her cigarette. I watched as its tip glowed red. She withdrew it from her lips and exhaled nervously.

'Mr MacAuley was head of the ICS finance department in Bengal. But he was more than that. He was one of the L-G's inner circle, advising him on all sorts of policy matters. On a day-to-day level, he could be involved in anything from negotiating pay for post office workers to making sure the trains ran on time.' She said it like she'd memorised the words.

'I've worked for him for about three years,' she continued, 'since late 'sixteen when his previous secretary decided to do his bit for King and country and got himself killed in the desert somewhere near Baghdad.' She took another drag. 'As for Mr MacAuley, they say he'd been in Calcutta for a quarter of a century or more. A permanent fixture at the Bengal Club most evenings.' She looked past me, as though speaking to the wall. 'He didn't have many friends. He wasn't the type to have friends.'

I could sympathise. I had precious few friends left alive myself these days.

'Then what type was he?'

'The type who saw you in terms of what you could do for him. If you were rich, he'd seek to charm the pants off you. If you weren't, he wouldn't give you the time of day.' She gave a short laugh. 'It seemed to work for him, too. He was close to some very influential men.'

'Such as?'

'Well, there's the L-G, of course. But that was business. There was no friendship there. There's no way the Lieutenant Governor of Bengal, the deputy to the Viceroy of all India, is going to socialise with the likes of MacAuley, no matter how useful he could be.'

'Useful in what way?'

She gave me a look that suggested she thought the question, or possibly me, to be stupid. 'MacAuley was the L-G's fixer, Captain. He came from working-class stock; a hard-nosed so-and-so who could get things done quickly and quietly, and didn't much care who got hurt in the process. Someone like that can be very useful to a politician like the L-G.'

I stayed silent, hoping she'd elaborate. People will often keep talking just to fill the void, but she wasn't that type. She just let the silence hang in the air.

'Who else was he close to?'

'James Buchan,' she said, as if the name should mean something to me. She read the look on my face and smiled. 'I take it you're new to Calcutta, Captain. Mr Buchan is one of our beloved merchant princes, one of the richest men in Calcutta. He's a jute baron, and a Scot like MacAuley. His family have been jute and rubber traders for over a century, since the days of the East India Company. They used to own several mills back in the old country. If you go down to the river, you'll probably see barges with the name *Buchan Works – Dundee* printed on them. They used to ship the raw jute from East Bengal, through Calcutta and on to Scotland. There they'd weave it into everything from rope to wagon tarpaulins. Buchan's brainwave was to shift his mills from Dundee and start production here. All the things he used to make in Scotland, he now makes here at a fraction of the cost. The story goes he trebled his profits at a stroke. He's a millionaire many times over. He owns some mills about ten miles upriver, at a place called Serampore, and a mansion the size of a maharaja's palace.'

'You've been there?'

She nodded. 'He practically runs that town.'

'And how does he do that?'

'Money talks, Captain. He has all of the local officials in his pocket, probably the police too. I don't know what it's like back in England, but here, anyone can be bought for the right amount of rupees. Almost everyone up there owes their position to him in one way or another. He's even shipped in several hundred of his own people from Scotland to run his operations upriver. Dundee on the Hooghly, they call it. You should take a walk along Chowringhee on a Sunday afternoon, Captain. Every second person you see strutting along will probably be one of Buchan's people from Serampore, down in the big city for the day. No better than working-class labourers back home, here they have their own servants and swagger about like lords.'

'Chowringhee? The road opposite the park?'

'Really, Captain,' she teased, 'just when did you arrive here? Chowringhee is our Piccadilly. It's where the great and the good come out to play.' She paused. 'I'd be glad to show you it some time.'

That sounded good. The prospect of going anywhere with her sounded good. But I instantly regretted the thought and reproached myself. I was a man in mourning, after all. Still, I'd never met a girl in England who was ever this forward. But then Miss Grant wasn't English.

I tried to focus. 'What was Buchan's relationship with MacAuley?'

'Mr MacAuley always said he was the only man Buchan trusted. Something to do with them coming from the same town. Buchan never had any issues about socialising with him. They'd often get hopelessly drunk together. MacAuley would regularly come into the office at ten or eleven in the morning after a night out with Buchan. That man knows how to throw a party.'

'They were close friends?'

She thought for a moment. 'I'm not sure, Captain. MacAuley was definitely closer to Buchan than he was to the L-G, but it's not as though Buchan ever treated him as an equal. I got the impression that MacAuley was Buchan's man. He would get things done for Buchan, a permit here, a by-law changed there. Buchan probably looked after him handsomely for it too, though I've no proof, of course.'

'Anyone else he considered a friend?'

'Not that I can think of. Like I said, he wasn't a popular man . . . There was that preacher, though; I think his name's Dunne or Gunn, or something. MacAuley was never the religious type, but about six months ago he met this preacher, I think he'd only recently arrived in Calcutta. A common enough sort – fresh off the boat, here to do God's work saving little brown souls from the fires of hell . . . *Zealots*,' she said distastefully. 'Anyway, I think he runs an orphan- age.' She stubbed out her cigarette in a tin ashtray on the desk. 'MacAuley would go and help out now and again. That came as a shock to a lot of people round here, me included. Then, about two months ago, he started attending church. Began talking more and more about sin and redemption. I think something changed inside him. It was as if he'd become a different person. It's funny,' she said, her lips forming a thin smile, 'a man like MacAuley can spend his whole life being a swine and then find God just before he dies. Clean slate, all sins forgiven. Is there any justice in that, Captain?'

I could have pointed out that there was a certain justice in his being found stabbed to death in a gutter, but it seemed better just to ask her a few more questions.

'Did he have any enemies?' I asked. 'Anyone who would benefit from seeing him dead?'

She gave a small laugh. 'Half the people in this building hated him, but I can't see any of them killing him. Other than that, there's probably a whole heap of people he must have ruined to help his patrons, but I couldn't tell you who they are.'

'What about Indians? Did he have any enemies amongst them?'

'I dare say he did. There were quite a few native landowners and jute agents who were bankrupted by MacAuley's actions on behalf of Buchan. Not to mention those affected when Bengal was partitioned by Lord Curzon. It might have been Curzon's name on the order but MacAuley was the one who drew up the report and its recommendations. It was fifteen years ago but a great many Bengalis still haven't forgotten. Or forgiven.'

Could that have been a motive? At the time, I'd read in the papers about the protests in Calcutta when the partition was announced. The then Viceroy, Lord Curzon, had decided to split the Bengal Presidency in two. He'd justified it on the grounds that Bengal was just too big to govern effectively. There was some truth to this – the province was larger than France with almost twice the population – but the natives saw it as an attempt to divide and rule. They'd reacted with fury. But why would anyone wait fifteen years before taking revenge? They do say our eastern cousins have long memories but if one of them were to wait quite so long for vengeance, I'd have expected something more elaborate than a back-alley stabbing.

My mind was wandering. I'd grown to recognise the signs. In a few hours the cold sweats would start. I needed to focus.

'Did he have any female friends?' I asked. 'A companion maybe?'

'Not to my knowledge,' she said. 'He wasn't a very attractive man.'
That much was true, especially with his eyes pecked out.

'He was a confirmed bachelor by all accounts,' she continued. 'At any rate, he never mentioned any companions to me. I kept his diary for three years and I don't recall him ever asking me to make a dinner reservation or buy flowers for anyone.'

I took out the photo I'd found in MacAuley's wallet and showed it to her. 'What about this woman? Do you recognise her?'

She shook her head.

'I can't say that I do. Is it important?'

'I'm not sure,' I said. 'It could be. Did MacAuley have any appointments yesterday?'

She opened a desk drawer, pulled out a large gilt-edged diary, and thumbed through the pages.

'He'd a ten a.m. with the L-G. They've been meeting a lot recently. It's the same at this time every year. Always so much to organise before the L-G and his retinue decamp for Darjeeling. Then he had lunch with Sir Godfrey Soames of the Landowners' Association. That was at the Great Eastern. He returned here at around four, rather the worse for wear, and left pretty soon after that. I expect he went home to sleep it off.' She continued to read. 'Then he had some function at the Bengal Club at nine p.m. One of Mr Buchan's soirées, I believe.'

'Are Buchan's parties a common occurrence?'

'Oh yes,' she said, picking up the pencil once again from the desk. 'Once or twice a month, generally. I think it's got much to do with the climate and the Scottish temperament. If the mercury so much as touches eighty-five, they all go half-mad, resort to drink and raise hell.'

It didn't sound such a bad life to me. That MacAuley was at one of Buchan's parties last night would also explain the clothes he'd been found in, though not what he was doing in Black Town, miles away from the Bengal Club.

'Any idea why he might have been up in Cossipore last night?'

She shook her head. 'None at all, I'm afraid. He would never venture into a native area without good reason, though. The only place he visited up there was the orphanage run by that preacher, but it's in Dum Dum, not Cossipore.'

'Dum Dum?' The name sounded like it should mean something to me.

'It's a suburb out near the new aerodrome, about ten miles from here. There's a munitions factory there, home to the dum-dum bullet. I expect you've heard of it.'

'Of course,' I said, as I remembered a demonstration of that particularly nasty munition at a Scotland Yard weapons range. The dum-dum was one of the world's first soft-point bullets, designed to expand on hitting a human torso in order to cause maximum damage. As such, the dum-dum didn't so much hit its target as obliterate it. Before the war, we'd been especially fond of using them to put down local tribal disturbances in Africa. They were later banned by international convention, something a few of our generals found rather inconvenient.

'In any case,' she continued, 'he'd no cause to go out to the orphanage last night.'

And even if he had, I thought, he'd hardly have gone there in black tie.

'What did he have in his diary for today?'

'He was supposed to join the L-G at nine for a briefing on next term's budget, then he had a lunch appointment with a director of one of the local banks. Otherwise his diary was empty.'

'When MacAuley failed to show up for the nine o'clock meeting, did anyone telephone from the L-G's office asking where he was?'

She thought for a moment, then shook her head. 'No. I was here from eight. The first call came through from the L-G's office around eleven, when my friend telephoned to tell me they'd found his body.'

'What about military intelligence?' I asked. 'Did MacAuley have any dealings with them?'

Her eyes widened. 'Not as far as I'm aware, Captain. If he did, he kept it very quiet.'

I'd run out of useful questions. I considered asking some useless ones too, but it's best not to outstay your welcome with a beautiful woman. The longer you hang around, the greater the chance she'll see through you. I thanked her for her time and stood up to leave. She rose and led me to the door.

'And Captain,' she said, 'if I can be of any further assistance, please let me know.'

I thanked her, took one last surreptitious glance at those smooth, tanned legs, then heard myself saying, 'And, if it's still open, I might take you up on your offer to show me Chowringhee.'

She smiled. 'Of course, Captain. I look forward to it.'

I stood on the steps of the building, lit a cigarette and stared into the distance. The sun was now just a red disc off to the west and the temperature was dropping. That didn't mean it was comfortable, just less hot. By common consent, dusk was the best time of day out here, not that it lasted long. Night falls like a stone in the tropics. Broad daylight to darkness in less than an hour.

I watched as a flock of birds flew overhead and landed on the pool at the centre of the square. Crossing over the road, I leaned on the low railing, looked down at the water and considered what I'd learned from the beautiful Miss Grant. Alexander MacAuley, a Scot from somewhere near Dundee, a twenty-five-year India-man with few friends and no family. A fixer for powerful men – something that had made him many enemies. A nasty piece of work whose own secretary thought he was a bastard. Then, in the last few months, he finds God and becomes a different person.

As for who might want him dead, though, I wasn't much wiser. I flicked the cigarette butt into the water below and watched it land with a hiss. Other than discovering MacAuley's links to Buchan and why he'd been found wearing a penguin suit, I hadn't really made much progress. Apart from meeting Annie Grant, of course. In some ways, that felt like the most progress I'd made since leaving London.

The street lamps were being lit. They glowed orange, then bright white. The government departments and mercantile houses were shutting up shop for the night. Office buildings disgorged bureaucrats and *boxwallahs* into the gloom as I made my way back to Lal Bazar along pavements jammed with salarymen, jostling in the half-light for space on the trams to take them home.

The lights were blazing at Lal Bazar and shafts of yellow broke through the slats of shuttered windows. On my desk was a note from Surrender-not. I telephoned the pit and asked the desk sergeant to tell him to join me. Minutes later, he was knocking on my door. He entered, saluted and stood to attention like an oversized tin soldier.

'This isn't a parade ground, Surrender-not,' I said.

'Sir?'

'At ease, Sergeant. You don't need to salute every time you enter the office.'

The poor boy furrowed his brow. 'No, sir; sorry, sir. I wished to provide you with an update. I've instructed a guard to be posted at the morgue as per your orders. Access to the body has been restricted to authorised personnel only.'

'Good,' I said, 'and the post-mortem?'

'Scheduled for tomorrow afternoon, sir. There's only one pathologist. He claims to have a backlog of several weeks' worth of cadavers, but I impressed upon him the urgency and delicacy of this particular case and requested, in the most steadfast terms, that he make this a priority. He was not especially enamoured of my request, however he did eventually agree to make a one-off dispensation and fit it in tomorrow.'

'You must have been pretty convincing.'

'I may have mentioned the Commissioner's name a few times. It's possible that helped.'

'Of course,' I said, impressed. 'I forgot that you and he are on first-name terms now. Anything else?'

'Sub-inspector Digby was looking for you earlier, sir. I informed him you were over at Writers' Building interviewing MacAuley's secretary. He said it could wait till the morning.'

'Do you know what he wanted?'

'I think he may have a lead.'

The news came as a jolt. Whenever a colleague had a lead, I tended to experience an odd, bittersweet feeling: the thrill of potential progress tinged with a certain resentment that someone else's efforts may have eclipsed my own. I put it down to my natural competitiveness. That and a certain insecurity.

'If it's a lead, he should have waited and told me tonight, or at least left a message. Where is he now?'

The sergeant shrugged. 'I don't know, sir.'

'Very well. I'll speak to him first thing,' I said. 'And Surrendernot, there's a whole host of things we need to progress tomorrow. I want to have a chat with Mr James Buchan. See if you can find out where he is and set up an appointment. I also want to speak to some people who knew MacAuley: his servants and colleagues. Get me names and addresses. Finally, I need you to track down a Christian minister. His name is Gunn or Dunne or something similar. He runs an orphanage up in Dum Dum.'

Banerjee pulled a small notepad and pencil from his breast pocket and quickly took down my instructions. 'Yes, sir,' he said. 'I'll see to it immediately.'

It was another sultry evening. Humidity so high, the very air seemed wet. Despite this, I decided to walk the mile or so to my lodgings rather than take a rickshaw. Not that I objected to rickshaws, even though Calcutta only had the sort pulled by a man on foot. I didn't particularly like them, but I didn't object to them either. There's nothing dishonourable about pulling a rickshaw. It's a job, and any job gives a man dignity and puts food on his table. No, I set off on foot because, as any beat copper could tell you, the only way to really know a city is to walk every square inch of it.

I chose a meandering route back. First along Bow Bazaar, then left onto College Street, an avenue of a thousand rabbit-warren-like bookshops, past the whitewashed porticos of Medical College Hospital, then up towards Machua Bazaar Street. These were the environs of Calcutta University. *Established 1857*, proclaimed a sign outside. *The oldest university in Asia.* I guessed that was true, so long as you didn't count the native institutions, and it probably was best not to, as some of them were a few thousand years older.

The Royal Belvedere Guest House was situated on Marcus Square and exuded the atmosphere of a seaside guest house back home. The mores of Bournemouth exported to the heat of Bengal. Despite the name, it wasn't really the sort of place patronised by royalty, but it was clean enough and handy for the office. Above all, it was cheap. One of Lord Taggart's minions had booked me a room for a month. Enough time, hopefully, to find more permanent lodgings.

The place was owned by a battleship of a woman called Mrs Tebbit, the wife of a Colonel Tebbit of the Indian Army (retired). She and the Colonel ran a tight ship. Breakfast was served between six thirty and seven thirty sharp, and dinner in the evenings between seven and eight thirty. The food itself made army rations taste like dinner at the Savoy Grill, and sat in the stomach like a sack of stones. The front doors were locked at ten p.m. sharp. However, on account of my war record and position with the Imperial Police, I was afforded the singular honour of my own key.

I went straight up to my room. It was small and spartan, like a monk's cell without the proximity to God. A bed, a wardrobe, a corner sink, a desk and a chair. On the wall a print of an English country scene, and a window with a view of the house next door. My few belongings added little in the way of clutter. They were all easily packed into the large Pukka trunk that Sarah had bought for me from Harrods before I left for France. The thing was vast, with compartments for everything a gentleman might need when adventuring overseas. Strong, too. It could have taken a direct hit from a Boche shell and still kept your clothes from getting creased.

Removing my belt and holster, I draped them on the back of the chair and walked over to the sink, turned on the tap and splashed tepid water on my face.

Taking off the rest of my uniform, I went and lay face up on the bed. My hands were shaking. The cravings were getting stronger. I told myself I didn't have much longer to wait, just a few more hours.

I turned over, buried my hands under the pillow and contemplated, not for the first time, just what I was doing here.

Nothing, save maybe for war, quite prepares you for Calcutta. Not the horrors recounted by returning India-men in the smoke-filled rooms of Pall Mall, not the writings of journalists and novelists, not even a five-thousand-mile sea voyage with stops in Alexandria and Aden. Calcutta, when it arrives, is on a scale more alien than anything the imagination of an Englishman can conjure up. Clive of India had called it *the most wicked place in the Universe*, and his was one of the more positive reviews.

There was something about the place. It wasn't just the heat or the god-awful humidity. I was beginning to suspect it was something to do with the people. There's a special arrogance to be found in the Calcutta Englishman, something you don't find in many other outposts of empire. It may be born of familiarity. After all, the English have been top dog in Bengal for a hundred and fifty years, and seemed to consider the natives, especially the Bengalis, as rather contemptible. Colonel Tebbit had expounded on it over dinner the previous evening: 'Of all the races of the empire, Bengalis are the worst. No loyalty, you see. Not like the warriors of the Punjab who'd gladly rush headlong to their deaths if ordered to by a *sahib*. No, your Bengali is a very different fish, too smart for his own good. Always scheming and plotting . . . and talking. Why use one word when a paragraph will do? That's the Bengali way.'

He was right about the Punjabis. They really would rush headlong to their deaths if ordered to. I'd seen them do it. Still, white or brown, there was something supremely depressing about men willing to sacrifice themselves at the whim of their superiors, and if the Bengalis weren't minded to do so, that was all right with me. Moreover, as a policeman, I quite liked the idea of a people who preferred talking to fighting.

Still, if the Colonel was to be believed, the Raj was threatened more by ten Bengalis with a printing press than a dozen armed regiments of Sikhs and Pathans. Not that I underestimated the capacity of the written word to stir up passions. I'd seen enough propaganda in my time to know better. Nevertheless, the fact that even now, back home, British censors were busy banning Fenian books and mutilating newsprint on an industrial scale didn't sit well with me. But India wasn't Ireland, and maybe we needed to be tougher here. After all, the note found stuffed in MacAuley's mouth was a somewhat unsubtle metaphor for the power of words.

The aroma of fried fish drifting up from the dining room roused me from such thoughts. My watch read twenty past eight. I considered skipping dinner, maybe substituting it with a couple of glasses of whisky. The best part of a bottle of Talisker still lay on the floor beside the bed. But whisky made me maudlin, and there was no guarantee I'd stop after a couple.

Instead I got up, put on a shirt, steeled myself and went down to dinner. A few other guests were still seated around the long dining table, with the Colonel at the far end holding court. I made my apologies.

'Don't you worry, Captain Wyndham,' said Mrs Tebbit as she rose to serve me. 'We know you're a busy man. Besides, there's plenty left for you.' She liked to make a fuss of me. After all, it wasn't every guest house that could boast a police officer among its residents. Most of the others had to make do with the usual procession of travelling salesmen and up-country traders. She heaped a portion of grey fish and greyer vegetables onto my plate and I thanked her and contemplated how best to tackle it.

Opposite sat a flame-haired Irishman called Byrne whom I'd met at dinner the previous night. He was a salesman for a Manchester textile concern and spent most of his time travelling across the country selling his wares to local retailers. The two weeks in Calcutta were apparently the highlight of his year. To my right sat a waspish gentleman called Peters, a solicitor from Patna, in town for a case at the High Court. Both acknowledged my arrival with a nod before resuming their conversation.

'Y'really should visit 'em,' said Byrne energetically, 'miles and miles of tea plantations. As far as the eye can see.' He turned to me. 'Captain Wyndham, I was just telling yer man Peters here that I'm off to the tea gardens in Assam this Friday. Very different they are to the ones we have up in Darjeeling. See, the ones in Assam are low lyin', on the banks of the Brahmapootra river, not up in the hills.' He turned back to Peters, who at that moment was preoccupied hiding a piece of fish under some of the vegetables on his plate. 'And somethin' else that'll surprise you.' He grinned. '*The time!*' He made a show of looking at his watch. 'The time here in Calcutta is now half past eight. That's the same time in Bombay and Karachi and Delhi. Sure, it's even the same time in all the towns of Assam. But that's not the time on the tea plantations. No, sir! D'you know what time it is there?'

Peters didn't look like he cared.

'Half past nine!' crowed Byrne. 'That's right. An hour ahead of the rest of the country! *Tea Garden Time*, they call it.'

'Why is that, Mr Byrne?' asked Mrs Tebbit, rising to put another piece of fish on Peters' plate. She considered herself quite the hostess, on a par with the London set, and took it upon herself to stimulate genteel discussion between her paying guests.

'Ah well, y'see, Mrs Tebbit,' he replied, 'it's all about the daylight. As you know yourself, the tea pickers are out in the fields from first light till sundown. But Assam is so far to the east that the sun rises at four o'clock, when it's still dark in Calcutta and sets at about four thirty in the afternoon. Now that's no good to the plantation

58

owners. They don't want their workers getting up in what is officially the middle of the night. So, they set the clocks an hour ahead.'

Mrs Tebbit turned to me. 'What do you make of it, Captain?'

I didn't really give a damn about Tea Garden Time, but social mores dictate that a truthful reply such as that is considered ill-mannered. Instead, I swallowed and gave what I hoped was a more palatable answer, certainly one more palatable than Mrs Tebbit's fish.

'I suppose it's a sensible solution.'

'Nonsense!' snorted the Colonel from the far end of the table. 'My dear boy, it's anything but sensible. It's soft, that's what it is! In my day, we would think nothing of getting up at *three* in the morning if we were ordered to. That's the problem these days. No discipline. The country's gone to the dogs!'

The table fell silent. Byrne and Peters were nodding, though whether in agreement or just to shut the old duffer up was open to interpretation. Either way, it seemed a sensible strategy.

After dinner, the Tebbits retired to their rooms while Byrne and Peters invited me to the parlour for a smoke. I made my excuses. The truth is that since the war, I'm hardly good company at the best of times, let alone when craving a hit. Instead, I went up to my room, locked the door and switched on the ceiling fan. I kicked off my shoes and lay on the bed with my hands behind my head, staring up as the fan made its languorous circuit. Sleep was far from my thoughts. It was an oppressive night and I was on edge. I checked my watch for what felt like the hundredth time. It would still be at least an hour before everyone else in the house had retired to bed.

Time inched forward. I badly needed a hit. My body and mind cried out for it. Without it my dreams were haunted, and always by the same nightmare. Our trench, under an endless artillery barrage. The screams of wounded men. A shell lands almost on top of me and I'm knocked off my feet. Suddenly I'm on my back on the trench floor, drowning under thick black water. I try to surface, struggling to regain my feet, but it's no use. The mud has me and I'm sinking deeper, scrabbling around ever more frantically, searching for a handhold, a foothold, anything solid, but there's nothing, except slick, putrid mud. My strength begins to fail. My lungs about to explode. I feel death close around my throat. I'm going to die, drowned in the devilish, stinking ooze at the bottom of a trench. My vision blurs. Blackness closes in. I stop struggling. I'm resigned to it. No, not resigned but reconciled. Death will be a release. I can hold my breath no longer. I shall open my lungs and end it. Then, at the final moment, powerful hands grip me. I am being pulled upwards. I break the surface, choking but alive. The shells are still falling. I am dumped unceremoniously against the trench wall. I don't see the faces of my rescuers. I catch my breath. Beside me lies a body, its face covered with soil. Fear grips me. I clamber over to it. Desperately, madly, I wipe the dirt from its face. Sarah stares up at me with cold, dead eyes.

FIVE

It was time.

Wrenching myself off the bed, I stumbled over to the sink and washed the sweat from my face. I pulled on a nondescript shirt and trousers, then silently left the room, made my way downstairs and out the front door, locking it carefully behind me. Several rickshaw *wallahs* were lounging at the corner of the square, engrossed in some heated discussion. They eyed me warily as I walked over, their conversation dying away mid sentence.

'English?' I asked.

'I speak English, *sahib*,' answered the youngest, a wiry sort in a yellowing vest and red checked *lunghi*.

I looked him over. Black eyes and skin the colour of the cheroot he held between two tobacco-stained fingers. He raised it to his lips and took a long hard pull. His cheeks hollowed, accentuating an angular, pockmarked face.

'I need to go to Tangra,' I said.

The other rickshaw *wallahs* laughed, exchanging incomprehensible words in some damnable foreign tongue. The youngster shook his head and smiled in the manner the natives all do when about to impart bad news.

'Tangra is far, *sahib*. Too far for rickshaw.'

I cursed. That was stupid of me. I should have realised a rickshaw was never going to take me the five miles to Tangra. I obviously wasn't thinking straight. But I'm not the type to give up easily. Especially where opium's concerned.

'Take me to a tonga rank, then.'

He nodded and helped me onto the rickshaw and moments later we were moving, passing briskly through the streets around Marcus Square.

'Why you want to go Tangra now, *sahib*?' he asked as he pulled.

'I want to go to Chinatown.'

There was only one reason for a European to go to Chinatown in the dead of night. But it would be out of place for a native to say so out loud.

'*Sahib*,' he said, 'I can take you to little Chinatown. Is in Tiretta Bazaar, near Coolootolah. Everything you find in Chinatown you will find also in Tiretta Bazaar. Chinese food . . . Chinese *medicine* . . .'

The man was no fool.

'All right,' I said, 'take me there.'

I smiled grimly at the thought of what Mrs Tebbit would say if she knew where her prize lodger was off to at this hour. Still, the way I saw it, she was partly responsible. If she hadn't given me the key to the front door, I'd still have been in bed.

That was a lie. The cravings were too strong. If she hadn't given me the key, I'd have found some other means of escape, probably involving windows, bedsheets and drainpipes. One of the practical benefits of attending an English boarding school is that one receives a first-class education in the surreptitious access and egress from almost any premises.

Anyway, Mrs Tebbit's hypothetical displeasure was irrelevant. What I was doing wasn't illegal. Very few things are strictly illegal for an Englishman in India. Visiting an opium den certainly isn't. Opium's only really illegal for Burmese workers. Even registered Indians can get hold of it. And as for the Chinese, well we could hardly make it illegal for them, seeing as we'd fought two wars against their emperors for the right to peddle the damn stuff in their country. And peddle it we did. So much so that we managed to make addicts out of a quarter of the male population. If you thought about it, that probably made Queen Victoria the greatest drug peddler in history.

———

The city was quiet at this hour, as quiet as Calcutta gets at any rate. Travelling south, the roads became narrower and the houses shabbier. The back streets seemed inhabited mainly by stray dogs and stray sailors, who staggered from *shebeen* to brothel, eager to part with whatever back pay they had left before shipping out on the next tide.

We turned into a nondescript alley and stopped outside a decrepit doorway. No windows, no signs, just a door in a wall beside one of those paper lanterns the Chinese love so much. I got down and paid the man. No words were spoken. My mind was on other things. He just nodded his thanks and pressed his palms together in *pranaam*, then walked over to the door, knocked loudly and called out. The door was opened by a squat Chinaman in a greasy shirt and khaki shorts that revealed podgy knees and made him look like a Boy Scout gone to seed.

He looked me up and down, assessing me in the way a farmer does a lame horse before deciding whether or not to shoot it, then beckoned me inside.

'Quickly quickly,' he snapped, looking past me into the alley, as though the whole exercise of conversation was distasteful to him.

After a week of dealing with obsequious Indians, his attitude was oddly refreshing.

I followed him through a dimly lit hall and down a narrow stairway into a small corridor, at the far end of which stood a doorway covered by a faded curtain. The smell of opium smoke, sweet and resinous and earthy, hung heavy in the air and sparked something in my brain. It wouldn't be long now.

The Chinaman held out a hand. I'd no idea as to the going rate, so I just took out a bunch of dirty notes and handed them over. He counted them and smiled. 'You wait here,' he said, before disappearing behind the curtain. The minutes passed and I grew restless. Lifting the veil, I peered inside. Bare walls and stubby little cots of wood and string stood illuminated in the flickering glow of a hurricane lamp. This was no den for the sophisticate. No silken beds, gilded pipes or pretty girls here. This was a place for real addicts: little men with little to live for. It was the right sort of place for me. Not that I considered myself an addict. My usage was purely medicinal. I just needed the O to help me sleep, and for such a purpose, a back-alley shit-hole was better than any upmarket premises, even if it did lack the pretty girls. The problem with a high-class establishment is the quality of the opium. It's just too good. Pure opium is energising. You get a buzz from it. I didn't want a buzz. I wanted oblivion, and for that, you need the cheap stuff: the rough, impure, adulterated filth they'd serve in a dive like this, cut with ash and God knows what else. The end result is euphoria followed by anaesthetising, deadening, stupor. Blessed O. After morphine, it's the next best thing in the world.

From an anteroom appeared a young, moon-faced oriental woman. Her lips and nails were painted blood red and she wore a dress as black and silken as the hair that flowed over her slender shoulders and onto her back. A slit ran up one side of the dress all the way to her thigh and made me think I might have been hasty in judging the place.

'Please come with me, *sahib*,' she said. It jarred hearing an Oriental use the Indian term. Like a Frenchman singing 'God Save the King'. Nevertheless, I followed her to a *charpoy*, near the back of the dingy room.

'Please make yourself comfortable,' she said, gesturing to the rickety wooden cot. *Comfortable* would be an achievement, but I lay down on the low bed. She disappeared, returning moments later carrying a wooden tray on which stood a simple bamboo opium pipe, long stemmed and with a metal saddle which connected to a small ceramic pipe bowl. Beside it sat a spirit lamp, a long needle and finally a little black ball of opium resin, not much larger than a pea. She set the tray on the floor and, taking a candle that lay close by, proceeded to light the spirit lamp. Then, picking up the ball of opium, she deftly placed it on the end of the needle.

'Bengal opium,' she said. 'Much better than Chinese opium. Gives more pleasure for *sahib*.'

She took the needle and held it over the flame. The O swelled and turned from black to molten red. Working with the finesse of a glass blower, she teased it, first stretching it, then rolling it back into a ball. This went on, until finally, happy that the O was cooked, she once more rolled it up and quickly inserted it into the pipe bowl, before passing me the pipe with all the deference of a samurai handing over a sword. I took it and held the bowl close to the spirit lamp, close enough for a tongue of flame to lick the ball of O. I took a pull of the pipe, a long steady pull, and inhaled deeply the smooth, syrup scented smoke. I breathed it in until there was nothing left.

And then at last I slept.

———

I awoke some hours later. I checked my watch, but as usual it had stopped and read a quarter to two. It always stopped around that time, and as a rule was generally unreliable any time after nine p.m. It had been my father's. He'd given it to me on my eighteenth birthday and it was about the only family heirloom I had. I'd worn it constantly since then, including the years in France. It had been problematic for some time now, ever since the Germans had tried to take my head off with a high-explosive shell at the Somme in '16. I was thrown clear by the force of the blast and, by some miracle, survived unscathed. The watch, however, had been less fortunate. Its face was cracked and the casing dented. I'd had it patched up on my next leave, but, like many an old soldier, it had never been quite the same since. There was some problem with the mechanism, which meant that it would slow down and fail to keep proper time about twelve hours after winding. After the war I'd taken it to some of the finest horologists in Hatton Garden. They'd tinker with it and eventually proclaim success, but after a week it would always revert to type – regular as clockwork.

I sat up on the *charpoy*, my shirt drenched with perspiration. The candles had burned out and were now nothing more than pools of melted wax, fossilised on the floor. By the light of the hurricane lamp, one or two other patrons were visible, lying on their sides, passed out on their cots. There was no sign of the girl. Slowly, I rose to my feet and staggered out, back up the stairs and out onto the street.

An industrial fog had settled and the night air smelled foul and reminded me of London. It was only now that I pondered how to get back to the guest house. The chances of finding transport at this hour were slim. Walking was the only real option. Or at least it would have been, if I'd had any idea of where I actually was. I cursed myself for not having had the presence of mind to tell the rickshaw *wallah* to wait. Suddenly it occurred to me that MacAuley had met his end in a similarly unsavoury neighbourhood almost exactly twenty-four hours earlier. It would be ironic for the man charged with investigating his murder to himself be murdered in similar circumstances so soon after. Ironic and not particularly pleasant.

I set off in the direction I hoped was north, groping my way towards a solitary light that in the mist was little more than an orange blur. From somewhere behind me there came a sound. I spun round and reached for my revolver, realising as I did so, that it was still slung over the back of the chair in my room. I cursed myself once again.

'Who's there?' I called out, hoping to mask the fear in my voice.

There was silence. A fat sewer rat scurried out of the gloom and into an open drain. I gave a sigh of relief. The city was making me jumpy.

As I turned back, I felt something. Nothing tangible, just a change in the air and a shifting of shadows. I peered into the black, and, for an instant, thought I heard the faintest of whispers. A shiver ran down my spine. I told myself it was nothing, that I was being paranoid. People often thought they heard things after smoking O. In hindsight, I wished I'd just stayed at the Belvedere instead of venturing out into the middle of nowhere. But hindsight's a commodity that's generally in short supply when you're craving a hit.

Then came another noise. A metallic scraping, louder and closer. Without thinking I backed away and began to hurry in the opposite direction. I turned a corner and collided with a man, knocking him off his feet.

'*Sahib?*'

It was the young rickshaw *wallah* who'd brought me here.

'*Sahib*,' he said, struggling for breath, 'I did not see you exit the premises.' He smiled as I helped him to his feet, then pointed to his rickshaw, which lay close by.

'Guest house?'

I considered going back to investigate the noises, but decided against it. After all, discretion *is* the better part of valour. Doubly so when your gun is sitting in a room half a mile away.

———

Fifteen minutes later we were back in Marcus Square. I got down outside the Belvedere, pulled a one-rupee note from my pocket and handed it to him. He brought out a battered leather purse and began to rummage for change. I stopped him and he looked perplexed.

'Fare is only two annas, *sahib*.'

'The rest is for waiting time,' I said.

He smiled, and pressed his palms together. 'Thank you, *sahib*.'

'What's your name?' I asked.

'Salman.'

'You're a Mohammedan?'

'Yes, *sahib*.'

'Have you lived here all your life?'

'No *sahib*, I originally am coming from Noakhali, in East Bengal. But many years now I am living in Calcutta.'

'So you know the city well?'

'Most certainly, sir,' he said, shaking his head in the Indian fashion.

'I need a good rickshaw *wallah*,' I said. 'One I can call on at short notice. Do you fancy the job?'

'I am always here only,' he said, pointing to the rickshaw stand at the corner of the square.

'Good,' I said, rummaging in my pocket, this time for a five-rupee note. I handed it to him. 'Consider this a retainer.'

———

I let myself back into the guest house and crept silently up to my room. Undressing in the dark, I sat on the bed and rested my back against the headboard. On the floor next to me sat the bottle of whisky and a tooth glass. I picked them up and poured out a measure. Just a nightcap, no more. Swirling the whisky gently round the glass, I let the antiseptic scent envelop me. Feeling calmer than I had in days, I sipped slowly and reflected on events. Only my second week in Calcutta and I already had my first murder. A high-profile one too.

I wondered why Lord Taggart had given me the case. Surely there were a few seasoned inspectors in Calcutta to whom he could have turned? Was he testing me? The proverbial baptism of fire? I pondered the alternatives but made precious little progress in figuring out his motives. Instead, I finished the whisky, lay down and tried to think of other things. I succeeded too, finally falling asleep to the memory of Sarah on the Mile End omnibus.

SIX

Thursday, 10 April 1919

Sometimes it's better not to wake up at all.

But that's impossible in Calcutta. The sun is up at five, heralding a cacophony of dogs, crows and cockerels, and just as the animals get tired, the muezzins kick off, their call to prayer emanating from every minaret in the city. With all the noise, the only Europeans not awake by five thirty are the ones entombed in the Park Street cemetery.

Once more I awoke to the smell of fish. I'd slept fitfully, bothered by the high-pitched whine of a mosquito. Mrs Tebbit had assured me that none had ever crossed the threshold of the Belvedere, but I guess this one hadn't received the memorandum. I rose, showered and shaved, before dressing and heading down to breakfast. The dining room was empty, save for the maidservant, so I sat down at the table and began to set my watch by the clock on the mantelpiece. Mrs Tebbit came in as I was winding it. She carried a plate of what I assumed was kedgeree, probably prepared from the wreckage of the previous night's meal, and proceeded to place it in front of me with a degree of ceremony that the dish really didn't warrant.

'I'm going to have to give it a miss, I'm afraid, Mrs Tebbit,' I said. 'Bit of dicky tummy this morning.' It was a conceit, but it was in a good cause.

'Oh, that *is* a shame, Captain.' She frowned. 'Did it trouble you during the night?'

'I'm afraid so.'

'You poor dear! I thought I heard someone on the stairs last night. Was that you?'

'Probably,' I agreed. It was a perfectly good excuse; one I could use the next time I fancied a midnight sojourn to Tiretta Bazaar.

I opted instead for a cup of black coffee and a glance at the morning's *Statesman*, which lay on the table. It was folded so that only half the front page headline was visible, but it was enough to grab my attention. I unfolded it and read the top story:

SENIOR GOVERNMENT OFFICIAL SLAIN IN COSSIPORE

There followed a report on the crime scene and a description of the state of MacAuley's body that might have caused some of the paper's readers to choke on their morning kedgeree. It was a fulsome and florid report. Accurate, too. Right down to the detail of the bloody note found in his mouth. That he'd been found yards away from a brothel, however, had curiously been omitted. The piece was sure to enflame white opinion, as was the paper's editorial, which had no doubts as to the perpetrators. *Terrorists and revolutionaries!* it screamed, out to overthrow the legitimate rule of law, and it demanded swift and merciless justice.

That worried me. Of course the paper was entitled to its opinion, and to be honest I had no issue with the 'merciless' part. It was the 'swift' part that was the problem, as that depended on me and my team, and if yesterday was anything to go by, it didn't look like we'd be achieving anything much in a hurry.

They'd got hold of the story surprisingly quickly. So much for the L-G's attempt to keep a lid on things by sending in military intelligence. Now that the lurid details of MacAuley's death had been splashed all over the front page, the spotlight would be well and truly on us. Public opinion could always be relied upon to panic at the first hint of trouble. It would demand instant results. Though that wouldn't be a bad thing if it forced the L-G to give me my crime scene back.

———

An hour later I was at my desk looking across at Digby. I'd arrived to find him waiting for me, in a state of some excitement.

'Wyndham!' he'd said. 'I think I may have a breakthrough!'

I took Digby's news on the chin, led him into my office and made myself comfortable while he paced the floor.

'Tell me what you've got.'

He leaned over the desk. 'One of my informants has something. Says he's heard things about who might have killed MacAuley. He claims he's got a name.'

'And you trust him?'

'Of course not,' he snorted, 'he's an Indian. But I pay him, and what he gives me is usually reliable.'

'Where is he?'

'Up in Black Town. He's a *paan* seller. Goes by the name of Vikram. He has a patch near Shyambazar.'

'Okay,' I said, 'check out a motor car. We'll head up there.'

Digby smiled. 'We can't just stroll over there, old boy. Being seen talking to a couple of *sahib* police *wallahs* could have a severe impact on his usefulness, not to mention his life expectancy.'

'So when then?'

'Relax,' he said, tapping his nose, 'I've got it all arranged for this evening.'

Sitting around all day waiting to speak to Digby's snitch was not something I was keen on doing. It was unlikely to meet the *Statesman*'s definition of 'swift and merciless justice' and I doubted the Commissioner would be impressed either.

'You can't make it earlier?'

'Trust me,' he replied, 'it's safer under cover of darkness.'

Grudgingly, I nodded my approval.

'Great!' said Digby, clapping his hands together. 'Will there be anything else, old chap?'

I told him to sit, then briefed him on my conversation with Miss Grant the previous afternoon.

'Her take on MacAuley seems spot on to me,' he said. 'He always was a bit of an odd fish.'

'You knew him pretty well, then?' I asked. 'Shouldn't you have mentioned that before?'

'Well, I never really *knew* him,' he stammered. 'I met him a few times, obviously, but that's all. Calcutta's a small place, and, well, you know how people talk. The chaps at the club would say he was a bit off, if you know what I mean.'

I'd no idea what he meant, and told him so.

He hesitated. 'Well . . . he didn't really mix with many people. Don't get me wrong, I'm sure he was a good pen-pusher, kept the natives in their place and all that, but he wasn't really . . . one of us. They say his father was a *coal miner*.' His tone suggested that, in his eyes at least, it made the man little better than a coolie.

'And what about this fellow Buchan?' I asked. 'Do you know him?'

Digby paused. 'Not well. I've met him once or twice at functions, but that's about it.'

'And would you say he is *one of us*?'

He laughed. 'He's a millionaire. He can be one of us whenever he wants to be. Now if you don't mind, old boy, I'd better get on with things.'

He left, closing the door behind him. I considered my priorities. Waiting till nightfall to question Digby's informant was hardly appealing. Instead, I decided to stick to my original plan. That meant interviewing Buchan, as well as some of MacAuley's colleagues and servants, attending the post-mortem, sorting out a meeting with the L-G and tracking down the preacher Miss Grant had mentioned. Most importantly, I wanted to question the girl, Devi, again. There was something she wasn't telling us and I needed to know what it was. To do that, though, I'd have to get her away from the formidable Mrs Bose.

I telephoned the pit and asked to be put through to Banerjee. The desk sergeant shouted across the room and some moments later, Banerjee came on the line.

'What have you got for me, Sergeant?'

'Well, sir,' he said in that cut-glass accent that made him sound like the Archbishop of Canterbury, 'I placed a telephone call to Mr Buchan's mill works in Serampore. His secretary informed me that Mr Buchan had not been *in situ* for several days and that he gave no indication of a date for his return. The secretary provided me with a telephone number for Mr Buchan's residence. I tried that and was informed that Mr Buchan was down in Calcutta for the week, in residence at his club.'

'Which one?'

'The Bengal Club, sir. I took the liberty of telephoning the reception desk. The clerk informed me that Mr Buchan was indeed in residence, but that he had given instructions not to be disturbed before ten o'clock. He also mentioned that Mr Buchan usually takes a late breakfast at around eleven. We may be able to catch him then.'

'Good,' I said. 'That saves us having to go upriver. See if you can requisition a car and driver. I want to catch our friend Buchan before he leaves the club.'

'Yes, sir.'

'What about the preacher?' I asked. 'Any luck tracking him down?'

'Not at present, sir. I telephoned the *thana* at Dum Dum Cantonment. They informed me that there are several orphanages and Christian missions in the locale. They are making inquiries and will report to me post-haste.'

'Anything else?' I asked.

'One final thing, sir,' he said. 'I've located an address for MacAuley, should you wish to interview his servants.'

'Very good, Sergeant,' I said, noting it down on a scrap of paper. 'Let me know when you've organised the motor car.'

No sooner had I replaced the receiver than the telephone rang again. I expected Banerjee had forgotten to tell me something, but instead was surprised to hear the voice of Daniels, the Commissioner's secretary.

'Wyndham,' he said frantically, 'please come to the Commissioner's office at once. It's urgent!'

SEVEN

'I can't believe Taggart thinks this is a good use of our time,' complained Digby, mopping the perspiration from his forehead with a sodden handkerchief. I had some sympathy with him, and not just because of the temperature, which was around a hundred and ten in the shade. Or at least, it would have been, had there been any.

April wasn't a pleasant month in Calcutta. Not many months are, but April was the start of summer and about as bad as it got. The land was smothered under a torrid blanket of heat, and both Englishman and native stewed during the interminable, exasperating wait for the monsoon rains still two months away.

The three of us – Digby, Banerjee and I – were in the countryside an hour's drive north of the city. Green fields stretched out on all sides. In the distance, time stood still, and men tilled the soil, leading bullock-drawn ploughs across rutted pastures. The driver had pulled over at the roadside and we were now clambering up a steep bank raised some twenty feet above the pastures, on which sat railway tracks. Ahead of us, a stationary train, a coal-black locomotive, beached atop the bank like a fat metallic slug. Behind it, eight carriages, a mix of passenger compartments and goods vans, all painted in the livery of the Eastern Bengal Railway Company. A number of native constables milled around, doing their best to stay out of the sun. They wore khaki uniforms, as did almost all of the officers and men of the Imperial Police Force throughout India. But Calcutta was different. Within the city, our uniforms were white.

'How does he expect us to progress the MacAuley case if he sends us scurrying out to investigate the murder of every Tom, Dick and Harry?' he grumbled.

'I'm sure the Commissioner has his reasons,' I said, though I'd have been at a loss to say what they were.

'Couldn't he have found someone else? It's the death of a *coolie*, for Christ's sake. Surely the officers from the local *thana* could have handled it.' He was panting now, from the heat and the exertion of the climb up the bank.

On Taggart's orders, we'd been dispatched here to investigate a murder. Initial reports spoke of an attack by *dacoits* on a train, an attempted robbery that had gone wrong and resulted in the death of a native railway guard. While the colour of a man's skin should have no bearing on the importance of the case, the reality was that it generally did, and I confess that, like Digby, I was surprised that Taggart had deemed it prudent to divert us from the MacAuley case to investigate what was essentially a botched robbery.

What activity there was seemed centred on the guards' van at the rear of the train. I ordered Banerjee to go up front and question the driver while Digby and I headed for the rear. Two constables were busy lowering a body, wrapped in a sheet, from the bogie and onto the ground below.

I ordered one of the constables to uncover the victim's head. It wasn't a pleasant sight: broken nose, face severely bruised and hair matted and sticky with blood. Whoever had done this wasn't shy about using their fists. I nodded to the constable to cover him up.

Inside the guards' van, two men stood silhouetted and in the midst, it seemed, of a heated discussion. The shorter of the two, a man in a peaked cap, looked the more agitated, gesticulating, then pointing a fat finger at the chest of the other. I assumed he was the senior officer on site. It came as a shock then to find that he wore not the uniform of a policeman, but of a railway conductor. He looked Anglo-Indian, and the man he was busy berating was a native police sergeant. Both seemed relieved to see us.

'English officers!' exclaimed the railwayman. 'Maybe now we'll get somewhere.'

I ignored him and turned to the sergeant, who seemed cut from the same cloth as Banerjee: thin, bespectacled, and almost as depressed-looking.

'What happened here?' I asked.

The railwayman interjected before the Indian could reply. 'If you want to know that,' he said, 'I'm the one to tell you, on account of me being the ranking railway officer and seeing as I was actually here when it happened.'

I sighed. I never enjoyed dealing with minor public officials. They tended to have rather inflated opinions of their own importance, and the ones in peaked caps tended to be the worst.

'And you are?'

'Perkins, sir. Albert Perkins,' he said, puffing out his chest and rising to his full height of five foot five, plus cap. 'Senior guard on this train.'

'In that case, Mr Perkins, you'd better tell us what happened. From the beginning.'

'Well,' said Perkins, 'if you want it from the beginning, then that's where I'll start. We were scheduled to leave Sealdah station last night at a half past one,' he began, 'but were delayed by about ninety minutes, so it was after three a.m. by the time we finally got underway. For an hour or so, everything went as normal. Then as we reached this spot, someone pulled the communication cord. Of course the driver immediately brought the engine to a halt.

'I made my way through the carriages to see what the problem was. I don't mind telling you, it's not often you get someone pulling the cord on a night train. It was when I reached the second-class passenger compartment that the trouble started. Two Indians stood up, respectable-looking types in suits, they were. One of them pointed a gun in my face and ordered me to lie face down on the floor. Of course, I did as I was told. Some of the passengers began to panic, but one of the men shouted something in Bengali and got them to shut up. I couldn't see much from the floor, but I'm sure the other fellow then left the carriage. About a minute later, I heard voices coming from down on the tracks: natives, and quite a few of them by the sound of it. There was a bit of a commotion going on outside. I expected them to pass through the compartments robbing the passengers of their valuables, but they didn't. Not even the first-class carriage. According to the driver, they just placed one of their men in each of the carriages and a couple up front in the locomotive, while the rest of them came here to the rear of the train.'

'What happened then?'

Perkins shrugged. 'I don't rightly know. The scoundrel kept me on the floor the whole time. All the while I could hear shouting coming from the rear. Eventually, it must have been just before five o'clock, there was a shout and the *dacoit* in our compartment went outside. I expected him to come back with some of his compatriots, but he didn't. He and the rest of them just melted away.'

'What did you do then?'

'I didn't do anything, not till the driver and his mate came looking for me. How was I to know the bastards had scarpered? After that, I left the carriage with Evans, that's the driver. He's a real

79

Englishman, you know. From London, so he says. Been driving the number forty-three for almost twenty years now. Once I'd confirmed with him that the miscreants had made a run for it, I began checking each compartment in turn. Several English ladies in first class were quite distressed by the whole episode, but none had been harmed. It was only when I'd passed through the entire train and reached the guards' van that I found young Pal's body.' He pointed down to the tracks, to the body wrapped in the sheet.

'That was his name, was it?'

Perkins nodded solemnly. 'Hiren Pal.'

I surveyed the van. The compartment was divided in two by a wire grille, with a door allowing movement between both halves. On this side of the grille stood a small desk with papers strewn over it. On the floor beside it an overturned chair, a smashed hurricane lamp and some papers that had fallen and become stuck in the pool of coagulating blood. On the other side sat a dozen or so heavy-looking burlap sacks, and beside them two large safes, both open.

'Why d'you think they attacked him?' asked Digby.

'I don't know,' replied the conductor.

'What did they take?' I asked.

The railwayman removed his cap and scratched his head. 'That's the thing. As far as I can tell, they didn't take anything.'

'Nothing?' asked Digby. 'A bunch of *dacoits* attack a train, kill a guard and then leave with nothing? That's ridiculous.'

'I'm telling you,' said Perkins vehemently, 'all the mail sacks are still here, and as I said before, they didn't rob the passengers.'

'What about those safes?' I asked. 'What was in them?'

'Last night, nothing,' said Perkins.

'Is that usual?'

'Some nights they're full. Other nights they're empty. This is the forty-three *down* after all.'

He read our expressions.

'The forty-three *down* is the Darjeeling Mail,' he said by way of clarification. 'It's the main service between Calcutta and North Bengal. Most everything going up there, from people to livestock to official government correspondence, goes on the forty-three *down*.'

'And how did you raise the alarm?' I asked.

'The twenty-six *up* passed by about ten minutes after the *dacoits* had fled. We flagged it down and told the conductor what had transpired. They offered to help, then went up the line to Naihati and got the word out.'

I turned back to the Indian sergeant. 'Where are the passengers?' I asked.

'The second- and third-class passengers have been removed to the station at Bandel Junction for questioning,' he replied. 'The first-class passengers were all Europeans, sir. They were also taken to Bandel but allowed to continue their journeys. We have names and addresses for all of them, though.'

The first-class passengers had been white. As such, there was little prospect of them following the order of a native officer to hang around for hours in the middle of nowhere for questioning. In India, it seemed, even the forces of law and order were subordinate to the hard fact of race.

I left Digby to take a full statement from the conductor while I crunched my way across the gravel to the front of the train. Banerjee was talking to the driver. On seeing me, he clambered down from the locomotive.

'Have you got much out of him?' I asked.

'I've been taking a statement from him, sir, but it's proving most challenging. His English isn't so good.'

'Odd,' I said. 'The conductor said he was an Englishman.'

'I fear he may be correct, sir. You may wish to question him yourself.'

Evans was a stocky man who looked as solid as the locomotive he drove. His face and overalls were flecked with coal dust and the creases of his face were lined with soot. I took an instant liking to him.

His version of events was similar to that of Perkins: around an hour out of Calcutta's Sealdah station, someone had pulled the communication cord and Evans had brought the train to a halt. But while Perkins had spent the rest of the attack making a close inspection of the floor of the second-class compartment, Evans, up front in the locomotive, had had a better view of what had then transpired.

'As soon as we was stopped,' he said, 'a whole load of the buggers came at us from all sides. From the front, from the left, from the right.'

'How many?' I asked.

Evans shrugged. 'Can't rightly say, Guv'nor, on account of it being pitch black, but there would've been at least ten of 'em, I'd say. Then one of 'em climbs up 'ere an' points a shooter at me. Tells me to put me 'ands up. Twenty years ago I'd 'ave took a swing at 'im, but I'm not exactly in me prime no more. Anyways, then the rest of 'em fans out along the train. I could 'ear the ladies in first class all shriekin'. Still, they quieted down smartish. I 'spect one of the wogs probably pulled a shooter on *them* an' all.'

'Could you make out what was going on in the guards' van?'

He shook his head. 'Nah. Too far away.'

'Then what happened?'

'The wog that was in 'ere with me an' Eric,' he pointed to his mate who was busy shovelling coal into the engine's furnace, 'he wanted us to get down off the engine, but we refused, didn't we,

Eric?' The coal man nodded and continued shovelling. 'I says to 'im, "You might as well bloody shoot me, cos I been drivin' the Darjeelin' Mail for more years than you been on God's green earth an' I ain't gettin' down off this engine till we reach Hardinge Bridge." In the end, the little bastard changed his mind an' let us stay up 'ere. It was all quite civil after that, just me an' Eric and the little wog wiv his gun trained on us. We could hear all sorts goin' on round the back but we couldn't see nuffink in the dark.

'After about an hour or so, just before the sun was comin' up, one of the bastards down on the track starts shoutin' summink. Then the whole bleedin' lot of 'em, includin' our little friend up 'ere, jump off the train an' scarper. Some of 'em headed off in that direction.' He pointed across the fields to the north. 'The rest of 'em went down there towards the road. They was all gone in a matter of minutes.'

'And then?'

'Well, me an' Eric, we waits a little while. By now the sun's comin' up, so we 'ave a look around, just to make sure the coast is clear an' that none of the bastards is still 'angin' about. We can't see any of 'em, so we jump down and make our way along the train lookin' for old Perkins. I was rather hopin' they'd have ruffed him up a little, but there he was, lyin' on the floor of the second-class carriage, like a baby 'avin' a nap. Anyway, once he'd got up off his belly, he told me to get back up to the engine while he checked the rest of the carriages. It was 'im who found poor Pal.'

'Tell me about him.'

Evans shrugged. 'Decent chap, came from a family of railway-men. 'E'd been workin' on the railways since 'e was a boy. Quiet lad, 'e was, wouldn't say boo to a goose. I can't imagine 'im standin' up to a gang of *dacoits*, though. Why they saw fit to beat *'im* up rather than Perkins, I can't rightly say.'

'You're not fond of the conductor?'

'Well, you've met 'im. Do you like 'im? Now imagine you 'ad to work with the old coot day in, day out, for the last seven years.'

I had one final question. 'Are *dacoit* attacks common in these parts?'

Evans shook his head. 'It's not un'eard of, specially in the wilds up-country or out in Bihar – which is the arse end of nowhere, by the way – but I ain't never 'eard of *dacoits* hittin' a train this close to Calcutta before.'

Thanking him, I jumped back down to the track and called over to Banerjee, who was talking to one of the local constables.

'Let's take a walk, Sergeant,' I said, heading towards the fields through which, according to Evans, some of the attackers had made off. For ten minutes we scoured the area to the north of the train, but other than some flattened grass, there was nothing.

Returning to the train, we headed south-east, towards a tarmac road, where the driver had said the rest of the *dacoits* had headed.

'What road is this?' I asked Banerjee.

'The Grand Trunk Road, sir.'

'Does it lead back to Calcutta?'

'Yes, sir.'

'And in the other direction?'

Banerjee smiled. 'It's over two thousand miles long, sir. It goes all the way to Delhi and then on to the Khyber Pass and Kabul.'

'I think we can discount the possibility of our culprits fleeing to Afghanistan, Sergeant,' I said. 'What I want to know is what's the next major town it passes through.'

'In the immediate vicinity, sir, I think it passes through Naryanpore.'

'How far is that?'

'No idea, sir. I'm not sure exactly where we are.'

We continued walking along the road for some minutes until we reached a small dirt lay-by.

'Look,' I said to Banerjee, pointing to some tracks in the earth.

'Tyre prints,' he said. 'A motorised vehicle was here, probably not too long ago. A car?'

'No,' I said. 'The tracks are too wide for car tyres. These were made by something larger, a lorry most likely.'

We continued to search for some time longer but found nothing. I checked my watch. It was almost nine thirty. We'd need to leave soon if we were to catch Mr Buchan at the Bengal Club. Reluctantly I called to Banerjee to head back to the train.

———

'Theories, gentlemen?' I asked as the car sped back towards Calcutta. All three of us were squashed into the back.

'It seems pretty clear to me, old boy,' said Digby. '*Dacoits* attack the mail train hoping to rob the safes. They find them empty and in their frustration attack the guard. When he dies, they take fright and flee. We should order the district police to round up the local miscreants. We're not dealing with the most sophisticated individuals here. One of them's bound to talk and give the whole game away.'

It was a tempting course of action. Chalk it down to incompetent bandits and get the local boys to deal with it. The problem was that particular scenario didn't fit the facts. From what I could tell, the attackers had been far from incompetent. Indeed, everything suggested they'd planned things meticulously. Everything except the outcome, of course, and that raised the biggest question of all. If robbery was their motive, why didn't they steal anything?

EIGHT

The Bengal Club was situated on the Esplanade, a wide avenue tucked between the L-G's residence of Government House and the Hooghly river. The gates were manned by two mountainous, bearded Sikhs, and given their size, there seemed little need for the gates themselves. Both wore uniforms of red and white and sported as much gold braid as an entire regiment of the Household Cavalry. Golden badges, affixed to their white turbans, glinted in the mid-morning sun.

As we approached, one of the hulking sentries stepped forward, raising a hand the size of a tennis racquet. The driver slowed to a stop and Banerjee got out and walked up to the man. He barely came up to the Sikh's chest. What happened next was unexpected. Banerjee began shouting and gesturing like a madman, and the startled guard immediately changed his attitude, bowing and frantically waving us through, while his colleague stood ram-rod straight and saluted. It was like watching a Jack Russell scare the life out of a Doberman.

'Good show, Surrender-not,' I said as the sergeant rejoined us. 'I feared for a moment he might squash you.'

The car crunched down a long gravel driveway between immaculate lawns. A number of native gardeners were busy cutting the already perfect grass, like barbers tending to a bald man. The club itself resembled a mini Blenheim Palace whitewashed and transported to the tropics, and was yet another example of us living out our imperial fantasies through architecture. British India, where every Englishman has a castle.

The car came to a stop outside a rather grand entrance. A brass plaque screwed to one of the columns read, *The Bengal Club, Est.1827*. Beside it stood a wooden sign, its perfect white letters bearing the message:

NO DOGS OR INDIANS BEYOND THIS POINT

Surrender-not noticed my distaste.

'Don't worry, sir,' he said. 'We Indians know our place. Besides, the British have achieved certain things in a hundred and fifty years that our civilisation didn't in over four thousand.'

'Absolutely,' chimed Digby.

'Such as?' I asked.

Banerjee's lips contorted in a thin smile. 'Well, we never managed to teach the dogs to read.' He suggested he take a walk round the grounds while Digby and I went in search of Buchan.

'Absolutely not,' I said. 'I'll be damned if you wait out here *slacking* while Digby and I do the hard work.'

He smiled. 'Yes, sir. Sorry, sir.'

'If I may, old boy,' said Digby, 'it might be better if the sergeant did remain out here. The last thing we want is to put people's backs up, especially if we'd like them to answer some questions.'

That might have been the tactful thing to do, but I wasn't much inclined to be tactful. Fortunately Surrender-not stepped in.

'Sir,' he said, 'perhaps I could question some of the grounds staff?'

'Very well, Sergeant,' I said, and Surrender-not set off across the lawns while Digby and I headed inside.

The lobby was cavernous, the decor comprising more marble, more columns and more busts on plinths than was strictly necessary in any building that wasn't the British Museum. If Julius Caesar or Plato had dropped in for a drink, they'd have felt quite at home. At the far end, marooned behind a reception desk, sat a middle-aged Indian in a black jacket emblazoned with the club's crest. While Digby enquired after Buchan, I took the chance to look around.

On one wall, a large oak panel listed the past presidents of the club: a roll-call of colonels, generals, knights of the realm and even the odd 'Right Honourable', all immortalised in golden type. The other walls sported the mounted heads of tigers, rhinos and more sets of antlers than you'd find on the heads of a whole herd of deer running around a Highland estate. The reception desk sat under another full-length portrait of George V, this time in full military regalia and looking slightly constipated. It always struck me how similar he looked to Kaiser Wilhelm. As far as I could tell, the only difference between them was their choice of facial hair. Dress them up in each other's uniforms and I doubt anyone would have noticed the difference. Even for cousins, the resemblance was uncanny. Sad then, that so many should have died for what was essentially a family squabble.

'Buchan's having breakfast on the first-floor veranda,' said Digby, walking towards an ornate staircase. 'This way.'

I followed him up, then through a mirrored landing to a large drawing room, empty save for a few grey-haired old duffers reading the papers. They reminded me of Colonel Tebbit: all moustaches and mutton chops and faces the colour of beetroot.

We continued onwards, through a set of French doors and onto a shaded veranda. Half a dozen tables and cane chairs were set out under an awning. All were empty, save for the one furthest from us, where sat a stocky gentleman in a white shirt and blue silk waistcoat, reading a newspaper. A plate of ripe yellow mangoes sat on the table in front of him. I didn't need Digby to point him out as our man. There was something about him, a barely concealed strength, like a retired boxer. He looked up at the sound of our footsteps and put the newspaper to one side. Steel-grey eyes, strong jaw and a sheer physical presence with an underlying hint of menace. He looked like a cliff face.

'Mr Buchan, sir,' said Digby, 'may we have a few minutes of your time?'

'Ah, Digby,' said Buchan, his voice rough as a tank engine. 'How the devil are ye, man?'

'Excellent, sir, excellent. Thank you for asking,' said Digby as though licking the boots of the Viceroy himself. He gestured to me. 'May I introduce Captain Sam Wyndham, formerly of Scotland Yard.'

Buchan acknowledged me with a slight nod of his shaved, bullet head.

'Mr Buchan,' I said, returning the gesture.

'Captain Wyndham and I were hoping to ask you a few questions, sir, regarding this MacAuley business,' said Digby, indicating the headline in Buchan's newspaper.

Buchan gestured to two empty wicker chairs. 'Of course, gentlemen. Please join me.'

A turbaned waiter appeared, unbidden, at our side.

'What'll ye have?' asked Buchan.

I shook my head. 'Nothing, sir.'

With a flick of his hand, Buchan dismissed the waiter, who melted away as unobtrusively as he'd materialised.

'Gentlemen, this is a bloody disgrace,' said Buchan, tapping the newspaper with one large hand. 'What's this country coming to when the wee bastards have the audacity to murder an aide to the

Lieutenant Governor? And here, of all places! Right in the middle o' Calcutta!'

'We're on the case, sir,' insisted Digby. 'You can be sure of that.'

Buchan ignored his protestations. 'And what have our *good* friends in the Indian Congress Party had tae say about it? *Nothin'*. These preachers of "non-violence"? How many o' them have come out and condemned this act of supreme violence? Not a single one . . . Bloody hypocrites. I tell ye, gentlemen, an example needs to be made of whoever did this. We have tae send a message to the natives that this sort of *mendacity* will be met without mercy. Hang half a dozen of 'em and their families and you can be sure they'll no' try something like that again in a hurry.'

He picked up a folding knife that lay on the table and proceeded to expertly slice off a piece of mango, raising it to his mouth with the knife-point.

'We're going to apprehend whoever was responsible,' I said. 'That's why we're here. We'd like to ask you some questions.'

'Aye,' he said, 'and what would ye like to know?'

'Mr MacAuley was a friend of yours?' I asked.

Buchan nodded. 'That's right,' he growled. 'A good friend, and I'm no' ashamed to say it . . . unlike some.'

'Tell me about him.'

'What d'ye want to know?'

'How long had you known him?'

'I guess it must be nigh on twenty years.' He sighed.

'And did you meet in India?'

'Aye.' He nodded. 'Met him in Calcutta; right here in this very club, as it happens. It's odd, we grew up down the road frae each other back in Scotland, but we never met there. I'd just come back from negotiatin' a large jute purchase out near Dacca and was on my way back tae Dundee. Thought I'd stop off in Calcutta for some creature comforts afore the long voyage home. It was a party hosted by the Viceroy, if I'm no' mistaken. I moved out here soon after. Looked him up when I got here.'

'You looked him up specifically?'

'Aye. He may have been just a junior clerk back then but he was already marked out as a rising man. An' he was a Taysider like mysel'. Don't we all crave the familiar when we're far from home, Captain?'

That was probably true. You only had to look around for confirmation. One glance at Calcutta, that little piece of England dropped slap bang into a Bengal bog, would tell you that we British probably craved the familiar a good deal more than most.

'What sort of a man was he?' I asked.

Buchan thought for a moment. 'A decent man,' he replied. 'A hard-workin' servant o' the Crown. He did as much as a'body in helping to improve this place. An' it was no easy job, 'specially no' in the last few years when he had to deal wi' growin' demands for the *Indianisation* of every bloody thing.' He screwed up his face in disgust.

'You don't think that's a good idea, sir?'

'On the contrary, Captain. It *is* a good idea, at least on paper. Make some concessions, let the Indians gradually take over some of the responsibility for running this country so that one day, they can take their seat at the table o' nations in the empire, beside Australia and Canada and the like. But in practice? You have to remember that the Indian is an Asiatic. He cannae be relied on in the way you could an Australian or a Canadian – or even a South African, for that matter. All that our reforms have done is open a Pandora's box. We've given them a taste o' power and rather than being grateful, all they want is more, and then more still. They won't be satisfied until they control everything we've built here. That's what MacAuley had to deal with.'

'How did it affect him?'

'Take that whole Champaran business a couple of years ago. When that rabble-rousing wee lawyer frae Gujurat came over and brought the place to a standstill for months. The peasants stopped paying their rent or harvesting the indigo. *Non-violent civil disobedience*, they called it. More like blackmail. The Viceroy ordered the L-G to sort it out and, as usual, that chinless wonder didnae have a clue what to do. So it was up to MacAuley to deal wi' it all. The poor man had to force the landowners to give in to most o' the peasants' demands. A lot o' them weren't happy with him, felt he'd railroaded them into a settlement just to save the Viceroy embarrassment. And you'd think the Indians would hae been thankful for the deal he'd got them, but no. No' a bit of it! That was just the beginnin'. Every few months now they make some new attempt to grab more concessions. You should see the number of strikes I have to deal with at my mills. An' each time they're successful, it just makes 'em worse. They think they can get away wi' anything. I suppose it was only a matter o' time before they tried somethin' like this,' he said, tapping the newspaper headline.

'Was MacAuley ever in your employment?' I asked.

Buchan ate another piece of mango before answering. 'He'd been in the ICS as long as I'd known him.'

The choice of words was interesting.

'And did your friend ever do you any favours?'

The question hung in the air like a bad smell. Digby squirmed awkwardly in his seat as Buchan fixed me with a stare. I didn't mind. I was hoping to incite a reaction. He looked down at his plate. Slowly and deliberately, he took his knife and drove it deep into a fresh mango, expertly slicing it into quarters around the stone at its heart. When he looked up, his expression was once again calm.

'Well, Captain, as you say, he was a friend. He sometimes gave me an insight on the thinking inside government circles if they had a certain impact on business matters.'

I had to give the man credit. He wasn't about to let himself be provoked. He'd sized me up and decided that the friendly approach was best. After all, I was just a policeman here to find out who'd killed his friend. Still, his reaction was telling. It was the reaction of a politician.

'And did that include insights into government policy on the partition of Bengal?' I asked.

Buchan rubbed the back of his neck with one hand. 'I don't see how that's in any way relevant, Captain. It happened fifteen years ago.'

'We're working on a theory that MacAuley may have been killed by someone who held a grudge against him. Possibly linked to his role in pushing through the Curzon partition. I understand a lot of people were ruined by it.'

'Aye!' he said irritably. 'A lot of the old *zamindars* took a big hit. An' I'll admit, we did talk about it at the time. Hell, it was the biggest thing to happen in this part o' the world since the Battle of Plassey! It was the only thing *anyone* was talkin' about back then. In fact, it would have been strange if he hadn't discussed it with me. But we only chatted about it, that's all. He certainly didn't seek my opinion.'

He turned to Digby. 'I hope you an' the captain didn't just come here for a history lesson. Surely you've got more pertinent questions for me? Somethin' relevant to a murder inquiry? I'd hate to have to tell Taggart that his officers are wasting my time on ancient history when they should be out catching the bastards who did this.'

Digby spluttered protestations to the contrary. I ignored whatever it was he was saying.

'Did he have many other friends?' I asked.

Buchan took another piece of mango. 'Not really. An' before you ask, Captain, I don't know why. I guess he just wasnae that sociable.'

'Do you think it had anything to do with his background?'

'You mean, being frae Tayside? I doubt it, Captain, it's never done *me* any harm.'

'I meant his social class.'

Buchan thought about it. 'Aye, I can see why you might think that. But to be honest, Calcutta's the kind of place where a man who has the ear of the Lieutenant Governor will never be short of friends – of a certain sort, at any rate. I think it would be more accurate to say he just didn't want them.'

That at least chimed with what Annie Grant had told me. I changed tack.

'Did you notice any change in his behaviour over the last few months? I understand he may have had a religious conversion?'

Buchan's expression darkened again. 'You mean all the nonsense that preacher was fillin' his head with?'

I nodded.

'What can I tell ye? Some time ago, some Calvinist minister by the name o' Gunn arrived here from South Africa. One o' those earnest types that believes we've a God-given duty to save the heathens from themselves. He'd known MacAuley from way back. He'd even known MacAuley's wife.'

'MacAuley's married?'

'*Was* married,' said Buchan. 'She died a long time ago, back in Scotland. It may have been why he decided to come out here in the first place.'

It seemed that MacAuley and I may have come to Calcutta for the same reason. It wasn't a particularly inspiring precedent.

94

I tried to focus. Buchan was still talking. 'Anyway, before long he's attendin' church every Sunday and talkin' about giving up the drink. As you can imagine, Captain, that's a pretty serious step for a Scotsman.'

'What can you tell me about this chap, Gunn?' I asked.

'Not much. I've only met him a few times. Let's just say we don't have much in common.' He took a gold pocket watch from his waistcoat and made a show of checking the time. 'Gentlemen,' he said, 'I don't mean to be rude, but I have to be back in Serampore by two, so I'm afraid we'll need to wrap this up.'

'Of course, sir,' said Digby, ever obliging. He made to rise from his chair. I put a hand on his shoulder.

'Just one or two more questions, sir. If you wouldn't mind.'

Buchan nodded.

'We understand that on the evening of his murder, MacAuley attended a party here, hosted by you?'

'That's right,' he said, looking out over the gardens below. 'I was having a wee soirée for a few Americans who were looking to place a large order. I thought a party wi' the cream of Calcutta society might impress them. I'd even have got the Viceroy over, had he been in town. You know how Americans are, so proud of their republic but then so quick to fawn over anyone with a title. I've often thought I'd have made a lot more money out of Americans if I'd have been born a lord.'

'What time did MacAuley leave?'

'I cannae say for sure. I was busy seeing to my other guests, but it was probably some time between ten and eleven.'

'Do you know where he was going?'

He shook his head. 'Not a clue, Captain, I assumed he was going home.'

'Any idea what he was doing up in Black Town?'

95

'None at all,' said Buchan. He sounded peeved. 'Maybe you should ask Gunn? For all I know, MacAuley was up there helpin' him save heathens.' He gave a hollow laugh. 'And now, gentlemen, I really must be going.' He rose and held out his hand for me to shake.

'I'm havin' another wee get-together next week, Captain,' he said, walking towards the French doors. 'Come along if you're free. I'd be happy to introduce you to some o' Calcutta's finest. You too, of course, Digby. I'll have my secretary send you the details.'

Once he'd departed, Digby and I sat back down. I looked out over the veranda. In the distance, Surrender-not was talking to a gardener.

'What do you make of that, old boy?' asked Digby, smiling.

'The religious angle is curious,' I said. 'We may need to look into that.'

'You think some local hotheads might have knocked him off for preaching?'

That was unlikely. I had trouble picturing a bunch of fundamentalist natives killing MacAuley for preaching the Good News. In fact, there was probably more chance of the good Lord himself deciding to smite MacAuley with a bolt of lightning for a bit of a laugh. In my experience, the Almighty could be capricious like that. Nevertheless, I wasn't going to share any more of my thinking with Digby just yet. I was missing something – a connection I was failing to make. Maybe it was down to the heat, or the O, or Mrs Tebbit's food, but for whatever reason, I wasn't yet as sharp as I should be.

'I think we need to be open to all possibilities,' I said.

Back at the entrance, Digby signalled for the driver while I went looking for Surrender-not. The heat of the day was fierce now and I found him sitting on a bench in the shade of a jacaranda tree, holding one of its purple flowers and lost in thought. I called over to him and he snapped out of his reverie, dropping the flower. He stood up and hurriedly made his way over.

'I thought we agreed *no slacking*?'

'Sorry, sir, I was just . . .'

We walked back across the lawns to the entrance. The motor car was waiting with its engine idling. Digby was seated in the back, watching us.

'Did you find out anything useful?'

'Possibly,' he replied, almost breaking into a run to keep pace with me. 'I had a cigarette with one of the bearers who was on duty the night before last.'

'The night of Mr Buchan's party?'

'Yes, sir. Apparently this was one of Mr Buchan's more sedate soirées. Normally they continue till two or three in the morning. This one was over by midnight.'

'And did he see MacAuley leave, by any chance?'

'He did. He believes it was around eleven, and this is the interesting part: he intimated that before MacAuley departed, Buchan and he left the other guests and went into another room for fifteen minutes. When they came out, Buchan was red faced and MacAuley left without a word to anyone else. Buchan then made a call from the members' telephone.'

'Did he hear any of what they were talking about?'

'Unfortunately not, sir. He says the doors were closed and he had no business listening anyway.'

'What about Buchan's telephone call?'

'Again, no, sir.'

That was unfortunate, though what the sergeant had discovered was still interesting. Curious that Buchan should neglect to mention his last conversation with MacAuley.

I turned to Banerjee. 'I've got one more task for you, Sergeant.'

'Yes, sir?'

'I want you to hang around here for a little while longer. Speak to your new friend again and find out if Buchan himself left the club at any time after the party the other night. Also, try to question some more of the staff, especially that chap at reception. That telephone call Buchan made – see if you can find out if anyone placed it for him. I want to know who he called.'

Banerjee nodded, before jogging back in the direction we'd just come. I joined Digby in the car.

'Did the sergeant find out anything useful?' he asked.

I gave him a summary, telling him about MacAuley's departure from the party at around eleven p.m., and his private conversation with Buchan.

'So at this point,' I said, 'that makes Buchan the last person to see him alive.'

NINE

The traffic round the Esplanade was at a standstill. A bullock cart, loaded with vegetables, had overturned, shedding its cargo and blocking the road. Buses and cars stood gridlocked, their drivers blowing their horns impotently. A decent-sized crowd of natives had gathered to gawk at the spectacle and a couple of street urchins were taking the opportunity to liberate some cauliflowers from the stricken cart while its owner's attention was elsewhere. Even the rickshaws were stuck, but their passengers simply got out and walked. The rickshaw *wallahs* seemed to take it quite philosophically, which was more than I was doing.

It had been over thirty hours since we'd found the body, and in that time all I'd achieved was to rack up a series of unanswered questions. Of these, why Buchan had omitted to mention his late-night chat with MacAuley was just the latest. It was in good company. I still wanted to know how the L-G had found out about MacAuley's murder so quickly, and why he'd ordered Section H to take over the crime scene. Then there was the small matter of what the prostitute was concealing from us. On top of it all, I now had the added headache of figuring out why *dacoits* would hit a train, kill a man and not bother to steal anything. The more I thought about it, the muddier it all got.

I punched the seat in frustration. I'm not exactly a patient man these days, my full measure of restraint having been expended sitting in a trench for several years acting as target practice for German artillery. Luckily I had an idea. I pulled out the scrap of paper with the address that Surrender-not had given me earlier.

'Where's Princep Street?' I asked Digby.

'Not far from here, old boy, just off Bentinck Street.'

I ordered him back to headquarters while I got out and set off for MacAuley's lodgings. I headed along the Esplanade and turned left onto Bentinck Street, past venerable old office buildings, homes to the merchant houses that had built Calcutta. On the right stood Chowringhee Square, dominated by the grand offices of the *Statesman*, with its circular portico. As I approached, I was surprised to see Annie Grant emerge through the building's revolving doors. She was preoccupied, otherwise she'd have seen me as she turned and walked briskly in the direction of Writers' Building.

I cautioned myself against jumping to any conclusions. For all I knew she might have been there for any number of reasons, but I couldn't shake the feeling that her visit had something to do with MacAuley's murder. The *Statesman* had got hold of the story pretty damn quickly and published a surprisingly accurate account. What better source than the victim's secretary? I thought about confronting her but that was a hare-brained idea. What was I going to do? Accuse her of selling information to the press? Even if I was right, she'd probably deny it and I couldn't prove a thing. And it wasn't a crime to talk to the press. At least, I didn't think so. It wasn't clear to me just how far the Rowlatt Acts went. If I was wrong, she might think I was following her. Either way, it would kill any chance I had of getting to know her better. So I left it, and continued to Princep Street.

MacAuley's flat was located in a grey mansion block opposite a park. The entrance was manned by a surly *durwan* who directed me to the third floor. The stairwell smelled of respectability. In truth, it smelled of disinfectant, but in Calcutta that's pretty much the same thing. I knocked on the door of number seven and it was opened by an anxious-looking native, dressed neatly in shirt and trousers. He eyed me cautiously.

'Can I help you, sir?'

'You are Mr MacAuley's manservant?'

The man nodded watchfully.

I introduced myself and told him I had some questions about his erstwhile employer. He seemed somewhat surprised.

'But I already have spoken yesterday to *police*.' He pronounced the word '*pooleesh*'.

'Well, *I* need you to answer some more questions for me,' I replied.

He nodded, then led the way down a darkened hallway and into an austere lounge, which contained a threadbare sofa, some chairs, a dining table and a nondescript view out of the window. It was the living room of a man who mostly lived elsewhere. On the table sat a pile of files tied together with red ribbons.

'*Cha, sahib?*'

I declined, took a seat on one of the chairs and beckoned the manservant to the sofa.

'What's your name?'

'Sandesh,' he answered nervously.

'How long have you worked for Mr MacAuley?'

He thought for a moment. 'Almost fifteen years I have been working for Master *sahib*. Since before he is moving to these lodgings.'

'And how did you come to be in his employment?'

'Excuse me, *sahib*?'

'How did you get the job?'

'I was given recommendation by the manservant of one of Master *sahib*'s former colleagues.'

'And was MacAuley *sahib* a good employer?'

He smiled. 'Most definitely. He was very fair and scrupulous man. Always he is upstanding in his dealings with me and also other staff.'

'Other staff?'

'There is also a cook and a maid in Master *sahib*'s employ.'

'Are they here?'

'No, *sahib*. Maid only comes three times per week. Cook is here in mornings, but I tell him yesterday he is no longer required. No one else is here to cook for.'

'MacAuley lived here alone?'

'Yes, *sahib*,' he nodded, 'always Master *sahib* is living alone. Though I am having quarters behind the kitchen.'

'Did he have any family in Calcutta?'

He shook his head. 'No family. Not only in Calcutta, *sahib*, but also no family elsewhere. He is having one nephew, son of his deceased brother, but nephew is being killed in war, two years previous. Nephew's death is causing Master *sahib* much distress. Master *sahib* now last of family line and he is having no *issue*, so family name dying out upon passing of himself.'

'*Issue?*' I asked.

He looked puzzled. '*Issue* is not correct English word, *sahib*? I am told it is meaning, eh, childrens?'

I guessed he was probably correct. Something I was beginning to learn about Calcutta – the Indians, other than Surrender-not with his twenty-four-carat diction, generally favoured a form of English that seemed an odd mix of Victorian expressions and a perpetual present tense.

'What about friends?' I asked. 'Did he have many visitors?'

'Again no, *sahib*. Visitors are calling here most rarely.'

'And women? Did he have any particular lady friends?'

He laughed awkwardly. 'Master *sahib* is never having the lady callers. Only lady who is coming occasionally is his secretary, Miss Grant. *Memsahib* is coming for work purposes.' He pointed to the files on the table. 'She is coming again last evening only, and is removing certain files and documentations.'

'Do you know what files she took?'

'I am sorry, *sahib*. These matters are outwith my purview.'

That was interesting. Once again Miss Grant had unexpectedly entered the picture. It may have been innocent coincidence, but I'm not a man who generally believes in them. She hadn't mentioned anything about needing to go to MacAuley's flat when I'd interviewed her. But then again, why would she?

'Did MacAuley *sahib* have any enemies?'

'Master *sahib* is most upstanding person,' he retorted, 'admired by all.'

I pressed him. 'Was there anyone he didn't like?'

The servant thought for a moment. 'Stevens *sahib*,' he said, 'number two to Master *sahib* in office. I am overhearing Master *sahib* often saying that Stevens *sahib* is no good rascal. Master *sahib* always keeping close eye on machinations of Stevens *sahib*. He is saying Stevens *sahib* is covetous of Master *sahib*'s good standing with L-G *sahib*.'

'Did you notice anything unusual in MacAuley *sahib*'s behaviour recently?'

The servant paused and rubbed the skin on the back of his neck.

'I do not wish to speak ill of Master *sahib*.'

I changed my tone. Sometimes it helps to take a stronger line. 'Your employer was murdered and this is a police investigation. Now answer the question.'

The man flinched, then his story trickled out.

'For last three-four months,' he said, 'Master *sahib* is behaving in most unorthodox fashion. He is making late-night trips, returning at all hours. First he is eschewing all liquor, then in last month he is once again partaking most heavily.'

'Do you have any idea what might have caused the changes in his behaviour?'

He shook his head. 'That I am sadly not knowing, *sahib*.'

'And when was the last time you saw MacAuley?'

He thought for a moment. 'Tuesday, in the evening. Before he is going to Bengal Club.'

'And did he tell you what time he expected to return?'

'No, *sahib*. Unless he is wanting me to make preparations for him, Master *sahib* is usually not sharing with me his timings.'

'Did he say he was planning to go up to Cossipore that night?'

'Absolutely no, *sahib*.'

There was something about the vehemence of the denial that made me wonder.

'Did he *ever* go up there?'

The guarded look was back. Behind his eyes the shutters had come down. 'I don't know,' he said emphatically. 'Already I am telling all this to the inspector *sahib* who came yesterday.'

A *sahib*? When, at the door, he'd said he'd already spoken to the police, I'd assumed he'd meant the native constables who'd have come to inform him of the death of his employer. I'd certainly not dispatched any *sahib* officer to the scene, and other than Lord Taggart, I couldn't think of anyone else who would.

'What was the inspector's name?' I asked.

'I do not know, *sahib*.'

'Can you describe him?'

'He is looking like you, tall and having same colour hair but he is sporting moustaches. Also he is wearing uniform much like yours.'

Could it have been Digby? It was possible, but no one would have said he looked like me. Then again, to Indian eyes, maybe we all looked the same?

'What did the inspector ask you?'

The servant hesitated. 'He is asking mainly about Master *sahib* and Cossipore. He is being most insistent but I am telling him I know nothing of such things. Eventually he is accepting my protestations. Then he is searching through Master *sahib*'s files,' he pointed once more to the table, 'and also his personal papers.'

'Where are these personal papers?' I asked.

'In Master *sahib*'s study.'

He led me through to a windowless room, little bigger than a walk-in wardrobe. Most of the space was taken up by a wooden desk and shelves. Files and papers were strewn haphazardly on the desk.

'I have not had chance to replace files after inspector *sahib*'s examination,' he apologised.

I looked through some of the papers on the desk. Most appeared to be correspondence of a business nature: appeals to MacAuley from a variety of people to intervene in land deals, tax issues and the like. The names of the appellants were unfamiliar to me. On the shelf above the desk, however, were several buff-coloured files, all titled 'Buchan'.

I pulled one of the files down and flipped through it. The correspondence dated from 1915; mainly letters from James Buchan, some typed, others handwritten, and copies of MacAuley's replies, all in that curious black charcoal that comes from carbon paper. As far as I could tell, they too dealt with business matters: a strike at one of Buchan's jute mills, riverine transportation problems Buchan was facing in getting the rubber out of one of his plantations in East Bengal, nothing that appeared incriminating. Then again, I didn't know what I was looking for.

'Did the inspector take any files away?' I asked.

The servant nodded. 'Yes, *sahib*. Three files, all from that shelf.'

'Were they also marked "Buchan"?'

'I do not recall, *sahib*. Maybe you can be asking him?'

I'd have loved to, if I'd known who the hell he was.

'I need to ensure the inspector *sahib* took all the relevant files,' I lied. 'Did he review them thoroughly?'

'No, *sahib*. He is picking up those particular files without opening them. Then he is looking though all remaining correspondences. He is also examining files in dining room and also searching Master *sahib*'s bedroom, but he is taking no other documentations.'

'Did he arrive before Miss Grant?'

'No, *sahib*. He is arriving much later. After eight o'clock in evening. Grant *memsahib*, she is coming six o'clock.'

I recreated the events in my mind. My meeting with Miss Grant, during which she'd made no mention of needing to go to MacAuley's apartment, had ended at around five p.m. An hour later she was here, removing a file. If she was simply taking government documents back to the office, why not take all the files that were on the table? Why take just one?

Two hours later, a uniformed Englishman turns up claiming to be a police inspector, asks questions about Cossipore and goes through MacAuley's papers. He takes three files, all from a shelf where the remaining files are correspondence with James Buchan. That he went on to search the bedroom suggested he might not have found everything he was looking for. Maybe he was searching for the file that Miss Grant had removed? That was just speculation, but there were enough unanswered questions to justify me speaking to

Miss Grant again. And the prospect of that made me happier than it should have done.

'Show me MacAuley *sahib*'s bedroom,' I said, returning to the matter in hand.

The room was littered with crates half filled with the clothes and other possessions that had given colour to MacAuley's life. It was the only room in the flat that seemed to have any real imprint of him. On a dresser, a framed photograph of MacAuley and a lady. It was the same woman as in the picture I'd removed from his wallet.

'What will happen to his possessions?' I asked.

The servant shrugged. 'I do not know, *sahib*. I am packing only.'

A wave of depression descended on me. Admittedly, the use of O had started to affect my mood, but this felt different. I picked up the photograph, sat down on the bed and stared at it.

Two days ago, MacAuley had been one of the most important men in Bengal; respected and feared, it seemed, in equal measure. Now his memory was already halfway to being erased. All that was left of him, the sum total of a life of fifty-odd years, was wrapped in yesterday's newspaper, ready to be packed away and forgotten about.

The thought scared me. After all, what was left of any of us after death? A special few might be immortalised in bronze or stone or in the pages of history, but for the rest of us, what trace remains other than in the memories of loved ones, a few sepia-toned photographs and some paltry possessions we may have amassed? What was left of Sarah? My memories could never do justice to her intellect, nor the photographs honour her beauty. And yet, at least she did live on in *my* memory. If I died, who would remember *me*? The parallel with MacAuley was too obvious to ignore.

'Pack everything into the crates,' I said, 'including the files in the study. I'll have some constables come and take possession of it all. They may contain evidence.'

It was an odd thing to do, and even at the time I wasn't sure exactly why I'd ordered it. Whatever evidence there might have been had likely already been removed by the *sahib* who'd come round last night. The truth was there was probably no evidence left to safeguard. What I was doing, I realised, was protecting the memory of a dead man, a man I'd never even met – at least, not while he was alive. And why? Was it that his past echoed mine? It didn't matter. I wasn't going to let his memory fade away quite so easily. My homage would be to find his killer.

I thanked the manservant who showed me back through the hall.

'What will you do now you no longer have an employer?' I asked.

He smiled weakly. 'Who knows? If I am fortunate I may get new position. Otherwise I will be forced to return to my native place.' He pointed upwards. 'It is in the hands of the gods.'

TEN

Back at Lal Bazar I found another note from Daniels on my desk. Lord Taggart probably wanted an update. There wasn't much to tell him yet, and I didn't fancy the thought of Daniels coming down looking for me. Over the years, though, I'd learned that the best way to deal with such a situation was to ignore it and head for lunch. The problem was I didn't know where to go. This wasn't London. Here in the tropics, where an Englishman could come down with dysentery by so much as looking the wrong way at a sandwich, the choice of eating establishment was potentially a matter of life and death.

On a whim I picked up the telephone and asked to be put through to Annie Grant at Writers' Building. She answered on the third ring.

'Miss Grant?'

'Captain Wyndham? What can I do for you?' She sounded distracted.

'Would you care to join me for some lunch? If you're free, that is?' I told myself I'd use lunch as a pretext for questioning her further, but that was only half the story at best. I felt a gnawing in the pit of my stomach. It was ridiculous. How does a man survive three years of bombing, shelling and machine-gun fire and yet still tremble with nerves when asking a woman out for lunch? For a moment the line went silent. I held my breath and felt disgusted with myself.

'I suppose I could make some time, Captain, but I'm not sure there's much more I can say about Mr MacAuley that I didn't tell you yesterday.'

'Sorry, Miss Grant, perhaps I wasn't being clear. I just thought it might be nice to have lunch . . . I don't know many places here and wondered if you might be able to show me some . . . if you're free, that is . . . my treat.' Why did I need to make a conscious effort to stop talking?

Her voice brightened. 'Well, in that case, Captain, of course. Just give me fifteen minutes. I'll see you on the steps outside my office.'

———

Fifteen minutes later, I was waiting on the steps of the Writers' Building and looking out over the square. She came up behind me and tapped me on the shoulder.

'Captain Wyndham.' She smiled.

'Please,' I said, 'call me Sam.'

'Well, Sam,' she said, taking my arm and leading me down the steps, 'shall we start your introduction to the culinary delights of Calcutta?'

That sounded good to me, as did the word 'introduction'. It suggested the promise of more to come.

'How about that new place, the Red Elephant, on Park Street?' she said. 'It's all the rage at the moment. I've been waiting for somebody to take me there.'

I'd never heard of it. Not that it mattered. Whatever she suggested would have been fine with me, even a three-course meal at Mrs Tebbit's.

'Let's go,' I said, so eagerly that she laughed like a schoolgirl on a picnic and I felt an irrational swell of pride. I suspected the laugh was for my benefit, but I didn't care. Taking my hand, she led me to the street and hailed a passing tonga. And all the while I couldn't help thinking how strange it felt holding another woman's hand.

The tonga *wallah* pulled on the reins and brought the contraption to a halt at the kerbside. He was a lean fellow, just muscle and sinew and skin tanned black by the Bengal sun. I helped Annie up on to the banquette, then climbed aboard myself.

'Park Street *chalo*,' she said. The tonga *wallah* gave another pull on the reins and pulled out into the stream of traffic. We headed in the direction of the Esplanade, away from the choked streets around Dalhousie Square and were soon travelling down Mayo Road towards the genteel thoroughfare that was Park Street.

The Red Elephant was a discreet little place occupying the ground floor of a large four-storey building. There wasn't much to see from the outside, just smoked-glass windows and a solid wooden door, in front of which stood an equally solid Sikh doorman. At times it felt as though every second Sikh in Calcutta was a doorman. You could understand why. They were so much bigger than the native Bengalis. As long as there were doors in Calcutta, a Sikh would never be short of employment. The fellow gave a curt nod and ushered us inside.

The interior was dark and shiny, like some fashionable funeral parlour. Black marble floors, smoked-mirrored walls, ebony tables and against one wall, a bar, complete with black barstools and black barman.

'Colourful place,' I said.

Annie laughed. 'Once you get to know Calcutta, Sam, you'll realise that the darker the restaurant, the more exclusive it is.'

In that case, I reflected, the Red Elephant must have been as exclusive as they came.

The trouble started with the maître d', a pint-sized European, who materialised as if out of nowhere and barred our path. He was five feet four, maybe slightly taller with his nose in the air, and his demeanour was as dark as the rest of the place.

'Do you have a reservation?' he asked, the way a doctor might ask if you had syphilis. Judging by the number of empty tables, the lack of a reservation shouldn't have been a problem. Nevertheless, he took a sharp intake of breath when we replied in the negative and consulted a ledger almost as tall as himself.

'I'm afraid it could be difficult,' he said, in a manner that suggested I'd just asked him to perform surgery.

'You don't look that busy,' I said.

The man shook his head. 'I'm afraid I've nothing till at least three o'clock.'

'You don't have a single table till then?'

'I'm afraid not,' he said, then turned to Annie. 'Maybe you should try somewhere further down the street?'

Her expression changed abruptly, as though the man had slapped her.

'Come on,' she said, taking my arm, 'let's try somewhere else.'

'Wait,' I said, turning to the maître d'. 'Surely you must be able to squeeze us in somewhere?'

He shook his head again. 'I fear sir may be new to Calcutta.'

People had been saying that to me a lot, as though Calcutta was so very different from everywhere else in the empire. It was getting to be annoying.

'Where do you think I'm from,' I asked, 'Timbuktu?'

'Please, Sam,' Annie said, 'just leave it. For my sake?'

I wasn't about to argue with her. Instead, I glowered at the maître d', then turned and followed Annie out.

'What was his problem?' I asked when we were back on the street. She didn't answer, just kept walking with her back to me. I'm not exactly the most accomplished reader of women, but I could tell she was upset. 'Are you all right?'

She turned towards me. 'I'm fine,' she said.

'I think you should tell me the truth.'

She hesitated.

'Honestly, I'm fine,' she said. 'It's not as though it's the first time.'

I still had no idea what she was talking about. 'Not the first time for what?'

She looked at me. 'You really are an innocent, aren't you, Sam?' She sighed. 'There was no table for us because it doesn't set the right tone for my sort to be seen there. Let's just say you'd have had no trouble if you'd turned up with an English girl.'

My blood boiled. 'That's ridiculous,' I said. 'All that nonsense because you're part Indian?'

I might have been new to Calcutta and a stranger to its ways, but this was grotesque and I'd had enough of it. I turned to go back inside, not entirely sure what I was going to do, but I was a police-man and throwing your weight around was something you learned pretty early in the job.

She took my arm. 'Please, Sam. Don't,' she said wearily, her eyes glistening with the first hint of tears. It was enough to take the wind out of my sails.

'All right,' I said eventually, 'but we still need to eat.'

She thought for a moment, then her face lit up. 'There *is* a place near here you might like. It's nothing fancy, though.'

If it made her happy, it was fine by me. She turned and hailed a couple of rickshaws.

———

We pulled up outside a shabby little building whose front opened on to the pavement. A hoarding mounted on the first floor read, '*The Glamorgan Hotel*'. The place was packed. White-shirted waiters buzzed between diners squashed in around small square tables. The restaurant covered two floors, a main area and a mezzanine. The decor was simple, whitewashed walls and checked tablecloths, and all around the smell of honest cooking. A bank of fans whirred from the ceiling high above.

I paid the rickshaw *wallahs* as Annie led the way into the restaurant. A rotund Anglo-Indian in a grimy apron and a handle-bar moustache came over and greeted her like an old friend.

'Miss Grant!' he gushed. 'What a pleasure to see you again. It's been such a long time I was beginning to worry!'

'Hello, Albert,' she said, taking his hand and giving him the sort of smile I'd hoped was reserved just for me. 'This is my friend, Captain Wyndham. He's new in town and I thought I'd take him to the best restaurant in all Calcutta.'

'You are too kind, Miss Grant!' he effused. Then, taking my hand, he shook it vigorously, 'An honour to make your acquaintance, sir!'

'Albert,' said Annie, patting him on the shoulder, 'is a Calcutta institution. His family have been running this place for almost forty years.'

Albert beamed at her, then led us up the sagging steps of a narrow staircase to the mezzanine, where fewer tables were occupied. He selected one that offered a view of the restaurant below. 'Special section,' he effused, 'reserved for my favourite customers!'

He left and returned some moments later with two dog-eared menus. The general hubbub of conversation floated up from the tables below. I looked down a list of dishes that read more like incantations from some foreign holy book than items on any menu I was used to.

'Maybe you should order for both of us?' I said.

She smiled and summoned a waiter who was hovering nearby and ordered a couple of dishes. The waiter nodded and disappeared down the stairs.

'Glamorgan?' I said. 'Strange name for a restaurant.'

'It's an interesting saga,' she replied. 'The tale, as Albert tells it, is that his grandfather Harold was from around those parts. He came to Calcutta as a sailor on one of the old clippers. One night he got so drunk that he never made it back to the docks and his ship set sail without him. At first, he tried to sign on as a crewman on another ship heading west – he had a wife and family back home – but it was coming up to monsoon season and there were precious few vessels prepared to risk the voyage. Of those that did, none were prepared to take on a crewman with Grandpa Harry's reputation. Finally he gave up, and reconciled himself to waiting several months in Calcutta before heading home. In the meantime, however, fate intervened. One day he met a Bengali girl, a *nauch* dancer. Poor Harry was smitten, captivated by her dancing. Forgetting about his family back in Wales, he set about wooing the girl, which was no mean feat for a penniless sailor, but he must have managed it because he ended up marrying her – not in a church, of course, but in a Hindu ceremony for whatever that's worth – and spent the rest of his life in Calcutta. His sailing days were over and the only other thing he was any good at was cooking. So with what money he managed to scrape together, he opened this place and named it after his homeland. It still serves the best Anglo-Indian food in the city.'

'A love story?' I said. 'That's nice to hear. From what I've seen, most British and Indians tend to be at each other's throats.'

She smiled. 'There was a time, Sam, when the Indians and the British got on extremely well. The *sahibs* wore Indian clothes and followed local customs. And, of course, they took native wives. It was good for the Indians, too. The British brought with them new ideas that led to an explosion of culture among the Bengalis. It triggered what they like to call the *Bengal Renaissance*. Over the last hundred years, this little place has churned out more artists, poets, philosophers and scientists than half of Europe. At least, that's what the Bengalis would tell you.

'The irony is that the new ideas brought by the British, of democracy and empirical reasoning, the ones they were so proud of and which the Bengalis took to heart so keenly, are the very ideas that the government now finds so dangerous when they're espoused by people with brown skin.'

'What changed?'

'Who knows?' She sighed. 'Maybe it was the Mutiny? Maybe it was just time? After all, they say familiarity breeds contempt. I sometimes think the British and the Indians are like an old married couple. They've been together for what seems like forever; they fight and might think they hate each other, but at heart there will always be some mutual love there. Once you've been here a bit longer I think you'll notice it too. They're kindred spirits.'

She was insightful, and obviously an intelligent woman. Beauty and intellect – it was a powerful combination. In that respect, she reminded me somewhat of Sarah.

'And what about you, Miss Grant?' I asked. 'Are you British or Indian?'

She gave a hollow laugh. 'If an Indian doesn't see me as Indian and an Englishman doesn't see me as British, then does it really matter what *I* think I am? To be honest, Sam, I'm neither. I'm just a product of that first doomed flowering of British and Indian affection a hundred years ago, when there was nothing wrong with Englishmen marrying Indian women. Now we're just an embarrassment; a visible reminder to the British that they didn't always think of themselves as superior to the natives. You know what they call us, don't you? *Domiciled Europeans.* That's the official term. It sounds almost dignified until you consider what it actually means. We're acknowledged as European but we have no home in Europe. You see, that fraction of Indian blood condemns us as outsiders, generation after generation.

'And as for the Indians, they look upon us with a mixture of loathing and disgust. We're the symbol of their precious Indian womanhood abandoning its culture and purity, and the inability of Indian men to stop it. To them we're out-castes, quite literally; the physical embodiment of their impotence.

'The worst of it is the hypocrisy. To our faces, both the English and the Indians can be perfectly pleasant, but in their own way, they each despise us. But then, this is a land of hypocrites. The British pretend they're here to bring the benefits of western civilisation to an ungovernable bunch of savages, while, in reality it's only ever really been about petty commercial gain. And the Indians? The educated elite claim they want to rid India of British tyranny for the benefit of all Indians, but what do they know or care about the needs of the millions of Indians in the villages? They just want to replace the British as the ruling class.'

'And the Anglo-Indians?' I asked.

She laughed. 'We're as bad as the rest of them. We call ourselves British, mimic your ways and talk about Britain as the "old country", when the closest most of us have ever been to England is Bombay. And we're positively beastly to the natives, calling them things like *wog* and *coolie*, as though by treating them in such a fashion we're showing *you* how different we are to them. And we're ever so patriotic. Did you know that our most common Christian names are Victoria and Albert? We're the most loyal people in the empire. And why? Because we're terrified of what will happen to us if and when the real British *do* leave.'

'A whole country of hypocrites and liars?' I said. 'Maybe you need to be less cynical, Miss Grant?'

She smiled that wonderful smile at me as Albert arrived with our desserts.

'Well, maybe not everyone,' she said, placing a hand on Albert's arm as he set down the plates. 'As far as I'm aware, when Albert here says he makes the finest caramel custard in India, he's telling the truth.'

We finished lunch and made small talk over coffee. She asked about my family. I told her I had none. It was the truth, or at least a version of it.

Till now we'd studiously avoided any mention of MacAuley. Still, his presence hung over the table like Banquo's ghost. In the end, I'd no choice but to raise it as subtly as I could.

'How are things at the office?' I asked.

'Pretty chaotic,' she said. 'Though nowhere near as bad as yesterday. There's so much that Mr MacAuley was dealing with, so many things that required his signature, that half the department came to a standstill without him. But things are getting better slowly.'

'Has his successor been appointed yet?'

'Not officially, but it's clear that Mr Stevens will be getting the job. He's taken on most of Mr MacAuley's responsibilities and I've already been appointed his secretary.'

'That's fortunate. I'll need to interview him. Can you arrange an appointment for me?'

She nodded. 'I'll get on to it as soon as I get back to the office, but it might take a while. He's snowed under with work.'

'What's he like, by the way?' I asked, recalling what MacAuley's manservant had said.

'Mr Stevens? Nice enough, I suppose. He's one of the younger generation, keen on modernising everything.'

'Did he get on with MacAuley?'

She smiled. 'Let's just say they didn't always see eye to eye. MacAuley was rather set in his ways. He didn't care for some of the suggestions that Stevens made.'

'Did they ever argue?'

'Now and again.'

'Recently?'

She hesitated.

'Please, Annie,' I said. 'You're not betraying any confidences and it's important you tell me.'

She stirred her coffee. 'Last week,' she said, 'Thursday or Friday, I forget exactly when. Stevens barged into MacAuley's office. It's next door to mine and the connecting door was ajar. He all but accused MacAuley of doctoring some legislation.'

'Did he threaten him at all?'

She hesitated again. 'Not in so many words, but he did suggest MacAuley would regret it.'

That was interesting.

'And how did MacAuley respond?'

'Well, he was hardly a shrinking violet.' She laughed. 'He gave as good as he got.'

'Do you know what the legislation related to?' I asked.

'Rubber,' she replied. 'Something to do with importation duties from Burma, I think.'

'They had an argument about tax rates?' I asked, deflated. So much for the possibility that MacAuley had been bumped off by a jealous colleague. Civil servants weren't exactly known for their passions, and even if they were, a disagreement over rubber taxes hardly seemed to constitute grounds for murder. I changed tack.

'Did MacAuley ever take work home with him?'

'All the time, unfortunately,' she said. 'The man lived for his work.'

For some reason, the phrase made me uncomfortable.

'Why *unfortunately*?'

'Because documents would occasionally go missing and I never knew whether they'd been lost, mis-filed or if MacAuley had them at home.'

'So his death must have complicated things.'

'It's caused a few problems,' she continued. 'As I told you yesterday, MacAuley was responsible for a whole raft of matters. A lot of things in the department don't move without his signature. Suddenly, we couldn't find certain documents that Mr Stevens urgently needed to sign in MacAuley's stead. In the end, I had to go round to Mr MacAuley's flat to see if they were there.'

'Did you find them?'

'Yes, thankfully. There'd have been hell to pay if I hadn't. But Stevens didn't get round to signing them till this morning. In the end, all we had was a delay of a day or so. Not ideal, but not the end of the world either.'

That explained her presence at MacAuley's flat. I breathed a sigh of relief, and with it, my doubts about Miss Grant gratefully dissolved.

'So how's your investigation going?' she asked.

I considered giving her the usual flannel. It would have been the proper thing to do. But I have a weakness when it comes to beautiful women. They disarm me. Or maybe it's just that I don't like to disappoint them. I finished my coffee and told her the truth: that so far, my inquiries had generated more heat than light and that I felt people were holding things back.

'I hope you don't mean me, Sam?' she said.

'Of course not,' I said hastily. 'I think you're about the only one who hasn't.'

ELEVEN

I left Annie on the steps of Writers' Building and walked back to Lal Bazar, making best use of whatever shade was offered by the buildings en route.

There were three new yellow chits waiting on my desk and I was starting to suspect that my office might double as a post office sorting room when I was away. The first was another note from Daniels, asking to see me. This one was marked 'URGENT' and I crushed it and filed it in the bin.

The next was from Banerjee. He'd spoken to the bearer at the Bengal Club who'd stated that on the night of MacAuley's murder, Buchan had retired to bed immediately after his guests had left, emerging for breakfast at around ten o'clock the following morning. As for who Buchan had spoken to that night, the sergeant had drawn a blank, with the receptionist either unwilling or unable to divulge the information.

The third was from Digby. Military intelligence had granted the Commissioner's request that we once again be given access to the crime scene. 'Any and all assistance' would be provided to us. That was a nice touch; like someone punching you in the face, then asking what they could do to help stop the bleeding.

I lifted the receiver and telephoned Digby's office. The line rang out. I was about to go looking for him when Banerjee knocked and entered.

'The post-mortem, sir. It's scheduled for three o'clock. Will you be attending?'

I nodded.

'And I'd like you there too.'

Halfway up College Street sits the Medical College Hospital, with the Imperial Police morgue in its basement. Morgues always seem to be in basements, as though being physically underground is a good first step towards the grave. This one was no different to the others: white tiled walls and floor, no natural light, and everywhere, the sickly stench of formaldehyde and raw flesh.

We were met by a cadaverous-looking pathologist who introduced himself as Dr Lamb. He appeared to be in his fifties, his skin pallid, almost grey, as though he'd started resembling the bodies he worked on. He was kitted out in gumboots and rubber gloves, with a white apron over a blue shirt and red spotted bow tie, and from a distance looked a bit like a retired circus clown.

He kept the pleasantries brief, then hurried us into the post-mortem theatre. Inside the smell was acrid and the floor slick with water. In the centre of the room stood the dissection table, a large marble slab on which lay MacAuley's mortal remains, still dressed in his bloodstained tuxedo. The slab was angled downwards on one side towards a drainage channel. On a table next to it were the doctor's tools of the trade: a collection of hacksaws, drills and knives on loan from the Dark Ages. Two other men were already waiting. The first was a police photographer, replete with box camera, flash bulbs, tripod and plates. The second I took to be Dr Lamb's assistant, there to transcribe the doctor's observations; a secretary for the most macabre dictation.

'Right, gentlemen,' said the doctor jovially, 'shall we get down to business?'

He started by cutting through MacAuley's clothing with a large pair of scissors, like a tailor working lovingly over a mannequin. Once the clothing had been removed, he set to work measuring the body, noting the usual descriptive details, height, hair colour, distinguishing marks, all of which his assistant duly recorded. Methodically, he described MacAuley's wounds, starting from the missing eyeball and working downwards. As he spoke, he pointed them out to the photographer, who took close-up shots.

'Slight laceration of the tongue, some bruising and discoloration around the mouth. Clear-cut incision on the neck. Most likely caused by a long-bladed knife, moderately sharp. Incision is five inches in length. Commencing two inches below the angle of the jaw. Incision is clean, deviating slightly downwards. Arteries severed.'

He moved on to the chest. 'Large puncture wound, three inches wide. Again probably caused by a long-bladed knife. Appears to have punctured a lung.'

He checked MacAuley's hands. 'No defensive cuts.'

To my left, Banerjee was making odd noises. I looked over. The young sergeant was reciting some heathen mantra under his breath and the colour had drained from his face.

'Is this your first post-mortem, Sergeant?'

He smiled sheepishly, 'My second, sir.'

That was a pity. It's the second that's usually the worst. The first, while gruesome, at least has the saving grace of surprise. You don't really know what's coming. The second one has no such silver lining. You know exactly what to expect but you're still not quite prepared for it.

'How did your first one go?'

'I had to leave part way through.'

I nodded. 'Well done, Sergeant.' I watched as he blushed, but I have a habit of teasing subordinates. In my book it's a compliment.

Dr Lamb had moved on to washing the body, humming in a deep baritone, like some Inca priest anointing a victim before cutting his heart out. Then, taking a knife, he made an incision from MacAuley's throat to his abdomen. There was very little blood. He broke open the ribcage, exposing the major organs, and proceeded to remove them one by one. Beside me Banerjee shifted awkwardly. It was never any one thing that tipped you over the edge, it was always a combination: the smells and sounds coming together and reaching a macabre crescendo. Banerjee covered his mouth, then turned and headed hastily for the exit.

My first few post-mortems I'd been sick as a dog. I couldn't say why. After all, it wasn't that different from being in a slaughterhouse. But there's something about the human psyche that rebels against the physical act of watching a person being reduced to a pile of meat. But human beings adapt. It's one of our great strengths. Natural reactions can be switched off or, as in my case, destroyed. Three years of watching men being butchered will do that to you. I envied Banerjee his reaction. Rather, I envied him his ability *to* react.

I stayed a few minutes longer, watching the good doctor go about his work. Quiet and efficient, as if it were no more mundane than a dentist removing teeth. While he worked, I built a picture of what might have transpired. Bruising around the mouth, no defensive cuts on the hands. It suggested MacAuley's killer had approached him from behind. Taken him by surprise. Probably covered his mouth to prevent him from calling out. Then slit his throat, judging by the blood splatter at the scene.

One thing puzzled me, though. The killer clearly knew what he was doing. The incision had been clean, severing the arteries and the windpipe. MacAuley would have been dead in less than a minute. So why the second wound? Why the stab to the chest? The killer must have known MacAuley was as good as dead. Why waste time stabbing him?

That tied in with something else that had been bothering me. The note. Why ball it up and stick it in MacAuley's mouth? Surely if you were making a political point, the logical thing to do would have been to leave it visible? I'd originally assumed it was done to make sure it wasn't lost somehow, but now I wasn't so sure.

I'd seen what I needed to see. Anything else of interest would be in the post-mortem report. I turned and headed out in search of Surrender-not and found him sitting on the steps of the college building, his head in his hands. I sat down next to him and offered him a cigarette, extracting one for myself. He accepted gratefully, taking the cigarette in a shaky hand, and for a minute we sat in silence, letting the smoke do its work.

'Does it get any easier?' he asked.

'Yes.'

'I'm not sure I will ever get used to it.'

'That might not be such a bad thing.'

I finished my cigarette and flicked the butt away. Banerjee still appeared shaken by the experience. That wasn't good. I needed him to focus, and the best way of doing that was to get him back to work. We had two murders to solve, one of which I couldn't figure out a motive for, and the other for which I had a surfeit of motives, but as yet no solid leads.

'Come on, Sergeant,' I said, 'we've got work to do.'

TWELVE

'You didn't happen to go round to MacAuley's flat last night, did you?'

In response, Digby almost spat out his tea. 'What? Why the devil would I do that?' We were in my cramped office. Surrender-not was in there too, making it nice and cosy. 'Why d'you ask, old boy?'

'Something MacAuley's manservant said this morning. He told me some *sahib* officer had shown up at the flat around eight p.m. asking questions about MacAuley and Cossipore, then left with a load of files from MacAuley's study.'

'Could he describe the fellow?'

'Tall, blond, moustachioed. That's why I hoped it might have been you.'

Digby smiled. 'Me and about half the officers on the force.'

'You don't think Taggart's allocated any other officers to the case, do you?'

'I doubt it,' he replied. 'Anyway, you're his golden boy. You think he'd tell me before he told you?'

It was a fair point, but I had to make sure. Banerjee stuck up his hand. Both Digby and I stared at him.

'You don't need permission, Surrender-not. Just speak if you've got something to say.'

'Thank you, sir,' he replied. 'I was just wondering how the servant was sure it was a policeman?'

'The man was in uniform.'

'With respect, sir, the military also have white dress uniforms, which look very much like ours. To the untrained eye, there's not much difference between a white police uniform and a military one.'

'What are you suggesting, Sergeant?' asked Digby.

'Nothing, sir. I was merely speculating that the officer may not have been a policeman. He may have been military personnel. After all, military intelligence did commandeer the crime scene.'

It was an interesting observation, one that got me thinking.

'Did you get much else out of the man?' asked Digby.

'Not really,' I said. 'Only that something was troubling MacAuley in recent months. He'd been going out at odd hours, had given up the drink but was recently back on the sauce.'

'Any enemies?'

'To listen to his servant, you'd have thought MacAuley was a saint. Having said that, he doesn't seem to have got on particularly well with his number two, some fellow called Stevens.'

'Would you like me to organise an interview with him, sir?' asked Banerjee.

'I've already asked MacAuley's secretary to do so,' I replied in what I hoped was a neutral tone. 'There *is* something I do need you to follow up on, though. I want you to post a guard at MacAuley's flat. Make sure no one other than the domestic help enters or leaves without our permission, and even they are to be checked to ensure that nothing is removed from the apartment.'

'Yes, sir,' said Banerjee, scribbling the instructions into his notebook.

'And where are we in terms of tracking down the Reverend Gunn?' I asked.

'Mixed news on that front, I'm afraid, sir. Our colleagues in Dum Dum inform me that he is the minister at St Andrew's Church up there, but that he is presently out of town. I understand he is scheduled to return this Saturday.'

It was yet another delay. It seemed nothing to do with this case would be straightforward. I turned to Digby.

'Everything organised for tonight?'

'Yes, old boy. All set for nine o'clock. We should depart here around eight-ish. That'll give us plenty of time.'

'Good,' I said. 'That just leaves the small matters of interviewing the L-G and having a proper chat with that prostitute.'

'Do you want me to bring her in for questioning?' asked Digby.

'No,' I said, looking at my watch. 'I think a softer approach is called for. I'll head up there myself. Anyway, there's something else I need you to do. Do you know anyone in military intelligence?'

I noticed a momentary tightening in the muscles of his jaw.

'Yes,' he said, 'the chap who heads up the anti-terrorist unit. Goes by the name of Dawson. He's a hard-nosed bastard. Why do you ask?'

'Would he be their man dealing with the MacAuley case?'

'Probably.'

'I want you to set up a meeting with him for me, the sooner the better.'

'Very well,' he said, 'but I should warn you, he's not the most cooperative of chaps.'

There wasn't much more to discuss on the MacAuley case. In truth, all three of us were on edge. The chances of solving a case are greatly diminished if there's no breakthrough within forty-eight hours. After that, potential witnesses, evidence and momentum all tend to disperse like cigarette smoke on the breeze and the trail goes cold. We were getting close to the two-day mark and still had nothing. We sorely needed a break and I hoped the meeting with Digby's snitch would provide it.

I turned to the little matter of the murdered railwayman.

'Have you pulled the file on Pal?' I asked.

'Yes, sir,' replied Banerjee. He flipped through his notebook. 'Hiren Pal, aged twenty, an employee of the Eastern Bengal Railway Company. Comes from a family of railwaymen – his father is a station master's assistant up at Dum Dum Cantonment. He'd been employed by the railways in various capacities for the last nine years, most recently as a guard—'

'He's been working on the railways since he was eleven?' I interrupted. 'Isn't that a trifle young?'

Banerjee gave a wry smile. 'The authorities are somewhat *lackadaisical* when it comes to recording the births of much of the non-European population. The chances are he was at least several years older. I understand it's quite common for railway workers to lower their ages on official documents.'

Digby laughed. 'You see what sort of people we're dealing with here, Wyndham! That's the vanity of the Bengali for you. Even the bloody coolies lie about their age!'

Banerjee squirmed. 'If I may, sir. I doubt vanity has much to do with it. The fact is, the railways impose a policy of retirement at the age of fifty-eight. Unfortunately, the pension provided to native Indians is generally too meagre for a family to live on. By lowering their ages on the forms I believe the men hope to work for a few years more and thus provide for their families just that little bit longer.'

'That's fascinating, Sergeant,' said Digby, 'but it has little to do with why the chap was killed.'

'Why *was* he killed?' I asked.

'It's obvious, isn't it?' said Digby. 'As I said before, it's a botched robbery. *Dacoits* attack the train on the off chance of finding cash in the safes. When they discover there isn't any, they take out their frustration on the guard. He dies, they panic and run off.'

Banerjee shook his head. 'But they were there for an hour. Why not rob the passengers or take the mail sacks? If you know what to look for, those sacks probably contain a lot of value.'

'Remember, Sergeant,' said Digby, 'your average illiterate *dacoit* won't have the first clue about the value of the mail sacks.'

I had trouble believing this was the work of illiterate peasants. For one thing, it was too well planned. For another, there were those tyre tracks leaving the scene. Peasants would be lucky to have access to a bullock cart, let alone motorised transport.

'I think the whole enterprise was planned extremely thoroughly,' I said. 'The two men on the train knew exactly when and where to pull the communication cord so that their accomplices could storm the train.'

'So why kill the guard, and why not take anything?' asked Digby.

'I don't know,' I said.

'Maybe they hit the train specifically to kill the guard?' ventured Banerjee.

'Unlikely,' I replied. 'To organise such a complex operation simply to kill a railway guard seems far-fetched.'

'Then why?' asked Digby.

A theory began to form in my head. 'That they didn't rob the passengers or take the mail sacks suggests they were looking for something specific, something they thought was on the train. When they couldn't find it, they beat up the guard in the hope that he might tell them where it was. But he wouldn't have known anything and they ended up killing him. My guess is they'd have started on Perkins, the conductor, next, but they ran out of time.'

Digby sucked his teeth. 'How can you possibly know that?'

'I don't. It's a guess. But the whole thing seems to have been planned meticulously. They must have had a railway timetable. Remember, the train was running late. If it was on time, it would have been attacked over an hour earlier. That would have given them at least two hours of darkness to complete whatever it was they wanted to do. It can't be coincidence that they pulled out just before sunrise and ten minutes before another train arrived on the scene. From what the driver told us, they left methodically and on a schedule.'

'Let's say you're right, old boy,' said Digby sceptically, 'and these fellows weren't just petty *dacoits* hoping to get lucky. If they'd planned things so exceedingly well, why didn't they know the safes on the train would be empty last night? It seems rather a huge oversight.'

It was a good question. One I didn't have an answer for.

'Maybe there *should* have been something in them?' said Banerjee.

Digby snorted. 'Fine. Let's assume they expect to find something in the safes, but don't. Why not just take the mail sacks? If they're not illiterate peasants, they'd know there was value in the mail. You can't have it both ways. You want me to believe they were a sophisticated gang who, in all their detailed planning, managed to bungle the operation by hitting the train on a night when what they were looking for wasn't there and when it's running an hour late. Then they fail to take the mail sacks or rob the passengers and finally end up accidentally killing a guard.'

He turned to me. 'You're overthinking this, Wyndham. It's not your fault. You're probably used to cases in England where the villains are a lot smarter than they are here. Trust me, this is just a random robbery gone wrong.'

He was probably right, but I didn't appreciate being lectured.

'There's one way to find out,' I said. 'Sergeant, get down to Sealdah station. Speak to the station master. I want the baggage manifest for last night's train. Find out if there was anything that should have been on the train that wasn't. And find out the reason for the delay in its departure.'

Banerjee nodded and scribbled the instructions down into his little pad. As he did, the telephone rang. I answered it and was asked by the switchboard operator to hold while the connection was made to Annie Grant at Writers' Building. Something jumped in the pit of my stomach. I told her to wait while I hastily dismissed my officers: Digby to set up a meeting with Dawson of Section H, and Banerjee to Sealdah station by way of posting the guard at MacAuley's flat.

———

'Yes, Miss Grant?' I asked after the door had closed behind them.

'Captain Wyndham,' she said, her tone bearing none of the warmth it had over lunch. 'You requested a meeting with Mr Stevens. I'm afraid things are still quite chaotic here. Mr Stevens apologises but he will not be able to see you today.'

I guessed he was in the room with her. He might even have been standing over her shoulder.

'How about tomorrow?' I asked.

There was a pause. 'He has an opening at one o'clock. Would that suit you?'

'That's fine,' I said. 'Good day to you, Miss Grant.'

'Good day, Captain Wyndham.'

I replaced the receiver, then picked it up a second later, asked to be put through to the car pool and requested a vehicle and driver be made ready for a trip to Cossipore. It was time to have a proper chat with Devi the prostitute.

Just as I strapped on my cross-belt and gathered my cap, the door to my office flew open and in charged Lord Taggart's secretary, Daniels, looking like he'd been pursued by a bear.

'Wyndham,' he puffed, 'thank goodness.'

'Is there a fire, Daniels?'

'What? No. Didn't you get my messages? The Commissioner's organised a meeting for you with the L-G.'

'That's good news,' I said. 'When?'

'Ten minutes ago.'

THIRTEEN

Government House. In the City of Palaces, this one was the biggest.
Four vast wings around a central core, a symphony of columns and
cornices, topped by a silver dome. All very impressive, and if the
sight of it didn't take your breath away, climbing the stairs to the
entrance probably would.

Its occupier was the most important man this side of Delhi.
More powerful than any maharaja. He was also a civil servant.

I was met on the stairs by a pale-looking chap attired in morning suit and cravat. I assumed he was some mid-level functionary,
maybe even upper-mid level, given the cravat. He didn't give me his
name, which was fine as I'd only have forgotten it.

Instead, he led me inside towards the administrative wing. We
passed the throne room, where once the King Emperor would sit
with his local satraps in attendance. Now that the capital had moved
to Delhi, it was doubtful the throne would ever be sat in much
again, at least not by a royal posterior.

'His Honour will see you in the Blue Drawing Room,' said the
functionary as we passed through one of several sets of double doors,
each opened by a pair of turbaned flunkies in red and gold livery.
I nodded, as though well versed in the colours of the rooms of the
L-G's inner sanctum.

The room itself was about twice the size of Lord Taggart's office back at Lal Bazar and smaller than I'd expected. Behind a desk the size of a rowing boat sat Sir Stewart Campbell, the Lieutenant-Governor of the Bengal Presidency, pen in hand and poring over documents. Beside him stood another functionary in morning suit and cravat. As we entered, the functionary whispered something to him. The L-G looked up. He had a hard face, not brutal, but severe. The face of a man accustomed to power, used to governing countless masses for their own good. A beak of a nose, pinched features and eyes that showed a businesslike determination. Together they gave him a look of mild irritation, as though there was some noxious odour in the room and he was the only one who could smell it.

'Captain Wyndham,' he said, betraying a curiously nasal accent, 'you're late.'

I walked across an acre of polished floor to the desk and took a seat opposite him. He looked slightly surprised.

'I was under the impression there would be two of you?'

'I'm afraid my colleague had to be elsewhere,' I said.

'Very well,' he said. 'I understand you're new to Calcutta.' It was a statement rather than a question. 'I'd have expected a seasoned hand for a case such as this, but Taggart assures me you're ex-Scotland Yard and the right man for the job.' Again, I said nothing, which was fine as the man didn't seem to want an answer. 'The Viceroy himself has been informed of the regrettable incident of two nights ago,' he continued. 'He's deemed it a matter of imperial importance that the criminals be apprehended swiftly and without further disruption to the organs of state. Anything you need, you will have.'

I thanked him. 'If I may, Your Honour, I'd like to ask you a few questions about MacAuley and his role in the administration here.'

The L-G smiled. 'Of course. MacAuley was indispensable to the government here.' He paused, then corrected himself. 'No, that's not quite true. No man is "indispensable" but he was an important and integral part of the machinery of government in Bengal.'

'What exactly was his role?'

'Technically he was in charge of government finances, but in reality, his remit was far wider and covered many things, from planning to policy execution.'

'I assume it was a high-pressure role.'

'Very much so. But MacAuley was well used to it.'

'And do you know if he was under any unusual strain recently?'

'Tell me, Captain,' the L-G said, 'did you ever happen to see a German P.O.W. camp during the war?'

I wondered where this was going. 'I was lucky enough to avoid such a fate, sir.'

'No matter,' he said. 'I once met the commandant of one of them. He told me the Boche liked to use Alsatians as guard dogs in their camps . . . all except for the one he ran, that is. He preferred Rottweilers. You see he didn't trust Alsatians. Good dogs they undoubtedly are, but they have a better nature. If they're treated with kindness, over time they'll reciprocate. Rottweilers, on the other hand, have no better natures. They're fiercely loyal to their masters and will obey every command, no matter what. MacAuley was this administration's Rottweiler. He wasn't the type to succumb to strain, unusual or otherwise.'

'I expect that made him quite a few enemies,' I said.

'Oh undoubtedly,' he said, '*zamindars* and *babus* but they're not the sort to have done this kind of thing. Are you familiar with the term "*bhadralok*"?'

'No, sir.'

'It's a Bengali word. It means "the civilised people", what we'd call "gentlemen". It refers mainly to the upper-caste Hindus who hold prominence among the natives. They're all soft and fat. It's just not in their nature to commit this sort of act.'

'What about whites? Someone with a grudge against MacAuley personally?'

'You're not serious, are you?' he said, a thin smile forming on his grey lips. 'This isn't the 1750s when *sahibs* conducted duels on the *Maidan*. We certainly don't solve our disputes by knocking one another off. No, it's inconceivable. This is clearly the work of terrorists. I believe there was a note found on MacAuley's person confirming as much. That is where you must concentrate your efforts.'

'Do you have any idea why he might have been up in Cossipore on the night he was murdered?'

The L-G scratched distractedly at one ear. 'None whatsoever. I wouldn't have imagined any European would venture up there after dark.'

'He wasn't up there in an official capacity, then?'

'Not that I know of.' He shrugged. 'It's possible, though highly unlikely. Nevertheless, do check with his colleagues at Writers' Building.'

'I will do. It's a rather delicate matter, though.'

'How so?'

I hesitated. 'You do know his body was found behind a brothel? It might just be a coincidence but . . .' I trailed off.

'Do you have a question to ask, Captain?'

'No, sir,' I said. 'I was merely thinking aloud.'

'Good. Remember, Captain, the man those terrorists assassinated was a British official, not some moral degenerate. Speculation to the contrary would reflect terribly badly upon us all.'

I could have pointed out that the two weren't exactly mutually exclusive, but instead I opted to change tack. 'Did you attend Mr Buchan's function at the Bengal Club on Tuesday night?'

'Sorry?'

'I was wondering whether you attended Mr Buchan's function. MacAuley had been there earlier that night. We think he may have gone to Cossipore straight from the club.'

The L-G stepped his bony fingers together and touched them to his lips.

'No, I did not. He may be one of our great captains of industry, but there are some matters more pressing to the interests of His Majesty's administration than assisting Mr Buchan in closing yet another contract.'

There was a knock at the door and another secretary entered. The L-G rose from his chair. 'Unfortunately we will have to end our conversation there. Humphries here will see you out.'

I thanked him for his time.

'This case is your top priority, Captain,' he said. 'Solve it quickly.'

I checked my watch as I followed the secretary back down the corridor. Exactly fifteen minutes since I'd entered the room. It's what Taggart told me I could expect. Still, the precision was impressive.

Back outside, I lit a cigarette and considered what I'd learned. MacAuley was a hundred per cent loyal. A Rottweiler. Well, the L-G was wrong about one thing: Rottweilers do have better natures. And if Miss Grant was correct about him finding God, so too it seemed, did MacAuley. There was only one man who could tell me if that was true. I needed to speak to the Reverend Gunn.

FOURTEEN

The smell of wood fires burning reminded me of home. The thick, silver smoke that rises from village hearths on crisp winter nights, fills your nostrils, dries your throat and all but calls out for a whisky to clear the soot from your gullet. Here, though, in the warmth of a moonlit Bengal night, it came not from chimneys but from the fires of a thousand native cooking stoves.

Black Town seemed to come alive in the evenings. Just as the avenues of White Town emptied, its citizens repairing to their clubs or retreating behind high, whitewashed walls, the inhabitants of Black Town took to the streets, flocking to pavement tea stalls or gathering on verandas to smoke and discuss politics. At least the men did.

Digby, Banerjee and I were in *mufti*, dressed in native clothes and sandals, walking silently along a lane near the Bagbazar road.

We'd met up at Lal Bazar, where Banerjee had given me more bad news. The baggage manifest for last night's Darjeeling Mail was missing. Of the two copies, one had been on the train and had probably been taken by the attackers. The other should have been filed at Sealdah station but couldn't be located. He'd been assured that these things often took a few days to be entered into the filing system and that the station master would pull out all the stops to locate it.

From Lal Bazar, Digby had driven us to Grey Street, half a mile away. There weren't many cars in this part of town and driving any further would have drawn attention, so we continued on foot through the busy, ill-lit streets. Digby and I had our heads covered with hooded cloaks over rudimentary turbans which one of the Sikh constables back at Lal Bazar had tied, much to the amusement of his colleagues. I drew the cowl close over my head. The sight of a couple of *sahibs* wandering through Bagbazar at this time of night would have generated as much unwanted interest as the car, possibly more. So we moved surreptitiously, taking advantage of the darkness. Or rather Digby and I did. Surrender-not, without the need to mask his appearance, walked comfortably in plain sight a few paces ahead of us, making sure the path was clear. I could have sworn the sergeant was taking some perverse pleasure in being able to walk freely in the street while we Englishmen were forced to skulk in the shadows.

We turned into an alley, not much different from the one MacAuley had been found in. A pack of stray dogs lay dozing across our path. One of them eyed Banerjee and yawned lazily. Carefully, the sergeant began to pick a path between them. As he did so, two bicycles suddenly turned the corner into the alley a few yards away. Distracted by the dogs, Banerjee must have failed to hear them approach and noticed them too late to warn us. Digby grew nervous as the glow from their lights drew closer. The two men would soon be right on top of us.

'How close are we to the safe house?' I whispered.

'Too close to risk being seen,' muttered Digby. 'We'll have to abort.'

It was a scenario we'd discussed in advance. Being spotted and identified as *sahibs* in the vicinity of the safe house carried with it the risk that Digby's informant's cover might be blown, a risk

Digby wasn't willing to take. There was a good chance the two men would just cycle past without paying us the slightest attention, but Digby had made it quite clear that when it came to the natives, nothing could be assumed and no one could be trusted. In the current climate, two *sahibs* in the wrong part of town could make a tempting target for anything from a robbery to a lynching. If spotted, we'd have to turn back, at least for a couple of hours. In keeping with protocol, though, the informant would only remain at the safe house for an hour. Any longer was considered too risky. If we aborted now, we'd have to wait another twenty-four hours before trying again and I'd be damned if I was going to sacrifice another day. Frantically I scoured for cover, but there was nowhere to hide.

The bicycles came closer, almost in line with Banerjee. Just before they drew level with him, the sergeant seemed to have an idea. He raised a foot and stamped it down heavily on the tail of one of the dogs. The animal let out a shriek of pain and bolted down the lane as if electrocuted, straight into the path of the oncoming cyclists. He hit one at full pelt, knocking the rider a clean ten feet across his handlebars. The other dogs, roused by their comrade's howls, immediately rushed forward, surrounding the riders and barking furiously. While Banerjee went to the aid of the stricken fellows, Digby and I took advantage of the ensuing chaos to hurry past unnoticed. We stopped a little further ahead and waited for Banerjee to catch up. Digby bent down, as if fiddling with the buckle of his sandal while I turned towards the wall and pretended to relieve myself into the open gutter. Finally, Banerjee sauntered over to us, grinning like a dervish.

'Good show, Sergeant,' I whispered.

'Thank you, sir,' he replied. 'It would seem that sometimes, it is better *not* to let sleeping dogs lie.'

Minutes later we were stood in the shadows of a dilapidated house while Digby quietly undid a rusty padlock and chain that fastened the two halves of its front door. He ushered us in to the pitch-black interior before barring the doors with a wooden beam. I guessed he'd been here before as he had no trouble locating the beam in the darkness. He extracted a book of matches and lit one. It flared briefly before subsiding to a gentle glow that dimly illuminated a decrepit, dust-filled room that smelled of mould. Digby wasted no time and led the way through to the back of the building where he unlocked another door, this one old and worn and held shut by a flimsy latch. He stepped out into a walled compound and made for the far end.

'Wait here,' he whispered as we reached the wall. He went off to one side and began rummaging in the waist-high grass, returning momentarily with a wooden crate. Banerjee helped him place the crate beside the wall. He climbed onto it, then pulled himself over the wall, beckoning Banerjee and me to follow. We landed in another walled garden, at the far end of which stood a door lit from above by a hurricane lamp suspended from a crooked nail. Digby silently crossed the yard and knocked on the door. It opened a crack and a wary eye examined us before opening the door further, scraping it along the ground.

It was now that I caught sight of our host, a balding, middle-aged native with hard, black eyes set in a fat head, like spots on a potato. He was smoking a *bidi*, a rolled leaf filled with tobacco and tied with string at one end. A poor man's cigarette.

'You're late,' he rasped, nervously taking a drag, 'I was about to—'

Digby silenced him with a stare. 'We had to take a few precautions. Or maybe you'd rather we just turn up on time with a couple of Congress *wallahs* in tow?'

The man raised his hands in surrender. 'No, no. Of course not!' He ran a hand across his scalp, flattening strands of greasy black hair onto his head. 'Come, this way,' he said, leading us to a stairwell and down to a claustrophobic cellar that stank of sweat and camphor. He pointed us to some wicker mats scattered around a low wooden table, while he retrieved a bottle and some glasses from a rough-hewn cupboard that looked like it had seen better days.

'What do you say, Sub-inspector?' said the Indian, raising the bottle. 'A little drink before we do business?'

'Fine,' said Digby.

He set down the glasses on the table and filled each of them with a golden-brown liquid from the bottle.

'What is it?' I asked.

'Arrak,' he replied with a smile. 'Very good liquor it is and no mistake. It comes from the South only.'

Digby nodded and took a sip. I followed his lead. It was fiery stuff. Enough to put hairs on your chest, or burn them off if you spilled some.

'Not for me,' said Banerjee, pushing his glass away.

'You do not partake of the strong liquor?' asked the native. 'Indians all should drink liquor. And eat meat also. Red meat, especially the beef. The Britishers,' he said, pointing at Digby and me, 'all are partaking of the liquor and beef, even *memsahibs*. That is why they are strong. We Indians, alas, are too much teetotal and vegetarian. That is why we are in state of subjugation.'

'Enough of this,' said Digby tersely. 'What have you got for us, Vikram?'

The Indian gave a sly grin. 'This MacAuley business. Very upsetting it is to the Britishers. Your English papers are calling it "outrageous calamity" and demanding killers be caught and urgently made example of.'

It was clear where this was heading. Vikram had information – a commodity he knew we wanted. He would try to talk up the value of what he had to sell. It was simple supply and demand. Whether it was London or Calcutta made no difference: a snitch was a snitch and economics was universal.

'The *sahibs* and the *memsahibs*,' Vikram continued, 'verily they are consumed by state of panic.'

'Get to the point, Vikram,' said Digby.

'There is much talk,' continued the Indian, 'up Cossipore way. Much gossip, much speculation. You know, Sub-inspector, how we damn Indians like to talk. You Britishers are even passing the laws to stop us talking, but still we persist. And people are always gossiping with their local *paan wallah*. I am hearing things—'

Digby cut him off. 'I'm not interested in gossip, Vikram. Either you have something or you don't. Stop wasting my time.' He made to rise from his seat.

'Wait!' cried the Indian. 'You know I am having good sources. Value of my informations is tip top!'

Digby looked the native in the eye, then slowly sat back down. 'So, what have you got?'

The Indian hesitated, no doubt pondering his next move. Selling information is like selling sex. You have to tease the customer. Reveal just enough to whet his appetite, but leave enough to the imagination so that the fool buys the goods.

'Two nights previous, on the night of unfortunate demise of the *burra sahib*, there was proscribed meeting in a house in Cossipore. Some no-good rascals spouting all manner of seditious what-nots to crowd of locals. Fiery speeches and big-big talk about the need to send a message to the Britishers. I have all informations on the meeting, and also of what is transpiring thereafter. I am thinking these informations would be of value to you, Sub-inspector?'

'Do you have names?' asked Digby.

'One especial name has been mentioned to me jointly and severally.'

Now it was Digby's turn to ponder.

'Okay. You'll get the usual amount. Now let's hear it.'

The snitch gave a servile laugh. 'Please, Sub-inspector, with my informations you will surely be putting the miscreants behind bars. And with big case like this, the *burra sahibs* will give you promotion and no mistake!' He rubbed the thumb and fingers of one hand together. 'I am thinking that is worth "extra" to you?'

Digby made a decent show of nonchalance, but we all knew it was a bluff. 'All right,' he said finally, 'an extra twenty.'

'Fifty,' the Indian shot back.

Digby snorted. 'An extra thirty and that's more than you're worth. Take it or leave it.'

An oily smile broke out across the snitch's face. Instead of a reply, he simply nodded his head in that peculiar way Indians have, like a figure of eight, which leaves you wondering whether they're agreeing, disagreeing or merely reserving the option to decide later.

Digby took out his wallet and counted out eighty rupees in notes and passed them across the table. It was a little over five pounds, not cheap, but still good value if the snitch's information was as good as he was claiming.

'Right,' he said, 'let's have it. Chapter and verse.'

Vikram quickly pocketed the cash, then picked up the bottle. He refilled the glasses and toasted our health before continuing.

'So, the meeting in Cossipore,' he said, 'it is taking place at the abode of one fellow by the name of Amarnath Dutta, a most fiery radical. Previously he is running Bengali news-sheet called *New Dawn*, then Britishers are shutting it down. But Dutta is still involved in whole "freedom struggle" business.' He gave a wave of his hand. 'All nonsense, obviously. Nevertheless, I am hearing that some fifteen men were in attendance, all good types: traders, engineers, lawyers. Dutta is giving speech, but all had really come to hear one different person: Benoy Sen.'

'Sen?' said Digby, suddenly animated. 'So he's back in Calcutta, is he?'

Vikram nodded, keen to please. 'Oh yes, and no mistake! Apparently Sen is giving speech about need for strong actions in face of British aggression. He is saying there is need to send a message that Britishers cannot ignore. All the listeners became most thrilled by his hot-tempered agitations! Then Mr Dutta is telling all people to heed Sen's call for vigorous combat, after which meeting is dissolving.'

'What happened then?' I asked.

Vikram smiled. 'That is the most intriguing aspect, Inspector *sahib*! When body is being found next day, people are saying it must be the doing of Sen.'

'Why not one of the others at the meeting?' I asked.

The snitch shook his head. 'It is not possible, *sahib*. Those men all are lawyers and accountants; what you Britishers are calling the armchair revolutionists.'

'What do you think?' I asked Digby.

'I agree with Vikram,' he replied. 'Calcutta's full of that sort of Bengali: all mouth and no trousers. Their idea of action is writing a stiffly worded letter to the Viceroy. They'd never actually kill anyone. No, it has to be Sen.' He turned to Vikram. 'And where is he now?'

The snitch made a show of looking dismayed, 'Alas, *sahib*, this I do not know. I can try to find out, but these types of informations are not coming cheap. It would be most efficacious if I am having some advance to cover expenses?'

Digby threw another ten on the table. Vikram smiled and pocketed the note.

We left the snitch and headed back over the wall and into the safe house, and from there retraced our steps back to the car on Grey Street.

It was late but Digby was bouncing about like a Hun in a sausage factory. We all sensed a possible breakthrough in the case, but he was the most excited. In a gesture of bonhomie, he offered to drop me off at the guest house. He even offered to drop Banerjee at a rickshaw stand en route.

'Tell me about Benoy Sen,' I said to Digby, after we'd left the sergeant at the stand.

'He's the de facto leader of Jugantor,' he replied, 'one of countless revolutionary groups trying to kick us out of India. Nasty chaps, responsible for assassinating quite a few policemen. During the war, they hatched a plan to smuggle in weapons from the Boche. They hoped to launch an armed insurrection and start a mutiny by native army regiments. The plot was quite sophisticated and would have caused countless deaths if Section H hadn't got wind of it. In the end, we were waiting for the shipments as they arrived. Managed to take the ringleaders by surprise. Most of Jugantor's high command were arrested or shot trying to escape. Sen was the one that got away. Rumour had it he'd gone into hiding somewhere up in the hill country near Chittagong. They must be planning something pretty big for him to risk coming back here.'

As Digby dropped me off outside the Belvedere, I brooded on whether I'd been a trifle unfair to him. He'd impressed me tonight, handling his snitch with aplomb. If I was being honest, he was responsible for pretty much every advance we'd made, from identifying the body and calling it as a political crime, to now identifying a chief suspect. Underneath the bluster and colonial pretence, he was actually a pretty decent officer. It made me wonder why he was still only a detective sub-inspector.

———

The lights were still on in the parlour as I let myself in. Dinner had finished almost two hours ago but it sounded like Mrs Tebbit and several of the guests were still up. I sensed they were waiting for me. They'd probably seen the headlines in the *Statesman* and wanted the inside gen. I closed the front door as softly as I could and tiptoed across the hallway, hoping to slip unnoticed to my room like some errant schoolboy returning to dorms after lights-out. I made it as far as the staircase when the parlour door swung open and light streamed into the hallway, outlining the unmistakable silhouette of Mrs Tebbit. It seemed everything about that woman was formidable, even her shadow.

'Ah, Captain Wyndham, there you are!' she cried as if greeting the second coming of the Lord. 'I thought you'd be working late, so I saved you a cold supper. You must be ever so hungry.'

'Very kind of you, Mrs Tebbit,' I said, 'but I'm fine, thank you.'

'Oh come now, Captain, you've got to keep your strength up. After all, we're relying on you to protect us from those nefarious natives in these uncertain times.'

From where I was standing, it looked as though she'd be perfectly capable of protecting herself from the natives, nefarious or otherwise. And given the heft of the woman, if anything it would probably be the natives who'd need protecting. However, short of being rude, there seemed little chance of avoiding her food or her questions, so I surrendered to the inevitable. At least I was trained to deal with the questions. I smiled, followed her into the dining room and sat down as she poured me a glass of wine and brought over a cold meat pie with a few slices of bread and butter. Simple fare. Hopefully that meant there was less chance of her getting it wrong. As I cut into the pie, Byrne and Peters traipsed in, ostensibly to keep me company. Mrs Tebbit poured them both a glass of wine, taking a small sherry for herself.

'Abominable business this MacAuley affair,' said Peters to no one in particular.

'Absolutely dreadful,' tutted Mrs Tebbit. 'It makes you wonder if any of us are safe in our beds.'

I could have pointed out that MacAuley hadn't been murdered in his bed, but five miles away in an alley behind a whore house. But I suspected they wouldn't want to hear that. Instead, I concentrated on the meat pie.

'It's a disgrace, that's what it is, Mrs Tebbit,' Peters continued. 'The gall of it. To kill a representative of the King Emperor, in cold blood, here in the empire's second city. I don't know where these bloody *wogs* get the nerve.'

He continued in this vein for some minutes, working himself up into a lather while Mrs Tebbit clucked in agreement.

Mrs Tebbit turned to me. 'You couldn't put our minds at ease, could you, Captain?'

I gave her the usual flannel – we're doing all we can; investigating the crime thoroughly, no stone left unturned, et cetera, but that didn't seem enough for her, so I followed up with: 'There's nothing for you to concern yourself about.'

'That's all well and good, Captain,' she said, 'but what if this is the start of a concerted campaign? If it continues, Europeans will be afraid to walk the streets after dark.'

'That's not going to happen,' I said. 'Besides, I'm surprised at you, Mrs Tebbit. A fine woman of good English stock. I'd have expected you to be the last person to be intimidated by the actions of some disgruntled natives. You need to stiffen your upper lip, madam!'

That did the trick. When logic fails, I've found that a naked appeal to patriotism often has the desired effect.

'Oh, of course not,' she gabbled, 'I didn't mean . . .'

'The Captain's right,' said Byrne. 'Ah sure, you know yourself, Mrs Tebbit, we've seen this sort of thing before. Besides, if you ask me, the violent ones aren't the problem. It's the ones preaching *non-violence* that are the real issue altogether. They might call it "peaceful non-cooperation" but economic warfare's what it really is. This boycott of British cloth. It's hurtin' the trade somethin' fierce. Sure, my orders are down thirty per cent on last year, *fifty* per cent in some parts. If it carries on like this, I'll be out of a job by the summer.

'Christ almighty, it's not just happenin' here in Bengal, but all over the country. And the worst of it is there's nothin' we can do about it. I mean, it's not as though you can lock folk up for not buying cloth.'

A sombre mood seemed to settle over the table as Byrne's words sunk in. Mrs Tebbit looked as though her world was collapsing. Peters just fumed. I had some sympathy for them. In their eyes, they and their kind had built this country and now everything they'd made was threatened. It was the impudence of it all that they couldn't understand. How, after everything they'd done for this land, could the natives have the effrontery to want to send them all packing back to Blighty? At the heart of it, I recognised the real fear. Mrs Tebbit and her kind might think of themselves as British, but India was the only life they really knew; a life of garden parties and cocktails at the club. They were like a hybrid flower transplanted to India and acclimatised to such an extent that if returned to Britain, it'd probably wither and die.

I cleared my plate and Mrs Tebbit whisked it away.

'It's late,' said Peters, 'I'd better call it a night.' He rose and bade us goodnight, his tired footsteps echoing slowly as he traipsed up the stairs. Mrs Tebbit, realising there was no more information to be gleaned, also made her excuses and retired. That left Byrne and me and half a bottle of red wine. He pulled out a couple of cigarettes and offered me one. I took it and lit up.

'Are you very much involved yourself in the MacAuley case, Captain?' he asked. Not that he sounded particularly interested. I got the feeling he just wanted to fill the silence.

'I'm afraid so,' I replied, 'but I can't tell you any more than I told the others.'

'I can appreciate that.' He nodded. 'It's just that, security wise, things seemed to be improving. I'd hoped we'd seen an end to all the independence nonsense when the war finished.'

'You've no sympathy for their cause?' I asked. 'I'd imagine a lot of your countrymen might have a slightly different opinion.'

'As a textiles salesman, I can tell you I have absolutely no sympathy for them at all. As an Irishman, though . . .' He smiled. 'Well, sure now, that's a different matter.'

He raised his glass in a toast.

'The thing is,' he continued, 'for the most part your average Indian terrorist, at least the Bengali ones, are somewhat incompetent. They spend a lot of their time fightin' each other, an' when they're not – most of the time, thankfully – they manage to blow themselves up without hurtin' anyone else. When, on occasion, they do actually manage to kill someone, as often as not it's some innocent passer-by rather than the feller they were aimin' for. All in all, it's usually not long before they get caught or shot themselves. Rest assured, Captain, they could carry on like this for another hundred years without making the slightest dent in the foundations of the Raj. The problem, y'see, is this: your classic Bengali revolutionary is a dilettante. Look at them – they're all uppercaste, upper-class toffs who look on the whole thing as some sort of noble, romantic struggle. Now that's all fine an' dandy in a university debatin' chamber, but sure if you want to end over a hundred years of British rule, you need real hard-men. Working-class lads that know how to get the job done. Not a bunch of effete intellectuals who have trouble tellin' one end of a Mauser from the other.'

'If they're as incompetent as you say,' I asked, 'why has MacAuley's murder got everyone so spooked?'

Byrne ruminated, taking a sip of wine before replying. 'D'you know how many British there are in India, Captain?'

'Half a million?' I guessed.

'One hundred an' fifty thousand. That's all. An' d'you know how many Indians there are? I'll tell ye – three hundred million. Now how d'ye suppose one hundred and fifty thousand British keep control of three hundred million Indians?'

I said nothing.

'Moral superiority.' He let the phrase sink in. 'For such a small number to rule over so many, the rulers need to project an aura of superiority over the ruled. Not just physical or military superiority mind, but also *moral* superiority. More importantly, their subjects must in turn *believe* themselves to be inferior; that they need to be ruled for their own benefit.

'It seems everything we've done since the Battle of Plassey has been with a view to keepin' the natives in their place, convincing them they need our guidance, and our education. Their culture must be shown to be barbaric, their religions built on false gods, even their architecture must be inferior to ours. Why else would we build that bloody great monstrosity the Victoria Memorial out of white marble and make it bigger than the Taj Mahal?

'Christ we don't even let *facts* get in the way if it might harm the image we want to maintain. Take a look at any Indian primary school atlas. They put Britain and India next to one another, each takin' up a full page. We don't even show them to scale, lest little brown children realise how tiny Britain is compared to India!

'The problem, Captain, is that over the last two hundred years, we've come to swallow our own propaganda. We do feel we're superior to the bastards we rule. An' anything that threatens that fiction is a threat to the whole edifice. That's why MacAuley's murder has caused such a stink. It's an attack on two levels. First it shows us that some Indians at least no longer think themselves inferior, so much so that they can successfully pull off the murder of such a high-profile member of the ruling class, and secondly because it shatters our own fiction of superiority.'

He finished the last dregs of wine.

'You don't believe in the superiority of the white man, then?' I asked.

'In over fifteen years here, I've yet to see any proof of it. Look, I'm an Irishman, Captain. There are enough of your own people back in London who would think me a stupid Paddy. Sure if I don't accept that, what would give me the right to claim superiority over another race? And times are changin', Captain. The old order is collapsing. You only need to take a look at the map of Europe to see that. Poland, Czechoslovakia, all the other newly independent nations. If we believe in their right to self-determination, sure why should it be different in the case of India?'

I lit a cigarette as he finished the last of the wine.

'Anyway,' he said, 'it's gettin' late. I best be off to bed.'

He rose and bade me goodnight.

'I guess I should bid you farewell,' I said. 'You're off to Assam tomorrow, aren't you? To the tea gardens?'

'Oh, right so.' He smiled. 'No. Change of plans, I'm afraid. I'm stuck in town for a few more days.'

I said goodnight and sat alone, smoking. Byrne had certainly made an interesting point. I could have assured him, though, that any notions I may have once held about British superiority had died back in Flanders alongside my friends. Not that it changed anything. Neither self-determination nor moral superiority was my concern. A man had been murdered and it was my job to find his killers. I'd leave the politics to others.

FIFTEEN

The electric fan creaked slowly round on the ceiling and made not a jot of difference to the temperature in the room. It had been several days since I'd realised its presence was more decorative than functional, but I'd switched it on anyway, more in hope than expectation.

Another torrid Bengal night. The humidity was suffocating. You could taste it in the air. Perspiration dripped off my body and drenched the bed. I'd opened the window in an attempt to encourage some sort of breeze to circulate, but all it did was allow free access to the mosquitoes Mrs Tebbit insisted didn't exist.

I checked my watch. It read twelve forty. I shook it and held it up to my ear. It was still ticking, though somewhat irregularly and I guessed the correct time was probably closer to two. I turned over, trying to make myself comfortable on the damp mattress, but the battle was already lost. Sleep wasn't going to come tonight.

The urge to pay another visit to my new friends in Tiretta Bazaar was growing and the lure of oblivion was hard to ignore. But the O was my servant, not my mistress, and it was best to keep it that way. She could be insidious, and it was essential to respect her or she'd turn the tables on you. Others didn't realise that, and she took them. Completely. Discipline was key. It was like crossing a river on the back of a crocodile: people might consider it foolhardy, but if you knew what you were doing, it'd get you where you wanted to go. The trick, obviously, was to not get eaten, and to do that you had to stay in control. And, I told myself, I was in control. So I stayed in the room, and lay on the bed, and watched the fan turn monotonously on the ceiling.

I leaned over and reached for the bottle of whisky on the floor, but it wasn't there. I cursed, panicking that the bloody maid had thrown it out, but that was unlikely. After a lifetime in the service of Mrs Tebbit, independent action of that magnitude was frankly beyond her. I sat up and scoured the room. The bottle was sat on a corner of the desk, its label glinting in the moonlight.

Pulling myself off the bed, I staggered to the table and poured out a double measure, then added a dash of water from the sink. As I did so, I recalled Mrs Tebbit's warnings about drinking water straight from the tap. I cursed once again and looked at the tooth glass, then took a sip and walked back to the bed. I'd take my chances with cholera before I threw out good single malt.

I sat back on the bed and, not for the first time, questioned what I was doing out here, in this country where the natives despised you and the climate drove you mad and the water could kill you. And not just the water, pretty much everything out here seemed designed to kill an Englishman: the food, the insects, the weather. It was as though India itself were reacting to our presence as one's immune defences react to invasion by a foreign body. Indeed, it was a wonder men like MacAuley survived as long as they did before succumbing. And it was as true to say he'd been killed by India as it was to say he'd been murdered by a native in an alley. They both amounted to the same thing.

And yet, here we were and here we stayed, noble Englishmen and women standing resolute in the face of implacable hostility from both nature and native. We told ourselves we'd tamed this savage land with railroads and breach-loading rifles and, it seemed, we'd be damned if we were going to leave any time soon, whatever the cost to us in dead civil servants and gin-soaked *memsahibs*. We were doing the Lord's work, after all. Bringing the word of God and the glories of the free market to these poor souls. And if we made a profit in the process, surely that was God's will too.

I felt a great heaviness. India was depressing me, as it appeared to depress pretty much everyone. No one seemed very happy. The British weren't happy. Not Digby, or Buchan or Mrs Tebbit or Peters. They all seemed angry or scared or despondent, sometimes all at once. The Indians – the educated ones, at least – appeared no more content, be it Mrs Bose and her sullen acceptance of our hegemony over her country, or Surrender-not with his earnest, melancholy, hang-dog face.

Then, of course, there was Annie. She fell into neither camp, but she didn't seem happy either. There was a certain sadness to her. She tried to hide it under a cloak of forced good humour and that beguiling smile of hers, but every now and again, as happened outside the Red Elephant, the mask would slip and the sadness would surface. She was like a bird trapped in a rusting cage.

If there was such a thing as happiness in India, it was probably to be found among the poor, illiterate classes who had little to do with either the British or the Indian elite. People like Salman the rickshaw *wallah*. For him, happiness meant a full belly and a *bidi* before bed and it mattered not a jot whether it was *sahibs* in suits or *babus* in *dhotis* who sat in Writers' Building and ran the country.

My thoughts wandered. At some point they turned to Sarah, as they always do. In the months since her death, I'd realised I hardly knew her. In three years of marriage, we'd spent a total of five weeks together. Five weeks. Too short a time for anything other than her memory to be indelibly scratched into my mind. The bile rose in my stomach. Fate had cheated me of her. *Fate*. Not God. For I no longer believed in the Almighty. In truth, I'd begun to doubt his existence while in the trenches – it's hard not to ask where he is when your comrades are being blown to pieces – but I still prayed to him in the hope he'd see me through to the other side, as though my prayers mattered more than those of the millions who weren't so lucky. But it was Sarah's death that finally shattered my faith. It's funny how one can believe in the existence of a deity until you lose the one closest to you.

———

Before daybreak my thoughts turned to Byrne. He was a funny old fish. Most of the time he seemed an amiable buffoon, drivelling on about textiles and tea gardens, but when you got him on his own, like tonight, he came across as clever and surprisingly insightful. I reflected on what he'd said about Bengali revolutionaries, their ridiculous notions of noble struggle and their general haplessness. He was right. Men like that had no idea what war meant. Real war was blood and slaughter and the screams of the dying. It had no place for ideals. Real war was hell, and spared neither friend nor foe.

The thought triggered something. The attack on the Darjeeling Mail. Suddenly, and only for an instant, there was a terrible clarity. I jumped to my feet and in a daze threw on my uniform. It was still dark outside but I needed to get to the office. I knew why the passengers on the train hadn't been robbed. I also had a theory for why the mail sacks hadn't been taken, and if I was right, we had a much bigger problem than the death of a railway guard to deal with.

SIXTEEN

Friday, 11 April 1919

I left the guest house and ran towards the rickshaw stand on the corner. Salman was sprawled on a mat under his rickshaw. At the sound of my footsteps he opened his eyes and hauled himself to his feet. He gave a hacking cough and spat into the roadside gutter.

'Office, *sahib*?'

I nodded and climbed aboard the rickshaw. With one finger of his right hand, Salman rang a battered little tin bell that hung from a string tied around his wrist. It tinkled like a child's toy. Then we were off.

The roads were busy despite the early hour. The morning was humid and still and the sky was already turning from pinks and oranges to the hazy blue that brought with it the portent of another broiling day.

———

There was a note from Daniels waiting on my desk, imploring me to call him, at my earliest convenience, to arrange a time to brief the Commissioner. That was fine by me. I was more than happy to do so, now that I actually had something to tell him.

I telephoned Daniels' office but no one answered. It was only six o'clock and the man was probably still in his bed and I took a perverse pleasure in writing him an angry note, telling him I'd tried to contact him several times as I needed to brief the Commissioner urgently on developments. I called in a *peon* from the corridor outside and dispatched him to Daniels' office with the note.

Once confident he was headed in the right direction, I telephoned the pit and asked the duty officer to take a message for Surrender-not. The sergeant was already at his desk, so I asked him to join me, bringing with him all the files we had on Benoy Sen and the terrorist group Jugantor.

Ten minutes later he knocked and entered the office, carrying a pile of fat buff-coloured folders. He let out a sigh as he dropped the lot onto the desk. 'Here you are, sir,' he said. 'The thick ones are on Jugantor. They go back about ten years. The thin one is on Sen himself.'

'Good work, Sergeant,' I said. 'Any news on that missing baggage manifest for the Darjeeling Mail?'

'I'm afraid not, sir. I'll keep pushing.'

I dismissed him and began reading through the Jugantor files. They told the classic tale of an outfit which, from innocuous beginnings, had developed into a major terrorist threat. The early files comprised mainly scene-of-crime reports, detailing petty theft and thuggery. The later files showed a graduation to gun attacks and much more sophisticated felonies. They'd started out robbing taxi cabs and ended up robbing banks. The proceeds of these raids were used to pay for guns and parts for bombs. As for assassinations, they were mainly of policemen, most of them natives, and a few minor British government officials. What was interesting, though, was the number of failed assassination attempts recorded in the file. On many occasions the terrorists hadn't even come close to achieving their objectives, either through laughably poor execution or faulty weaponry or because they'd been infiltrated by security service informants.

Alongside the scene-of-crime reports were a small number of intelligence reports. These speculated on the hierarchy and operating structure of the organisation, together with what was known about the group's regional cells throughout Bengal, and their contacts with terrorist factions in other parts of India. The group's leader had been a Bengali named Jatindranath Mukherjee, whom the natives referred to as 'Bagha Jatin' – 'the Tiger'.

There was a significant increase in Jugantor's activities during the war, with several of the later files devoted solely to a period between 1914 and 1917. The Tiger seemed to have looked on the war as a golden opportunity to try to force the British out of India and there were several reports on a raid that he and his men had carried out on the warehouses of a company called Rodda & Co, which held one of the biggest arms stores in Calcutta. They'd managed to escape with ten cases of arms and ammunition, including fifty Mauser pistols and forty-six thousand rounds of ammunition.

Most of the files, though, focused on what they termed 'the German Conspiracy', detailing a plot to acquire weapons from the Kaiser, seize Calcutta and foment insurrection of the native regiments of the Indian army throughout India. They described the group's links to seditious Indian organisations as far afield as Berlin and San Francisco, detailing how funds were channelled through these organisations to pay for arms shipments. In the end, the group had been fatally compromised by a number of spies acting for Section H, and the insurrections in Bengal and the Punjab were strangled at birth. Mukherjee and five of his comrades had gone into hiding and were discovered near Balasore, betrayed by locals. Section H moved in and Mukherjee and two others were mortally wounded. Two more were captured. Only one man escaped. Benoy Sen.

I turned to Sen's file. There were few hard facts and no photographs or sketches of the man. Most of it was just speculation about his involvement in raids in the movement's early days. Later there were rumours of him having a role in the group's strategic planning, but nothing concrete. Section H, with their greater resources and spies within Jugantor, would probably have a better picture of the man. I'd make sure to ask them for access to their files on him. It would be interesting to see whether their commitment to provide 'any and all assistance' would stretch that far. Somehow I doubted it.

The telephone began to ring. I picked up the receiver. On the other end, Daniels was breathing heavily. The Commissioner would see me in his office in ten minutes.

I sat facing Lord Taggart's empty chair, listening to the clock in his office tick slowly by. Lord Taggart was running late and Daniels had offered no explanation as to why. So I sat there as the sublime countenance of the King Emperor George V gazed down on me from his exalted position on the wall. The doors opened and Lord Taggart strode in, the silver buttons on his freshly pressed uniform glinting in the sunlight.

'My apologies, Sam,' he said, gesturing for me to sit and dropping down into his leather chair. 'Now, what have you got for me?'

I told him of the meeting with Digby's informant and that we now had a prime suspect in the form of Benoy Sen.

His ears pricked up at the mention of Sen.

'So the old fox has finally come home,' he said, more to himself than to me. 'That's good work, Sam,' he continued. 'You have my permission to call on whatever resources you need to track him down. Do whatever you have to. I've waited a long time for this and I don't want him slipping through our fingers again. In the meantime, I'll inform the L-G of your progress.'

'It may be better to wait until we have Sen in custody,' I ventured.

Taggart shook his head. 'No. That might seem like the prudent thing to do, Sam, but it would be a severely career-limiting move for all of us if the L-G found out we'd been keeping information from him. Besides, his other sources might be able to help find Sen.'

'There's something else,' I said. 'I think Sen might be linked to the attack on the Darjeeling Mail.'

'Go on,' said Taggart calmly, as though what I'd suggested was the most natural thing in the world.

'I suspect the attack was carried out by terrorists rather than mere *dacoits*. It's the only explanation that makes sense. The attackers were searching for something specific, something they expected to find in the safes on board. Fortunately those safes were empty. *Dacoits* wouldn't have left empty handed. They'd at least have robbed the passengers of their valuables. Terrorists, though, wouldn't be interested in petty theft. From what I'm told, it would probably offend their sensibilities.'

'So what *were* they looking for, Sam?' said the Commissioner. It felt as though he was leading me to an answer he already knew.

'My guess is they were looking for cash. And a lot of it. They were expecting to find it in the safes.'

'Then why not take the mail sacks?'

'Time.' I said. 'Monetising the valuables in the mail would take time.'

'That would imply their need for the cash is urgent,' said Taggart. 'What does that suggest to you?'

The answer was obvious. 'They're looking to conclude an arms deal. If this man Sen's suddenly come back to Calcutta, and he *is* behind the attack, that suggests MacAuley's assassination is just the first shot in a much larger, bloodier campaign.'

'You need to share your concerns with Section H,' said Taggart. 'If you're right, we're facing something far more dangerous than I'd anticipated. Sen and his cohorts must be stopped before they get the chance to launch a real terror campaign. Get to it, Captain.'

I rose and walked towards the door, but stopped halfway and turned.

'You knew, didn't you, sir?' I said.

Taggart looked up from his desk. 'Knew what, Sam?'

'The attack on the Darjeeling Mail, that it wasn't just a botched robbery by some *dacoits*.'

'I *suspected*, Sam. I didn't *know*. For that matter, I still don't.'

'Why didn't you voice your suspicions before?'

'I trusted your judgement. Besides, one whiff of suspicion that this might have been the work of terrorists and the case would have been handed to Section H. You wouldn't have got a sniff of it, and, by extension, neither would I.'

I thanked him for his candour and headed back to my office. The situation was grave, but as I saw it, we had one thing in our favour. The safes had been empty. That suggested Sen still hadn't the funds to purchase the arms. It meant we had a window of opportunity. We just had to find him before he found the cash.

SEVENTEEN

On the riverbank to the south of town sits Fort William. Home to the army's eastern command, it's also the headquarters of its intelligence function, Section H. I was sat with Banerjee in the back of a police car speeding towards it.

'General Clive had it rebuilt after the Battle of Plassey,' marvelled Banerjee, as we drove down a palm-lined avenue towards the Fort's Treasury Gate. 'Apparently at a cost of over two million pounds. What's more, it's never fired a shot in anger.'

It was unlike any military base I'd seen before. For a start it had its own golf course, which might begin to explain why it had cost so much.

'What do the natives make of Benoy Sen?' I asked.

'Well,' said Banerjee hesitantly, 'ever since the death of Bagha Jatin, Sen's become a folk hero. There are reports of him turning up everywhere between Sylhet and the Sundarbans, preaching to villagers and putting the fear of God into corrupt officials. They call him "the Ghost". Half Robin Hood, half Lord Krishna. The peasants love him. That's how he's managed to stay on the run for nearly four years despite a substantial reward for his capture.'

'Any rumours of him being behind terrorist activities recently?'

'Not to my knowledge, sir, though it's not the sort of thing people would tell a policeman.'

'What's *your* impression of the man?'

Banerjee thought for a moment.

'I think, with the death of Jatin and the other leaders, the people have created a legend around Sen to serve their own purposes. For those who seek violent revolution, he's the freedom fighter who's managed to outsmart the British and galvanise the people. He's a symbol that the struggle continues. They need him for their own dignity.

'At the same time, for the British, at least for the *Statesman* and its readers, he's a bogeyman. The embodiment of everything they're scared of, a bloodthirsty communist who won't be happy till every last Englishman has been killed or sent packing. He's their justification for things like the Rowlatt Acts. My own opinion is that he's probably neither.'

We pulled up to the guardhouse at the Treasury Gate. Fort William was certainly impressive. A star-fort covering three square miles, it was a huge brick and mortar structure, housing thousands of troops and ancillary staff. It was also the site of the infamous Black Hole of Calcutta, well known to every English schoolboy as a symbol of eternal native perfidy.

The driver presented our papers to a stiff sentry who made a show of scrutinising them before waving us through, past red walls several feet thick. Inside, we passed some three-storey buildings which I took to be barracks, then neat rows of officers' bungalows, followed by a high street of shops, a post office and a cinema. At the centre sat St Peter's Church, complete with towers and flying buttresses. Indeed, the whole place looked more like a Sussex village than a military garrison.

I had a healthy distrust of the intelligence services, carefully honed over many years, starting with my time at Special Branch and then later during the war, when I was a cog in their machinery. True, they were smart, resourceful people, working, as they saw it, to defend the nation and the empire. But if the cause was noble, the means often weren't. As a policeman, steeped in the rule of law, I often found their methods unsavoury, immoral and, worst of all, un-English. Nevertheless, it was a relief to be able to call on them now. Their resources would be vital if we really were looking at thwarting a concerted terrorist campaign.

I briefed Banerjee on my theory that MacAuley's murder and the attack on the Darjeeling Mail were linked, that Jugantor were behind both and that we were going to solicit whatever help we could from Section H in tracking Sen down.

Banerjee's face darkened.

'Do you have a problem with that, Sergeant?'

He shifted nervously in his seat.

'May I speak freely, sir?'

I nodded. 'Please do.'

'Are you honestly interested in getting to the truth behind this murder?'

I was surprised by the question.

'It's our duty to get to the truth, without fear or favour,' I replied, 'and that's exactly what we're going to do.'

'Forgive me,' said Banerjee, 'but if that really is your intention, then bringing Sen in for questioning would be vital. Is that not correct, sir?'

'Obviously.'

'In that case, sir, I would advocate caution in what you share with Section H. They have a reputation for being rather heavy handed.'

'Are you suggesting I keep this information from Section H?'

'I'm saying, sir, that if you want Sen alive, then it's critical we find him before Section H does.'

———

We pulled up outside a large admin block, Banerjee's words still ringing in my head. Instinctively I shared his concern, but what he asked was impossible. I'd no option but to share everything with Section H. The stakes were too high. Besides, I'd already told Lord Taggart everything, and he'd be briefing the L-G. Anything I didn't divulge, they'd find out anyway.

That left me with the small headache of what to do with Banerjee. I'd planned on taking him with me to meet Colonel Dawson, but now I wasn't so sure. Besides, Dawson might be more guarded in his conversation with me if there was a native in the room. In the end I got out, leaving Banerjee with the driver.

Entering the building past two wilting sentries, I knocked on the first door I came across and asked a junior officer where I might find Colonel Dawson. He directed me to Room 207 on the second floor.

The room turned out to be a large open-plan office, humming with activity. There were desks for a dozen officers and their assistants. Pinned to one wall were several large maps of India, Bengal and a city that I presumed was Calcutta. Each was covered with a variety of flags, crosses and circles. What with the din of voices and typewriters, no one took much notice of my entrance. I asked a pretty young secretary in a khaki uniform where I could find Dawson. She pointed to a cubicle with frosted-glass partitions in one corner of the room. I thanked her, walked over to the cubicle and knocked.

'Enter,' boomed a stentorian voice. I did as requested and found myself enveloped in a fog of pipe smoke.

'Colonel Dawson?' I asked, peering through the haze at a well-built, moustachioed officer with a pipe clamped between his jaws. He was about forty, I guessed, with coarse, copper-coloured skin and brown hair flecked grey at the temples. He looked up from reading a typed report.

'Ah, Captain Wyndham,' he said, rising to shake my hand. 'Please, have a seat.'

Obviously, he knew who I was. There was a certainty in his tone as though we'd met before. Not that it should have come as a surprise. The man worked in intelligence, after all.

'Would you care for some refreshment?' he asked, raising a thick, bronzed forearm and studying his watch. 'Too early for a proper drink alas. How about a cup of tea? Miss Braithwaite!' he thundered, without bothering to wait for a reply. A waspish woman with a face like a disgruntled horse stuck her head round the door. 'Two teas please, Marjorie.'

The woman nodded sourly and disappeared, closing the door heavily behind her.

'Now, Captain,' he continued, 'I understand you're new to Calcutta. How do you like our fair city?'

I guessed he'd done his homework on me. Chances were he'd already seen my wartime personnel file. In which case he'd know of my wounding and discharge, and maybe personal details too. He probably knew more about me than even *I* cared to remember.

'I like it just fine,' I replied.

'Good, good.' He took a puff of his pipe. 'I don't suppose you've had much of a chance to do any sightseeing as yet?'

'I wasn't aware there was much to see.'

Dawson grinned. 'That depends on your point of view. I'd recommend a visit to the temple at Dakhineshwar. It's a Hindu shrine to the goddess Kali. They call her The Destroyer, and an interesting sight she is too. Black as night, her eyes bloodshot, garland of skulls round her throat and her tongue lolling out in an ecstasy of violence. The Bengalis revere her. That should tell you everything you need to know about the sort of people we're dealing with. They make blood sacrifices to her. Goats and sheep these days, but they weren't always quite so civilised. Some say the city takes its name from her. Calcutta, the city of Kali.' He paused, smiling. 'Ironic, isn't it? Beneath our modern metropolis still beats the black heart of the heathen goddess of destruction.' He seemed far away for a moment. 'Anyway,' he said, focusing, 'I think you might appreciate it.'

Miss Braithwaite returned carrying a tray. She set it down noisily, spilling some of the tea from the cups. Dawson glared at her and she glowered back, then left the room.

'Milk and sugar, Captain?'

'Black is fine,' I replied, taking a cup from the tray, leaving a ring of liquid in its place.

'So, Captain, I understand you saw a bit of action in the war.'

I nodded. 'I did my bit. Joined up in 'fifteen and made it in one piece through three years before the Hun got lucky and bounced a high-explosive shell off my head.'

Dawson nodded as though I was merely confirming facts he already knew.

'And what about you, Colonel?' I asked. 'Were you at the Front?'

His expression soured. 'No, Captain. I never had that honour. Unfortunately my duties kept me here in India for the duration.'

He took a puff of his pipe and leaned forward.

'So, how can I help you?' he said, pouring some milk from a small porcelain jug and stirring it into his tea.

'The MacAuley murder. I'd like an update on everything you've found at the crime scene.'

'Of course,' he said, laying the pipe on his desk and taking a sip of tea. 'There's not much to tell, I'm afraid. A lot of blood but not much else. It's a shame the dogs got to the body before your men did. Which reminds me, we did manage to find one of his fingers. It's been packed and sent to the morgue for you.'

'Can I have a copy of your report?'

'Of course, Captain,' he said. 'I'll make sure a copy is sent to your office.'

'And are your men still guarding the scene?' I asked.

'Naturally, and what's more they'll stay there until the Lieutenant Governor says otherwise. Don't worry. They won't let anyone tamper with the site.'

'That's most reassuring,' I said. 'If you don't mind, I'd like some of my men to carry out a fingertip search of the alley. Maybe they'll be able to find something that's been missed.'

Dawson's avuncular manner evaporated.

'I hope you don't think my men aren't competent enough to carry out such a search.'

'Not at all,' I replied. 'It's just that sometimes things are overlooked in the heat of the moment.'

'Not by *my* men,' he said brusquely. 'Still, get your men to liaise with Marjorie. She'll sort out access for them. Now, is there anything else I can help you with?'

'There is one other matter.'

'Oh yes?' he replied, picking up the report he'd been reading when I'd entered.

I told him about the meeting at the house of Amarnath Dutta, and Benoy Sen's presence in Calcutta. I hoped the disclosure would allay any concerns he might have that I didn't trust him, which I didn't.

The Colonel betrayed no emotion on hearing Sen's name. He simply nodded and puffed away on his pipe.

'There's more,' I said. 'The Darjeeling Mail was attacked in the early hours of Thursday morning. Initial reports were of an attempted robbery by *dacoits*, but I fear it was the work of terrorists, specifically Sen. I think they were looking for cash to fund an arms deal. I expect I don't need to tell you what that means.'

Dawson suddenly looked as though I'd hit him in the face with a four iron. For the first time I felt I'd told him something he didn't already know. It felt good.

'This is more serious than I anticipated,' he said finally. 'What do you know of Sen, Captain?'

'Not much,' I confessed. 'Our file on him is thin on detail. I was hoping you might grant me access to yours.'

Dawson thought for a moment.

'I regret that won't be possible, but I will tell you this. Benoy Sen is an extremely dangerous individual. I take it you've read about his involvement in the German Conspiracy? What you won't know is that a key part of that plot was to incite the native regiments of the Calcutta garrison to rise up against us. As I recall it was the 14th Jat regiment at the time. They were billeted here in the fort. If the revolt had succeeded, every white man here would likely have had his throat cut. Now Sen's evaded us once already. I don't intend to let him do it a second time.'

'I trust we have your assistance in tracking him down?'

'Oh, you can depend on that,' said Dawson. 'My men'll get on it immediately.'

'And you'll inform me the minute you have something?' I asked.

Dawson gave a thin smile. 'Of course, if it's feasible. But I can't guarantee we'll be able to wait till we've informed you before we take action, especially if, as you surmise, he's plotting a larger campaign. The man's been on the run for four years and if we don't get him while he's still in Calcutta, we might lose him for another four.'

'I understand,' I said, painfully aware that the first notification I'd get from Dawson would be when Sen was either dead or in a military prison somewhere. Either way, if Section H got to him first, there'd be precious little chance of me questioning him.

I thanked the Colonel for his time, finished the tea and took my leave.

I walked back down and out into the sun. Surrender-not was standing in the shade of a large banyan tree, smoking a cigarette. On seeing me, he quickly stubbed it out and flicked the butt into the grass. He saluted and made his way over.

'We've got a problem, Sergeant,' I said, 'and I'm going to need your help to sort it out.'

'Of course, sir,' he replied as I led him back towards the building.

We climbed the stairs and headed back to Room 207.

'Listen closely,' I said, 'I'm going to introduce you to a lovely lady called Marjorie Braithwaite. You're going to sweet-talk her.'

'Sir?'

'You're going to make small talk with Miss Braithwaite and while you're chatting to her, I want you to get a good look at her boss. He's the man in the office at the end of the room. And make sure he doesn't notice you. D'you think you can manage that?'

Banerjee swallowed hard. He looked queasy.

'I'm not sure, sir,' he said, tugging at the collar of his shirt. 'I've never been particularly good at talking to English women.'

'Come on, Surrender-not,' I said. 'It can't be that different from talking to Indian women.'

'To be honest, sir, I'm not particularly good at talking to them either.' He looked like a man on his way to his own funeral. 'In our culture, contact between the sexes is strictly limited. I never know quite what to say to women . . . unless they like cricket,' he brightened, 'in which case I don't have a problem.'

Miss Braithwaite didn't look the type to be impressed by an explanation of the difference between short leg and silly point. 'On second thoughts,' I said, 'just ask her about arranging access to the MacAuley murder site. D'you think you can manage that?'

Banerjee nodded apprehensively.

'That's the spirit, Sergeant,' I said.

We entered Room 207. I looked over to Dawson's office. The door was closed, with only his silhouette visible through the frosted glass. I prodded Banerjee in the direction of Miss Braithwaite and made the introductions.

'Pleased to meet your acquaintance,' he stammered, before standing there, mouth open, staring alternately at me and Dawson's closed door, like a goldfish at a tennis match.

'Miss Braithwaite,' I said, 'I forgot to ask Colonel Dawson something. If you don't mind, can you explain to the sergeant here what he needs to do to gain access to the MacAuley crime scene while I pop my head round the Colonel's door for a minute?'

Without waiting for a reply, I marched over to Dawson's office, knocked and opened the door wide.

'Sorry to bother you, Colonel,' I said, 'I've forgotten the name of that temple you mentioned.'

He was on the telephone and didn't look amused by the interruption.

'The Kali temple at Dakhineshwar,' he said, covering the mouthpiece of the receiver with one hand, 'It's on the road to Barrackpore. Your driver will know it.'

I thanked him again and made to leave. I looked across the room to Surrender-not. He saw me and nodded and I closed Dawson's door and rejoined him. Miss Braithwaite wrote something on a scrap of paper and handed it to him. Surrender-not smiled and thanked her.

'Did you get a good look at the Colonel?' I asked as we headed back down the stairs.

'Yes, sir.'

'Good work, Sergeant. And was that her home telephone number I saw Miss Braithwaite pass you?'

Banerjee blushed. 'No, sir,' he stammered, 'it was an entry chit to show the guards at the crime scene.'

'Good,' I said, 'though next time I task you with sweet-talking a woman, I expect you to at least obtain her telephone number, if not an actual date for dinner.'

'Here's what I need you to do, Sergeant,' I began, as we sat in the back of the car. 'That man you saw in the office is Colonel Dawson. He's going to start his own search for our fugitive, and with his resources, there's a damn good chance he's going to beat us to Sen. That's why I need you to tail him and let me know the minute you think he might have tracked Sen down.'

Banerjee stared at me wide-eyed. 'You want me to follow a senior Section H officer?'

'That's right,' I replied. 'I expect you'll find it a whole lot easier than talking to Miss Braithwaite.'

'You want me to spy on a spy? Isn't he trained in that sort of thing? He'll spot me a mile off.'

'I don't think so. Right now he's only interested in Sen. I'm hoping he'll be too preoccupied to notice you.'

'But how am I supposed to tail him? He's sitting inside the most secure location in the whole of India and there are at least five exits to the place.'

'Then we're going to have to take a chance,' I said. 'Assuming Sen's still in the city, where's he most likely to hide?'

Banerjee thought for a moment.

'Among Indians,' he said. 'Among his own kind. That probably means either North Calcutta or across the river in Howrah.'

'So, if and when Dawson discovers Sen's location, we'd expect him and his men to head straight there by the quickest route. Probably in several cars. Maybe even with a truckload of soldiers in tow.'

Banerjee followed my train of thought.

'In that case, I should position myself outside the Plassey Gate. It's the closest gate to the main roads north. There's a police *thana* on the Plassey Gate Road. I can use that as a base of operations. I'll also arrange for a watch on the bridge, in case he's over in Howrah. It's the only crossing for cars and trucks.'

'Good,' I said. 'I'd expect Dawson to lead the raid himself, but even if he doesn't, what you need to look out for are several vehicles that look like they're going somewhere in a hell of a hurry.'

It wasn't a perfect plan, but it was the best we had. If we were lucky, it would be enough. In any case, I hoped it would take Section H at least a day or two to locate Sen. That might give us a chance to come up with something better. And there was still the hope that Digby's informants might find him first. They did, after all, have a few hours' head start.

Banerjee ordered the driver to take the Chowringhee Gate, then drive north to the *thana* on Plassey Gate Road. I instructed Surrender-not to organise the watch on the Howrah Bridge and to contact me the minute he had anything to report. Leaving him there, I ordered the driver to take me back to Lal Bazar, then return and await Banerjee's instructions.

Back at headquarters, I waited ten minutes before summoning Digby to my office.

'Any progress locating Sen?' I asked.

'Not so far. Vikram made contact earlier. He's got feelers out across Black Town, all the way up to Bara Nagar and Dum Dum, but it's early days, old boy.'

'What about your other informants?'

'Same story, I'm afraid. I've contacted those I think might be able to help, but they're not *politicals*, it's really not their thing. Besides, these chaps have their own twisted morality. They're quite happy to make a bit of money snitching on their own kind, but it's another matter for them to turn in someone like Sen. They seem to regard him as some sort of hero.'

He looked almost apologetic. 'Did you have any luck with Dawson?' he asked.

I recounted the highlights for him.

'Well,' he said, 'it's good that they're going to help track Sen down.'

'I hope so,' I replied. 'Though I have my doubts as to the level of cooperation we can expect from our new friends. Still, we need to be ready should they locate Sen, and I'm going to need your help with that.'

'Just tell me what you need, old boy.'

'I want to understand how Section H goes about organising a raid.'

He stared at me quizzically. 'You mean, how they plan it?'

'More how they organise the raid itself, what personnel they use, where their resources are based, what sort of protocols they have. That sort of thing.'

'Well,' said Digby, 'from what I've seen, they prefer to use their own personnel. I'm not sure of their exact numbers but they're not often short handed. When they do need additional manpower, they'll use military resources before they come to us.'

'And all based up at Fort William?'

Digby nodded. 'As far as I'm aware. Obviously they've got a lot of agents out in the field, but the officers are all based up at the fort.'

'And how do they liaise with us?'

'That depends on whether they need something or not. If they want something from us, they generally just take it.'

'But the police aren't answerable to the military,' I said.

'This isn't England, old boy,' he replied. 'Out here all roads ultimately lead to one place: the Viceroy. And in Bengal, all channels to the Viceroy go through the Lieutenant Governor. Section H works for the L-G. If they want something from us, the L-G simply sends an order to the Commissioner and we comply. Take your crime scene, for instance. How long did it take them to pull that away from us? A couple of hours?'

'And Taggart's happy with this?'

'Of course not. But what can he do? Who's he going to complain to? The Viceroy? He sits in Delhi hob-nobbing with princelings and maharajas. He's got no idea what goes on down here and he cares even less. He's more than happy for the L-G to do whatever the hell he likes so long as he keeps a lid on the separatists and revolutionaries. No, old Taggart's just got to accept it.'

'And what if we need something from them?'

Digby gave a snort. 'Then it comes down to how well you know one of their officers and whether they're willing to do you a favour.'

'Have you ever dealt with them?'

Digby tensed slightly. 'Once, and only in a minor capacity. It was some years ago now, during the war. I was based up in Raiganj at the time, officer in charge of the whole district. Section H had tracked down a terrorist to a nearby village. I never found out what they wanted him for. Anyway, they ordered us to set up roadblocks on all routes in and out of the village till they could get their troops up there. Naturally, I took control of it personally. For the best part of a day, we manned the checkpoints and kept watch over the fields. Finally, just before nightfall, several truck loads of troops arrived. They spent the night forming a ring of steel round the village, then moved in at first light.'

'And they caught him?'

Digby looked away. 'In a sense. He was shot resisting arrest. Along with several villagers.'

'Did you investigate their deaths?' I asked.

'The major in charge of the operation informed me that their deaths couldn't have been prevented. He confirmed they were harbouring a suspected terrorist.'

'And what did the other villagers have to say about it?'

He gave a short, bitter laugh. 'A bunch of terrified peasants who've just seen half their village razed to the ground? What do you think they said, Captain? They said nothing. They were too scared.' He paused before continuing. 'There was no case for me to investigate.'

EIGHTEEN

I sat in MacAuley's office. Except it wasn't MacAuley's office any more. It was a room in transition: Stevens' belongings, neatly boxed, sat next to the desk, ready to be unpacked. Meanwhile MacAuley's things had been thrown haphazardly into crates, ready for God knows what.

I'd no idea where Stevens was. Miss Grant had told me her new boss would be along *presently*. That was ten minutes ago. After five minutes, I'd grown tired of staring at the photograph on the desk of Stevens and his wife and instead took to staring out of the window. It was far more interesting. The whole of Dalhousie Square was laid out below. It looked better from up here, away from the heat and the smell. The best views are often the preserve of powerful men.

'Impressive, isn't it?'

I turned to find Stevens walking towards me. There was a grin on his face, like a child with a new toy.

'The view or the office?' I asked.

'The view, of course. The office is, well, . . .' His voice trailed off.

He looked to be in his thirties, young for someone so senior, and there was a nervous energy about him, a jerkiness to his movements that suggested a man not wholly at ease.

'Captain Wyndham, is it?' he said, directing me to a chair. He sat down behind his desk, adjusting the high-backed leather chair and raising it a few inches. 'You've caught me at a rather difficult juncture. The L-G moves to Darjeeling next week before it gets too hot, and half of Government House is going with him. Of course, it's up to us here at Writers' to sort everything out for them. This unfortunate business with MacAuley couldn't have come at a worse time.'

'Yes,' I said, 'his murder must have been inconvenient for you.'

He stared at me, trying to gauge the sentiment behind the comment. I wondered what he'd make of it, especially as I wasn't sure myself.

'What can I do for you, Captain?' he said finally. 'I can't spare long, I'm afraid. I've an urgent meeting with Sir Evelyn Crisp this afternoon.'

The name meant nothing to me. Not that it made a difference. He could have been best man at my wedding and I'd still have feigned ignorance, just to see Stevens' reaction.

'He's the managing director of the Bengal and Burma Banking Corporation,' he clarified. I applied what I thought was an appropriate expression of awe. It seemed Stevens was the type of man who liked to drop names. That was good. A confident man would have no need to tell me who he was meeting afterwards.

'I'll get to the point,' I said. 'How long had you worked for MacAuley?'

'Too long.' He laughed. The comment was in bad taste and he realised as much. His tone became serious. 'That's to say, I reported to him for the last three years. Prior to that I was posted elsewhere.'

'Where was that?'

'Rangoon.'

'And your relationship with Mr MacAuley? How would you characterise it?'

'Professional.'

'Not warm? You worked together for three years.'

Stevens picked up a fountain pen and distractedly tapped it on the desk. 'He wasn't the easiest of men to work with.'

'In what sense?'

'Let's just say he was rather set in his ways. There was never any room for discussion with MacAuley. Things always had to be done his way. It was as though he regarded the exercise of independent thought by others as a personal affront.'

'You found it difficult to work with him?'

'No more than anyone else did.' He examined the pen in his hand, as though seeing it for the first time. Maybe he was. Maybe it was MacAuley's.

'Any disagreements between the two of you recently?'

He shook his head. 'Not that I recall.'

I thought back to what Annie had said – of MacAuley and Stevens arguing the previous week about import taxes. Odd that Stevens should forget such a thing.

'What about others? Did he have any enemies?'

'It's possible. As I say, he was unpopular, even for a Scotsman.'

'Did he display any odd behaviour recently?'

'He came in drunk once or twice in the last month. I thought it strange as I'd heard he'd given up alcohol.'

'Did anyone call him up on it?'

'Of course not. MacAuley wasn't just the head of finance – he was the L-G's special friend. That made him bulletproof.'

It was another poor choice of words. Bulletproof he may have been, but he'd certainly been susceptible to knives.

'And are you taking over all of MacAuley's responsibilities?'

'On the finance front at least. In fact, that's more than enough to be getting on with. It's been a mission keeping things moving over the last few days.'

'I expect MacAuley was vital to the running of things.'

'That depends on how you look at it.' He laughed. 'In terms of work, the department functioned perfectly well without him. However, MacAuley's authorisation was required for certain things – all payments and movements of funds above a hundred thousand rupees, for example. Money oils the wheels of government and without his signature, nothing could move. Not a good position to be in when half the government's moving up to Darjeeling.'

'And that power of authorisation couldn't simply be transferred to someone else?'

'Oh it was. The L-G transferred signing powers to me within hours on Wednesday morning. The only problem was we couldn't find a lot of the requisite documents that needed authorisation. Turned out the old man had taken them home with him.'

'The documents Miss Grant was dispatched to bring back from MacAuley's flat?'

'What?' he said, flustered. 'Yes, I suppose so, in part.'

'What did they relate to?'

'The usual things.' He shrugged. 'Authorisation for salaries payments mainly and for transfers of funds. MacAuley should have signed the papers on Monday but he took them home and sat on them. I wouldn't be surprised if he got drunk and forgot he had them. By the time we got them back, we'd begun receiving urgent telegrams from up-country wondering where the hell their wages were.'

'What about policy matters?' I asked. 'I understand MacAuley played a role in formalising fiscal policy. Is that another area you'll be taking over?'

His eyes lit up. 'I hope so. There's a lot to be done in that sphere. But that's up to the L-G.'

'Such as?' I asked. Like most men, I didn't much care for tax policy, but it can get a certain breed of bureaucrat very excited. MacAuley and Stevens had argued over it, and it would be useful to know if it was just an accountants' tiff or if there was something deeper.

'Lots,' he replied. 'Where do I start? Many of our taxes are regressive and as for our import tariffs, some of them are nonsensical. They positively hinder business.'

There was a knock on the door and Annie entered.

'Sir Evelyn to see you, sir.'

'Ah good,' said Stevens, rising from behind his desk. 'Tell him I won't be a moment.'

He turned to me. 'I hope you don't mind, Captain, but I'm afraid we're out of time. If you've any more questions, please feel free to speak to Miss Grant about scheduling another meeting when things are calmer.'

I walked back to Lal Bazar in a daze. In my head, a picture was forming. It was still blurred, like the image through a camera lens before it's focused, but something seemed to be taking shape. I reached the office and immediately telephoned Surrender-not at the Plassey Gate *thana*.

'Any news?'

'No, sir. There's been very little traffic leaving the fort as yet. I've also placed a watch on the bridge.'

'Okay,' I said. 'There's something else I need you to do. I want you to take a look at the business interests of Stevens, MacAuley's former deputy, especially anything to do with Burma.'

'I'll have a constable check at Companies House,' said Banerjee.

'Let me know the moment you hear back.'

'There's one other thing, sir. Ten minutes ago, I received a rather irate message from the station master at Sealdah station, telling me he was doing his best to locate the baggage manifest, and asking why we had requested the military to requisition all his records for the last fortnight.'

'But we did no such thing.'

'I know, sir. I don't understand it.'

'I think I do,' I said. 'Section H. I mentioned the attack on the Darjeeling Mail to Dawson. He must have given the order to seize the records. Without the baggage manifest, we'll never know what, if anything, was supposed to be on that train.'

'Yes, sir. Sorry, sir.' It sounded like he blamed himself, not that there was anything he could have done about it. That was the trouble with the boy. He was always falling on his sword over something or other.

I sighed. 'Why are you apologising, Sergeant? It was my fault, if anything. I was the one who told Dawson about the attack.'

'Still, if the manifest had been filed at the right time, we'd have received it before Section H ever got involved.'

Something in my brain clicked. 'What did you say, Sergeant?'

The question seemed to take him by surprise. 'Just that, if the railways personnel hadn't mislaid the paperwork, the baggage manifest would have been filed at the right time and we'd have got a hold of it by now.'

'Bloody hell, Surrender-not! You're a genius!' I said as I dropped the phone, grabbed my hat and ran out of the office.

For once I didn't notice the heat as I raced back to Dalhousie Square and up the stairs at the front of Writers' Building.

I burst into Annie Grant's office, dripping sweat on the carpet.

'Captain Wyndham,' she said, startled, 'did you forget something?'

I caught my breath. 'In a manner of speaking.'

'I'm afraid Mr Stevens is in another meeting. I'm not sure when he'll be able to see you.'

'It's you I came to see, Miss Grant,' I panted. 'Those papers you retrieved from MacAuley's apartment. Did they include documents authorising the transfer of funds?'

She looked at me curiously. 'Why yes, as it happens. They were authorisation for the transfer of funds up to Darjeeling in anticipation of the L-G's move next week.'

'Can you tell me how much?'

'Two hundred and seven thousand rupees. It was to be transferred from the treasury in Calcutta up to Darjeeling.'

'And was the transfer of funds delayed because MacAuley had taken the documents home?'

'Yes, but only by a day.'

'Let me guess. Were the funds supposed to be dispatched on Wednesday night's Darjeeling Mail?'

She stared at me as if I was some clairvoyant Indian *fakir*. 'Why yes. But how did you—'

'How many people knew that the funds were supposed to be transferred on Wednesday night?'

'Lots.' She shrugged. 'Almost everyone here in the finance department, a lot of people in the L-G's office, railway officials, the military who provide the security. It's not exactly a secret, it happens every year.'

Two hundred and seven thousand rupees. Enough cash to keep Sen and his gang in arms and explosives for a very long time. And they'd have had it too, if MacAuley hadn't taken the documents home and then got himself killed. My head buzzed. Suddenly I had all the pieces. All I needed now was to find Sen.

NINETEEN

It was four p.m. when the telephone rang.

Lal Bazar was an oven, but it was still preferable to being outside. I was in my office, reading through the post-mortem report that Dr Lamb had sent through. I set it down and picked up the receiver. It was Banerjee. He was breathing heavily.

'Sir,' he said, 'they're on the move!'

'Section H?'

'Yes, sir; two cars and a truck. They were spotted approaching the Howrah Bridge about five minutes ago.'

'Can your men catch them up?'

'I think so, sir. There's always a bottleneck at the approaches to the bridge. At this time of day, it'll probably take them around thirty minutes to get across and through the jam at the other side. A man on a bicycle should be able to catch them.'

'Good,' I said. 'Order your men to keep them in sight and to report to you at Lal Bazar. Give them their orders, then get back here as soon as possible.'

Section H had managed to track Sen down far quicker than I'd expected. They must have had informants everywhere. It was a testament to the size of their budget if nothing else, and made me wonder how they'd failed to track him down over the last four years. But that was a question I didn't have time to worry about.

The next few minutes passed in a blur. I called through to Digby, relayed Banerjee's message and told him to be ready to leave in five minutes. I then wrote a note for Lord Taggart. What I wanted was too complicated to explain to a *peon* without the aid of a diagram and several dictionaries, so I ran up to Taggart's office with it myself, taking the stairs two at a time. I burst in to Daniels' anteroom and startled the man for the second time in three days. It was becoming a habit. I thrust the note at him and ordered that he wait ten minutes before delivering it to his boss, giving me enough time to leave the building. After that, even if Taggart wanted to stop me, it would be too late.

I ran back down to my office and checked my Webley. It was clean and loaded. Banerjee arrived as I reholstered it. His breathing was ragged.

'Any news, Sergeant?'

'Not yet, sir.'

'Right,' I said. 'Call ahead to the *thana* at Howrah. Tell your men to forward the message there. We can pick it up when we get across the river.'

'Yes, sir.'

'Have you got a gun?'

'No, sir, but I've had rifle training.'

'In that case check out a Lee Enfield and meet me at the car.'

———

Within minutes, Digby, Banerjee and I were racing along the Strand Road, heading for the Howrah Bridge. The bridge itself was no more than a metalled road laid across two dozen floating pontoons, the central sections opening to allow ships to pass up- and downriver.

As Banerjee had surmised, the approaches were clogged with all manner of traffic.

'We should get out here and make our way across on foot,' he said. 'I've arranged for a car from Howrah *thana* to meet us on the other side.'

We jumped out and began running towards the bridge. Before us lay the Hooghly. It was a distributary of the Ganges, not that the natives distinguished between the two. Coming from a small country, it was hard to appreciate the scale of the Hooghly. Even here, eighty miles from the sea, it was still about ten times wider than the Thames at London. It stretched all the way to the horizon, a great brown gash across the landscape. Now, running over the bridge under the glare of the Bengal sun, it seemed we would never reach the other side. As we approached the central section, the reason for the congestion became clear. Traffic had been stopped so that the bridge could be opened to allow a steamer to pass downriver. I ran up to the official who looked to be in charge and ordered him to stop. He was an Anglo-Indian in a peaked cap bearing the badge of the Calcutta Port Authority. Any thoughts he may have had of remonstrating were quickly shelved as I unbuttoned my holster. Frantically, he shouted at a number of native coolies to close the bridge. They stared back in confusion until a stream of invective jolted them into action.

Another ten minutes and we were across the bridge, all three of us drenched in sweat and breathing heavily. In front of us lay the squat structure of Howrah station. Banerjee pointed to a police car, which hurtled down the road and screeched to a halt beside us. Exhausted, the three of us piled into the back and the car took off towards Howrah *thana* with its siren wailing.

If Calcutta was the belle of Bengal, then Howrah was its ugly sister. A town of lean-tos and go-downs, the whole place looked like one giant marshalling yard. We drove past innumerable warehouses before skidding to a halt outside a small police station. Banerjee scrambled out and ran into the *thana*, returning a few moments later clutching a scrap of paper.

'They've stopped,' he said, panting.

'Where?'

'Kona. About five miles from here, on the Benares road.'

'Let's go.'

He jumped in and barked directions to the driver, who quickly reversed the car and accelerated back down the road. We left Howrah behind, passing swiftly through suburban townships before emerging into open country. Our progress should have been rapid, but the road soon turned into little more than a dirt track, pitted with potholes large enough to swallow an elephant or two. Not that the driver seemed to notice. He just ploughed on like a man possessed, and, whether through divine providence or some native sixth sense, managed to get to Kona without killing us all.

———

We reached the village in darkness. There was no sign telling us we'd come to the right place, but then we didn't need one. A throng of villagers were gathered in the middle of the road. Men were shouting. From somewhere close by came the growl of engines. We headed on in the direction of the commotion, villagers scattering in front of us. The headlights illuminated clouds of dust recently churned into the air. From around a corner came the glow of lamps and I ordered the driver to make towards it. There, in the headlight beams of a military truck, an agitated crowd had gathered. Angry voices shouted at impassive sepoys who, with bayonets at the ready, blocked them from advancing any further. We drove up to the edge of the cordon and the sepoys opened a gap and waved us through.

In the darkness, the sight of two *sahibs* in uniform was all the identification they needed.

We stopped next to a couple of stationary vehicles. Colonel Dawson stood a few yards away, in conversation with a group of officers. Pipe in hand, he gestured towards a building in the distance. I turned to Banerjee.

'Find the nearest building with a telephone line and get a message to Lord Taggart,' I said. 'Give him a sit rep and our location.'

He saluted and hurried off in the direction of some telephone poles while Digby and I headed for Dawson. Suddenly, a bottle came flying out of the darkness and crashed at the feet of one of the soldiers. Shards of glass splintered, striking him in the leg. He cried out in pain and turned to his superior, a *subedar* with a white handlebar moustache, who stepped forward and glared at the mob. If he'd hoped to cow them he was soon disabused as first a stone, then a brick, and then a hail of objects came hurtling towards them. The *subedar* flinched and his sepoys fell back a few paces. He turned towards Colonel Dawson, who with pipe clamped tightly between his jaws, gave a curt nod. The *subedar* immediately barked a string of orders. They were aimed as much at the crowd as at his men, though I doubt many of them heard it over the noise. There was no mistaking what followed, though: the rhythmic clicking of rifles being readied for firing. Another shouted command. The sepoys raised their weapons, and took aim at the crowd. There was a sudden hush followed by a collective groan, like the sound of a wounded beast, as people realised what was happening. Those at the front frantically began to turn and push backwards.

'Fire!' shouted the *subedar*.

A thunder of rifle shots. Then screaming terror. Men and women trampled one another in an attempt to escape. Minutes later the street was all but deserted and a ghostly quiet had settled. I expected to see perhaps a dozen dead or wounded, but other than a few villagers picking themselves up off the ground, there didn't seem to be any injuries. The sepoys must have raised their rifles at the last second and fired overhead.

The acrid smell of cordite filled the air. Suddenly I was back in 1915, the sound of shellfire ringing in my ears. I screwed my eyelids shut against the avalanche of mud and earth that would rain down on me any second. But none came. Instead, the scent changed to pipe tobacco.

'I'm glad you're here, Captain.'

I opened my eyes to see Colonel Dawson walking over. If he'd been surprised to see us, he hid it well.

'Illegal gathering,' he said. 'We'd have been within our rights to shoot 'em, but we've got bigger fish to fry.'

I pulled myself together.

'Sen?'

Dawson nodded.

'We've found him.'

Found him was good. It meant they hadn't arrested him yet. *Found him* was better than *got him*. And much better than *shot him*.

'Where?'

'He's holed up in there,' said Dawson, pointing with his pipe to a nearby building.

By the light of the moon, I made out a squat, single-storey, flat-roofed house, surrounded by a low wall on three sides. It looked like the fourth side backed directly onto a canal. The place was in darkness, the door barred and the windows shuttered.

'You're sure he's in there?'

'Almost certain. Our man saw him go in. Hasn't seen anyone come out. Of course, there's a chance he left by another way before we got here in force, but it's unlikely. We've set up a perimeter around the house.' He pointed to several places where his soldiers had taken up position. 'All the exits are covered.'

'Anyone with him?'

'We think he has two, maybe three, accomplices.'

'Armed?'

'No doubt.'

'Are your men in place?'

He gestured with his pipe once more. 'That's the last of them moving into position now. We were about to issue him with an ultimatum when you arrived.'

'Any civilians inside?'

'What's your definition of *civilian*, Captain? Because as far as I'm concerned, anyone in that house is abetting a terrorist.'

'What about women and children?' I asked. 'If Sen decides to ignore your ultimatum, we should make an offer of safe passage to anyone else who wants to leave. Besides, we might glean some information from them on the building's layout . . . and whether Sen's actually in there.'

Dawson fixed me with a stare. His face was expressionless, but behind it he was clearly assessing the options.

'Okay,' he said at last, 'we'll do it your way.'

He called over to a sepoy holding a loud hailer who was crouched behind a wall at the front of the house. The soldier ran over, bent low. Dawson spoke to him in his native tongue and the sepoy saluted and returned to his position.

'Here goes,' said Dawson.

The sepoy called out to the occupants, the loud hailer lending his voice a hollow tone. There was no movement from the house. A minute later he repeated his message. This time a shot rang out from the building. The bullet hit the wall not far from the sepoy, and a brick exploded in a shower of dust and splinters.

'There's your answer,' said Dawson.

He called over the *subedar* and gave the order to open fire. Immediately, a volley of shots rang out from soldiers positioned around the building. Plasterwork and wood splintered along the façade of the house. The fugitives inside returned fire, their bullets ricocheting off the walls and vehicles.

On a nod from Dawson, the sepoys attempted to rush the building. Any veteran of the trenches could have told them it was a mistake; that the enemy needed to be worn down before attempting a frontal assault. But Dawson wasn't a veteran and his men were cocky. Within seconds, two sepoys had been hit: one left screaming on the ground, the other mercifully dead. The rest pulled back to relative safety behind the perimeter walls.

'This won't end until everyone in there is dead,' Dawson said with a sigh.

'Let's hope they run out of ammunition before that,' I replied.

Dawson laughed drily. 'If they do, they'll save the last bullets for themselves.'

Banerjee returned from placing the call to Lord Taggart and crouched beside me. The shooting subsided. The terrorists were conserving their resources, only returning fire when they saw movement on our side. The wounded sepoy's screams turned to cries. I didn't understand the language, but I didn't need to. A mortally wounded man only ever cries out for one of two things, his god or his mother. His comrades tried to reach him but were forced back by fire from the house. Then he fell silent. I knew his death would mark a point of no return. His comrades would seek revenge and no prisoners would be taken. If I wanted Sen alive, I'd need to take matters into my own hands.

I left Dawson's position, taking Digby and Banerjee with me and scouted out the perimeter. Dawson's troops were arranged behind the wall around the house, covering its front and sides. At the rear of the building was the canal. There were only two windows at the back of the house, both shuttered. No shots had come from these, and Dawson had placed only a few screening troops on the far bank to guard against the possibility of escape by that route. These men were laid out on the grass, their weapons trained on the shuttered windows.

I dropped to my stomach and crawled slowly towards the canal bank. Digby and Banerjee followed. The water smelled of something unholy. One of the soldiers on the opposite bank spotted us and raised his rifle, then realised he was aiming at *sahib* officers and quickly lowered it again. The three of us slipped into the warm, stagnant water and swam across to the other bank. Once across, I gestured to my colleagues to take up position with the troops covering the windows. Then I asked Banerjee for his bayonet before returning to the canal and swimming back to the bank immediately under one of the windows.

Against the bank was a shallow ledge. Standing on it allowed me to keep my head above water. There, I waited. Things seemed to have gone quiet. I assumed Dawson was reassessing the situation. A few minutes later, shots again began to ring out at the front of the house. It sounded like the sepoys were preparing for another assault. I looked up. The window was about eight feet above me. From inside came snatches of foreign conversation, a muffled cry then frantic, staccato shouts. My heart was racing. It was now or never.

I took Banerjee's bayonet and rammed it into the wall above my head. The blade was strong and sharp and easily cut through the plasterwork, lodging firmly into the brick beneath. Holding it with one hand, I used the other to find a handhold and pulled myself up. I then pulled out the bayonet and smashed it back in, further up the wall. Once secure, I reached up towards the window frame. As I did so, one of the shutters opened. Metal glinted in the moonlight: the barrel of a rifle. I flattened myself against the wall. A woman appeared and looked down. She saw me and instantly swung the rifle downward. I closed my eyes. There was precious little else I could do. A shot rang out . . .

They say that when you're about to die, your life flashes before you, a tableau of treasured memories flitting across the mind's eye. In my case there was nothing. Not a single flash. Not even the image of Sarah's face. I flinched, expecting the end. Half welcoming it. But there was to be no end. Above me I heard the woman groan, then slump forward. I looked up at her lifeless hand hanging over the ledge.

I dragged myself up on to the ledge and only now realised that there were iron bars across the window. They hadn't been visible with the shutters closed. The woman lay slumped against them. I cursed my stupidity. I'd assumed the window would be empty behind the shutters. For a moment I sat dripping on the ledge, considering what to do. The only option was to keep climbing. I stood up. Above the window was another concrete ledge somewhat thinner than the one I was standing on. I guessed it acted as some sort of protection from the monsoon rains. I reached up, took a hold and pulled myself up on to it. The roof was now only six or so feet above me. I continued my ascent, using the bayonet and any cracks in the crumbling plasterwork as handholds, and finally wrenched myself over the lip of the flat roof.

I reached over and retrieved the bayonet, then took a minute to catch my breath and get my bearings. The firing seemed to be intensifying. Ahead of me was the outline of a door, which I assumed led to the stairwell into the house. Beyond that lay a body, slumped against the far wall.

Pulling out my Webley, I ran to the door, gently pushed it open and stood back. No shots rang out. I peered into the stairwell. All was dark. Slowly, I crept down the stone stairs and into a hallway. To one side, a passageway led to the rear. To the other, two doors, both open, led to the front rooms. In the gloom, I made out the shape of two figures: one on the floor, hardly moving and possibly wounded; the other, nearer the window, holding a rifle and firing outward. The shouts outside were louder now. It sounded like Dawson's men were moving in for the kill.

I ran into the room, my pistol at the ready, and shouted for the figure to drop the weapon. The man spun round. It might have been Sen. I'd no way of knowing, and I hadn't come all this way to kill my prime suspect. I aimed for his leg and pulled the trigger. The gun jammed. The firing mechanism must have clogged while I was in the canal. The terrorist hesitated, then fired. I dived to the floor as a searing pain tore up my left arm.

The man began frantically to reload. Time seemed to slow down. I heard the front door smash open. Boots in the hallway. They weren't going to reach me in time. The man finished reloading and raised his rifle. I had one chance. I reached for Banerjee's bayonet with my right hand and hurled it at my attacker. He saw it coming and deflected it with the muzzle of his gun. So much for a last-ditch reprieve. All I'd done was buy a few more seconds. But it was enough. A soldier entered and fired. The man fell back, a hole in his chest. The soldier turned and took aim at the other body, prone on the floor.

'Wait!' I shouted.

He spun round, his rifle cocked. 'This man is under arrest,' I said, pointing to the wounded fugitive. The sepoy kept his weapon trained on me, till suddenly the room seemed to fill with soldiers. Digby was with them.

'Are you all right, old boy?' he asked, dropping to my side.

'Is this Sen?' I asked, pointing to the man lying on the floor.

'Get me some light!' he shouted, and a sepoy hurriedly brought over a hurricane lamp.

Digby bent over to take a closer look. The man was sweating, his face contorted in pain, eyes screwed shut beneath a pair of metal-rimmed spectacles.

'Could be. He fits the general description.'

I pulled out a pair of handcuffs and cuffed myself to the wounded Indian. There was no way I was going to let Section H spirit him away after what I'd gone through.

Several orderlies now arrived and attended to the man. His breathing was shallow and the floor was slick with his blood. Another orderly bandaged my arm. He told me I'd been lucky – it was only a flesh wound. Still, it hurt like hell. I'd managed to survive three years in France without getting shot. In Calcutta, I hadn't made it to three weeks.

Still handcuffed to me, the man was stretchered out to a waiting ambulance. There seemed to be the best part of a hundred military personnel outside. Lord Taggart was standing beside Dawson. That was a relief. I'd need his support if I was going to keep my prisoner.

Both men noticed me at the same time and hurried over.

'Commissioner,' I began, 'this man has been arrested in connection with the murder of Alexander MacAuley and the attack on the Darjeeling Mail. I intend to question him once his wounds have been seen to.'

Taggart looked over at Colonel Dawson.

'Is it Sen?'

Dawson bent down for a closer look, then nodded.

'Thank God,' said Taggart. 'Good show, Captain. You seem to have bagged yourself the—'

'If I may, Lord Taggart,' Dawson interrupted, 'I'm afraid I'm going to have to take custody of the prisoner. We need to interrogate him about a number of attacks.'

Taggart paused. 'Colonel,' he said, 'this man has been lawfully arrested by one of my officers in relation to a matter that the Lieutenant Governor has classified as top priority. He will remain in our custody unless and until you can provide me with written orders to the contrary. Of course, my officers and I thank you for the assistance you and your men have rendered in apprehending the suspect and will share with you any and all information obtained from him during questioning.'

The Colonel glared at him, then nodded curtly, turned and stalked off. Taggart turned to me.

'Thank you, Captain. I've been wanting to do that for a long time. You'd better get Sen to hospital and put under police guard. Question and charge him as soon as you can. I'm not sure how long I'll be able to hold Dawson and his superiors off.'

'Yes, sir,' I said, as the orderlies lifted Sen's stretcher. I winced as a stab of pain ran up my arm.

'And Sam,' said Taggart nodding at my wounded arm, 'get that seen to properly.'

With that, he turned and walked back to a waiting motor car. The driver saluted and opened the rear door.

Digby and Banerjee walked over, both soaking wet.

'Look at us,' beamed Digby, 'heroes of the hour.'

'Like the three bloody musketeers,' I replied.

Digby laughed. 'Yes, I like that. Athos, Porthos and Banerjee. It's got a certain ring to it don't you think, Sergeant?'

Surrender-not said nothing.

TWENTY

The rear of the ambulance was windowless. Inside, Sen lay on a stretcher, his eyes closed, groaning now and again. His skin was grey but his breathing was less ragged than before. That was good. It would have been a shame if he'd died before we got a chance to hang him.

An Indian orderly silently ministered to him a bit too tenderly, and I tried to stay out of his way and nursed my wounded arm. My head was spinning. A combination of blood loss and lack of food probably. At that point, even Mrs Tebbit's cooking held a certain appeal, though not as much as a hit of O did.

Somewhere along the road I lost my bearings. Eventually there came the rhythmic bumping that indicated we were crossing the bridge back over the Hooghly.

We reached Medical College Hospital shortly after ten. Someone must have told them we were coming as there was quite a party waiting for us, including half a dozen medical personnel and an armed police detachment. Two native orderlies, pristine in white shirts and trousers, gently lowered Sen onto a gurney. A white doctor briskly took his pulse, then held his eyelids open with thumb and forefinger and shone a light in each eye while a nurse wrote down his observations on a clipboard.

The doctor turned to me and held out his hand. Maybe it was the loss of blood, but I had no idea what he wanted. Was I supposed to pay him? Was that the custom here? I reached into my pocket and pulled out the remains of a sodden ten-rupee note. My swim in the canal had rendered it little more than mush. I handed it to him apologetically.

He looked at me like I was an idiot.

'The key,' he said forcefully. 'You're still handcuffed to the patient. Now, unless you propose to accompany him into the operating theatre, I suggest you give me the key so that I can uncuff him.'

I did as ordered. The doctor deftly unlocked the cuffs, freeing Sen's wrist. He handed them back to me along with the remains of my ten-rupee note. The medical team quickly took charge of Sen and a gaggle of white coats wheeled him inside, the guards following. With the cavalcade gone, I was suddenly alone. The exhilaration of the chase and capture of Sen had quickly dissipated and now I stood there, damp and bleeding. As heroes' welcomes go, it left quite a lot to be desired.

I looked around. The orderly from the ambulance was leaning against the building, smoking. He eyed me sullenly as I walked over to him.

'I need to get my arm seen to.'

He stubbed out the cigarette and let the butt fall.

'Come with me, *sahib*.'

I followed him into the hospital reception, through swing doors and along a dimly lit passageway, his shoes squeaking on the tiled floor. An overpowering smell of disinfectant clawed at my throat. Someone had used it liberally, like a priest sprinkling holy water to ward off disease.

We entered a narrow corridor, one side of which was lined with wooden chairs, worn through use. The orderly instructed me to wait while he went off to fetch a doctor. He returned a few minutes later in the company of a middle-aged Indian in a white coat who introduced himself as Dr Rao. He was about five feet ten – tall for an Indian – with a head shaved smooth as an egg.

'Please come with me,' he said, gesturing down the corridor.

We entered a room off the hallway. The stench of chemicals permeated even here. He switched on the light, illuminating a small windowless office that was little more than a glorified cupboard.

I sat on a banquette while he removed the makeshift bandage the orderlies had applied back in Kona.

'Can you remove your jacket?'

I did so with some difficulty. It was still soaking wet and felt like it weighed a tonne. He took out a scalpel and cut off my blood-soaked shirtsleeve.

'That should make things easier,' he said. 'Please remove the rest of it.'

He made a cursory examination of the wound, then led me to the sink in the far corner of the room and washed it. I winced. The water stung like ice.

'Come now.' He smiled. 'A big man like you should not be acting like a woman.'

His bedside manner wasn't going to win him any prizes. And the comment was hardly fair, given I'd just arrested a wanted fugitive and possibly foiled a terrorist campaign. Still, any resentment I may have had towards him didn't last long.

'I'm going to give you something for the pain,' he said, directing me back to the banquette. 'Lie down please.'

'What is it?' I asked.

'Morphine.'

It was the best thing anyone had said to me all day.

I don't remember much more. Just the doctor unlocking the steel cabinet in the corner of the room and extracting a syringe. The strong smell of antiseptic. Then nothing.

———

I woke up on the banquette and noticed my arm was in a sling. I guessed my wound had been sewn and bandaged. The doctor was writing some notes at his desk.

'Ah,' he said as I sat up, 'so you're back with us. Good, good.' He walked over and handed me a tube of ointment. 'Remove the bandage when you bathe. Reapply this cream and re-bandage afterwards. You can probably dispense with the sling after a day or so.'

The doctor seemed a good man. At that moment he'd even replaced Surrender-not as my favourite native. It's difficult not to feel predisposed towards someone who gives you the gift of morphine. He was a kind man, and if there was one thing the war had taught me, it was that when you meet such a person, the sensible thing to do is to take advantage of them as much as possible, for you never know when you'll come across such a gift-horse again.

'Can you give me something for the pain?' I asked.

He thought for a moment, then went over to the steel cabinet and unlocked it.

'I'm going to give you some tablets. Use them *extremely* sparingly. One at a time and only when you absolutely need to. They contain morphine. Do you understand what that means?'

I nodded and tried to look earnest, which was difficult when what I really wanted to do was hug the man.

'Morphine is highly addictive,' he cautioned.

Yes, I thought. *Like all good things.*

I thanked the doctor as he draped my jacket over my shoulders, then I made my way back to reception. There I asked the duty nurse where I could find the patient who'd been brought in under armed guard earlier. She consulted the log before directing me to a room on the first floor.

Sen's room wasn't hard to find. It was the one with the armed gorilla standing outside. On seeing me, the constable saluted and opened the door, the tattered remains of my uniform being all the identification he seemed to need. There was only one bed, screened off by curtains. Another constable stood guard at the foot of the bed. Beside him stood Surrender-not, his uniform still damp from his swim in the canal.

'What news, Sergeant?'

'They've just brought him up from the operating theatre. The doctors removed some shrapnel from his leg and back. They say he lost quite a lot of blood. But he'll live.'

'Can we question him?'

'Not before morning, apparently. They'll monitor him through the night and give us an assessment at eight a.m.'

That wasn't ideal. 'Who knows what'll happen by the morning?' I said. 'Colonel Dawson could turn up with several detachments of the Madras Light Infantry and lay siege to the hospital till we give him up.'

Banerjee's brows furrowed. 'I don't believe the Madras Light Infantry is billeted in Calcutta,' he said, 'or anywhere else in Bengal for that matter, sir. They're probably in Madras.'

'My point, Sergeant, is that by the morning Colonel Dawson might have obtained an order from the L-G commanding us to hand Sen over.'

'In that case, sir, maybe you could speak to Lord Taggart and request him to purchase us as much time as possible before Section H force our hand?'

It was a good point. We'd also need to get Sen out of the hospital and to somewhere more secure. Guarded or not, it would be too easy for Section H to get hold of him here.

The curtains around Sen's bed parted and a bean-pole of a European in a white coat came out. He looked altogether too young to be a doctor. Then again everyone these days looked either too young or too old. The chap was sallow and clean shaven, not that it looked like he needed to shave more than once a month. Wide eyed, he appraised my bandaged arm, then effusively introduced himself as Dr Bird.

'You must be the arresting officer.'

'Captain Wyndham,' I said, shaking his hand. It was limp and clammy. Like shaking a fish.

'Jolly glad to meet you, Captain,' he gushed. He pointed to his patient lying prone behind the curtain. 'From what I hear, you saved this man's life.'

He was wrong about that. I'd done nothing of the sort. I'd merely bought him a stay of execution. He was going to hang. I'd see to it myself, assuming Section H gave me the time to file charges. If not, *they'd* kill him. Either way, he was a dead man. But I wasn't about to let Section H take my prisoner without a fight. I'd prefer to avoid it, though, and for that I needed the young doctor's unwitting help.

'I'm not sure he's out of the woods yet,' I said.

'What?' he stammered. 'I can assure you, Captain, he's out of immediate danger. He should recover quite quickly.'

'What I mean, Doctor, is that it may not be safe to keep him here. His comrades might try to break him out.'

What colour there was quickly drained from the young man's face. 'But you've posted an armed guard?' he spluttered. 'Surely they wouldn't try anything here?'

'I hope not, but you can never be sure. These are desperate men, Doctor. The last thing I want is a gun battle in a hospital. I'd be a lot happier if he were at Lal Bazar. We could protect him there. And it would remove any threat to your other patients.'

The doctor rubbed his hands together nervously. That medical oath of his probably told him that Sen should remain here. After all, he had a duty to safeguard the health of his patient. But his patient was a terrorist and his presence here endangered the lives of others, not to mention that of the good doctor himself. In the end, enlightened self-interest won the day.

'You should be able to move him in an hour or so,' he said. 'But he'll need to be accompanied by one of my staff, and you'll have to guarantee adequate facilities for his recuperation.'

'Whatever he needs, Doctor.'

An hour later, Sen and I were back in an ambulance, this time for the short trip to a basement cell at Lal Bazar. An Indian doctor would remain with the guards to check on the prisoner every thirty minutes. It was only once Sen was securely ensconced in his cell and I was happy as to the security, that I decided to head back to the Belvedere.

My watch read one thirty, so it was probably some time after four a.m. that a police driver dropped me off outside the Belvedere. The house was in darkness and the noise of the car engine failed to arouse anyone indoors. It did, however, wake the rickshaw *wallahs* at the corner of the square. Salman began to rise from his mat before I gestured to him to return to his bed.

I let myself in, quietly locked the door and made my way upstairs. In the darkness, I stripped out of the remains of my damp uniform and left the clothes where they fell. With my good arm, I poured myself a large measure of whisky and sipped it neat. I felt I'd deserved it. My other arm was aching again. I considered another drink to help dull the pain, then remembered I had something better. I retrieved the small glass bottle of tablets that Dr Rao had given me, unscrewed the lid and gently tapped out a couple of the chalky white discs. I considered swallowing both, but on second thoughts returned one to the bottle. There were only five tablets in all. The doctor had purposely rationed my supply. These things were precious and I'd have to make them last as long as possible – until I could find another source or, better still, obtain a repeat prescription. I popped the tablet into my mouth and washed it down with the last of the whisky.

TWENTY-ONE

Saturday, 12 April 1919

I awoke to what's euphemistically called birdsong. It was more of a bloody racket, nine parts screeching to one part singing. In England the dawn chorus is genteel and melodious and inspires poets to wax lyrical about sparrows and larks ascending. It's blessedly short too. The poor creatures, demoralised by the damp and cold, sing a few bars to prove they're still alive then pack it in and get on with the day. Things are different in Calcutta. There are no larks here, just big, fat greasy crows that start squawking at first light and go on for hours without a break. Nobody will ever write poetry about them.

My whole body hurt, the smallest movement resulting in a crescendo of pain. I reached down for the bottle of whisky on the floor but merely managed to knock it over. I cursed as it rolled under the bed. Lying back, I sighed and closed my eyes, hoping to placate whoever was using my skull for batting practice, and gave serious consideration to just lying there and not moving all day. It wouldn't have been a bad option if the crows would just shut up.

But there was Sen to consider, lying in a cell at Lal Bazar. I hauled myself up and stumbled to the sink, splashed tepid water on my head, then looked at the tramp with the crumpled face staring at me from the mirror.

I bathed, then reapplied the ointment and bandaged the wound as best I could. What was left of my uniform still lay in a heap on the floor. I didn't have a spare. A new one wouldn't be cheap, though I'd been told of a tailor on Park Street who did a special on officers' uniforms. In the meantime, I dressed in civvies like a proper CID man: a pair of trousers and a shirt that could have done with a wash. Fumbling with the sling, I eventually managed to adjust it so that my arm ached as little as possible.

Downstairs, the maid was already up and about, rushing around, preparing things before Ma Tebbit appeared.

'Morning,' I said. She gave a little shriek of surprise. Maybe she hadn't heard me come in. More likely she was just shocked at the state of me.

'Please, sir,' she said, 'breakfast is not served till half past six.' I must have looked a particularly wretched sight as she seemed to have a change of heart. She looked towards the clock on the mantelpiece, then at the door behind me. 'Come through,' she said. 'I can make you some toast and tea?'

'Is Mrs Tebbit awake yet?' I asked.

She shook her head. '*Memsahib* will not come down for another half an hour, sir.'

'In that case, I'd very much appreciate some toast and tea.'

I wolfed down the toast, partly through hunger and partly from a desire to be out of there before Mrs Tebbit made an entrance. I managed it too, exiting the premises just as I heard her footsteps on the first-floor landing. Salman was at the corner of the square, sharing a smoke with a few of his rickshaw *wallah* chums. I called over to him. He nodded and took a final drag of his *bidi* before sauntering over with his rickshaw. He noticed my arm in the sling, looked like he was about to say something but then seemed to think better of it. Instead, he lowered the rickshaw and helped me up.

'Police station, *sahib*?'

———

The streets were still quiet, with few Europeans about. At this hour, it was the menial workers of the Calcutta City Council who predominated, clearing gutters and washing down pavements. We went along in silence. You get precious little in the way of conversation from a rickshaw *wallah*. That's understandable. It's not easy making small talk while you're pulling twice your own body weight.

On reaching Lal Bazar, I went straight down to the holding cells. To my surprise, Surrender-not lay snoring on a bench in the corridor outside. He was dressed only in a thin cotton vest and a pair of shorts, his shirt rolled up under his head. Around his body hung a thin cotton string: the *sacred thread*, symbol of the priestly, Brahmin caste. It looked like he'd been there all night. I considered waking him, just to see his reaction to being roused by a *sahib* officer while dressed in his underwear, but I feared the shock might have killed him. Instead, better angels persuaded me to let him sleep a little longer and I continued on to the holding cells.

Fifteen feet by ten, with barred doors fronting onto both sides of a long corridor, the cells weren't quite the Ritz, though they did boast en suite facilities in the form of a bucket in the corner. Sen was lying on a cot in a cell at the far end, a police blanket pulled up around his chin. The doctor assigned to monitor him dozed quietly on a chair outside. Not far away the duty officer, a pot-bellied Indian, sat slumbering behind a desk, fat arms folded over a vast gut, his head resting on his chest. I walked up and rapped loudly on the desk, waking both him and the doctor. Startled, he heaved his bulk onto his feet and in a single deft movement, raised one chubby arm, wiped the dribble from his chin and saluted. It was surprisingly graceful for a fat man.

I walked over to the cell and gestured to the duty officer, who rushed over with a ring of large iron keys. He unlocked the door and it swung open with a metallic clang. Sen turned to face me. A slight smile appeared at the corners of his mouth. He tried to sit up, but the effort was too much. The strain showed in his face and the doctor, who'd followed me in, forced him to lie back down.

'How is he?' I asked.

The doctor's reply was acerbic.

'As comfortable as can be expected for someone who's spent a night in a cell, hours after surgery.'

'I need him to answer some questions.'

He looked at me in horror. 'This man almost died last night. He's in no state to be interrogated.'

Sen raised a hand and beckoned us closer. The doctor and I broke off our conversation.

'May I have some water?'

His voice was just a whisper. I nodded to the guard who left the cell and returned with a jug and a battered enamel mug. The doctor helped Sen to sit up, then took the mug from the guard and held it gently to Sen's lips. The prisoner took small, shallow sips, then nodded his thanks.

'Please,' he whispered, 'can you tell me where I am?'

'You're in a holding cell at Lal Bazar,' I said.

'Not Fort William, then? A pity. I've always wanted to see the inside of Fort William.' He gave a small laugh, which ended in a fit of coughs and caused the doctor to rush to support him.

'Don't worry,' I said, 'there's a good chance you'll get to see it before too long.'

The doctor turned angrily towards me.

'This man is obviously not fit to answer any questions now. Please leave.'

I admired his determination, but the man he was protecting was a terrorist, and an Indian one at that. He was about to go down for the murder of an Englishman. The idea that this doctor could keep me from questioning him was laughable. Still, I preferred to wait till Digby and Surrender-not were present, and there was no point in antagonising the man needlessly.

'He can rest for a few hours more, Doctor,' I said, 'but I will question him later this morning.'

I left the cells and returned to the corridor. Banerjee was no longer on the bench but as I stood there he returned, his face and hair wet. He still wore only his vest and shorts.

'Not in uniform today, Surrender-not?' I asked.

He might have asked me the same question, but instead he froze on the spot, water dripping from his head onto his vest.

'Sorry, sir,' he stammered. 'I was just washing my face.'

'Have you been here all night?'

'Yes, sir. I thought it best. In case there was some deterioration in Sen's condition.'

'So you're a doctor now?'

'No, sir. What I mean to say is that I thought I should be close by in case there was any emergency. You yourself stressed the importance of questioning him quickly.'

'Good,' I said, 'because I don't need you showing concern for the man. What with the attitude of the doctor in the cell there with him, to say nothing of the medical staff last night, I'm beginning to think we've arrested the Dalai Lama rather than a terrorist. I trust I don't need to remind you that this man most likely murdered a British civil servant, to say nothing of his other crimes?'

His face fell. 'No, sir.'

It was harsh of me, and, I quickly realised, unwarranted. I hadn't meant to tear a strip off the sergeant, but I was dog tired. I'd had precious little sleep since the night I'd visited the opium den and it was affecting my mood. Getting shot probably hadn't helped either.

That reminded me of something.

'Sergeant,' I asked, 'you remember when I was climbing up the back of that house last night? When one of Sen's accomplices was about to fire at me from the window?'

'Yes, sir.'

'Was it you or Digby who shot them?'

Surrender-not fiddled with the cotton thread hanging from his shoulder.

'It was me, sir. I was the one with the rifle. I'm sure the Sub-inspector would have done the same, but he only had his pistol and that wouldn't have been as accurate.'

'Well,' I said briskly, 'I'm glad you paid attention during training. Get some rest now. We've got a few hours before we question Sen.'

I felt embarrassed. I was indebted to him, but somehow found it hard to say 'thank you'. That was the thing about India. It's difficult for an Englishman to thank an Indian. Of course, it's easy enough to thank them when they do something menial, like fetch a drink or clean your boots, but when it comes to more important matters, such as when one of them saves your life, it's different. The thought left a bitter taste in my mouth.

———

I walked wearily up the stairs to my office and dropped into my chair. The pain was getting worse. Fishing out the bottle of morphine tablets, I placed them on the desk and contemplated the worst of trade-offs. The pain in my shoulder was intense, yet I needed to keep a clear head. Lal Bazar wasn't Scotland Yard, but even here, interrogating a suspect while out of your head on morphine was probably frowned upon. Reluctantly, I returned the bottle to my pocket and instead telephoned Daniels to arrange a meeting with the Commissioner. He answered on the second ring and went out of his way to be helpful, so much so that I thought I might have dialled the wrong number.

'Lord Taggart is expected in at eight o'clock, Captain Wyndham. I've put you in his diary and I'll inform you as soon as he's ready.'

I thanked him and replaced the receiver. My stock was rising. News of the previous night's arrest must have reached the secretary. I afforded myself a dry smile. With luck, we might get a confession out of Sen and I'd be able to close the case. Even if the bastard didn't confess, the testimony from Digby's snitch, together with Sen's attempt to evade capture, would be enough for me to bring charges. It might have been too flimsy a case for an English jury, but under the Rowlett Acts there was no need for one. Terrorists like Sen were supposed to feel the full force of British justice. Building a case beyond reasonable doubt would merely complicate things.

Once he'd been charged, the matter would be out of my hands and what happened afterwards wasn't my concern. Taggart would most likely hand him over to Section H. They'd extract whatever other information he possessed, like squeezing the juice out of a lemon, and then would come a jury-less trial and a swift execution. All in all, a nice efficient process.

I leaned back in my chair and closed my eyes. The lack of sleep must have caught up with me as the next thing I knew, Digby was shaking me awake.

'Come on, old boy, we've got to get a move on. Taggart's waiting for us.'

'What time is it?' I asked, groggy with sleep.

'Just gone eight thirty.'

'I thought Daniels was going to telephone me?' I said, shaking the cobwebs from my head.

'He tried, but you didn't pick up. So he telephoned *me*. By the way, old boy, you do realise you're in civvies?'

'I only had the one uniform,' I said, 'and there's not much left of it. I haven't had time to get any more made yet.'

'It's probably best if you borrow one of mine, then. I'll get you a spare jacket from my office. By the way, there's a good tailor in Park Street that'll do you a special.'

I followed him out of the room and down the corridor. He ducked into his own office, reappearing with his spare jacket, which he helped me put on over the sling.

Daniels was waiting in the corridor outside his anteroom. He gave me a nod as we approached.

'The Commissioner's waiting for you,' he said, leading us through to Taggart's office. The Commissioner had his back to us, staring out of the French windows, but when he turned to greet us, there was a broad smile on his face. He ushered me to a Chesterfield.

'How's the arm, Sam?' he asked.

'Not too bad, sir.'

'That's good to hear, my boy. You were lucky last night. You're not planning to make these sort of heroics a regular occurrence, are you?'

'No, sir.'

'I hope so, for your sake. This isn't England, Sam. There are a lot more guns here. Us, the military, the terrorists – everyone's got them. Stunts like the one you pulled last night could very easily end up with you being killed, if not by the terrorists then very possibly by our friends in Section H. I dare say you're not their favourite policeman right now.'

'I'll watch my step, sir.'

'Make sure you do, Captain. I didn't bring you all the way out here just so you could get yourself killed within a fortnight. You're no use to me dead.'

'Yes, sir. I'd not wish to cause you any inconvenience, sir.'

He eyed me for a moment before letting the comment pass. 'Right then,' he continued, 'let's get down to business. That was some good work by you both yesterday.' He turned to Digby, 'I haven't forgotten it was your informant who put us on Sen's trail in the first place.'

'Thank you, sir,' said Digby with a nod of acknowledgement.

'As for putting a tail on Colonel Dawson,' Taggart continued, 'that was a rather inspired course of action.'

'We got lucky, that's all,' I replied.

'Never underestimate the value of luck, Sam. I'd rather have a lucky officer than a brilliant one. The lucky ones tend to live longer. Be that as it may, I don't think we should advertise the fact that you put a tail on a senior Section H officer. The L-G might not approve. You'll need to come up with a more *acceptable* explanation for how you just happened to come up on the scene so quickly.'

'We could tell them that we learned of Sen's location from a tip-off from one of our own snitches,' I said. 'After all, it must be how Section H found him. Hopefully it'll make them think more highly of our own network of informants.'

Taggart took a handkerchief from his pocket and slowly cleaned his glasses.

'All right,' he said, 'that'll work. All the same, the next time you consider putting a tail on a high-ranking military officer, please let me know beforehand.'

I nodded.

'So where are we with Sen?' he continued.

'He was taken to the Medical College Hospital,' said Digby. 'They patched him up last night.'

'When can we move him from the hospital?'

'He's already here,' I replied. Both men stared at me in surprise. 'He's in the cells downstairs. We moved him last night.'

'How did you manage that?' asked Taggart. 'I'd have thought the doctors would have screamed bloody murder if you tried to shift one of their patients into a cell so soon after an operation.'

'I appealed to their common sense.'

'Well, that's a relief,' said Taggart, 'the last thing we needed was for a potential stand-off at the hospital with Section H. If they want him now, they'll have to go through the L-G.'

'How long do you think we have, sir?' I asked.

Taggart shook his head. 'Hard to say. I expect Dawson would have spoken to his superiors last night; they'd be on the telephone to the L-G first thing this morning. The L-G will probably check with his advisers. If they think we should hand Sen over, we'll probably get an order some time this afternoon. We can probably stall them for a while. I'll speak to Daniels, make myself "uncontactable" for the day, but we'll have to hand him over by tomorrow morning at the latest. You should work from the assumption that you've got twenty-four hours at most.'

'I plan on questioning him as soon as we've finished here,' I said.

'Good. I want him charged by tonight. Get him to cooperate if possible. Tell him that if he doesn't, we'll hand him straight over to Section H. It'll happen anyway, of course, but he doesn't need to know that. Is there anything else, gentlemen?'

'Sir,' said Digby, 'what should we tell the press? By now they'll have got wind of last night's fireworks. They'll want us to comment.'

'If they ask, tell them that we're progressing with our inquiries and that we'll have a fuller statement soon. I don't want anything specific getting out until we've charged Sen. Now, gentlemen,' he said, rising from his chair, 'if there's nothing further, I'm going to have to make preparations to "disappear" for the rest of the day. Let Daniels know if you need to speak to me urgently. Otherwise, I'll contact you for a progress report at six p.m. sharp.'

———

'Interview commencing at ten o'clock, 12th April 1919.'

The room was small and airless and twenty degrees too hot. Five of us were crammed into a space better suited to two and the tang of sweat punctuated the air. Sen, his doctor beside him, sat staring at the floor. I was flanked by Digby. Between us, a battered metal table. Banerjee, with a yellow pad and a fountain pen in his hands, sat to one side.

The introductions were entered into the record: *Interview led by Detective Inspector Captain Samuel Wyndham. Detective Sub-inspector John Digby and Sergeant S. Banerjee, assisting.*

Lack of sleep and a hole in my arm were not exactly ideal preparation for an interrogation. If there was a consolation, it was that Sen looked worse. He was dressed in the standard-issue prison clothes, loose draw-string trousers and shirt. Khaki with black markings. His hands were manacled in his lap.

'Please state your name for the record.'

'Sen,' he said, 'Benoy Sen.' He sounded tired.

'Do you know why you've been arrested?'

'Do you need a reason?'

'You have been arrested on suspicion of murder.'

Sen didn't flinch.

'When did you return to Calcutta?'

No response.

'Can you explain your movements on the night of 8th April last?'

Again silence.

I didn't have the time or the inclination to indulge him.

'Look, Sen,' I said, 'maybe you don't appreciate your good fortune. You've been lucky enough to be arrested by the police rather than the military. That means you get to be questioned in these pleasant surroundings with a doctor by your side and everything is written down for the record. If you don't afford us some cooperation, I may as well turn you over to our friends at Fort William and they're somewhat less keen on playing by the rules the way we do.'

Sen raised his eyes from the floor and gave a snort of derision.

'You talk of rules, Captain. Tell me, why don't your rules apply to them?'

'You're not asking the questions here, Sen.'

He smiled.

'I'll ask you again, when did you return to Calcutta?'

He stared at me, as though sizing me up, then raised his hands and rested them on the table. There was a soft scrape as metal hit metal. 'I arrived in the city last Monday.'

I nodded.

'And why did you return?'

'I am a Bengali, born and raised in Calcutta. It is my home. Why should I need a reason to return?'

I wasn't interested in polemics. 'Just tell me why you came back. Why *now*?'

'I returned because I was invited.'

'Invited by whom? And for what purpose?'

'I'm sorry, Captain. I will not divulge the names of other patriots.'

'We know you gave a speech at the house of a Mr Amarnath Dutta.'

That shook him up. 'You must congratulate your spies,' he replied. 'I admit that I did indeed give a speech. I spoke to an assembly of forward-thinking men about the need for independence.'

'And you are aware that such an assembly is illegal?' I asked.

'I am aware that under your law such an assembly is illegal and such a speech is labelled seditious. Under this law, Indians are banned from meeting in their own homes to discuss their desire for freedom in their own country. It was passed by Englishmen without the consent of the Indians to whom it applies. Wouldn't you agree that such a law is unjust? Or do you believe that an Indian, unlike a European, should not have the right to determine his own destiny?'

'This isn't a political discussion,' I said. 'Just answer the question.'

Sen laughed, thumping his hands down on the table. 'But it is, Captain! How could it not be? You are a police officer. I am an Indian. You are a defender of a system that keeps my people in subjugation. I am a man who seeks freedom. The only type of discussion we *could* have is a political one.'

God, I hated politicals. Give me a psychopath or a mass murderer any day. Compared to a political, interrogating them was refreshingly straightforward. They were generally all too eager to confess their crimes. Politicals, on the other hand, almost always felt the need to obfuscate, to justify their actions, convince you that they worked for justice and the greater good and that you couldn't make an omelette without breaking heads.

'The rights and wrongs of the political system are not my concern, Sen. My job is to investigate a murder. That is all I am interested in doing. Tell me, what was the content of your speech at Mr Dutta's house?'

Sen thought for a moment. 'I stressed the need for unity. And the need for a new course of action.'

'And what was this "new course of action" to be?'

'Are you sure you want to hear, Captain? You might think I'm trying to engage you in a political discussion.'

'Watch yourself, Sen!' interjected Digby. 'We're not interested in a lecture from a bloody *babu*!'

Sen ignored him and kept his eyes firmly locked on mine.

'Carry on,' I said.

'As you are no doubt aware, Inspector, until I returned to Calcutta, I had been keeping a low profile for several years. During that period, I had plenty of time to reflect on matters. It became clear to me that though we fought for the freedom of all Indians, in over twenty-five years of struggle we had made precious little progress. I began to consider the reasons for this failure.

'Of course there were the obvious explanations: the peasants, so ground down by toil and daily survival that they lack all political consciousness; the infighting between our many groups, which you and your lackeys ruthlessly exploit; the fact that your spies are able to infiltrate our organisations, compromising our plans; but always I came back to one fundamental question: if our cause is just, why do the people not rally to us? Why do your spies not realise that we fight in their interests as well as our own? This was the question that vexed me and which I spent many hours a day contemplating.

'When you are in hiding, one thing you have plenty of is time. I read widely. As much as I could. Books, newspaper cuttings, anything I could find on freedom struggles across the world. The fight to abolish slavery in America, the struggle for Indian rights in South Africa. I read the writings of M. K. Gandhi especially closely. He posed a different question. He asked, "If our cause is just, why do our oppressors not realise it?" He argued that once the oppressor, in his heart of hearts, admits to himself that he is wrong, he will lose the will to continue his oppression.

'At first I laughed at the notion. By his logic, all we had to do was to point out to you the evil of your actions and you would recoil in horror, repent and go home. To my jaundiced eye, it was nothing more than the delusions of a hopeless naif. If only we appealed to your better natures, you yourselves would see the error of your ways!'

He laughed at the absurdity, then continued, 'For one thing, I didn't believe you even had better natures.

'I'd watched as your troops butchered my friends. In my eyes, you were all soulless demons. But time and solitude have a way of making one see reason. As my period in hiding continued, my anger subsided. I thought more on what Gandhi and men like him were advocating. Then one day, it struck me; I still remember the moment, I was pumping water from a tube well. The process was monotonous and my mind wandered. That's when I realised. I was guilty of the very actions that I ascribed to the British. If I accused you of treating the Indian as inferior, then it must follow that I cannot adjudge the Indian to be superior to the Englishman. We must be equal. And if we are equal, I must ascribe to you the same dignity I ascribe to Indians. If I believe that Indians have a conscience and a moral compass, in essence that we are *good*, then I must equally accept that most Englishmen are also good. Once that is accepted, it follows that at least some Englishmen will be open to see the error of their ways, if only they can be pointed out to them.

'I realised then, that our actions – the actions of Jugantor and other groups – only served to justify your repression. Every bomb blast, every bullet, provides you with an excuse to tighten your control over us. I came to see that the only way to end British rule in India was to strip away these excuses and reveal to you the true nature of your occupation of my country. That was the message I had come back to deliver; that only through unity, among all Indians, and by reaching out to the better nature of our oppressors through non-violent non-cooperation, can we hope to gain our freedom.'

Digby leaned back in his chair and snorted. 'Fine words, Sen. If there's one thing this country is not short of, it's Bengalis making speeches. You people are never at a loss for words, are you? Always happy to argue black is white and day is night.' He turned to me.

'We have a saying in these parts, Captain: *God save us from the fury of the Afghan and the rhetoric of the Bengali!*'

Once again Sen ignored Digby and directed his words at me.

'May I ask, Captain, which of the two the sub-inspector here believes is worse?'

Digby turned red. By talking only to me, Sen was goading him expertly.

'This isn't a debate, Sen,' said Digby angrily, 'but since you ask, the uppity Bengali is far worse!'

Sen smiled. 'It has been my experience, Captain, that many of your kinsmen reserve a special dislike for Bengalis, more so than they do for other Indians. I profess I am at a loss to say precisely why. Maybe the sub-inspector here could enlighten me?'

'Maybe it's because you all talk so bloody much?' Digby retorted.

'In that case,' said Sen, 'we truly are all in trouble. For over a century now we Bengalis have been told how lucky we are that you British were good enough to bestow upon us the wonderful English language and your vaunted western education, first here in our land before the rest of India. But having learned at your feet for all these years, when we avail ourselves of your gifts, we are accused of thinking and talking too much. Maybe, that western education was not such a good idea after all? Maybe it has given us "uppity Bengalis" ideas above our station? It seems the sub-inspector here believes that the only *good* Indians are ones that know their place.'

I cut in before Digby had a chance to formulate anything coherent. Time was running out and I needed to get answers from Sen.

'If you'd come to preach the gospel of non-violence,' I asked, 'why didn't you just surrender when it was obvious you were surrounded last night?'

'I considered it. I even tried to persuade my comrades to do just that. But I was in a minority.'

'But you were their leader, Sen. Are you telling me they wouldn't listen to you? You're a persuasive man. You tell us you came back to persuade people towards the path of non-violence, yet you expect me to believe you couldn't even persuade your own men?'

'Have you been present at a raid carried out by your colleagues in military intelligence before?' he asked. 'If so, you might be aware of their reputation for being rather trigger happy. Things happen in the dark. There have been many cases where men trying to surrender have been gunned down. My comrades decided it was better to die like men than like dogs.'

'And you expect me to believe that?'

Sen sat back and sighed. He stared into my eyes. 'I have no way of convincing you, Captain.'

'I think you're lying,' I said. 'I think your "new course of action" was to instigate a terror campaign starting with the assassination of a high-ranking British official.'

'Why do you continue with this farce, Captain? Your spies had obviously infiltrated the meeting. They must have confirmed everything I've told you.'

'Our informants have reported on your meeting,' said Digby. 'They made no mention of your miraculous conversion on the road from Dacca.'

'What time did your meeting at Dutta's house finish?' I asked.

'Just after midnight.'

'And what did you do then?'

'I talked with Mr Dutta for about half an hour. Then I left for the safe house in Kona.'

'Did anyone go with you?'

'I was accompanied by a comrade. Your troops killed him last night.'

'And you went straight there?'

'Yes.'

I banged my fist down on the table – it was a stupid thing to do – sending a jolt of pain stabbing through my wounded arm. 'Do you take me for a fool?' I shouted. 'I know you left Dutta's house with an accomplice. I know you found MacAuley wandering the streets, I know you killed him and stuffed a note in his mouth. What I want to know is whether you specifically targeted him that night or whether he was just the first white man who had the misfortune to cross your path?'

Sen's doctor was on his feet. 'Captain, I must protest! This man is recovering from surgery. His health is in a delicate position. Please stop this interrogation now!'

Sen waved him to sit. 'Thank you, Doctor, but I am willing to continue this conversation.' He turned to me and smiled. 'I think I may have been rather naive. You're not interested in the truth, are you? This is about being able to say you've caught a terrorist who killed a government official and that the streets are safe once again for the good citizens of Calcutta – the white ones, at any rate. You don't give a damn about finding the real killer. All you want is a scapegoat. And who better than a freedom fighter? It gives you the justification to continue your repression.'

I turned to Banerjee. 'Sergeant, please pass me exhibit A.'

From a buff-coloured box file on the floor beside him, Banerjee removed the bloodstained note that had been found stuffed in MacAuley's mouth. He flattened it out and passed it to me.

The ink had run somewhat and the stains had turned reddish brown, but the words were still clear. I laid the note flat on the table in front of Sen.

'Do you recognise this? It was found in the mouth of the deceased.'

Sen looked at it, then laughed bitterly. 'This is your evidence, Captain? This scrap of paper?' He nodded towards Banerjee. 'Has your lackey read it?'

I realised that I hadn't shared it with Surrender-not. It had been stupid of me not to, but I hadn't met the sergeant when I'd found it and, with all that had happened since, I'd neglected to share it with him afterward.

Sen read the look on my face. 'No? I didn't think so. Maybe you should show it to him? He'll tell you that I wouldn't have written that note – unless he's totally craven, of course.'

Behind me, Banerjee drew a sharp intake of breath. I held out a hand before he had a chance to rise further to the bait. I wasn't about to let Sen dictate the terms of the interview, and I certainly wasn't about to admit to him that Banerjee hadn't seen the note.

'Why did you write the note, Sen?' I asked.

'You must know that I didn't. I shouldn't think any Bengali wrote that note. It was obviously written by your people in an attempt to frame me.'

'I can assure you that's not the case. I found the note myself.'

Sen sighed. 'Then we have a problem, Captain. You claim not to believe me when I tell you I didn't write that note. And I cannot believe you when you say your men didn't write it to implicate an innocent Indian. We are back to our fundamental problem, a lack of trust. We both believe the other to be lying. Maybe one of us is, but then again, it is possible we are both telling the truth. It falls to one of us to believe in the better nature of the other.

'Let me ask you a question, Captain. If, as you say, I wrote that note as a warning to the British, why would I write it in Bengali?' He pointed to Digby. 'As so vexed the sub-inspector here, I have had the benefit of an English education. Why wouldn't I write it in English?'

'It's obvious, isn't it?' Digby interjected. 'To cast doubt on your guilt should you be captured.'

Sen shook his head as though disappointed with a particularly obtuse child. He turned to me. 'Really, Captain, is it plausible that I would do such a thing in the hope that, should I be caught, it might sow doubt in the minds of my accusers? What good would that do me? Am I to appeal to the great British sense of fair play? Will I get to plead my case in front of a jury? Of course not! All I will get is a mockery of a trial followed by a bullet or the hangman's noose. But I'm not afraid to die, Captain. I resigned myself to a martyr's death long ago. I just ask to be martyred for my own actions rather than as a scapegoat for someone else's.'

I sat back. The interview was going nowhere. Any expectation on my part of a speedy confession had been desperately naive.

'Tell me about the attack on the Darjeeling Mail,' I said. 'What exactly were you looking for?'

Sen stared. 'I don't know what you're talking about.'

'So you know nothing about the attack on that train in the early hours of Thursday morning?'

'Are you going to try to pin all your unsolved crimes on me?' he asked. 'As I've told you, I returned to spread the message of non-violence. Neither the assassination of the Englishman nor the attack on this train you mentioned have anything to do with me or my associates.'

I checked my watch. We had been at this for almost an hour. It was time to try a change of tack. I took out a packet of Capstans and offered one to Sen. He accepted it with a shaking hand. Banerjee brought out a box of matches, lit one and offered it to him. Sen stared at him in disgust and laid the cigarette down. The match burned down to Banerjee's thumb. He shook it, extinguishing the flame.

Sen turned to me. 'I'm sorry, I won't accept anything from some-one I consider a traitor to his people.'

'But you'll accept a cigarette from me?'

'You and I are on opposite sides,' he said. 'We may have our differences, but I acknowledge your right to defend your principles. Just as you should acknowledge my right to stand up for what I believe is right. *He*, on the other hand,' he gestured towards Banerjee, 'is an accessory to the enslavement of his own people. I will not accept anything from him.'

Banerjee flinched. I saw his fists clench, and though he held his tongue, there was the first spark of anger in his eyes.

'Surely,' I said, 'given your new mantra of tolerance and understanding, you should consider the sergeant's reasons for joining the police force before you condemn him? I should also tell you that if it wasn't for him, both you and I would probably have died last night.'

Sen paused. Finally he picked up the cigarette and held it out towards Banerjee. 'Forgive me, Sergeant. Old habits die hard. It was wrong of me to condemn you without proof. I only hope that your Captain here follows the same principle.'

Sen smoked, slowly savouring each drag. When a man has little left to live for, he takes his time over what few pleasures remain. I indulged him. In his position I'd have done the same. Once he'd finished, we started again; the same questions, the same replies. Again Sen denied any knowledge of MacAuley's murder or the attack on the mail train. Again he attested his new-found commitment to peaceful change, arguing with the passion of a convert. His logic was seductively appealing. More than once I was forced to remember I was dealing with a self-confessed terrorist whose organisation had maimed and killed both Englishmen and Indians, military and civilian. His supposed transformation to a man of peace was too convenient.

I felt sure he was capable of lying, telling me whatever would sow doubt in my mind. I was, after all, his enemy, the embodiment of everything he'd dedicated his life to overthrowing. And yet I *was* beginning to have doubts. Whether or not his story was true, there were some things that seemed odd, most obviously the note found in MacAuley's mouth. Why *would* Sen have written it in Bengali when he spoke and wrote English as well as anyone? And why was he so adamant that I show the note to Banerjee?

Then there was the paper itself. In the days after the murder, I'd not had the chance to examine it closely, but now, seeing it again raised questions. I'd forgotten its quality – it was luxurious, heavy, with a rich smoothness to it. The kind you'd find in the bedroom of a five-star hotel. From what I'd seen in Calcutta so far, such paper wasn't common. The paper used by Indians was generally flimsy and coarse. Even the paper used by the police was of a quality worse than back in England. Where then would a fugitive who'd been in hiding for four years get such paper? And why would he crush it into a ball and stuff it in his victim's mouth?

I called a halt to the interrogation. A guard led Sen and his doctor back down to the cells. Once they'd left, I turned to Digby and Surrender-not. Digby was shaking his head while Surrender-not just sat there wearing that hang-dog expression he always seemed to wear when upset.

'Well?' I asked.

'I'll say one thing for him,' said Digby, rising to his feet, 'he's got some imagination. All that rubbish about non-violence. You'd think we'd arrested a saint rather than a terrorist mastermind.'

'What about you?' I asked Banerjee.

He looked up from his thoughts. 'I'm not sure what to think, sir.'

'You should be under no doubts, Sergeant,' said Digby. 'I've seen his sort before and believe me, sonny, he'd as happily slit your throat as a white man's if he got the chance.'

Banerjee made no reply. Whatever he was thinking, he knew enough to keep his own counsel. The box file was on the table in front of me. I opened it, took out the bloodstained note, and passed it to him.

'I should have shown you this earlier, Sergeant. Digby tells me it's a note warning the British to quit India. Read it and tell me what you make of it.'

Banerjee examined the note.

'Sub-inspector Digby is correct.'

'There, you see!' said Digby.

'It's rather odd, though.'

'How exactly?'

'Well, sir, it's hard to explain to someone who doesn't speak Bengali. There are really two different types of Bengali. There is spoken Bengali and there is formal Bengali, similar to your notion of the King's English, but far more formulaic and excessively polite. This note is not written in standard, colloquial Bengali. It's formal Bengali.'

'Is that significant?' I asked.

Banerjee hesitated. 'Well . . . it would be like writing a note in English using "thou" and "thee" instead of "you". It's not wrong, just unusual. Especially when you're writing a threat.'

Digby continued to pace the room. 'Sen's an educated man. Maybe he prefers formal Bengali? I don't see why it should matter.'

'Maybe I'm not explaining it very well,' said Banerjee. 'If the note was written as a threat, it's the politest threat you could possibly send. What it literally says is: "I must apologise for there will be no further exhortations. The blood of those from overseas will flow in the streets. Kindly take your leave of India." I don't understand why Sen would have written that.'

Digby turned to me for reassurance.

'Look, Sen's a known terrorist, responsible for countless attacks. He shows up after four years in hiding. On his first night in town, he gives a speech calling for action against the British. On the same night, not ten minutes away from where he gives this speech, MacAuley is murdered. The next night, there's an attack on a train, which, by your own deduction, was a terrorist raid. You don't seriously think *all* of that is just a coincidence, do you? So the man writes an odd note. What of it? The fact is, the note is a threat, a warning of more violence to come. It's what Sen's dedicated his life to. The man is guilty. Whether he admits it or not is irrelevant.'

In one sense he was correct. Whether Sen admitted it or not *was* irrelevant. He would be pronounced guilty and hanged. Too many people had too much resting on his guilt for the verdict to be anything else. The press were up in arms. To them the murder was a direct attack on British authority in India. That put pressure on the L-G. He had to respond with an iron will; show the natives that such an act would be met with savage and public retribution. What better way to demonstrate British power than the swift arrest and execution of a terrorist? Section H wanted Sen dead to make up for the embarrassment of letting him escape when the rest of the Jugantor leadership were liquidated back in 1915. Even we in the Imperial Police Force had reason to see Sen convicted, for the simple fact that we were under pressure to close the case quickly and we had no other suspects.

There was only one problem. I couldn't be sure he'd done it.

It wasn't just concerns about the note. I still had no idea what MacAuley had been doing outside a brothel in Black Town in the first place. No one else, from the L-G to MacAuley's friend Buchan, knew or seemed to care much about that. I realised also that I'd been uneasy since the beginning. It was as though I was always two steps behind, following a trail of crumbs laid by someone else. Unfortunately Digby was right. How would I explain to Taggart that I had doubts about the guilt of a wanted terrorist who was in the vicinity of the crime on the night of the murder, just because of a rather eccentric note left at the scene? He would laugh me out of his office.

There was something else, though. A fear forming at the back of my mind. If Sen wasn't guilty of the attacks, then it meant that the perpetrators were still out there. If so, the threat of a full-blown terrorist insurrection was still very real and time was running out. I tried to put the thought out of my mind. Sen was guilty. I just had to prove it.

'Sir?' asked Banerjee. 'What are your orders?'

I told him to get his notes typed up. I wanted them ready so I could review them before I gave the Commissioner a progress report later on.

'What about Sen?' asked Digby. 'Do you want to have another go at him?'

'Do you think there's much point?' I asked.

'If it were up to me, I'd hand him over to Section H today. See what they can get out of him. They can be very persuasive when they want to.'

'Section H will get their hands on him soon enough,' I said. 'But in the meantime, I plan on holding on to him for as long as I can.'

TWENTY-TWO

I returned to my office, locked the door and collapsed into my chair. Throughout Sen's interrogation the pain in my arm had been gradually worsening to the point where I feared it had clouded my judgement. I'd gone in certain, and come out unsure about pretty much everything. The result was two precious hours wasted.

I had to focus. What little time I had was slipping away. I reached into my pocket and pulled out the bottle of morphine tablets. I took out two of the round white pills and swallowed them dry, then sat back and closed my eyes. Within minutes the pain started to ebb. But two tablets had been a mistake. I'd hoped the dose would remove the pain, allowing me to concentrate, but I'd misjudged it. The morphine was too powerful and I fell into a stupor.

I was floating serenely down the Hooghly. Past palm trees and paddy fields, an orange sun enveloping me in its warmth. My mind and body parted company. It was glorious. People were standing on the banks, gazing down at me as I passed. Sarah was there. Young, fresh and beautiful, the Sarah I'd first met. She said nothing, just looked on with the most caring of countenances. I wanted to go to her, but she was out of reach and I had no control over my body. I couldn't even call out. She faded from view and I kept floating downstream, past a train marooned on tracks halfway up to a tea garden, past more faces, past Lord Taggart and Mrs Tebbit, past Banerjee and Byrne, past Annie Grant. She looked concerned, but why wasn't clear. Beside her stood Benoy Sen, dressed in prison clothes, with his manacled hands held out in front of him, palms up. I tried to move, to rise from the river, but my body refused. Sen and Annie faded from view as the current pulled me along and into a cavern. It grew colder. Water dripped from the ceiling. There stood MacAuley, in black tie and bloodstained shirt, one glassy eye trained straight ahead. As best I could, I turned to see what he was staring at. Figures silhouetted in the darkness. I strained to get a better look, but without success. The gloom turned to blackness and I felt myself sinking.

———

I was swimming. Underwater. There was a noise coming from somewhere. A persistent hammering. A light was shining above the surface. I swam towards it. The noise grew louder, more focused, and I surfaced and found myself slumped in my chair. Someone was knocking at the door. Groggy, I rose and with some difficulty, made my way over and turned the key in the lock. Surrender-not stood in front of me. My appearance seemed to shock him.

'Sorry, Sergeant,' I said, 'the medication the doctors gave last night must have knocked me out.'

The poor boy's ears turned crimson. He held out a half-dozen sheets of closely typed paper.

'The notes from this morning's interrogation, sir.'

I thanked him, took them from him and returned to my desk. Banerjee loitered in the doorway, his hang-dog face on again.

'Is there something else?' I asked.

He stood there, nervously rubbing his chin.

'I was hoping to speak to you privately about the interview this morning.'

'You mean without Sub-inspector Digby being present?'

He nodded.

I gestured to him to sit.

He closed the door and took the chair across the desk from me.

'What's on your mind?'

Banerjee shifted in his seat.

'It's this MacAuley case, sir. I have certain misgivings.'

'You mean about Sen?'

'What if he's telling the truth?'

'That he just happened to be in the area that night, gave his speech and then headed straight off to Kona? He's got no alibi, Sergeant.'

'He claims we killed his alibi last night.'

'What would you expect him to say?'

Banerjee squirmed. 'What about the note, sir? Why write a note like that?'

I didn't have the answer to that. 'Maybe Digby's right,' I said. 'Maybe it's just a ploy to throw us off the scent.'

He grew tense. 'I don't believe that, sir, and, with respect, I don't believe you do either.'

It took courage for him to question me like that, but it was still out of order.

'Remember your place, Sergeant,' I said. 'That man is going to hang. If not for this, then for a raft of other crimes. You're dismissed.'

Banerjee held his tongue, though his eyes betrayed his frustration. He rose, saluted and marched out of the room.

I instantly regretted taking such a stern line with him. He was right, after all. The evidence we had was purely circumstantial. Nothing connected Sen directly to MacAuley's murder or the attack on the train. No court would have convicted an Englishman on what we had. But under the Rowlett Acts his reputation alone would be enough to send Sen to the gallows. It made me uneasy. The man was going to hang for crimes I wasn't wholly convinced he was guilty of. Before India, I'd never have contemplated such a thing. But now that was exactly what I was proposing to do. And why? Because it was easier to convict him than prove him innocent. Because it would help cement my reputation in a new job. Because the life of an Indian has less value than that of an Englishman.

Banerjee had dared to point out details that made me uncomfortable. Facts that my own conscience should have rebelled against and I'd rebuked him for it. Would I have done so with a white subordinate? Probably not, especially when I shared his concerns. But Banerjee was Indian, and even in the short time I'd spent in India, I knew that an Englishman should never show doubt in front of a native, lest it be interpreted as weakness. No one had explicitly told me, it had just sunk into my consciousness as if by osmosis. But why should my agreeing with Surrender-not be a sign of weakness?

Then I realised. It wasn't personal error I was afraid of, it was the possibility of an error by the state. Our justification for ruling India rested on the principles of impartial British justice and the rule of law. If we were willing to pervert the course of that justice, by hanging Sen for the murder of MacAuley without proof, then our justification for ruling, our moral superiority, would amount to naught.

Moral superiority. They had been the words of the Irishman, Byrne. He was right. Our rule in this country depended on our claims to moral superiority. It was often unspoken but obvious in everything we did. We believed in it. The empire was a force for good. It had to be, otherwise why were we here? But the empire's killing of Sen for the sake of expediency would undermine that claim. It would be an abrogation of our core values, and abandoning those values would make us hypocrites. I'd rebuked Banerjee because he was calling me out on my hypocrisy, and in that minute he'd lost his respect for me, and by extension for the empire that I represented. The problem was, while I could afford to live without his respect, the empire couldn't.

That left me with a choice. I could accept things as they were and watch Sen hang, or I could do my job; find proof that he was guilty, or if he wasn't, discover who was. I got up from behind my desk, slung Digby's jacket round my shoulders and headed out of the door and down to the cells.

It was feeding time, the dull aroma of cooked rice doing little to dispel the stench of the place. Sen had been returned to the same cell I'd found him in earlier. He was sitting on the floor next to the plank bed, beside him a battered metal pannikin containing rice and a thin yellow *daal* of lentils. There was no sign of the doctor who'd accompanied him earlier. Sen ate, deftly gathering a small portion of rice and lentils with his hand and lifting it to his mouth. He looked up as the warden unlocked the cell door, swallowed his mouthful of food, and smiled.

'Captain Wyndham. Is it time for my transfer to your colleagues in military intelligence? If so, would you mind waiting a few minutes for me to finish this repast? I believe the room service at Fort William is not as reliable as it is here.'

I smiled, despite myself. 'You seem very calm, Sen. Especially for a condemned man.'

'Is that what I am, Captain? Condemned without a trial? You are correct, of course. I am a condemned man. I'm sure there will be a trial though, and, like you, I have no doubt about its outcome. But as I told you earlier, I have reconciled myself to my fate. I am not scared of death.'

I sat down on the plank bed. 'Do you have any regrets? Anything you want to get off your chest?'

Sen scooped up another small mouthful of food and contemplated the question. He sighed. 'I have many regrets, Captain. I think what I might have made of my life had I been born under different circumstances. My father always maintained I was born under a very bad star. He was a good man, my father; a military engineer during the Afghan wars, respected by the British. They even gave him a medal – the Indian Order of Merit, second class. And he admired them greatly. It was he who made me join the Indian Civil Service. For a time I considered it the highest honour for an Indian.'

'What changed?'

'I grew up. I became involved in politics. It's what Bengalis do. It's our national hobby. You have gardening, we have politics. I grew interested in the writings of men such as Pal and Tilak. They opened my eyes to the true nature of your rule in my country. But I am sure you do not wish to hear about my journey from rising man to revolutionary.'

'You said you had regrets?'

Sen deftly picked up the last few lentils and grains of rice and transferred them to his mouth. He nodded. 'Yes, I have regrets, Captain. I regret thinking we could ever win our freedom through violence. That we could fight fire with fire. I regret every single life lost; the deaths of our foes as well as those of my comrades and the innocents. I regret what all the killing did to me. I lost my sense of compassion. I think any man who witnesses such things has to switch off a part of his humanity, otherwise he could not live with himself. And in doing so, I think he loses part of his soul. Maybe now you begin to understand why I say I am prepared for death. How can I be scared of it when the best part of my nature died long ago?'

I looked Sen in the eyes.

'Did you kill MacAuley?'

'No,' he replied. 'I had nothing to do with it, or the attack on that train.'

'You know they'll hang you anyway.'

'I know, Captain. But a man cannot cheat his *karma*. If it is written that I will hang, then so be it. I am ready.'

Experience had taught me to trust my instincts, and they were telling me that, whatever his other crimes, Sen hadn't murdered MacAuley or Pal, the railway guard.

I rose and called for the warden. He came shuffling along with the keys and unlocked the door. I looked at Sen, still sitting on the floor. I took his hand and helped him up on to the plank bed.

'May I ask you one thing before you go, Captain?' he asked. 'When will I be handed over to the military?'

'I don't know,' I said, 'but I doubt it'll be long.'

Sen considered this. 'Thank you for your candour,' he said.

A black cloud fell over me as I walked back to my office. I arrived to find a note from Daniels on my desk. The Commissioner wanted to see me at his residence at five o'clock. That gave me time to read the transcript of Banerjee's notes and mull over my options. I'd read a few pages when the telephone rang. A tinny voice ordered me to hold for a call from Writers' Building. Moments later I was connected to Annie Grant. The sound of her voice made me irrationally happy, like receiving those extra rations during the war, which signalled we'd be going over the top the next morning.

She sounded agitated. 'Sam? I've just heard the news. Are you all right? Everyone here's in a flap.'

'What have you heard?' I said.

'That you captured MacAuley's killer. Section H are saying the man's a known terrorist and that you refused to hand him over.'

'How did you hear all this?'

'The L-G wants him transferred to the military. The order was typed up by a friend of mine at Government House. She telephoned to tell me the news. She said you'd been injured.'

'I'm all right.'

'Are you sure? You sound exhausted.'

'I didn't get much sleep last night.'

'Is it true, then?' she asked. 'Have you caught the killer?'

I was wary about telling her too much. Seeing her outside the *Statesman*'s offices still bothered me. 'We've arrested a suspect,' I said. 'That's all I can say for the moment.'

'What's wrong, Sam? You sound . . . distant.'

'I'm just preoccupied, Annie. I've a lot to do.'

She was silent for a moment.

'I understand,' she said finally, though her tone suggested the opposite.

'Look,' I said, 'I'm sorry. I just have a hell of a lot to deal with right now. How about I take you to dinner tonight?'

Her voice brightened. 'Well, Captain Wyndham, I think I could manage that.'

I ended the call and forced myself to concentrate on MacAuley. The more I thought about it, the more I feared I'd been led like a dancing monkey down a path to Sen. Worse still, I'd gone down that path willingly. From the moment we'd met Digby's informant, I'd dropped all other avenues of inquiry. Christ, I hadn't even followed up on a search of the murder locus. The investigation, *my* investigation, had become a mere sideshow in someone else's game.

I telephoned the pit and asked Surrender-not to come to my office. A few minutes later he knocked and stuck his head round the door. He looked sullen.

'You requested my presence, sir?'

He was still upset with me.

'Yes, Sergeant, I asked to see you. Don't just stand there, come in, we have work to do.'

Surprised, Banerjee entered and closed the door behind him. He sat down at the desk and pulled notebook and pencil from his breast pocket.

'I've been thinking,' I said, 'about our conversation earlier. There are a number of questions about this case that remain to be answered. It seems to me we need to find those answers if we're going to be certain of Sen's guilt.'

'Or his innocence,' Banerjee interjected.

'We're going to conduct a proper inquiry,' I continued, 'get back to what we were doing before we ever heard of Sen. There's a lot to do. We need to find out exactly what MacAuley was doing up in Cossipore on Tuesday night. We need to speak to that prostitute you saw at the window. I also want a fingertip search of the crime scene carried out. We need to find the murder weapon if possible. And did you get a chance to take a look into the business interests of Mr Stevens, MacAuley's former deputy?'

'Not yet. I'll check with Companies House.'

'Good. Then there's MacAuley's friends. I want to talk to James Buchan again. And MacAuley's preacher friend.'

'The Reverend Gunn was due back in Calcutta today, sir.'

'Right,' I said, 'we'll head up there tomorrow.'

'What about Sub-inspector Digby?' asked Banerjee. 'He's convinced Sen is the killer.'

'Let me worry about Digby,' I said.

Banerjee finished his notes and looked up. 'Will there be anything else, sir?'

'That's all for now.'

As he left the room, my thoughts turned to Digby. He might be as pompous as the doorman at the Savoy, but the truth was I needed him. His local expertise was vital if I was to have any chance of finding out what had really happened to MacAuley, though convincing him that Sen wasn't guilty was going to be tough. What's more, the intelligence that Sen had returned to Calcutta had come from one of Digby's informants. A quick conviction might give Digby the promotion he probably deserved. At the very least he'd have the gratitude of some powerful friends in Section H. And all I had to convince him to the contrary were my instincts. I'd need a miracle. An appeal to St Jude, the patron saint of lost causes, might have helped, but I didn't have his number, so I picked up the telephone and called through to Digby's office instead.

———

'I can't believe we're even having this conversation,' he exclaimed, pacing the floor in front of my desk. 'The bastard's obviously guilty.'

'We can't prove it beyond reasonable doubt.'

'We don't *need* to prove it beyond reasonable doubt. Why do you think we have the Rowlatt Acts? So we can lock up terrorists like Sen and not worry about them getting off on technicalities. Besides, he's a wanted man, responsible for a whole host of previous crimes from sedition to murder. Are you telling me that means nothing to you?'

'Of course not,' I replied, 'but this is hardly a technicality. We have absolutely no solid evidence linking the man to MacAuley. And what if we're wrong and the killers are at large? We might still be looking at a terrorist campaign.'

Digby sighed. 'If it was terrorists that attacked that train – and it's a big "if" – you said yourself that they didn't find the cash they were looking for. Given that there haven't been any further attacks on mail trains in the last few days, it stands to reason that either Sen's gang was responsible and we've killed them all or the attack on the train was just a botched robbery by *dacoits*.'

He ran a hand through his hair. 'When are you going to start accepting you're not in England any more? Sen isn't some soap-box politician standing in the rain at Speakers' Corner on a Sunday. He and his ilk are trying to overthrow the legitimate government of India! It's a life-and-death struggle to them. If that means murdering a civil servant or blowing up a hospital, so be it. They'll stop at nothing to achieve their goal.'

'All I'm asking,' I said, 'is that we keep investigating till we've found the evidence we need to categorically confirm his guilt. I need your help for that.'

That seemed to calm him slightly.

'Look, old boy,' he said, 'it's a fool's errand. Sen's one of the most wanted men in the country. The press have already got a sniff of what's going on. They're not stupid, you know. That little pitched battle Section H orchestrated last night has tongues wagging all over Howrah. You think they're going to miss that? By tomorrow morning, the fact we've captured the bastard will be plastered all over the front pages. How do you think Taggart's going to react if you tell him you've got doubts? He'll hit the roof. And for what? We'll still be forced to hand Sen over to Section H and believe me, they'll have him charged and executed by the end of the week.'

'This discussion is over,' I said. 'If there's a death sentence hanging over a man, I want to make damn sure he's guilty before I stick his head in the noose. We're going to keep investigating. I will order you if necessary.'

He stared at me.

'Yes, sir,' he said icily. 'Just remember one thing. There *will* be a death sentence at the end of all this. Whether it falls on Sen or your career is up to you.'

TWENTY-THREE

South Calcutta. The heart of White Town.

Leafy suburbs sped past, wide avenues and whitewashed villas hidden behind high hedgerows. Hardly a native in sight, other than the *durwans*, of course, the surly Indian gatekeepers who controlled all access to their masters' houses. Occasionally, through gaps in iron gates, there was a fleeting glimpse of a gardener or two, hard at work tending emerald lawns.

South Calcutta, the preserve of first-rate men from second-rate towns like Guildford and Croydon. The home of colonial administrators, military officers and merchants made good. South Calcutta, with its endless rounds of golf and garden parties, its gymkhanas and gin on the veranda. It was a good life. Certainly better than Croydon.

On towards Alipore and Lord Taggart's residence. The driver slowed and turned into a wide gravel driveway, at the end of which stood a sprawling three-storey house set amidst flower beds and lawns. Only in Calcutta would such a mansion be called a bungalow.

The car pulled up gently under the portico at the entrance to the house. Green vines spiralled up the whitewashed columns. A uniformed constable ran up and swung open the door.

'Captain Wyndham to see Lord Taggart.'

'Of course, sir,' he replied. 'His Lordship is in the south garden. He's asked that you join him there. Please follow me.'

With a nod, he turned and set off across a pristine lawn. The scent of English flowers hung in the air. Roses and foxgloves, truly England in a corner of a foreign field, though more than just a corner, an acre or two at least. As we walked, I noticed armed troops discreetly positioned around the building. They were invisible from the road and unobtrusive from the house.

Taggart was enjoying the balmy weather. He was seated at a small cane table, shirt open at the neck, reviewing some papers. He looked up and greeted me with a smile.

'Hello, Sam. Good to see you, my boy.' His tone was as warm as the afternoon air. 'Have a seat,' he said, gesturing to a chair. 'What's your poison? Gin? Whisky?'

'Whisky, please.'

He summoned a manservant with the wave of a hand. 'A whisky for the Captain.' He turned to me. 'How do you take it?'

'Just a splash of water.'

'And a whisky and soda for me,' said Taggart.

The servant strode off and soon returned with the drinks.

We toasted each other's health.

The whisky was sweet and smooth. Not my usual choice, mainly because I couldn't afford it.

'What news, Sam?' he asked. 'Both the L-G and Section H are straining at the leash for us to hand Sen over. I'm not sure we can hold out much longer. Tell me you've got something out of the bastard so we can get it over with.'

I hesitated. I'd spent the journey from Lal Bazar wrestling with the dilemma of what to tell him, and what I was about to say would probably bring about a swift end to my short time in Calcutta. Maybe that wasn't such a bad thing. I took another sip, then bit the bullet.

'I don't think he killed MacAuley.'

My words hung in the air. I took another sip of whisky, a long one this time. If Taggart was about to kick me out, it would be a shame to let the stuff go to waste.

'What about the attack on the train?'

I shook my head. 'We've got nothing linking him to it.'

Seconds ticked by. In the distance, a green parrot in a pipal tree squawked loudly. Taggart's reply, when it came, was unexpected.

'I thought as much.'

That was it. No anger, no threats, no lecture. Of all possible responses, I'd never considered that Taggart might actually agree with me.

'Sir?' I said. 'You think he might be innocent too?'

'Hardly. He may not have killed MacAuley, but he certainly isn't innocent. And he'll be hanged for his crimes too. It's just that he'll take the blame for this one as well. In any case, the more pressing issue is the attack on the train. If it wasn't Sen and his men, then who?'

I was confused.

'You want me to charge Sen with the attacks even though someone else is probably responsible?'

'I want you to be smart, Sam. Have you actually found any evidence to support the theory that both crimes were committed by the same people?'

I thought about it. There was none. It had been clumsy presumption on my part. I'd assumed a single, monolithic enemy but there was little to justify it. Taggart sensed as much.

'There's nothing to say that the two crimes are linked,' he continued. 'So I want you to charge Sen only with MacAuley's death and hand him over to Section H. Hopefully that'll get them off your back. Tell them you don't think he was responsible for the train attack. Get *them* to hunt for the perpetrators. It's the sort of thing they're good at. Once their attention is elsewhere, I want you to keep investigating MacAuley's death. There's something odd going on there and I want to know what it is.'

'And the fact they'll hang Sen for something he didn't do doesn't bother you?'

Taggart sighed. 'We fight the battles we can win, Sam. I brought you out to Calcutta for a reason. The force is corrupt and it leaks like a bloody sieve. Most of the native men are on the take and half the white officers aren't much better. I need a man I can trust to help me clean things up. A professional, not beholden to anyone. I can't have you becoming a casualty in this whole affair. I need you, Sam.'

It wasn't much of a proposition. Sending an innocent man to the gallows was not what I'd define as a successful outcome, but at this point I had no other option but to accede to Taggart's request. At least it meant I could continue investigating.

'Okay,' I said, fighting down the bile. 'I'll do as you say.'

'Good man. But remember, Sam: Calcutta's a dangerous place. It's not just the terrorists you need to be wary of. There are influential people who'd think nothing of destroying you if they feel you threaten their interests. You'll need my protection to do your job, but I can only protect you so far. That's why you need to tread lightly. You've already made some powerful enemies within the military. Colonel Dawson's after your head. Another stunt like the one you pulled in Kona last night is out of the question.'

'What about my officers? Can I trust Digby?'

Taggart sipped his drink. 'I should think so. There's no love lost between him and Dawson. Back during the war, Digby wrote a report critical of the conduct of a policing action Dawson and his men carried out somewhere up north. Somehow, Section H got hold of it. They even have their spies within the police force. They put the report in front of the L-G. Made a case that it gave succour to the enemy during time of war. The L-G took their side, tore a strip off the previous commissioner, and made sure there was a black mark on Digby's permanent file. It's held back the poor bugger ever since. A man of his experience should have been a DCI by now.'

That was interesting. Maybe it wasn't just his general ill will towards all things Indian that blinded Digby to the possibility of Sen's innocence. Maybe he was scared to cross Section H again? After all, he'd done it once and been hung out to dry. As they say, once bitten, twice shy. There was a lesson in there for me too. As he'd already intimated, Taggart would only fight the battles he could win.

'There's something more you should know about Sen,' I said. 'He claims to have renounced violence.'

'Really?' said Taggart. He was about to take a sip of whisky, but stopped, his glass in mid-air.

'He says he did a lot of thinking while he was in hiding. Came to the conclusion that violent struggle was self-defeating.'

'Do you believe him?'

'He didn't strike me as a man who was lying. He says that's why he came back to Calcutta. Claims he was preaching the gospel of peaceful non-cooperation. Seems to have espoused it with all the zeal of St Paul post Damascus.'

Taggart took a long sip and reflected.

'Do our friends over at Section H know this?'

'I don't think so, but it won't take them long to find out after we hand him over.'

'Now that *is* interesting . . .'

It was half past seven and I was stood under the colonnaded arcade in front of the Great Eastern Hotel, choking on diesel fumes and watching the trams trundle by. I was dressed for dinner. Black tie, tux and a sling. Darkness had descended some time ago but the evening was still uncomfortably sticky. After the meeting with Taggart, I'd returned to the office and sought out Digby. I didn't tell him too much, just that Taggart had ordered Sen be charged and handed over to Section H. I told him to deal with the logistics. He'd looked relieved and assured me it was the right thing to do. I held off telling him that I was going to continue the investigation. After all, tomorrow was Sunday, his day off. Why spoil it? The news could wait till Monday. I could manage without him for twenty-four hours.

Banerjee was a different matter. He was more than happy to give up his Sunday for the cause. No surprise there. Besides, as a Hindu, he'd explained, Sunday held no special meaning for him. I'd agreed to meet him at ten the next morning. We'd sort out Sen and then set off for Dum Dum to track down the Reverend Gunn. But Dum Dum was the last thing on my mind now, as I watched Annie Grant slip between the traffic as she crossed the road. She wore a simple blue dress that came down to her knees and afforded me a view of those calves that I so admired.

The street was busy. Chock full of couples out for a Saturday night on the town. Judging by the red hair and redder faces, a fair few of them might have been from Dundee. Annie stood searching the crowd for me. I waved and she broke into a smile, then noticed my arm in a sling and the smile turned to consternation.

'Sam!' she exclaimed. 'What have you done to yourself? You said on the telephone that you weren't hurt.'

'It's nothing,' I said. 'I was just doing my duty. Besides, someone has to keep the good women of Calcutta safe.'

She kissed me tenderly on the cheek. 'That's just a little thank-you on behalf of the women of Calcutta,' she said, taking my arm and leading me towards the hotel.

Outside the entrance a British constable stood directing traffic.

'Isn't that odd?' I said. 'What's a white officer doing on traffic duty?'

Annie smiled. 'This is the Great Eastern, Sam, the finest hotel this side of Suez. This is where the cream of white society come out to play. It would hardly be proper for them to have to be cautioned by a native when they come out of the hotel roaring drunk now, would it? Just think of the scandal.'

We entered a foyer not much smaller than a cathedral. The room sparkled, decorated with crystal chandeliers and more marble than the Taj Mahal. Annie was right, the cream of Calcutta society had come out to play. Military officers in dress uniform, businessmen, fashionable young ladies in silk and satin. The room buzzed with the sound of conversation as a dozen native hotel staff fluttered around the distinguished guests, like those little fish that tend to sharks. Impeccably turned out in starched white uniforms, they waited discreetly, ready to be summoned to freshen a glass or refill a plate before fading once more into the background. Somewhere close by, a string quartet was playing some Viennese rubbish.

'How about a drink before dinner?' Annie asked.

'Why not?' I said. 'It might help get the taste of petrol out of my throat.'

I followed her down a glittering corridor, past hotel boutiques, a barbers and what looked like the entrance to Harrods department store boxed up, miniaturised and packed off to the tropics. At the end stood a set of swing doors, beside a brass plaque with the legend *Wilson's* affixed on the wall. We entered the bar. Like the Red Elephant, it was dark and subdued like a cellar. In one corner, a native dressed in black tie sat behind a grand piano and played softly. A long bar stretched the length of the room and at the far end stood an emaciated barman in a uniform that looked as though it belonged to someone a few sizes bigger. There weren't many patrons to keep him busy, just a few barflies nursing their drinks. In the shadows of a velvet-lined booth, a young couple whispered sweet nothings to each other. The barman made a show of cleaning a glass with a checked cloth, studiously ignoring us as we approached.

I rapped on the bar top to attract his attention while Annie perched herself on one of the high barstools. The barman kept polishing for a second longer than necessary, then walked over. The brass badge on his shirt read *Aziz*.

'Yes, sir?'

I turned to Annie. 'What'll you have?'

She made a show of examining the long line of bottles that sat on a mirrored shelf. 'Gin sling,' she said finally.

I ordered it and added a Laphroaig for myself.

The barman nodded curtly, poured out my whisky and sullenly set to work on Annie's cocktail.

'A warm welcome,' I said.

'Isn't it just?' she teased. 'I bring all my men friends here. If Aziz likes you, you'll get a second date.'

'I didn't realise he was a friend of yours,' I said. 'Maybe I should buy him a drink too?'

'Not a good idea, Sam. It's against his religion.'

'Odd that he chooses to work in a bar.'

'We all make odd choices sometimes,' she said. 'They tend to be for money.'

Aziz returned with the gin sling, placing it on the counter without a word. I thanked him and he smiled sourly.

Annie and I clinked glasses and moved to one of the empty booths.

'So are you going to tell me what happened?' she asked, pointing to the sling.

'Would you believe I fell off an elephant?'

She pouted, her red lips forming a delicate, exquisite 'O'. 'You poor man,' she said. 'Can't the Imperial Police Force stretch to providing you with a motor car?'

'I'm a new boy,' I replied. 'You need to be a senior before you get those sorts of perks. I was lucky they didn't start me off on a donkey.'

'I don't know,' she said, 'it's less of a fall from a donkey.'

I sipped my whisky.

'Seriously though, Sam,' she continued, 'I heard you were shot.'

'You should see the other chap,' I said. 'He's lying on a slab in the College Street morgue.'

Her eyes opened wide. 'You killed him?'

'No, someone else did. I managed to get through last night without killing anyone. In fact, I didn't even manage to shoot anybody.'

'Well, I'm glad,' she said, putting her hand on mine. 'You don't strike me as the trigger-happy type.'

That much was true. I'd seen more than enough death in my life already. I'd be more than content if I could get through the rest of it without having to shoot anyone else. My throat felt suddenly dry and I downed the rest of the whisky.

'Was anyone else hurt?' she asked. 'What about that English officer you work with?'

'Digby? No, he's fine. Got through it without a scratch. I didn't realise you knew him?'

'I don't,' she said, circling the rim of her glass with a manicured fingernail. 'I just know of him through a friend.'

She finished her drink and we headed to the restaurant for dinner.

The dining room was how the banqueting hall of a sultan's palace might look if it had been designed by a committee of Englishmen. The size of a ballroom, it was finished in white marble and gold leaf and split over two levels: a main floor and a raised terrace, separated by intricate golden railings. Despite its size, the place was packed. The string quartet was playing another Viennese waltz over the general noise. Several heads turned as the maître d' led us towards a table in the middle of the throng. I knew better than to think they were looking at me. The maître d' pulled out the chair for Annie and made a fuss over seating her. She thanked him and buried her head in the menu.

I ordered the wine, a bottle of South African white which I'd developed a taste for during the war. There had been a glut of the stuff at the time and it was often the cheapest you could find. As for food, Annie recommended I try the hilsa fish.

'Bengalis love fish,' she said. 'Hilsa's a local delicacy.'

I declined and ordered the steak. All I wanted was something straightforward with no surprises.

'You're brave,' she said.

I braced myself for bad news.

'You know there's a good chance your steak's going to be buffalo rather than beef? Remember, the cow is holy to Hindus. Most kitchen staff won't touch the stuff, and a lot of restaurants think it's easier just to serve buffalo instead, especially nowadays what with all these cow protection societies springing up all over the place. Still, this is the Great Eastern; perhaps you'll get lucky?' She smiled and suddenly I didn't care if my steak was buffalo or even baboon.

The wine arrived and we drank a toast.

She raised her glass. 'To new beginnings. Speaking of which,' she continued, 'have you found a place to live yet?'

'I haven't had time to think about it. The guest house is comfortable enough for the moment, though the food might kill me. Anyway,' I shrugged, 'I'm not sure it matters where I live.'

'Nonsense,' she said. 'You're not in London now, Sam. Here it's all about prestige. It won't do for an officer of the Imperial Police Force, a *pukka sahib*, to live in a guest house. You need rooms of your own. A nice apartment near Park Street, with servants of course.'

'How many servants?'

'As many as possible. The more the merrier.' She smiled.

'That sounds rather ostentatious.'

'Of course,' she teased. 'That's a good thing.'

'On my salary, I think I might be forced to opt for a rather truncated retinue.'

'That's not the Calcutta attitude, Sam. People here would rather sell their grandmother to the glue factory than part with a single member of the staff. What would people say if they found out Lady So-and-so had to get rid of a maid or two because of budgetary constraints? The scandal would be intolerable. Anyway, that's the thing about India; people are cheaper than animals. You could have a manservant, a cook *and* a maid for less than it would cost you to keep a horse.'

'In that case I'll advertise for all three first thing tomorrow. After all, I wouldn't know where to put a horse in an apartment.'

The evening unfolded as I'd hoped it would. The band played and the wine flowed. We ate and talked: about England, about the war, about India and Indians. During a pause in the conversation, I looked around. An awful lot of pale young women appeared to be sitting at tables with men who looked twice their age. I pointed it out to Annie.

'Those girls are the crew of what we call "the fishing fleet",' she laughed. 'Every year, boat loads of young Englishwomen with skin the colour of turnips arrive in search of husbands. They've been coming out here for years, though there's been a lot more of them since the war.'

'That's understandable,' I said.

'The system works well enough,' she continued, taking a sip. She held on to the wine glass, waving it gently to make her point. 'Something happens to nice English girls when they reach twenty-five. They get scared of being left on the shelf. So they get on a boat and come to India, where there are literally thousands of *sahibs* starved of home comforts who'll marry the first English rose they come across. It doesn't matter how plain or peculiar she might be, if she's got the right pedigree, she'll find a husband out here. It's the men I feel sorry for, the civil servants especially. Poor devils, they're expected to live like monks. You know it's still frowned upon for them to wed before thirty. And marrying a non-white would be career suicide.' Her tone grew harsh, steeled with what seemed the bitterness of a lifetime. The wine had loosened her tongue. 'The odd dalliance can be tolerated,' she continued, 'but marriage?' She waved one finger in the air. 'That's a no no.'

'What was his name?'

She looked at me in surprise. 'Who?'

'You know who.'

'His name's not important. Besides, it's ancient history now.' She took a sip of wine and I let the silence hang. I could see she wanted to unburden herself of the pain she carried, and sometimes the best thing a man can do for a woman is to listen.

'He was a clerk at Writers',' she continued. 'I met him when I was twenty-one. He'd just come out from England. Swept me off my feet. We were together for nearly a year. He promised to marry me.'

'What happened?'

'What always happens. India happened. The empire happened. It changes Englishmen. Stifles them. They come out here, wide eyed and full of good intentions. Soon enough, though, they become cynical and closed minded. They learn from the older hands and start to believe all the nonsense about British superiority and not consorting with racial inferiors. They begin to despise the natives. Anyone non-white is beneath them. The empire destroys good men, Sam.' She took another sip of wine. 'Mark my words, it'll happen to you too.'

'I don't think so,' I said. 'I've had my fill of British superiority.'

She laughed bitterly. 'Let's see how you feel in six months.'

She might have been right. The words had sounded hollow as soon as I'd said them. It was seductively easy to fall into the casual racism upon which the whole place seemed built. I'd done it myself only a few hours earlier. It was insidious. But I could be better than that: I could learn from this woman, this beautiful, intelligent woman, who saw through all the pretence and the hypocrisy.

'I'm serious,' I said, as much to convince myself, as her.

'Of course, Sam. You're not like all the others. *You're* different.' She drained her glass.

What was I supposed to say? Protest that I really *was* different? I feared I mightn't be that different anyway. For want of anything worthwhile to say, I just kept quiet and topped up her glass.

'I'm sorry,' she said. 'You didn't deserve that. It's just that I've seen it happen. Nice middle-class chaps from the Shires, they come out here and the power and the privilege go to their heads. All of a sudden they're being waited on hand and foot and being dressed by a manservant. They start to feel entitled.'

'Maybe I should forget about hiring the staff and just get the horse instead?'

She smiled. A beautiful, disarming smile that made me question how any man could put his career above a woman like her.

'So are you going to tell me what happened yesterday?' she asked.

'Like I said, there's not much to tell. We tracked down a suspect. He resisted arrest. I just did my job.'

'Do you think he killed MacAuley?'

I hesitated, then shook my head. 'I can't say any more, Annie. I wish I could.'

She smiled and brushed my hand gently with her own. 'I'm sorry. That was naughty of me.'

As she spoke, there was a commotion near the front of the room. The general conversation became hushed and eyes turned towards the door. A party of four entered, with the L-G at its head. He was dressed immaculately in black tie and starched white shirt and collar. Behind him trooped a portly gentleman in military uniform, a general, judging by his lapels, and two older ladies. The maître d' rushed over to intercept them. He bowed so low and long that I feared for his ability to get back up. When he did finally surface, he addressed the L-G with animation. From this distance I couldn't hear what was said but the oily smiles and exaggerated gestures suggested he wasn't exactly protesting against government policy.

The maître d' led the party in our direction between the mass of tables. They were heading for an empty table in a far corner, set apart from the others and offering a degree of privacy. They made halting progress, the L-G stopping at several tables as diners stood to greet him. A few quick words here, a handshake there. He spotted Annie, recognised her at once, and made a beeline for our table. We stood to meet him, just as the others at previous tables en route had done.

'Miss Grant,' he said, in that nasal tone that made him sound like an Edinburgh stock broker.

'Your Honour.'

'I just wanted to tell you how appalled I was to hear about what happened to poor MacAuley. Rest assured the perpetrators will face justice very soon.'

'Thank you, Your Honour,' she replied, lowering her gaze. 'That's most reassuring.'

'Tell me, my dear, how are you bearing up?'

She smiled weakly. 'I'm fine, thank you, though it took a little time for the shock to pass.'

'That's the spirit, my dear. Stiff upper lip and all that.'

Annie turned to introduce me. 'This is Captain Sam Wyndham, Your Honour. Recently—'

'Oh, I've already had the pleasure, my dear!' he said, interrupting her. He proffered me a hand. 'My dear boy, you're the hero of the hour. I understand we have you to thank for the apprehension of our old friend Benoy Sen.'

'I can't take the credit, sir,' I replied. 'It was a large operation.'

'Yes, so I hear. Have you got a confession out of him?'

'Not yet.'

He wrinkled his nose. 'Well, I can't say I'm surprised. You must hand him over to military intelligence. They have experience of dealing with customers like Sen.'

I nodded and told him we'd be transferring Sen in the morning.

He looked satisfied. 'In that case, I'll not take up any more of your evening. Miss Grant, Captain Wyndham.'

A curt nod to each of us and he was gone, back en route to his table. I sat down, took a sip of wine and turned to Annie.

'You never told me you were best friends with the L-G,' I said. 'What does Aziz the barman make of him?'

'He's hardly my friend, Sam. I met him a couple of times accompanying MacAuley to Government House. More importantly, is it true? Did you really arrest Benoy Sen?'

I kept quiet and smiled. When a woman's impressed with something she thinks you've done, the best course of action is often just to let her think what she wants and not spoil it with facts.

'That's quite a coup,' she gushed. 'He's been on the run for years.'

'You know I can't talk about the investigation,' I said.

'Oh, come on, Sam. The L-G himself has let the cat out of the bag. You've simply got to tell me now.'

I mulled it over. Drink always weakened my resolve, and I'd already had a skin full. What was the harm in telling her? It would probably be on the front page of the *Statesman* in a few hours anyway. Besides, the boy in me wanted to impress her. I raised one hand in a gesture of surrender.

'Okay,' I said, 'what do you want to know?'

'Everything!' she exclaimed. 'How you tracked him down, how you caught him, what he's like. Everything!'

'It's really not that interesting.'

'Of course it is,' she trilled. 'The gallant Captain Wyndham, in Calcutta for less than a fortnight and he captures one of the most wanted men in the country.'

'Like I told your friend the L-G, it wasn't just me. There were a lot of people involved.'

'But the L-G said you were the hero.'

I shook my head. 'I was just the one who arrested him.'

'And got yourself wounded in the process.'

'This?' I said, pointing to the sling. 'I told you, I got this falling off an elephant.'

I took out my cigarette case and offered her one. She gratefully accepted. I took one for myself and lit us both up.

'So why did he kill MacAuley?' she asked.

'That's just it,' I replied, 'I'm not sure he did.'

'Well, that *is* a surprise,' she said, wide eyed, 'and you didn't think to tell the L-G?'

I shook my head. 'It wouldn't make a difference. They'd still hang him. Sen's just a pawn in a bigger game.'

I could have told her I suspected I was too.

I expected her to be indignant. To ask me why I was letting a man wrongly accused go to the gallows. On some level I *wanted* her to be indignant, to be outraged that I could allow such a thing to happen. I wanted her to hold me to account and play the role my own conscience had abrogated. I was surprised when she said nothing. Surprised and slightly disappointed.

'You shouldn't feel bad about it, Sam,' she said, reading my thoughts. 'From what I hear, that man's a monster. He deserves everything he gets, whether he killed MacAuley or not.'

'I wish it were that simple,' I said.

She thought for a while. 'If you don't think Sen killed him, then who did?'

'I'm going to find out.'

'But if the L-G orders you to charge Sen, won't that mean the case is closed?'

'It won't matter. I'll do my job. Keep investigating. I didn't come to Calcutta to be anyone's lapdog.'

'So why *did* you come here, Sam?'

'To meet you, of course.'

She smiled and I felt like a schoolboy with a crush.

'Have you come to rescue me from this godforsaken place?' she asked. 'Because if you have, I feel I ought to warn you, I don't need rescuing.' She leaned forward and took a drag of her cigarette. 'Maybe you're here because it's *you* who needs rescuing?'

We left around eleven as the Great Eastern was disgorging its revellers. They gathered on the pavement outside, inebriated little groups of boisterous men and giggling women. The ladies of the fishing fleet seemed to have made a good catch.

The white constable was still there, trying to keep a low profile and wearing an expression that said, *Please God, don't let the bastards kick up a scene on my watch*. It was the same look his comrades wore half a world away in Mayfair and Chelsea on a Saturday night. After all, how does a poor working-class copper deal with a drunken mob of his social betters?

Heads turned as Annie and I walked past. I wasn't surprised. She was a beautiful girl, after all. The men stared, drinking her in. It didn't bother me. I've never been the jealous type. Jealousy is just the manifestation of insecurity, and a confident man has no truck with such things. In fact, it gave me an odd satisfaction. It's one of life's pleasures to see men look in envy at the girl on your arm. As they did so, their women cast malicious glances, their faces like sour milk. What were they thinking? Were they scandalised at the sight of a white man with a half-caste? Was it anger at their menfolk for staring at this *chee-chee*? Or were they just jealous? I guessed at a combination of all three and smiled to myself. Those men could keep their purebred English roses. I was more than happy being with Annie.

The night was cool. A pleasant breeze blew in off the river and a yellow moon hung low in the sky. She threaded her arm through mine. Ignoring the line of waiting hackney carriages we started walking, with no real purpose, in the direction of the *Maidan*, the large open space that sits between Fort William and Chowringhee. We passed the gates of Government House with its lion standing atop the archway. It was an odd-looking beast, a touch fat and ponderous with three of its four stumpy legs planted firmly on its plinth. If anything, it looked a bit tired, as though it could do with a sit down after standing up there for so many years. A few lights still blazed from windows in the palace beyond, though whether it was the masters of the Raj burning the midnight oil or simply the servants, I couldn't tell.

Ahead of us, street lamps glowed, stretching like pearls across the desiccated *Maidan*. The musky scent of marigolds wafted over. In the distance, illuminated by a dozen powerful arc lights, sat the vast white bulk of the Victoria Memorial, looking like some monstrous wedding cake that no one had the stomach to eat.

'I like Calcutta at this hour,' she said, 'it's almost beautiful.'

'The City of Palaces. Isn't that what they say?'

She laughed. 'Only people who don't live here. Or the people who actually live in palaces – people like Buchan and the L-G. Mind you, sometimes I don't think I could ever leave Calcutta. And why would I?' She smiled. 'All human life is here.'

'I confess, the place is starting to grow on me,' I said, 'though maybe that's down to the company I'm keeping.'

'Or maybe it's down to all the drink inside you?'

'Unlikely,' I said. 'I drank plenty in London and it never made me feel good about the place.'

She stopped and turned to face me, looking into my eyes as though searching for something. 'You're a curious man, Sam. In spite of everything you've been through, you're still an innocent, aren't you? I think maybe you *have* come to Calcutta to be saved. I—'

Before she could go any further, I held her and kissed her. That first kiss, unfamiliar, exquisite, like the first drops of autumn rain. The smell of her hair. The taste of her mouth.

The alcohol might not have changed my views of Calcutta, but it *had* helped me in other ways. Sometimes it takes a bit of Dutch courage to liberate an Englishman from himself. I looked at her now, seeing her as if for the first time. She took my face in her hands and kissed me back. There was a force to her kiss, an urgency. My breathing slowed. That second kiss was different, more important than the first. It seemed a release for both of us.

I hailed a hackney carriage.

'Where to, *sahib*?'

I looked at Annie. For an instant, I considered ordering the driver to take us to Marcus Square, but immediately my conscience rebelled. Besides, I doubted Miss Grant, for all her cosmopolitan talk, would have agreed any way.

'Bow Barracks,' I said to the driver, as I helped Annie up.

Annie said nothing, she just held my hand and rested her head on my good shoulder. I closed my eyes and breathed in the scent of her. The carriage stopped at the entrance to her lodgings, a flat in a grim, two-storey building, and I helped her out. She looked at me, then kissed me on the cheek and was gone without a word. I was too tired to make sense of any of it. Instead, I got back into the hackney and ordered the driver to take me to the Belvedere.

TWENTY-FOUR

Sunday, 13 April 1919

I awoke at dawn, feeling better than I had in quite a long while. My head was clear, the pain in my arm had dulled and everything had a warm glow. Even the crows outside sounded melodious. Odd how a kiss from a woman can change your perspective.

I lay there for some time, savouring the memory of the previous evening. Then my thoughts turned to Sen and the pleasant feelings evaporated. Twenty-four hours ago I thought I'd caught MacAuley's killer and averted a terrorist campaign. Twenty-four hours ago I was a bloody hero. Most people still thought I was, including the L-G. But life, my life at least, has never been quite so neat. The truth was I'd solved nothing and now time was running out. I had to decide what was more important: saving an innocent man's life or finding the real terrorists.

I got up, bathed, shaved and applied the ointment and dressing to my wound. I considered putting on the sling, but decided against it. The pain had lessened and I had a certain determination in my step. And if at some point that determination began to ebb, there were always the morphine tablets.

———

The dining room was busy with the sound of conversation. The Colonel was up. It was the first time I'd seen him at breakfast. He wore a starched collar and tie, and an irascible expression on his jowls. Across from him sat Mrs Tebbit, dressed in her Sunday best, and between them, Byrne and a young man whom I hadn't seen before.

'Here he is!' cried Mrs Tebbit rather too enthusiastically as I entered the room. 'Our Captain Wyndham!'

Our Captain Wyndham? I thought. Did she plan on adopting me?

'Captain,' she gushed, 'please come and sit, there's space here next to me.'

I did as ordered, taking a seat between her and the door.

'We've been reading about your exploits in the paper this morning,' she said, proudly brandishing a copy of the *Statesman*. The front page headline read:

MACAULEY MURDER: TERRORIST
SEN APPREHENDED

'It's all there,' chimed the Colonel, 'about how you shot and captured that wretched coolie. I dare say you taught him some manners.'

'I didn't shoot anyone, Colonel,' I said tiredly.

'Gave him *what for*, no doubt,' he chuckled. 'I'm sure you only did what you had to, my boy.'

I read the article, which, sure enough, mentioned me by name.

As the maid came over with my breakfast, the residents of the Royal Belvedere continued the inquisition.

'Tell us, Captain,' said Mrs Tebbit, 'has he confessed yet?'

'I can't comment on that, Mrs Tebbit.'

'I'll bet he hasn't,' she continued. 'Those people never do. They don't have the guts to admit their crimes and face justice. I'll bet he's been pleading for mercy. But you must be firm, Captain. Firmness is the only language these people understand. *Give them an inch and they'll take a mile.*' She looked at her husband. 'That's what the Colonel always says, isn't it, dear?'

The old man seemed not to hear a word of it.

I made a start on my omelette. It was cold and rubbery and a vast improvement on previous dishes that had came out the purgatory that was Mrs Tebbit's kitchen. I wolfed it down with the fervour of a Calvinist on Judgement Day and looked across at Byrne. He hadn't said a word since I'd arrived. Maybe he was just struggling with his meal. Or maybe the Tebbits hadn't let him get a word in edgeways.

'Where's Peters?' I asked him.

'Went back to Lucknow yesterday,' he replied, chewing on a mouthful of something. 'His case ended on Friday.' He took a sip of tea. 'So you caught the Ghost, did you, Captain? That's impressive. Sure, he's been on the run for years now.'

'Four years,' chimed Mrs Tebbit. 'Four years he's been on the run and they couldn't catch him. And now, *our* Captain Wyndham arrests him in less than a fortnight. I always said it wouldn't take long for a *real* Englishman to catch him. Ever since they started recruiting natives into senior ranks, the police force has gone to the dogs.'

'Like everything else,' snorted the Colonel.

I finished my breakfast and made my excuses.

'Of course, Captain,' said Mrs Tebbit. 'We quite understand. You have your work to do.' She turned to her husband. 'I can't wait to tell the vicar all about our Captain Wyndham shooting that wretched terrorist.'

Leaving them to their conversation, I made my way out to the street. The air was close. A storm was coming. Salman was sat with the other rickshaw *wallahs* gathered at the corner of the square. I called to him. He spoke briefly to his comrades before picking up his vehicle and heading over.

'Good morning, *sahib*,' he said, looking nervously skywards. He too seemed to have noticed the change in the air. He lowered the rickshaw and touched his forehead with his hand.

I nodded and got on.

'Lal Bazar, *chalo*.'

———

Surrender-not was waiting outside my office. Lost in thought, he leaned against the wall and tapped the floor with his *lathi*.

'Morning, Sergeant,' I said.

He quickly straightened up and saluted.

'Good morning, sir,' he said. He followed me in and hovered next to the door. Another yellow note was waiting on the desk. This time it was from Digby. I sat down and read it. It was dated the previous evening. He'd made arrangements with Section H for Sen's transfer. Their officers would arrive at nine a.m. to take custody of the prisoner. I crushed the note into a ball, threw it at the waste-paper bin and watched as it bounced off the rim and landed on the floor.

'Is everything all right, sir?' asked Surrender-not.

'Everything's fine,' I said. After all, it wasn't unexpected. Section H were always going to get their hands on Sen. But that didn't mean I had to like it. 'Military intelligence will be taking charge of Sen this morning,' I said. 'Let's go and break the news to him.'

We walked down to the basement. Overnight the cells had taken on an international flavour. A motley assortment of foreign sailors had joined the rag-bag of natives, and the stench of vomit and excrement was now all pervasive. The cells were packed. Calcutta is a port city, and that meant sailors on shore leave with nothing better to do than piss away their back pay on drink and whores. Europeans, Africans, even a few Orientals, all lay hung-over on the stone floors.

Sen, though, was a special case. As a political, he had a cell to himself. He lay awake on the plank bed and looked better than he'd done the day before. The colour had returned to his skin. With some difficulty, he dragged himself up onto his elbows.

'Good morning, gentlemen,' he said, a wry smile on his angular face. 'To what do I owe the pleasure?'

'You're to be transferred into the custody of military intelligence this morning,' I said. 'Looks like you'll be getting your wish to see Fort William.'

He accepted the news stoically. 'It is of no great consequence. Am I being charged with the murder of Mr MacAuley?'

'Final charges will be brought once you've been interviewed by Section H, but *yes*, provisionally that is one of the charges.'

He looked me in the eye. 'I understand, Captain.'

I left Banerjee with the guard to prepare Sen for the transfer and went off in search of a cup of coffee.

I didn't find it.

Instead, I was collared by a *peon*. It seemed Dawson and his men had arrived an hour early. Whatever else I felt towards them, I couldn't fault their enthusiasm. I made my way to the lobby where the Colonel was waiting with what appeared to be a whole platoon of gurkhas.

'I see you're not taking any chances,' I said. 'Trust me, he's really not that dangerous, so long as you don't let him make a speech.'

Dawson ignored the remark and handed me some type-written sheets.

'Transfer papers for the prisoner Benoy Sen.'

I made a show of reading every word, not that I doubted they were perfectly in order.

'Fine,' I said eventually. 'He's in the holding cells downstairs.' I called over to a constable and asked him to show Dawson's men the way. 'I'm afraid, though, I'm going to need a few minutes of your time, Colonel.'

'What?' He looked at me as though he suspected me of trying to trick him out of his prize, then gave his men the order to continue without him.

'Well?' he said as the soldiers trooped off.

'That train attack I mentioned the other day. I don't think Sen and his men were responsible.'

'You think it was *dacoits* now?'

'No. I just don't think it was Sen's gang.'

He stared at me, as though sizing me up.

'There's something you should know,' he said. 'There was an attack last night on a branch of the Bengal Burma Bank. Quite sophisticated: the perpetrators kidnapped the manager's wife, then forced him to open up the safe.'

'How much did they get away with?'

'Over two hundred thousand rupees.'

'Enough to fund an arms purchase.'

'And a lot more besides: training, printing presses, recruitment . . . Given the right climate, enough to fund a revolution.'

I swallowed hard as the full weight of his words sunk in. With the funds in their hands, it was only a matter of time before the terrorists would have the weapons to begin their campaign. Our only hope now lay in stopping them before they took delivery. But from the look on Dawson's face it seemed that even the vaunted Section H didn't know where to begin. Without a lead, it would be like looking for shadows in a darkened room.

One thing, however, was clear. It couldn't have been Jugantor. There was no way they could have mounted such an operation the day after their leader had been captured and his closest comrades dispatched.

'Have you any idea who was behind it?' I asked.

Dawson shrugged. 'Anyone from communists to Hindu nationalists. You can take your pick. Rest assured, we'll find out soon enough.'

His tone, though, was ambivalent.

'What can I do to help?' I asked.

The question seemed to hit him in the gut. 'What?' he said disgustedly. 'I'm not telling you this because I want your help, Captain. I'm telling you so that you know not to stick your nose where it's not wanted. This is a military matter. Remember that before you decide to do anything foolish.'

———

Half an hour later, Surrender-not knocked on my door.

'All done?' I asked.

'Yes, sir. They left about five minutes ago.'

'Take a seat, Sergeant.'

I passed him a sheet of paper on which I'd written a number of bullet points.

- MACAULEY
- SEN
- DEVI
- MRS BOSE

- BUCHAN
- STEVENS
- ATTACK ON DARJEELING MAIL
- BENGAL BURMA BANK ROBBERY

'What's the connection?' I asked.

Surrender-not stared hard at the paper then looked up.

'I'm sorry, sir. I can't see any.'

'That's a shame,' I said, 'neither can I. It looks like we're going to have to do this the old-fashioned way. Is the motor car ready?'

'The driver is waiting downstairs.'

'Right,' I said, 'let's get going.'

I rose from the chair, grabbed Digby's jacket and headed for the door.

———

Six miles to the north-west of the city centre lies Dum Dum, a shabby, nondescript suburb in a part of town not short of shabby, nondescript suburbs. It took an hour to make the journey from Lal Bazar, first up to the heaving streets of Shyambazar, then across the canal and along the train tracks at Belgachia, and finally on to the Jessore Road, lined with labourers in loin cloths, digging the new route out to the aerodrome.

The sky looked grim. It reflected my mood. I'd achieved nothing and time was fast running out. The attack on the Bengal Burma Bank suggested a fully-fledged terrorist campaign was imminent. Meanwhile, Sen was in the hands of Section H and MacAuley's killer was still at large. At the same time, I felt strangely empowered. I was conducting the inquiry the way *I* wanted to, not just chasing ghosts, and it was with a sense of anticipation that we approached our destination.

St Andrew's Church was a handsome, whitewashed chapel complete with bell tower and octagonal spire. It sat on one side of a leafy park, not far from the Central Jail. The driver pulled to a stop at the kerbside, attracting the attention of a group of urchins who were playing on the church steps. Their faces lit up at the sight of the car as they abandoned their game and ran over to examine the curious contraption. Leaving the driver to fend for himself, Surrender-not and I headed towards the church.

From inside came the sounds of the Sunday-morning service; English voices busy mangling some poor hymn. I imagined it was the same in every outpost of the empire, from Auckland to Vancouver. Each Sunday, that peculiarly dispiriting sound of piano or pipe-organ accompanying flat, discordant voices murdering the same songs resonated across the world. It was both depressing and oddly reassuring.

We entered through oversized wooden doors and sat in the last row of pews. I tried to remember the last time I'd been in a church other than for a funeral. Probably not since my wedding. Heads turned in our direction, then turned back and continued the business of singing 'Onward Christian Soldiers'.

I took in the surroundings. Scots like their churches austere. Arched windows set in bare walls, a dozen rows of wooden pews on either side of a central aisle. To the left, a small wooden staircase curved up to a raised pulpit in which stood the minister, a bull of a man with a thick neck, ruddy features and iron-grey hair. Above his black cassock, a clerical collar and a pair of starched white preaching tabs.

The music died and the congregation returned to their seats. The minister leaned forward in the pulpit, opened a large Bible which sat on a wooden lectern, and began reading. It was some Old Testament text, the days when God seemed more motivated by revenge than forgiveness. His voice, heavy with a Scots accent, echoed through the room like a thunderstorm.

'. . . *They provoked Him to jealousy with strange gods, with abominations provoked they him to anger.*

'They sacrificed unto devils, not to God . . .'

'Is that our man?' I whispered to Surrender-not.

'I don't know, sir, though the officer at the local *thana* said the minister generally gives the Sunday-morning sermon.'

'. . . *I will heap mischiefs upon them; I will spend mine arrows upon them.*

'They shall be burned with hunger, and devoured with burning heat, and with bitter destruction!'

You had to hand it to the Scots. They did fire and brimstone particularly well. Indeed, many of their clergy seemed fixated by the subject of hell. Maybe it was envy? After all, hell was a lot warmer than Scotland.

He came to the end of the reading and after a theatrical pause, started on his sermon, his voice rumbling like waves crashing on a beach. It grew louder, and if anything, deeper. Stewing in the torrid heat, my mind wandered back to countless other Sunday sermons. I had little time for God these days. If He couldn't be bothered to turn up at my wife's bedside when she needed Him, I didn't see any reason why I should have to turn up at His house every Sunday.

I stopped listening but the gist was clear. We were fallen creatures, saved only from the fires of hell by a merciful God.

There was no breeze from the windows and the congregation wilted in their buttoned-down Sunday best. Finally, the sermon drew to a close and a palpable wave of relief passed over the congregation as the minister called on them to stand in prayer. He ended with a final, 'Go in peace,' as most of his flock turned and headed straight for the exit. He descended from his pulpit to bid them farewell and I waited until the pews had cleared before walking over to him.

'Ah, a new face,' he said as he broke out in a broad smile. 'It's always a pleasure to see new folk in the congregation.'

I introduced myself.

'A pleasure to meet you, laddie,' he said, taking my hand. 'The name's Gunn. I hope ye enjoyed this morning's sermon.'

'It made quite an impression.'

'Good, good,' he mused. 'I expect you've just been posted to Calcutta, Captain. Well, we're a small kirk but I'm sure you'll be very happy here.'

He sensed my confusion.

'The congregation,' he explained. 'It's no' large, but we're very welcoming of newcomers.'

'I'm sorry, Reverend,' I said, 'I'm here on official business.'

'I see,' he said, his expression sobering. 'That's a pity. We can always do with new blood.' He gestured to Surrender-not. 'I don't suppose your native friend there would care to join?'

'I doubt it.'

'Aye, that's generally the case with the natives. It's always the Catholics that get them,' he said ruefully. 'I expect it's the theatricality of Catholicism that appeals to them. That and the incense. How am I supposed to save superstitious heathen souls for the *true* church, armed only with "Amazing Grace" and the King James Bible when the Catholics keep trotting out the bones of St Francis Xavier and new sightings of the Virgin Mary every other week?'

The true church. I wondered whether he meant all protestants or just the Church of Scotland? Judging by his sermon, it was probably the latter. If true, it raised the possibility that ninety-nine per cent of the people in heaven would be Scots. Suddenly hell didn't seem such a bad option.

'If I may, Reverend . . .'

'Oh, I'm sorry, son,' he said. 'Tell me, what can I do for you?'

'We have a few questions we'd like to ask you.'

'Of course. You don't mind if we continue this conversation while we walk? I'm needed at the orphanage in half an hour. It's just down the road.'

I'd no objection.

'I need to help out with the children's tiffin,' he said, striding towards the rear of the churchyard. He led the way across a dusty courtyard and into a small scrubby garden of yellow grass and a few tinder-dry shrubs.

'So how can I help you, Captain?'

'It concerns Mr Alexander MacAuley,' I said. 'I understand he was a friend of yours.'

'That's right,' he said, moving briskly, 'a good friend.'

'When did you see him last?'

'A few weeks ago, I think. Why? Is something wrong?'

'Mr MacAuley was murdered five nights ago.'

Gunn stopped in his tracks.

'I didn't know.' He stared at the ground. 'May the Lord have mercy on his soul.'

TWENTY-FIVE

Orphanages come in many shapes and sizes, all of them grim. This one was a rain-washed and tired-looking building exuding an aura of institutional neglect. It looked like it might once have been painted pink – depressing buildings such as these are often painted in bright colours – but that was a long time ago.

Gunn led the way up a flight of steps and into an unlit hallway. The sound of children's voices emanated from behind closed doors somewhere nearby. Opening a door he ushered us into a tiny office that smelled of mildew and good intentions and afforded a view over the garden. An oversized mahogany cross hung from one wall and dominated a room barely large enough for the desk, chairs and bookcase that had been crammed in.

Gunn threaded his way past the desk to the window beyond. For some moments, he simply stood there staring at the grass.

'Reverend?'

He snapped out of his reverie. 'I'm sorry,' he said, and made to take his seat behind the desk before suddenly stopping short. 'We seem to be one chair short.'

Surrender-not offered to stand, but Gunn would have none of it.

'Nonsense, laddie,' he said with a wave of an arm. 'Either we all sit or none of us do.'

He left the room and returned holding a small battered wooden chair, the kind made for schoolchildren. He placed it on the floor and sat down on it, leaving the full-sized chairs for Banerjee and me. He was a big man and shifted on the tiny seat, reminding me of a circus elephant balancing precariously on top of a brightly coloured ball. The sensible thing would have been to offer the chair to Banerjee, who was only slightly too big for it, but then religious men often have a streak of the martyr in them.

'So how can I help you?' he said eventually.

'How did you come to know Mr MacAuley?' I asked.

'Now *that*, Captain, is a long story.' He steepled his fingers and raised them to his mouth. 'I first met him in Glasgow, it must be about twenty-five years ago now. We were young men then. He was a clerk in one o' the shipping companies. I met him through Isobel, his wife, not that they were married then. She was a friend of mine. A beautiful lassie she was. I'd known her for years.' He paused, smiling to himself. 'I was keen on her mysel' but she never saw me in that light. Aye, she liked them tall did Isobel, and I was wee bit short for her. One day she introduced me to this new beau of hers, a fellow named MacAuley. I don't mind telling ye, at first I thought he was an arse. But as I got to know him, I have to say, I developed a grudging respect for him. He was smart as a whip, and idealistic too.'

'Idealistic?'

Gunn looked wistful.

'Aye,' he said. 'Idealistic, but godless. He'd bang on about the rights of the working classes, and quote Keir Hardie's speeches ver-batim. Glasgow's a radical place and Alec was in his element. As for Isobel, well, she worshipped him. He was tall and not bad lookin', and of course there was that brain of his. And he doted on her. They were married within a year. Isobel fell pregnant soon after and Alec was cock-a-hoop. He didnae earn much in those days, and life was hard for them, but they were happy. The problem was, he'd strayed from the Lord. When it came to his politics, sure he could pack in two or three meetings a week, but he'd no time for Church on a Sunday.

'Worse, he'd openly attack the Kirk, accusing it of being a mere tool to keep the working classes in their place. I warned him to change his ways. As the Good Book says, *For what shall it profit a man, if he shall gain the whole world, and lose his own soul?* I told him that if he carried on like that, the Lord would have His vengeance. And so it turned out.

'About two months before the baby was due, Isobel took ill. The doctor diagnosed typhus but there was nothin' to be done. Both she and the baby died. Alec was devastated. He shut himself off frae the world and things went from bad to worse. He took to the bottle, lost his job and fell behind with the rent. Eventually they kicked him out onto the street.' He stared out of the window. 'The Lord can be furious in His anger.'

From outside came the distant rumble of thunder.

'A storm's comin',' he said. 'Hopefully it'll break this oppressive heat.'

'What happened to MacAuley?'

'Well, Captain, God can also be merciful. I took Alec in. Over time he sobered up, but he became a different man. The deaths of Isobel and the bairn broke his spirit. He'd no more interest in politics – or anything else, for that matter. He'd just sit there brooding. Eventually I told him to leave Scotland for his own good, make a new start somewhere else. At the time, the Indian Civil Service was recruiting bachelors to come out and serve in Bengal. He applied and was taken on. We corresponded for a while but then lost touch. I eventually left Scotland myself, to do the Lord's work among the heathens, first in Natal, and then, six months ago, here.'

'And that's when you contacted him?'

'Almost,' he said. 'When I divined that it was the Lord's will that I come to Bengal, I wrote to a colleague here, a Reverend Mitchell, and asked him to look up my old friend Alec. Well, you can imagine my surprise when he replied telling me Alec was now a *high heid yin* in the ICS. The Lord works in mysterious ways. Anyway, I wrote to Alec, telling him of my arrival, and when I got to Calcutta, he was waiting on the pier-side.'

'How did MacAuley seem when you met him?'

Gunn smiled. 'It felt like old times,' he said. 'We hadn't seen each other in over twenty years but Alec was still a recalcitrant, ungodly old bastard. He offered to help me settle in and find my feet in Calcutta, and seemed put out when I told him Reverend Mitchell had already sorted out my accommodation. I think he wanted to show me what he'd made of his life. The first few weeks after my arrival, he took me round Calcutta, took me to that club of his, introduced me to the great and the good, but . . .' Gunn paused. 'It was all a wee bit hollow. It was difficult watching him toady up to the likes of the Lieutenant Governor. That's one fellow who's going straight to hell, you mark my words. The man acts like he's some modern-day satrap, and he treated Alec like a lackey.'

'What about his friend, James Buchan?'

'That snake?' he snorted. 'He was no friend of Alec's. A man like him doesn't have real friends. He measures folk in terms of what they can do for him. Just simple commodities to be bought and sold, like so much of his jute or rubber. The best that can be said of Mr James Buchan is that he's not particularly prejudiced against the natives. He treats them no more shamefully than he does his workers in Scotland.'

'He told us he was very close to MacAuley,' I said. 'He seemed upset at the news of his death.'

Gunn's face contorted. 'And did you believe him, Captain?' he spat. 'He was no more a friend of Alec's than the wolf is friends wi' the lamb! Both he and the Lieutenant Governor used Alec for their own purposes. Buchan was just a wee bit more pleasant to his face.'

'And what did Buchan use him for?'

He raked the fingers of one hand through his hair. 'That, Captain, is what it took me three months to find out.'

———

Gunn stood up and walked over to the window. Whatever he was about to say, it seemed to have been weighing on his mind for some time. He looked grave, as though about to administer the last rites, or at least he would have done had he been Catholic. He turned and leaned against the window sill.

'Maybe I should start from the beginning,' he sighed. 'As I said, Alec spent a lot of time with me during the fortnight after I arrived, but after that I didnae see him for about a month. I got stuck into my work here and no doubt he was busy too. Then out o' the blue, he turns up at my lodgings one night. He looked a mess, agitated and not making much sense. Kept mumbling something about *them* going too far. He'd been drinkin' pretty hard. Lord knows how he made it here in that state.

'I took him in and tried to calm him down, but he passed out almost at once, so I made up a bed for him. Next morning, once he'd sobered up, I asked him what he'd meant, but he just clammed up. Told me it was all drunken nonsense and to forget it. He was embarrassed by the whole thing. Before he left, I reminded him that I'd been his friend once and was a friend to his wife her whole life. I told him that I was there if he wanted to talk. It may have been underhand of me, bringing up Isobel like that, but it was in a good cause.'

'How did he respond?'

'He didn't. He just looked at me for a moment and then took my hand. About a week later, though, he turned up for the Sunday-morning service and afterwards we went for a walk to the park down the road. He told me he'd been thinking; that there were things he'd done that he wasn't best proud of, things that were an affront to Isobel's memory.

'I didn't press him. I told him I wasnae there to judge him and that he could make things right by Isobel by returning to the Lord and seeking His forgiveness. After that he started coming to church more regularly and I was certainly happy having such a high-profile addition to the congregation. Alec even started helping out here at the orphanage once in a while. All the time, I felt he was building up to something. Then, about a fortnight ago, he finally came out with it.

'It was a Tuesday night. Alec had come over to the orphanage to help wi' the children's dinner. After they'd been fed, we went out tae the veranda for a smoke. He seemed distracted. I remember his hands shaking when he lit his cigarette. I knew he wanted to unburden himself, so I came out and asked him what was troubling him so. And that's when he confessed.'

Gunn paused. He turned his back to us and once again looked out of the window. The first fat drops of rain had begun to fall, pockmarking the dusty garden as they landed. I pressed him, gently.

'What did he tell you?'

'He admitted he'd been procuring whores for that bastard, Buchan. Whenever Buchan needed to grease the wheels of a deal or had clients in town that he wanted to show a good time, he'd have Alec get hold of some high-class native courtesans for the evening.'

'MacAuley was running prostitutes for Buchan?'

Gunn's face turned as dark as the clouds outside. 'I'm afraid so.'
That made no sense to me.

'Why would a man in his position do it? Surely he'd have balked at such a thing?'

'I asked the same question,' said Gunn ruefully. 'He told me it wasnae a new thing. It had been goin' on for many years, from when Alec was a mere clerk. In the beginning he needed the money, and I dare say havin' an ally as powerful as Buchan probably did his career no harm either. It was Buchan's backing that helped him rise so quickly up the ranks. Eventually, Alec felt there was no way out. If he stopped, he'd lose Buchan's patronage. And if he came clean, he had more to lose than Buchan did. Buchan's a millionaire, after all. He could survive the scandal, but Alec would lose everything: his career, his reputation, everything.'

'So what made him decide he'd had enough?'

Gunn held up his hands. 'That I don't know. I got the impression, that first night he turned up drunk, that something had pushed him over the edge. And when he later confessed, I couldn't help but feel there was something else, something darker that he still wasn't telling me. I decided not to push him, hoping he'd confide in me when he felt ready.' Gunn paused. 'Well, that's no' gonnae happen now.'

'Did he say anything else about his relationship with Buchan?' asked Surrender-not.

'Not much. He seemed torn, though. There were obviously things he'd done for Buchan that he regretted. At the same time, he'd walked a long road beside Buchan all these years and he could-nae just cut him off.'

A bell rang in the hallway outside. Gunn checked his watch. The rain was starting to fall heavily now. The metallic smell of freshly moist soil hung in the air and a wild peacock called out forlornly somewhere.

'Gentlemen,' he said, 'I'm afraid I have to help wi' the children's meal. Would you mind if we continued this later?'

For the first time since finding MacAuley's body, I thought I was on to something. I wasn't about to end this conversation until I'd extracted every scrap of information the good reverend had. Indeed, I'd happily help cook the children's lunch if it meant Gunn volunteered anything more of use.

'A few more questions please, Reverend,' I said. 'Your friend's murder is a top priority.'

'Fair enough,' he said. 'I suppose I can give you another ten minutes – for Alec's sake.'

'You said there might be something else weighing on MacAuley's mind? Something he was keeping back?'

He nodded. 'Aye.'

'Any idea what it might have been?'

Gunn swallowed. 'I'm afraid not, but you can bet it's linked to Buchan in some way. Maybe you should ask *him*? All I can tell you is that the Alec MacAuley I found here was a profoundly bitter man. I think he was ashamed of what he'd become.'

'And what was that?' I asked.

Gunn smiled thinly. 'A hypocrite, Captain.'

He let the word hang in the air before continuing. 'Here was a man who'd once worked tirelessly to improve the lot of the poorest in society, and who now owed his position to doing the bidding of rich bloodsuckers. Still, if there's one thing I've learned since arrivin' here, it's that India makes hypocrites of us all. The Lord, in His wisdom, gave us dominion over this land so that we might do His bidding and bring the natives into the true faith; but what have *we* done? We've taken this bounty and used it for our own wicked ends. We've bled dry the land and stuffed our coffers in the process. We've sinned against the Lord, for it's not Him we've served but Mammon, and then we have the gall to lie to ourselves that we are here as protectors and not parasites.'

'You make it sound as if we are irredeemably evil,' I said.

He shook his head. 'No, Captain. If we were irredeemably evil, we'd have no need for the hypocrisy. We wouldn't even bother trying to justify our presence as masters in someone else's house. It's precisely because we seek redemption that we convince ourselves that we're here as benefactors. But the Lord is our salvation, Captain. He has made us redeemable, and our consciences urge us to be on the side of the angels. When we find we're not, we hate ourselves for it.'

He read my expression.

'You don't believe me? Tell me honestly, Captain. Other than the missionaries, how many of your countrymen have you met out here that are actually happy? They curse the natives and the climate and live out gin-soaked days in splendid isolation at their clubs, and why? So that they can live with the conceit that they're here for the good of the natives. It's all a lie, Captain. And it's ourselves we're lying to more than the Indians.' He pointed to Banerjee. 'The educated among them see us for what we are, and, when they seek Home Rule, we pretend we can't understand how they can be so ungrateful.'

The reverend, his face reddening, was straying into matters that I told myself were none of my concern, and which I hadn't the time for. Nevertheless, it struck a chord with something I'd picked up on over the last few days. I thanked him and asked to take our leave.

'Of course,' he said, calming somewhat. 'I hope I've been of some help to you. By the way, has the funeral taken place yet?'

'I'm sorry?'

'Alec's funeral. Has it occurred yet?'

It was a good question. The body should have been released to the next of kin soon after the post-mortem, but that would have been tricky seeing as how the man had none. For all I knew the body was still lying in a drawer at the Medical College morgue.

'If nothing's been arranged,' said Gunn, 'I'd like to organise the funeral.'

I nodded. 'We'll check on the situation and let you know.'

TWENTY-SIX

The rain continued to pour as we drove back towards town. The workmen on the Jessore road had downed tools and were sheltering under makeshift awnings of palm fronds, their excavations reduced to waterlogged pits of thick black mud that brought back memories of France. We headed for Cossipore. Back to Mrs Bose's high-class whore house.

The downpour had choked the sewers and transformed the roads into canals, turning Black Town into a poor-man's Venice, though with fewer gondolas and more drowned rats. The traffic had slowed to a crawl, only the natives didn't seem to mind. If anything, the rain seemed to energise them.

Maniktollah Lane was too narrow for cars, so Banerjee ordered the driver to stop in a street close by.

'We'll have to walk the rest of the way,' he said.

Walking was fine. I was just concerned we might have to swim. Black water reached well past my ankles. My shoes and socks were sodden and my trousers wet to the knees. Beside me, Surrendernot was having a better time of it. He held his shoes and socks in his hand and grinned like a child out for a paddle on Brighton beach. Wet trousers weren't a problem for him on account of the fact that he wasn't wearing any: regulations stipulated that native officers wear shorts rather than trousers, like junior boys at some prep school.

Wading up to the front of number 47, Surrender-not rapped loudly on the rickety wood. Eventually there came the shuffling of the manservant making his way to the door.

'*Kè?*'

'Police!' shouted Surrender-not. '*Dorja kholo!*'

'Wait. Wait,' the old man replied as he unbolted the door. '*Ha?*'

He didn't recognise us, either because his eyes or his brain were cloudy. Surrender-not addressed him roughly. I guessed he was asking to see Mrs Bose.

'Madam *bari-the nei.*'

'He says Madam is out.'

'When will she be back?'

'Madam *kokhon firbè?*' asked the sergeant.

The old man cupped his hand to his ear.

'*Kee?*'

Surrender-not shouted louder and the old man mumbled something in reply.

'He says not till late tonight.'

'What about Devi? Is she here?'

'He says she's out too.'

'Tell him we'll wait inside.'

The message didn't seem to go down well. The old man, still smiling, shook his head vehemently. Surrender-not raised his voice, maybe to intimidate the old man, or maybe just to make himself understood. Either way, the result was underwhelming.

'He says he's been instructed not to let in anyone he doesn't know. I could order him, sir?'

There was no point in that. Mrs Bose wouldn't be predisposed to assist us as it was. Finding us dripping on her drawing-room floor was unlikely to help her mood.

'Leave it,' I said. 'We'll come back later.'

We stepped back into the submerged lane and waded cautiously back towards the car. At the corner, Surrender-not pointed to a native woman approaching down the street. As she came closer, her features became clear. It was Devi. She'd turned one end of her sari into a makeshift bag, which she was using to carry something. She looked carefree, taking no notice of the rain. Then she saw us and her face fell. She stopped, and looked around frantically as though searching for an alternate route, but save for turning around, there was nowhere else for her to go. Before she could act, Surrender-not had set off in her direction. The girl stood there as if caught in a spotlight and waited for him.

———

Soon the three of us were sat in a dimly lit tea stall that opened on to the street. It was raised on stone blocks, just high enough to prevent the water from flooding in. It might even have been effective if the rain wasn't also seeping in through a ceiling that seemed more hole than roof. The place was empty save for the proprietor, a pot-bellied native in a moth-eaten vest and a blue checked *lunghi*, who sat on a stool and stared sullenly out at the rain, probably wondering how long we planned on staying. It was unlikely many other patrons would frequent his establishment while two policemen were in there drinking sweet tea.

We sat on benches around a rough wooden table, on which the girl had placed the vegetables she'd unwrapped from the folds of her sari. Surrender-not was speaking softly to her in her native tongue. Her responses were hesitant. She took a sip of *cha* from the small red clay cup in front of her. The hot tea seemed to help put her at ease. I sat back and let Surrender-not get on with it. Whatever he was saying, it looked to be working and eventually the girl smiled shyly.

Surrender-not broke off and turned towards me. 'She's agreed to answer some questions.'

'Ask her if she saw anything the night MacAuley was killed.'

Surrender-not repeated the question. The girl hesitated, but he pressed her gently. She nodded, stared down at the table and started to answer.

'She was between clients,' said Banerjee. 'She was at the window on her way back from the washroom and saw the whole thing.'

'Ask her what happened.'

'She says she saw MacAuley leave the house. As he turned to go, he was called into the alley by another *sahib*.'

'A white man?'

'Apparently.'

'She's certain?'

He asked her again. 'Yes. She says the *sahib* had been loitering. She thinks he was waiting for MacAuley. They talked for a few minutes then started arguing.'

So MacAuley *had* been in the brothel that night. He'd come out and, according to the girl, met someone who'd been waiting for him and who then killed him. If she was right and it *was* a *sahib*, that would put Sen in the clear, something he was sure to appreciate when they hanged him.

'What did they talk about?'

'She doesn't know. She says they were speaking in the language of the *firangi*. They argued for about five minutes.'

'Then what happened?'

Devi hesitated once again. When she answered, there were tears in her eyes. Banerjee translated as she spoke.

'She says the man who was killed, he made to end the conversation. He pushed away the other man and tried to leave. The other man pulled something from his pocket, she thinks it was a knife, grabbed MacAuley from behind and put it to his throat.'

'She's sure it was a knife?'

Banerjee translated and the girl nodded.

'Where did he get it from?'

'She thinks he pulled it from his coat.'

'Then what happened?'

'MacAuley stopped struggling. The other man released him and he fell to the ground. The man then stood there for some moments then put away the knife, wiped his hands on his trousers and ran off.'

'Ran off?' I asked. 'He didn't stab MacAuley in the chest? What about the note in MacAuley's mouth?'

Surrender-not asked the questions. The girl looked at him blankly, then answered.

'She says she didn't see him write any note or touch the body again. He just ran off.'

'And she's sure about that?'

'Positive,' said Banerjee.

I felt nauseous. It seemed this girl, my last best hope for ever getting to the truth of who killed MacAuley, was flatly contradicting the facts of the murder. I was tempted to hit my head against the wall, but if the roof was anything to go by, the damn thing would probably have collapsed. Instead, I persevered with the questions.

'Ask her if MacAuley was a regular at the brothel.'

The girl shook her head.

'She says she'd only seen him once before, but that she's new to Calcutta. She'd only been here a few weeks when she witnessed MacAuley's murder.'

'What about the killer? Did she get a look at him? Would she recognise him again?'

'She says it was dark. She didn't get much of a look at him, but she got the impression that he was no stranger to MacAuley.'

'Has she told anyone else what she saw?'

The girl looked worried, then replied slowly. Banerjee translated her reply.

'One person.'

'Mrs Bose?'

The girl shook her head.

'One of the other girls?'

She shook her head once more.

'Who then?'

'She won't say.'

'Ask her again.'

Surrender-not pressed her for an answer. Tears began to trickle down her cheeks.

'She won't tell us without first speaking to him. Apparently he's been kind to her.'

'A man? What, the old manservant?' That was great. The person she'd confided in, the only one who could corroborate her story, was half deaf and wholly senile.

'She says it's not him, it was another man who was also in the house when we went round the following morning. She assumed we'd already talked to him as he wasn't in the room when we questioned her and the others.'

'Did he also witness the murder?'

The girl trembled suddenly. She stood up quickly and said something to Banerjee. Before he could stop her, she'd gathered her vegetables, wrapped them in her sari, and run out into the street.

Another of the girls from the brothel was approaching in the distance. Devi wiped her face and walked hurriedly in her direction.

'She said she's been gone too long,' said Banerjee. 'One of the other girls has come to look for her and she's scared to be seen talking to us.'

I sipped cold tea.

'Do you think she's telling the truth?'

'Why would she lie, sir?'

'I don't know, but her story doesn't fit the facts.'

'You mean the stabbing and the threat? She was adamant the killer left no note. I suppose it's possible he went back later and left it.'

'But why? Why take the risk of going back and being caught? And why stab the body after he'd already killed the man?'

Surrender-not shrugged.

None of it made any sense.

'What about this man she confided in? You couldn't get a feel for who she might have meant?'

The sergeant had his hang-dog expression on again. 'I'm sorry, sir,' he replied. 'I should have pressed her harder.'

'Forget it,' I said. 'You did pretty well for a man who can't talk to women.'

───────

A half-hour later, I sent Surrender-not back to number 47 to see if Mrs Bose had returned. He came back shaking his head. We had another cup of tea to raise our spirits and then, in the gathering gloom, headed back to the car to keep a half-hearted watch on Maniktollah Lane. I wasn't sure what I hoped to see, maybe Mrs Bose riding home on a tandem bicycle with the man who was Devi's confidante on the back? Unfortunately Calcutta didn't seem to work that way. Instead, we sat through two hours of nothing before calling it a day. There was still no sign of the elusive Mrs Bose and, other than a dim light at one of the upstairs windows, the house looked dead. Besides, my arm was aching and my feet were sopping wet. Mrs Bose was going to have to wait till tomorrow.

The rain was still pissing down as I gave the order to head back to town.

The driver made for Shyambazar, home apparently to Calcutta's Bengali elite: the Boses, Banerjees, Chatterjees and Chukerbuttys. To British ears, at least, it seemed the higher the caste, the more comical the surname. There was nothing comical about their houses, though, many of which could give the best of White Town a run for their money. The Banerjee house, if indeed you could call a residence four storeys tall and several hundred yards wide a *house*, could hold its own against any of them. Surrender-not seemed embarrassed by the place. In my experience, the very rich and the very poor were often embarrassed by their dwellings. It was probably the only thing they had in common. The sergeant took great pains to explain that it was home to a whole extended family of cousins, aunts and uncles. Still, it hardly fitted my definition of living cheek by jowl.

'You have my sympathies,' I said. 'It must be hell having just the one wing to yourself.'

He smiled, got out of the car and walked to the front gate. A uniformed *durwan* promptly opened it and saluted as Surrender-not disappeared inside, his shoes and socks still in his hand.

———

It was after seven by the time the driver dropped me outside the Belvedere. The rain had stopped and in its wake, a curious chill hung in the air. The square was empty, with even the rickshaw *wallahs* absent from their normal spot. Inside, the lights were on in the parlour, though the door was mercifully closed. My luck held and I made it all the way to my room without anyone accosting me on the stairs and questioning the state of my footwear. Closing the door, I took off my wet clothes, changed for dinner, steeled myself and headed back down.

There was a festive air in the dining room that night, not that it seemed to have improved the food, which was the usual tussle between the bland and the inedible. Mrs Tebbit had ordered the cook to make a roast, it being Sunday, with real beef on account of my heroic actions as reported in the papers. It had the potential to be great, in much the same way that a frog has the potential to be a prince if kissed appropriately. The meat had been cooked to within an inch of its life, then cooked for several inches more and the Yorkshire puddings tasted as though they'd come from Yorkshire, though shipped to India the long way round. At least the wine was good. Better still, there was quite a lot of it. Toasts were drunk, many of them to my heroism and single-handed saving of the empire, and after a couple of bottles, who was I to disabuse them?

Little did I know that a mere twenty-four hours later we'd be toasting another British officer for exactly the same reason, and on just as fraudulent grounds.

After dinner, the party adjourned to the parlour for cigars and brandy. The Colonel held court, recounting tales of the second Afghan War. The way the old man told it, he'd been present at all the key battles, from Ali Masjid in '78 to Kandahar in '80, even turning up at battles when the rest of his regiment were a couple of hundred miles away. You couldn't fault his dedication. Indeed, if he was to be believed, we were damn lucky to have had him on our side.

He did well for a while, then started mixing up his Afghans. Was it Sher Ali Khan or Ayub Khan at the battle of Fatehabad? Mohammed Yakub Khan or Gazi Mohammed Jan Khan at the Siege of Sherpur? The saga tailed off into a confusion of Khans and soon the Colonel was snoring peacefully in his chair.

Mrs Tebbit was busy haranguing the new chap I'd seen at breakfast that morning. His name was Horace Meek, recently arrived from Mandalay, and he'd just committed the capital offence of spilling wine on one of Mrs Tebbit's rugs. When she did eventually notice the Colonel snoozing, she let out a shriek at a pitch most women emit when confronted by a murderer or a mouse, then rose and shooed her husband off to bed. Meek looked shell-shocked and Byrne tried to console him.

'Don't worry, son,' he said, 'she says they're Persian, but sure, I know they're made by a bunch of Biharis in a factory over in Howrah. The closest thing to Persian about them is the old Afghan trader she bought them off at the Hogg Market, and *he's* lived in Bengal his whole life. The old sod can't even speak Pashto.'

Meek, though, was taking no chances. He drained his glass and all but ran off to his room, just in case the lady of the house returned for another piece of him.

That left Byrne and me. On his own he could be pleasant company, at least when you got him away from talk of textiles. His cigar had gone out and I helped relight it from mine.

He seemed in better spirits than when I'd last spoken with him, though that may have been down to the wine.

'So,' I asked, 'how's business?'

'Oh, just grand.' He smiled. 'I should be out of here by Wednesday. Tell me, has your man confessed, yet?'

I decided to indulge him.

'No. Not to MacAuley's murder, at any rate. He's confessed to pretty much everything else, though.'

'Well, isn't that odd? That he should hold out on MacAuley while confessin' to all the other stuff?'

I poured us both another brandy.

'You don't think he might be tellin' the truth, do you? About MacAuley, I mean.'

'I doubt it,' I lied. 'Anyway, he's been transferred to the military. He's their problem now. No doubt they'll get to the truth.'

'Let's hope so,' chimed Byrne. 'So what's he been up to these past four years?'

'Hiding out,' I replied. 'Moving around in the east. By the sounds of it, he's been everywhere from Chittagong to Shilong. Claims he's been studying, that he's turned to the path of non-violence. I will say this for him, he's a fascinating man. I've met fanatics before, but Sen's different. He's calm. Unflappable. As if he's worked out all the answers and knows what has to happen.'

'And what would that be exactly?'

'That he has to die in the service of his cause.'

Byrne smiled. 'Sounds like the lad's got some ticket on himself. He's too intellectual for his own good.'

———

I finished my cigar, made my excuses and headed up to my room. Locking the door, I sat on the bed and contemplated taking a morphine tablet. It was tempting, but first I needed to think. This was no time for drugs. Drink, on the other hand . . . I reached for the whisky bottle on the floor beside me. There wasn't much left. Nevertheless I picked it up and poured out a measure. Taking a sip, I lay back and rested the glass on my chest. I needed to make sense of it all, and whisky generally helped.

If Devi was to be believed, MacAuley hadn't just been passing by Mrs Bose's brothel that night, he'd actually been inside. And by her account, it wasn't the first time either. The Reverend Gunn's statement corroborated that. But whether MacAuley went there for his own ends that night, or for Buchan's, still wasn't clear. What I knew for sure, though, was that MacAuley had gone there after an argument with Buchan at the Bengal Club. If Buchan had sent him to garner whores for his party, why hadn't the girls turned up at the club? Besides, if that had been his reason for going to Maniktollah Lane, surely Devi would have known about it? Wouldn't she have been one of the girls to be sent? That she wasn't suggested MacAuley went there for his own ends. But that would contradict the Reverend Gunn's claim that MacAuley had recently turned over a new leaf. Heading off to a brothel after a party wasn't really typical behaviour for a man who'd just found God.

But that wasn't the only puzzle. There was also the small matter of the killer. Devi thought she saw a *sahib*. That exonerated Sen and drove a coach and horses through my theory that the murder was linked to the attack on the Darjeeling Mail. But why would one white man kill another in the middle of Black Town and just how credible a witness was the young prostitute anyway? If she'd seen the whole thing, why hadn't she mentioned the note? I guessed she might be a fantasist, but then she didn't fit the profile. Fantasists were generally attention seekers. Devi, if anything, was terrified at the very thought of talking to us. For every question answered, another two seemed to rise up to take its place.

I thought back to the conversation with the Reverend Gunn. He'd said there was something else troubling MacAuley, something bigger, something that was connected to Buchan. But what? I felt a headache coming on.

I had only two suspects: Buchan and MacAuley's deputy, Stevens. So far, neither's motive seemed particularly strong. So Buchan used MacAuley to source prostitutes. In my book, keeping that fact concealed was weak grounds for murder, whatever the Reverend Gunn might think.

And as for Stevens, MacAuley's manservant, Sandesh, had said that MacAuley feared Stevens was after his job. According to Annie Grant, the two had argued over import duties on goods from Burma. Stevens had spent time in Rangoon and was presumably well connected there. It was probably nothing, but who knew what passions burned in the hearts of bureaucrats like Stevens? Men were strange creatures, after all. I'd once investigated the case of an accountant who'd murdered his wife of twenty years after becoming infatuated with a teenage shop assistant simply because she'd always smile at him when he entered the shop.

I sighed and took a sip. Things were not much clearer, even with the whisky. My mood was hardly helped by the thought that I'd been wrong about the attack on the Darjeeling Mail. It might not be linked to MacAuley's murder, but it probably *was* linked to the attack on the Bengal Burma Bank. If terrorists *were* behind both raids, they now had the funds they needed for their campaign. All that remained was for them to acquire the arms.

There wasn't much I could do about that. Dawson had warned me off in no uncertain terms. The problem was, once I get a sniff of a case, I find it difficult to keep my nose out of it. And I don't take kindly to threats.

TWENTY-SEVEN

Monday, 14 April 1919

Come the morning, everything changed.

I'd slept well on the back of a whisky and morphine cocktail, which proved an effective remedy for both pain and nightmares. No doubt some enterprising chap, an American most likely, would one day market the combination as a health tonic. To be fair, I'd buy it.

I awoke to silence. No voices from the street, no muezzin's call. Not even the usual chorus from the damn crows. I showered and dressed, avoided the dining room and went straight out into the street. Salman was missing from his usual spot. All of the rickshaw *wallahs* were. That was inconvenient. There was a lot to do and time was running out. Finally I felt like I was on to something. I needed to question Mrs Bose and Devi again and make the trip up to Serampore to confront Buchan. Of course the city also had bigger issues. If I was right, nationalist terrorists now had the funds to bankroll a campaign of violence. They had to be stopped before they could start waging their war. But that was no longer my problem. Not technically, anyway.

With little other option, I chose to walk the mile or so to Lal Bazar, through streets that were oddly quiet. They weren't entirely deserted, though, motor cars still sped to and fro, and the trams were running. There just seemed to be fewer natives than usual. The kiosk on Central Avenue where I sometimes bought coffee was closed and a number of the shops in College Street were still boarded up. I guessed at a public holiday or religious festival. Between them, the Hindus, Buddhists, Sikhs and Mohammedans could be relied upon to have some or other holy day at least once a week.

Lal Bazar, however, was bordering on panic. Officers barked orders to rows of *lathi*-wielding constables and frightened-looking *peons* hurried hither and thither, rushing notes from one desk to another. I ran up to Digby's office.

'What's going on?' I asked.

'Ah, there you are,' he said gravely. He leaned back in his chair. 'We were beginning to worry you'd got caught up in all the excitement outside.'

'Excitement?'

'Heightened state of alert. Seems there was an attempted insurrection yesterday.'

A chill ran down the length of my spine. It seemed the insurgency was already beginning. My worst fears were being realised.

'Where?'

'Amritsar. It's a thousand miles away from here. In the Punjab somewhere. No need to panic, though. The army seems to have nipped it in the bud. Still, Delhi's put the whole province under martial law.'

'Why the alert here?' I asked.

'Bengal's a hotbed of political agitation, old boy,' he replied. 'Rumours spread like wildfire. You can bet those rabble-rousing Congress *wallahs* are spreading tales of British brutality just to get the crowds onto the streets. There are already reports of rioting up near Baranagar. The L-G wants the city locked down, just in case there's any trouble.'

'I should tell you,' I said, 'I spoke to Dawson yesterday. He told me there had been a raid on a bank in town. They got away with over two hundred thousand rupees. He thinks it might be linked to the failed attack on the Darjeeling Mail.'

Digby's face fell. 'That rather complicates things, doesn't it? Maybe it's just as well the army's been called out. The Imperial Police Force really isn't equipped to handle a national uprising.'

That much was true. 'What about Cossipore?' I asked. 'Can we still get up there?'

Digby puffed out his cheeks. 'It's probably not a good idea to go running around right now. We should wait for the situation to stabilise. The L-G's called out the garrison at Fort William and I'm always nervous when there are armed natives on the streets. It doesn't matter if they're wearing our uniforms, they're still bloody Indians. Either deliberately or incompetently, one of them's bound to end up shooting at you.'

I left him and headed for my office. For once there were no notes on the desk, and no Surrender-not waiting at the door. I telephoned the pit. There was no answer. With nothing better to do, I made my way to the communications room on the top floor. The room was our eyes and ears, connecting us through telegraph, telephone and wireless radio to the rest of India and the world beyond.

The room itself was hot and cramped and smelled of burnt electrics. One wall was taken up by a colossal Marconi radio transmission and receiving device, its front a chaos of knobs, valves, gauges and glowing dials. Beside it several desks overflowed with telephones, an electrical telegraph machine and numerous wooden boxes with dials. A confusion of wires and twined cords stretched between the devices and onto the floor like the hanging roots of some monstrous mechanical banyan tree.

Three officers manned the equipment, a young Englishman and two native subordinates. One of the natives wore a large black headset. On the desk in front of him sat a heavy, steel-grey microphone. He furiously scribbled notes, before passing them to his colleague who typed them into official communications reports for the top brass. The place hummed like a well-oiled machine.

I read the raw reports as they came in. Things were still hazy, but a picture was forming. It looked as though Digby was right. Some time the previous afternoon, a detachment of Gurkhas under the command of a Brigadier General named Dyer had opened fire on a revolutionary mob, many thousands strong, at some place called Jallianwala Bagh in Amritsar. The Lieutenant Governor of the Punjab was crediting Dyer with averting an armed insurrection. He'd requested the Viceroy for permission to declare martial law throughout the province, permission that had been swiftly granted.

The more I read, though, the more the picture muddied. The first hint that things might not be quite so cut and dried came with news that the Viceroy had ordered a news blackout. Then came the casualty reports.

Initial estimates spoke of three hundred fatalities and over a thousand wounded, including women and children. In my experience, an armed mob planning insurrection weren't fond of taking their wives and children along to enjoy the spectacle. As for Dyer's Gurkhas, they hadn't suffered a single injury, not even a scratch. Impressive given there were only seventy-five of them facing a hostile enemy numbering in the thousands.

A feeling of dread began to well up in the pit of my stomach. Images of a massacre filled my head. If my fears were justified, it would explain the need for the news blackout. Not that you could keep something like that quiet. Not these days. This was the information age, after all; the same technology that allowed *us* to receive information from a thousand miles away in a matter of hours was also available to the natives. You could keep it out of newspapers and the wireless, but you couldn't stop Indians talking to each other on the telephone, not without paralysing the administration at the same time. It was probably too late, in any case. If the reports of riots in Baranagar were accurate, word had already reached the streets of Calcutta. If it had reached Calcutta, it would have reached Delhi, Bombay, Karachi, Madras and all points in between.

All of a sudden the L-G's decision to call out the army made a lot more sense. If I was correct, a tragedy was unfolding in the Punjab and its ramifications would be felt throughout the subcontinent and maybe beyond. This man Dyer may just have lit the match that would ignite a national revolution that could burn the Raj to the ground, and all of us with it. The problem was there was little I could do about it. Sometimes you just need to hold tight and hope the tide of history doesn't sweep you away.

———

Surrender-not was sat on the *peon*'s stool in the corridor outside my office when I returned. He looked more depressed than usual. I told him to take a seat inside while I fetched Digby. For a moment it looked like he wanted to say something, then thought better of it and morosely went and sat in my office.

Soon all three of us were crammed around my desk, Digby in a state of nervous excitement, Surrender-not looking as though someone had just shot his dog. There was no point in discussing the events in Amritsar or on the streets outside, so I cut to the chase.

'We're going to bring in Mrs Bose and the girl Devi for questioning.'

That wiped the smile off Digby's face.

'What for?' he spluttered.

I told him of the previous day's developments, about the Reverend Gunn's revelation that MacAuley had been providing prostitutes for Buchan and that, before he'd been murdered, he was going to come clean. I also mentioned Devi's account of seeing MacAuley leave the brothel and argue with a white man just before he'd been murdered. I left out my suspicions about the girl's reliability. Digby wasn't exactly convinced.

'Are you seriously suggesting that one of the most senior men in the ICS was running whores for Buchan, and that he was killed because he was going to stop?' he exclaimed. 'What absolute bloody rot. I don't know what hold that blasted native, Sen has over you, but you're clutching at straws.'

He was right. The theory had more holes than one of General Haig's battle plans. We were obviously missing something and I was determined to find out what.

'I know it sounds far-fetched,' I said. 'That's why we need to question Devi and Mrs Bose again. They're the key to this.'

Digby sighed. 'Right,' he said eventually. 'If that's your decision, I'll go and bring them in.'

'We'll all go,' I said firmly.

Surrender-not, who'd sat silently throughout, now decided to speak up. 'Sir,' he said, 'may I speak to you in private? It could take some time.'

'Can't it wait?' I asked. The whole country looked like it might be about to go up in flames and this was the time he needed to have a chat?

He looked green. 'I'm afraid it can't.'

'Look, old boy,' said Digby to me, 'I can go up to Cossipore with a couple of constables while you deal with the sergeant here.'

'Very well.' I nodded.

'I'll get going, then,' said Digby, rising from his chair. He left the room, closing the door behind him. I turned to Banerjee.

'What's on your mind, Sergeant?'

The poor boy fiddled with his pencil. He was sweating and looked like he was about to bring up his breakfast. He swallowed hard.

'I am afraid, sir, that the conduct of His Majesty's troops in enforcing the policing action in the city of Amritsar yesterday, utilising a force entirely disproportionate to the threat facing them or the government of Punjab province, without justification either legal or moral, has—'

I didn't have time for this. 'Look, Surrender-not,' I said, 'just tell me what's bothering you in words of two syllables or less.'

'I'm afraid I must resign, sir.'

He took a crumpled envelope from his pocket and placed it on the desk in front of me. It was damp with perspiration. 'My letter of resignation.'

'Because of what happened in Amritsar yesterday?'

'Yes, sir.'

'You do know that the reports are saying that an armed insurrection was put down?'

'With respect, sir, those reports are . . . erroneous. The stories we are hearing from Indian sources paint quite a different picture.'

'And what do these sources say, exactly?'

He squirmed in his seat. 'They say a peaceful, unarmed crowd was gunned down indiscriminately without warning or chance to disperse.'

'These people know that such gatherings are illegal under the Rowlatt Acts,' I said. 'They shouldn't have been there.'

'Sir,' he began. There was a steel in his voice that I hadn't registered before. 'I do not wish to debate the rights and wrongs of the current system of laws in this country. All I can say is that I no longer feel I can be a part of a system that treats the people of this country – my own people – in such a manner.'

I didn't blame him. In his position I'd have done pretty much the same thing. I might even have been tempted to take the law into my own hands and shoot a couple of my oppressors into the bargain. It was turning into quite a morning: a massacre in the Punjab, riots in Calcutta, and my most competent junior officer threatening to resign. And all before breakfast.

'What are you going to do afterwards?' I asked.

The boy looked surprised. 'I haven't given it much thought.'

That was a good sign. If he hadn't thought it through, there was a chance I might persuade him to reconsider. But sitting on opposite sides of a desk debating the rights and wrongs of British governance in India wasn't going to achieve much. If I was going to convince him to retract his resignation, I had to appeal to him somewhat more subtly.

We were in a coffee house in a lane near Lal Bazar. The place looked like it had seen better days. Then again, any day was probably better than today. It was a native joint, ill-frequented by Europeans, not that it was exactly packed with Indians this morning. In fact, the place was almost deserted and had the despondent air of a funeral parlour after the coffin's left for the cemetery. In one corner hovered a couple of waiters, studiously avoiding eye contact with the few patrons.

We were sat at a small table. One of its legs was shorter than the others, which caused the whole thing to list precariously when disturbed.

Surrender-not took a sip of his coffee and winced.

'Too hot?'

'Too bitter,' he said, adding a heap of sugar.

'You remember the day we met?' I said. 'I asked you why you joined the police force.'

'Yes, sir.'

'You told me it was because one day, you Indians would be in charge of your own affairs and when that day came, you'd need trained detectives, just as you'd need trained judges and army officers and engineers and everything else one needs to run a country.'

'Yes.'

'And what has happened to change your mind?'

Surrender-not spoke softly. 'Until now, I had believed in British justice and sense of fair play. Obviously there are bad Englishmen just as there are bad Indians, nevertheless I always imagined the *system* was fair. It would punish the wrongdoers and afford justice to the victims. I see now that my father was right. When one English woman is attacked, innocent Indian men are forced to crawl on their bellies in front of her. Meanwhile, hundreds if not thousands of unarmed Indians – men, women and children – are massacred, and the perpetrator is treated as a hero. Does British justice mean justice only for the British?'

What was I supposed to say? Tell him it was all lies and propaganda? That such an act would never have been sanctioned by a British officer? I could have said that. Maybe it's what I should have said, but I knew enough of the goings-on in Ireland to realise that, despite what we liked to believe, the British Army wasn't above committing the odd atrocity now and again.

Or I could have told him that *if* such a massacre had been committed, the perpetrator was a mad man and justice would be done. At least that statement had the advantage of being partly true. You probably did have to be mad to give the order to open fire on a crowd of unarmed civilians, but in my experience, madness had never been a barrier to high rank in the army, much less so now, after a war that had made madmen out of a great many. I expected Dyer was probably one of them. He wouldn't have seen the crowd of Indians as people, just as a problem to be solved.

As for justice, the truth was that whatever had happened would officially be swept under the carpet for a very long time. Byrne had been right. Our rule depended on us showing ourselves to be morally superior to those whom we ruled. You couldn't really do that if you admitted to shooting hundreds of women and children.

But I wasn't about to lie to the sergeant. He deserved better than that.

We both did.

The problem was, my investigation was heading the way of the *Lusitania* and I needed the young sergeant's help if I was ever going to right the ship.

'What's happened in Amritsar,' I said, '*if* it's happened as you say, is, I admit, a crime. But you resigning won't bring justice for those killed. If you stay, however, we can try to make a difference for at least one Indian.'

'You mean Sen?' He laughed bitterly and took a sip of coffee. 'He's already beyond help. They're going to hang him no matter what we do.'

'And your conscience could live with that? Knowing you'd given up on a man you knew to be innocent, just to protest something you can do nothing about?'

He said nothing, so I pressed the advantage.

'Sen doesn't have long left. A few days at most. You were the one who first suggested he might be innocent. If you still believe it, you owe it to him to keep investigating.'

The boy was wavering. I could see it in his eyes. It was time to offer him a compromise. 'I need your help, Surrender-not. I can't do this alone, and Digby would like nothing better than to see Sen hanged. After all, he'll get a bloody promotion out of it. All I'm asking is that you hold off on any decision till we've got to the bottom of this case.'

He drained his coffee cup.

'Very well,' he said finally, 'I shall defer my decision until this case has come to a conclusion.'

'That's the spirit,' I said emphatically.

He smiled. 'Besides you're right, my conscience wouldn't allow me to quit now.'

'Good man,' I said. 'I'm sure Sen would appreciate your commitment.'

'I'm not talking about Sen, sir,' he replied. 'I mean, I can hardly quit when there's a chance Sub-inspector Digby might get promoted and possibly become your superior officer . . . sir.'

———

We walked back to Lal Bazar amidst a frenzy of activity. Olive-green lorries loaded with soldiers sped past heading north, black smoke belching from their exhausts. Sepoys were moving into position around Dalhousie Square. Under the direction of a young British officer they were busy setting up checkpoints and laying sandbags around the entrances to Writers' Building, the post office and the telephone exchange.

Lal Bazar itself was practically deserted. Most of the uniformed officers and men had been dispatched to potential trouble spots and the administrative staff and the *peons* were the only ones left. Them and the detectives, of course. They'd only get involved after the balloon went up and people started dying. I left Surrender-not in my office and headed for the radio room. I wanted an update on the latest developments but, given his state of mind, taking the sergeant along didn't seem like a good idea. He was still wavering and the last thing I needed was him seeing unexpurgated reports of what was unfolding across the country and deciding to resign again.

As it happened, I didn't need to read the latest dispatches to know things were worsening. Just looking out the windows on the third floor was enough. To the north and east, thick plumes of black smoke were rising, darkening the sky like fat monsoon rain clouds.

It was almost midday now. The radio room was a furnace stoked by heat from the electrical devices. The shift had changed, the white officer and two native constables from earlier replaced by an identical team: another two natives and their white overseer. I read some of the more recent reports. Trouble was brewing in most of the major cities. From Delhi came confusion, the military authorities doubling down, praising Dyer as the saviour of the empire, the civilian authorities rather less vociferous. Mixed messages and the first hint of panic. From the Punjab, nothing. As if the province had simply disappeared.

I was halfway through a report on the situation in Bombay when Surrender-not burst into the room. He was panting. A trickle of perspiration ran down the side of his face.

'A message from Cossipore *thana*,' he gasped, 'from Sub-inspector Digby. It's bad news.'

TWENTY-EIGHT

The Wolseley wasn't in the vehicle compound. Neither was anything else. All of the Imperial Police's meagre stock of motorised vehicles had been dispatched to trouble spots around the city. There were a few horses left in the stables and I suggested we commandeer two. Surrender-not looked as though I'd just asked him to wrestle a bear.

'It's a trained police horse,' I said, 'not a wild bull.'

'It's not the horse's competence I'm questioning, sir,' he replied. 'I don't think the gods ever intended for Bengalis to ride horses.'

I could have ordered him to mount up, but there was no point. He might break his neck trying, or worse try to resign again.

'Have you got a better idea?' I asked.

It turned out he had, and ten minutes later we were on our way to Cossipore having hitched a lift on one of the military trucks heading north.

The lorry dropped us at Cossipore *thana*, from where we walked, down deserted streets, past houses with shuttered windows and boarded doors. A uniformed constable, armed with a *lathi*, stood at the entrance to number 47 Maniktollah Lane. On the step next to him sat the old manservant, Ratan. He was dressed, as always, in a *dhoti* and vest and was busy haranguing the constable about something. A stream of invective flowed from his gums, then suddenly dried up as though he'd lost his train of thought. Not that it seemed to matter much to the constable, who did a pretty good imitation of one of the sentries outside Buckingham Palace, standing ramrod straight and studiously ignoring him.

The interior echoed to the sound of officious voices. In a room at the end of the corridor, someone was barking orders. A native constable was stood at the foot of the stairs and snapped to attention as we entered. I asked to see Digby.

'Sub-inspector *sahib* upstairs,' he said, gesticulating with one raised finger.

Digby was on the first-floor landing, talking at a native constable.

'Ah, there you are, old boy,' he said. 'You'd better come through.'

He led the way down a corridor and stopped outside a room at the far end where another constable stood guard. Digby made a sweeping gesture with his arm.

'After you.'

The room was narrow and nondescript. Sparsely furnished – a bed and not much else, that is other than the body hanging from the ceiling. That would have been hard to miss even if there had been more furniture. It was the body of a girl, suspended from a cord attached to a hook on the ceiling. On the floor a few feet beneath her, an upturned chair. Her head was bent awkwardly to the side like a doll with its neck snapped, her features obscured by a mass of dishevelled black hair, but I didn't need to see the face to know who it was. She was wearing the same pastel-coloured sari she'd had on yesterday.

I touched her hand. The flesh was clammy. No sign yet of rigor.

'What do we know?' I asked Digby.

'Looks like suicide. She was dead when we got here. It's unclear exactly how long.'

'Who found her?'

'The maid,' he said. 'The lady of the house sent her to fetch the girl.'

'When exactly?'

'Just after we got here. Around eleven.'

'No one checked on her before eleven o'clock?'

'Working girls,' said Digby. 'It's not unusual for them to sleep late.'

'Where's Mrs Bose?'

'Downstairs. We've detained her in the drawing room.'

I nodded, then pointed to Devi's body. 'Get someone in here to cut her down, then organise transport to the morgue.'

Digby saluted and left the room. I took a closer look at the body hanging limp, then at the chair lying on the floor. There was something odd about it. I turned to Surrender-not. He too was staring intently up at the corpse.

'What do you see, Sergeant?' I asked.

He looked shaken. 'I'm not sure, sir,' he said. 'I've never seen a suicide before. It's not what I expected. It reminds me of an execution I once witnessed at Central Jail. That was a proper gallows hanging, though. They even weighted the body. His head almost came clean off when he dropped.'

He was right. It did look like a prison hanging. The problem was, it shouldn't have.

'I want a post-mortem carried out as soon as possible,' I said. 'Threaten the pathologist if you have to. I want to know the exact cause of death.'

'Yes, sir,' he said, turning to leave.

'One other thing,' I said. 'We need to find the man Devi confided in. With her dead, he could be our last hope of getting to the bottom of this. I want you to search every room. Make sure we haven't missed anyone.'

With that, I made my way downstairs. The drawing room was stuffy. Stiflingly hot. Mrs Bose was seated on the chaise longue, like a *maharani* holding court. Her maid and the other three girls stood close by. She looked up as I entered the room.

'Captain Wyndham,' she said, 'I wish I could say it is a pleasure to see you again, but under the circumstances . . .'

Her tone was measured. If she was distressed at the death of one of her girls, she betrayed no sign of it.

'You will forgive me,' she continued, 'if you find me a less than gracious hostess but it is hard to be hospitable when one is under arrest.'

'You're not under arrest, Mrs Bose,' I said. 'Not yet, anyway. We simply want you to come to Lal Bazar and answer some questions. Unfortunately, things seem to have been complicated somewhat by the tragedy upstairs.'

She remained silent.

'You wouldn't care to tell me what happened exactly?'

Mrs Bose smiled. 'I was hoping, Captain, that *you* might tell me. After all, I believe it was you she spoke to yesterday. What did you say to an impressionable young girl that would cause her to take her own life soon after? And what am I to tell her family?'

'She told you we spoke yesterday?'

'Oh, yes,' said Mrs Bose emphatically. She raised one bangled arm and moved a stray strand of hair from her face. 'My girls keep no secrets from me.'

'We'll continue this at Lal Bazar,' I said, and ordered Digby to take Mrs Bose into custody.

———

I walked out to the front of the building and lit a cigarette. The old man, Ratan was now sat quietly in the shade on the other side of the alley. He looked like he might be asleep. A small crowd had gathered, drawn by the sight of policemen like flies to shit. I scanned the faces in the crowd. The usual mix of loafers, gawkers and gossipers. One or two looked familiar. They'd probably been in the crowd the morning we found MacAuley. Surrender-not came out to join me and I offered him a cigarette.

'Any joy?'

'No, sir. Other than those in the drawing room, the whole house is empty. It looks as though we're back to square one.'

He lit the cigarette and took a despondent drag.

'Not quite,' I said. 'At least we know MacAuley was running girls for Buchan, that he was inside the brothel the night he was murdered and that he'd argued with Buchan earlier that night.'

'There's also the possibility,' said Banerjee, 'that the killer was white and that MacAuley knew him.'

I had to admit, Devi's death raised the question of whether she might actually have been telling the truth when she spoke to us the day before. The way forward lay through Mrs Bose. She knew far more than she was telling us, but I was under no illusions that getting the truth out of her would be one hell of a job. I finished my cigarette and flicked the butt into the open gutter.

TWENTY-NINE

We were back at Lal Bazar, in the same cramped room where we'd questioned Sen. This time it was Mrs Bose who sat opposite us. As usual the room was too hot. The ceiling fan wheezed around slowly for a few minutes, then spluttered and died. Beside me, Digby was sweating like a miner. Not that I was exactly fragrant myself. I could have done with a hit of O or better still, a morphine tablet, but they were long gone, though for some reason I'd kept the empty bottle in my pocket like a talisman. Surrender-not sat fanning himself with the pad he should have been using to take notes. I'd have admonished him, but the breeze was welcome. The only one who didn't seem affected was Mrs Bose who looked like she'd just arrived from taking tea with the Viceroy.

'Tell me what happened to Devi,' I asked.

'You don't mind if I trouble you for a glass of water first, do you, Captain? My throat is rather dry and if you're planning on asking me many questions, it may prove to be an inconvenience later.'

I nodded to Banerjee who stepped out and returned carrying a jug and glasses. He poured for Mrs Bose who thanked him, lifted it delicately to her lips and took the smallest of sips.

I asked her about Devi again.

'What can I tell you?' She shrugged. 'I returned home rather late last night. By the time I got back, Devi and the other girls were busy with clients. I expect she finished at around three or four in the morning. She would then have washed and eaten something before retiring to her bed.'

'Is it usual for you to go to bed while your girls are still working?'

'It happens from time to time. Especially if I've been out late. In those instances, my maid Meena oversees things. She wakes me if there is anything that needs my attention.'

'And where were you yesterday?'

Mrs Bose smiled. She clasped her hands together, then placed them on the battered metal table in front of her.

'Some of my older, long-standing clients are rather set in their ways. They sometimes prefer a personal service.'

'So you do house calls?' I asked.

'For certain clients. But don't we all bend the rules if the price is right, Captain?'

I ignored the question.

'Did anyone else see Devi before she went to bed last night?'

'I believe Saraswati saw her before she retired to her room.'

'Do all your girls have their own bedrooms? Isn't that a bit extravagant?'

She smiled. 'Obviously I can't vouch for the sort of places you are used to, Captain, but I run an exclusive establishment for a select clientele of Calcutta's finest gentlemen. My girls are the best, and they get the best. Let's just say the economics are slightly different from any old two-rupee whore house. I can afford the extra overhead.'

'Your girls are the best and they get the best?' I repeated. 'Any idea, then, why Devi would want to hang herself?'

Mrs Bose winced.

'As I told you, she seemed perfectly fine when I last saw her. But that was before she spoke to you.'

'Do you think her death might be linked in some way to MacAuley's murder?'

'I don't see how.' She shrugged again.

'So you think it's all just a coincidence?'

'I don't know what to think, Captain. Maybe she killed herself because of something you said to her?'

'I can assure you,' I retorted, 'what she said to me was far more interesting than anything I might have said to her.' I was hoping for some sort of reaction but she just sat there like some stone goddess.

I continued: 'Would you care to guess what she told us?'

Mrs Bose picked up the glass and took another sip of water. 'Given the unfortunate circumstances I find your little guessing game rather distasteful, Captain. Why don't you just tell me?'

'She told us MacAuley had been in your little brothel the night he was killed. In fact, he was murdered almost immediately after leaving it. Now is that true or was the poor girl lying?'

'It's true that the gentleman had been on the premises earlier.'

'And you didn't see fit to tell us that?'

She smiled coyly. 'As you will appreciate, Captain, my clients value their privacy. As the gentleman was not murdered in my house or on my property, I saw no need to sully his reputation.'

'You know it's a criminal offence to withhold information from the police?'

Mrs Bose sighed. 'I lose track of exactly what is and isn't illegal for Indians these days. From what we are hearing from the Punjab, it seems even peaceful gatherings are now a capital offence.'

'What exactly was MacAuley doing at your establishment last Tuesday night?' I asked.

'Oh, the usual, I expect. He was quite orthodox in terms of what he liked. No peccadilloes, no imagination; but in my experience that's quite normal for a Scotsman. At first I thought it may be due to the climate of their native land, which I understand is rather unpleasant for ten months of the year and downright inhospitable for the other two, but over the years I have come to the conclusion that it is down to that fundamentalist religion of theirs, which I believe considers almost everything enjoyable to be a sin.'

'So he wasn't there to procure girls for one of Mr Buchan's parties?'

She shook her head. 'I can assure you he was not.'

'Did he ever do so?'

She gave a derisive laugh. 'You don't really expect me to divulge that sort of information, do you?'

I could feel myself beginning to lose my temper. I felt as though I was banging my head against a wall. The heat wasn't helping. Neither was my need for a fix.

'Do I need to remind you that this is a murder inquiry? A *sahib* has been killed yards from your front door and one of your own girls is now dead. I can make things very unpleasant for you if you aren't a little more cooperative.'

'As you say, Captain, the man was killed *outside* of my premises, not in them. And as for Devi, you of all people don't need to remind me of the poor girl's fate.'

I had to admit, the woman had spirit. Under different circumstances I might have liked her, a lot. As it was, though, she was hampering a murder investigation and that rather soured things. It was time to show her I could be difficult too. Maybe a night in the cells would change her attitude.

'We'll continue this tomorrow,' I said. 'Hopefully you'll be feeling a little more cooperative then. If not, charges of obstructing a police investigation, and maybe others, will be laid against you.'

Digby led Mrs Bose off to a cell. I was on my way back to my office when Surrender-not pulled me to one side. He looked troubled.

'What is it, Sergeant?' I asked.

'There's one thing I don't understand sir. Mrs Bose knew that we'd talked to Devi yesterday. Back at the house she said that Devi told her personally. But now she says she never saw Devi after returning from her house call to her client. I'm wondering, then, how she could have known.'

The sergeant was right. The woman was lying to us.

'Would you like to recommence the interview?' he asked.

I thought about it and decided against. She'd only clam up, and time was fast running out.

'No,' I said. 'Let's keep that up our sleeve for now.'

THIRTY

There was a note on my desk. A summons to Lord Taggart's office. I made my way up there, and his secretary Daniels hurried me to a chair in the anteroom.

'His Lordship is being briefed on the situation in Black Town. He should be free shortly.'

The telephone on his desk buzzed and he picked up the receiver and listened with his eyes closed. I studied him more closely: dirty spectacles; lank, greasy hair plastered onto his skull. It looked like he hadn't slept for a week. The caller did most of the talking. Daniels tried to interject once or twice, but the voice on the other end cut him off. Finally, Daniels sighed and launched into a monologue of his own.

'I'm sorry,' he said, 'it's impossible. Even if we had any men left, which we don't, we couldn't dispatch them to South Calcutta. Not while Black Town is going up in flames.'

The door to Taggart's office burst open and several uniformed officers, military types by the look of them, strode out. Ignoring Daniels and me, they headed for the corridor. Without waiting for Daniels to finish his call, I put my head round the door. The Commissioner was standing behind his desk, poring over a map laid out in front of him. I coughed and he looked up.

'Come in, Sam,' he said. 'I hope you've got good news. It's been a rather trying day so far.'

The death of my only witness could hardly be described as good news, so it seemed better to change the subject.

'How bad are things up in Black Town?' I asked as I walked over. 'Any truth to what the natives are saying?'

Taggart looked up. 'What do you know about what the natives are saying?'

'One of my Indian officers threatened to resign earlier. I talked him out of it but he was quite upset. Claims what happened in the Punjab was a massacre.'

Taggart's face hardened. 'He may be right. Some damn fool of a general thought he could persuade a crowd of civilians to disperse by shooting at them in an enclosed space. The military are trying to put a gloss on it, but the truth is the whole thing's a bloody disaster. The imbecile thought a show of force would teach the natives a lesson. All he's done is throw the whole country into turmoil. Mark my words, thanks to that idiot, every white man and woman in India may soon be a target for revenge. And as for our dear city, I don't need to tell you how much of a tinderbox it is. This could be just the excuse the terrorists have been waiting for. We'll be extremely lucky if we can get through this without further bloodshed.'

'There's more bad news on that front,' I said, before repeating what Dawson had told me of the raid on the Bengal Burma Bank. 'Whoever it was got away with over two hundred thousand rupees.'

He looked grave. 'I see what you mean.'

He picked up the map, folded it in half and placed it to one side as he took his seat behind the desk.

'The reason I called you up here,' he said, 'is to see if you've made any progress on the MacAuley case.'

I apprised him of developments: the meeting with Reverend Gunn, MacAuley's sourcing of prostitutes for Buchan, and the Reverend's view that MacAuley had a darker secret which had pushed him over the edge. I told him of Devi's account that MacAuley had been in the brothel minutes before his murder and that she believed the killer was a white man. The good news, if it could be called that, was that I was now convinced of Sen's innocence and that there was no real link between MacAuley's death and the attack on the Darjeeling Mail. The other side of that coin, though, was that Section H, despite tracking down Sen in record time, didn't seem to have the first clue as to who might be behind the train attack or this latest attack on the bank.

'There's been a development on the Sen front,' said Taggart. 'His trial took place *in camera* this morning. He's to be hanged. The sentence is to be carried out the day after tomorrow at dawn.'

'That was fast,' I said. 'With half of Calcutta burning and a terrorist cell on the loose, I'd have thought Section H would have more pressing matters to attend to than staging some sham of a trial.'

'Yes, well,' he said, 'facts are facts. If you are going to get to the bottom of this, I suggest you do it quickly. Once Sen's executed I won't be able to justify any further investigation.'

'In that case, I'd like to pay Sen a visit. Can you get me permission?'

Taggart thought for a moment, then nodded. 'He's being held at Fort William until his execution. I'll have Daniels type up a note authorising your access to the prisoner. Use what time you have left wisely, Sam,' he said, rising from his seat. 'I think you're on to something but time's running out. Whatever you plan on doing, do it soon.'

———

324

Surrender-not and I followed several paces behind a stone-faced sepoy, along a corridor deep underneath Fort William. Footsteps echoed on the cobbled floor and across dank walls. To one side, iron doors barred the entrance to small cells. The place felt like a dungeon, the air was cool and damp but with none of the stench of vomit and urine that hangs over most holding cell blocks. On the contrary, this one smelled of disinfectant, as though it was regularly scrubbed clean. That was interesting. No one cleans a cell block so clinically unless they've something to hide.

Sen's cell was little more than an alcove built into one wall. He lay on a stone shelf which passed for a cot, and looked over as the guard unlocked the cell door, before slowly sitting up. His face was bruised, one eye swollen shut.

'Captain Wyndham,' he said, 'it seems you were right about the accommodation at Fort William. It's not quite five star.'

'From the look of you, it seems you've had a bit of a disagreement with the management.'

He laughed awkwardly. 'Still, I shouldn't be staying much longer.'

'I heard about the trial,' I said.

'Yes, it was all very . . . *efficient*. Done and dusted in a matter of minutes. Somehow I expected the wheels of justice to turn a little more sedately. Such haste appears somewhat unseemly, don't you think?'

'Did you have counsel?'

Sen smiled through a burst lip. 'Oh yes, a court-appointed chap. An Englishman. A nice fellow but he seemed rather unfamiliar with the basics of mounting a defence. At one point I feared he might apologise to the court for wasting its time. Not that there was much he could have done. I don't suppose the best barrister in India would have fared any better given the system of justice that operates in this country. You wouldn't happen to have a cigarette, would you?' He pointed to the sepoy who stood stern-faced at the cell door. 'These military *wallahs* haven't given me a single one.'

I fished out a crumpled packet of Capstans and handed it to him.

'Thank you,' he said, extracting one of the remaining cigarettes. 'I appreciate the gesture. I just hope these gentlemen's generosity will extend to offering me a light once you've gone.'

I lit a match and held it out for him. The flame illuminated the bruising and blood encrusted on Sen's lip.

'What happened to your face?' I asked.

'This?' he said, pointing to his closed eye. 'Your friends here were rather keen that I sign a confession.'

'Did you?'

Sen shook his head. 'No. They gave up after about an hour. To be honest, I think they were rather half-hearted about it. I suppose in the end they felt they didn't really need one. Seems they were right.'

'I've got some bad news,' I said. 'Your execution's been scheduled for six o'clock on Wednesday morning.' I watched as he took in the information. 'I suggest you get your counsel to lodge an appeal.'

'A wonderful idea, Captain,' Sen replied, 'assuming I had any ability to contact him.'

'You could seek alternative counsel?' Surrender-not suddenly interjected. 'An Indian maybe? There must be a dozen top barristers who'd jump at the chance of representing you, especially after yesterday's developments.'

Sen stared at him quizzically. It appeared the cells at Fort William were one place the government's news blackout had worked. I recounted the events in Amritsar to him, a sanitised version at any rate, though not as whitewashed as the official version. That seemed pointless with Surrender-not in the room.

'Unarmed civilians?' he asked.

'Possibly.'

'And the reaction?'

'There are reports of rioting from across the country. It doesn't look like your hopes for non-violent protest are going to be realised any time soon.'

He shook his head. 'A tragedy, Captain. For my people and yours. However, all it does is redouble the need for non-violence. The actions of this General Dyer are an act of weakness, motivated by fear. We must show him, and others like him, that they have nothing to fear from change.'

There was silence for a minute as Sen sucked on his cigarette.

'There's something else I need to ask you,' I said.

'Yes?'

'There was an attack on a bank on Saturday night. I suspect it's linked to the attack on the Darjeeling Mail. I think the perpetrators were looking for funds to buy arms and finance a terrorist campaign. With what's happened in Amritsar, an attack now could spiral into something uncontrollable and engulf the whole country. Thousands of innocents could die. If you truly believe what you say about non-violence, you need to tell me anything you know about who may be behind it, if not for me, then for the sake of your own conscience.'

Sen gave a short laugh.

'My conscience? Are you a priest come to give absolution for my sins, Captain? You forget, I'm not a Christian. My sins are part of my *karma*, and the law of *karma* does not allow for the possibility of forgiveness. Its consequences are inescapable.'

'I only meant that you might wish to tell me something that may help avert a potential bloodbath. Maybe the names of individuals who are still involved in the violent struggle?'

Sen shook his head. 'I'm sorry, Captain. I cannot do that. Maybe if I could be assured that they would receive a fair trial but under the circumstances . . .' He held a hand up to his bruised face. 'We both know that would be impossible. Anything I told you would simply lead to their execution. I cannot allow that to happen to former comrades just because I no longer agree with their methods.'

'What about foreigners?' I asked. 'Men who foment such violence for their own political ends?'

He looked at me like a professor lecturing a student. 'In my time, Captain, I have been accused by your press of being in the pay of whoever happens to be the foreign bogeyman of the day, everyone from the Kaiser to the Bolsheviks. I can tell you that neither I nor any other Indian patriot has ever acted in the interests of any nation other than Mother India. We may have taken assistance from outsiders, but we have never followed their agenda. I doubt you would act any differently if you were in our position. After all, don't you English say, *My enemy's enemy is my friend?*'

With that, he gave a mischievous smile and held out his hand. The meeting was over. He was reconciled to his fate. In truth, I suspected he was secretly happy with a martyr's death. It fitted nicely with what I was beginning to understand of the Bengali psyche. For him, there could be no finer outcome to a life of struggle against injustice, both real and imagined, than a pointless but glorious martyrdom. A death that might inspire others to take up the cause.

I took his hand and shook it.

The journey back to Lal Bazar was quick. We hitched another lift courtesy of the army, this time in a staff car. The roads were surprisingly quiet, and you might have been forgiven for thinking it was a Sunday. At least you would have if it wasn't for the sandbags and heavily armed troops at every street corner.

Surrender-not and I didn't speak much on the way. Too many things were troubling me, and the sergeant was hardly one for conversation at the best of times.

'We need to see Buchan again,' I said finally.

Surrender-not stared wide-eyed. 'You want to question him again?'

'I think "confront" may be a more appropriate term.'

'With what, sir? We've no evidence, just speculation, and our one and only witness is dead.'

He was right. We had precious little. Only the word of an old priest who stated that Buchan was involved, and who made no attempt to hide his contempt for the man. But confronting Buchan was the only card I had left. I had no choice but to play it.

'See if you can find out where he is,' I said. 'I want to see him as soon as possible.'

An hour later, Surrender-not knocked on my door. His face suggested even more bad news. Then again, it may have just been coincidence. His face always tended to look like that and the news always seemed to be bad.

'Buchan's uncontactable, sir.'

'Is he in Serampore?'

'No, sir. His secretary doesn't know where he is. He was supposed to return to Serampore today but his travel plans have been disrupted by the . . . situation in the country. He's hoping Mr Buchan will be back by tomorrow morning. Even then, the road and rail links to the north are closed. The only way up to Serampore will be by boat.'

That was less than ideal. Things seemed much easier back in England, where you could make pretty much any journey in a matter of hours. Hell, things were probably easier in wartime France, even with three million heavily armed Germans trying to get in your way.

'Very well. See if you can organise transport for tomorrow morning.'

'Yes, sir.'

'Anything else?'

'There is one thing, sir. The report from Companies House on Mr Stevens. He's not listed as a shareholder in any company that's registered in Calcutta or Rangoon . . . but his wife is.'

'Go on.'

'She's the majority shareholder in a rubber plantation near Mandalay. I only found out because Stevens is listed as the company secretary. I took the liberty of examining a copy of the accounts and it appears that the company is not in good shape. It's heavily indebted to several banks, primarily the Bengal Burma Banking Corporation.'

That made me sit up.

Suddenly Stevens had become a lot more interesting to me. His wife owned a rubber plantation in hock to the banks, and Annie had mentioned he'd argued with MacAuley over import tariffs on products from Burma. All at once he had a real motive: money. It was one of the unholy trinity of motives. The other two were sex and power. This case now had all three. At first, I'd thought it was about power on the largest possible scale, a murder aimed at changing who ruled the country. With Sen no longer my prime suspect, the focus had changed to sex, specifically Buchan and his procuring of prostitutes. Now, it seemed, I had another serious contender: Stevens' financial problems. That muddied the waters further.

'Come on,' I said to Banerjee as I rose and picked up my cap. 'Back to Writers' Building.'

THIRTY-ONE

'I don't care how busy he is, Miss Grant, I need to see him now.'

My tone was unnecessarily brusque. Much of it was for Banerjee's benefit, but much was also down to the fact that I felt as worn out as a rickshaw *wallah*'s shoes.

She looked tired too. No doubt today had been as manic at Writers' Building as it had at Lal Bazar.

'I'll see what I can do, Captain.' She rose and left the room, returning a few minutes later.

'Mr Stevens will see you both now,' she said, addressing her comments to Banerjee. It was a calculated snub and it needled me, though I couldn't say exactly why. The psychoanalysis, however, would have to wait.

We entered Stevens' office, and this time it truly was *his* office, with all trace of MacAuley having been removed.

'Make it quick, Captain,' he said from behind his desk. 'Things are extremely fraught. I've been in with the L-G's people most of the morning and in twenty minutes I've got—'

'Did you kill MacAuley?'

His pen fell to the desk and rolled onto the floor.

'What?'

'I asked you if you murdered Alexander MacAuley.'

'That's outrageous!' He was on his feet by now. 'You think I killed the man for his job?'

'No,' I said. 'I think you killed him for money.'

He laughed. 'Seriously, Captain? I did it for a pay rise?'

'I know about your business interests in Burma, and the parlous state of their finances.'

That wiped the smile off his face as abruptly as if I'd slapped him.

'You wanted to stop the imposition of the import duty on rubber, didn't you? It would have pushed the fortunes of your wife's plantation over the edge. When MacAuley rebuffed your attempts, you followed him to Cossipore and killed him. I'll bet you're already working on getting that tax shelved.'

He slumped back into his chair. 'Let me tell you something about Alexander MacAuley,' he said bitterly. 'He was a bastard. He engineered that bloody import tax just to get at *me*. When I arrived here from Rangoon, people warned me about him but I was too stupid to listen. My wife had just inherited the plantation, and in those days, due to the war, there was huge demand for rubber. The plantation was doing well and we weren't short of money. Life in Calcutta was good and MacAuley seemed like a most affable chap. I thought it couldn't hurt to be close to one's boss, so I began to see him socially. One night at his club, though, he got me plastered, then proceeded to flatter me, told me how well I seemed to be doing, especially on my salary. I let slip about the plantation, told him I'd married into money. Six months later he started work on that blasted import duty legislation. It made no sense commercially. India needs far more rubber than it produces and it's not as if Burma's a foreign country. It's British, for Christ's sake. Of course, it's going to hurt other producers, but I'm sure it was aimed at me.'

I could have pointed out there was another possible motive, that MacAuley had done it at the behest of his patron, Buchan, who owned rubber plantations of his own in India. A duty on Burmese rubber would make his Indian produce vastly more profitable. That seemed a more likely motive than some vendetta against Stevens. After all, wasn't that the sort of thing MacAuley had always done for Buchan? But MacAuley's motives for the tax were beside the point. All that mattered was whether Stevens had killed him in order to shelve it.

'Where were you between eleven p.m. last Tuesday and seven a.m. on Wednesday?'

'At home.'

'Can anyone corroborate that?'

' My wife and a half a dozen servants.' He wiped his brow with a white handkerchief. 'Look. You're right. I'm not sorry he's dead, and I'll get that blasted tax repealed just as soon as I can, but I swear to you, I didn't kill him.'

'Well, Mr Stevens,' I said, 'we'll check out your story. In the meantime, don't plan on going anywhere.'

THIRTY-TWO

There was nothing about Amritsar in the evening papers, but that didn't matter. The news had spread like a virus, and in the absence of hard facts the vacuum was filled by gossip and speculation. The rumours electrified Calcutta's citizens, both white and black, and the residents of the Royal Belvedere Guest House were no exception. The atmosphere in Mrs Tebbit's dining room that night resembled that of a crowd after a boxing match: levity, tinged with vindication and vindictiveness. Toasts were drunk to the gallant General Dyer, saviour of the Punjab and defender of the Raj.

I had no stomach for the conversation and even less for the food. That I was out of morphine tablets hardly helped. I decided to retire before I said something a better man might regret. Making my excuses, I headed for the hallway but stopped at the foot of the stairs. Though I'd no appetite for Mrs Tebbit's fare, I was still hungry. Maybe Annie would be free for a bite to eat? I turned and headed instead for the front door.

'Are ye off out, Captain?' called a voice from behind me. It was Byrne, coming down the stairs. 'Sure, I don't blame you. The conversation can get a bit monotonous at times.'

He was smiling, which was a surprise. I'd thought him more sensible than the others in the house.

'You seem to be in good spirits, Mr Byrne,' I said.

'Ah, yes,' he said. 'Good of you to notice. I've almost completed that big contract I was telling you about. All that's left is a little paperwork. I should be done tomorrow, and then it's off to pastures new. Much as I love Calcutta, I get itchy feet if I'm ever in one place for too long. What about you? Where're you off to at this hour?'

'I've work to do at the office,' I lied.

'Of course! That Sen feller. Any more luck gettin' a confession out o' the bastard?'

'I'm afraid not.'

'That's a surprise,' he said. 'From what I've read in the papers, these revolutionary types are generally only too happy to boast about what they've done. They see their actions as noble. But that's Bengalis for you. They're only really revolutionary from the neck up. I don't expect that Sen's any exception, strutting around with his glasses and goatee, like a little brown Leon Trotsky.'

'I really must be going,' I said.

'I quite understand, Captain,' he said, ushering me to the door. 'Please be on your way.'

I shut the door behind me and walked to the street corner. Thankfully the rickshaw *wallahs* were back at their post. I called over to Salman who looked up, and after a few moments, picked up his rickshaw and began to trot reluctantly over.

'Yes, *sahib*?' he asked, studiously avoiding eye contact.

'I need to go to Bow Barracks,' I said. 'Do you want to take me?'

Salman blew his nose between two fingers and flicked the mucus into the gutter, before wiping his hand on the folds of his *lunghi*. With that he gave a slow nod, and lowered the rickshaw.

As he silently navigated the quiet streets, I thought of Sen. It was true, he did look a lot like Leon Trotsky . . .

'Hold it, Salman!' I shouted. 'Change of plan. Lal Bazar *chalo. Jaldi, jaldi!'*

———

I told him to wait while I ran in and up to my office. I picked up the telephone and asked the operator to place a call through to Fort William.

'I need to speak to Colonel Dawson,' I said.

Miss Braithwaite was on the other end of the line. 'The Colonel isn't here at the moment.'

Frustration got the better of me as I uttered a few choice words I expected the prim Miss Braithwaite had probably never heard before, and even if she had, would never have admitted to. If she was shocked, though, there was no hint of it in her voice. I suppose keeping one's thoughts to oneself was a skill that secretaries to secret policemen learned early in their careers.

'Is there anything else I can do for you, Captain?'

'Can you tell me where he is?'

'I'm afraid I'm not at liberty to divulge that information.'

'It's imperative I speak to him.'

'As you will appreciate, Captain, tonight of all nights, the Colonel is extremely busy.'

There was no point in arguing with her. 'Please let him know I called and ask him to contact me as soon as possible. Tell him it's urgent.'

I hung up the phone, then spent the next forty-five minutes wearing through the varnish on the floorboards, anxiously waiting for Dawson to telephone back. But no call came. I've never been particularly good at standing around doing bugger all, and the frustration of waiting, coupled with a hunger-induced nausea, was beginning to take its toll. At this rate, it wouldn't matter when

Dawson came back to me as I'd probably be asleep and miss the call. Though it went against my instincts, in the end I decided I needed a short break. I could have a very quick dinner with Annie and be back here, refreshed, within the hour to see if Dawson had responded.

I returned to Salman in the courtyard.

'Guest house, *sahib*?'

'No,' I said. 'Bow Barracks.'

———

The streets were semi deserted and Salman made short work of the journey. I ordered him to pull up outside the grim, cement-grey two-storey building that housed Annie's flat. A balcony, reached by an external staircase, ran along the length of the floor. A number of stout wooden doors dotted the façade of both the ground and upper level.

I walked up the stairs and knocked on the door I thought was Annie's. In hindsight, maybe I should have turned up with flowers or something. It would have been the gentlemanly thing to do. Fortunately, though, I had a ready excuse in that there were unlikely to be many florists open that night. They don't tend to do much business during riots, though I expect their trade probably picks up again afterwards on the back of increased demand for wreaths.

A skinny Anglo-Indian girl of about twenty opened the door. Her dark hair was tied up in rollers.

'Can I help you?' she asked.

'I'm looking for Annie Grant,' I said.

She looked me up and down as though examining a fish that might be going off. 'And who are you exactly?' she sniffed.

I gave her my name and rank, just like the army taught us to do when interrogated by the enemy. Her eyes widened.

'Oh,' she exclaimed, 'so *you're* Captain Wyndham.' She smiled briefly before quickly regaining her comportment. 'I'm afraid Annie's out for the evening.'

'She does know that half the city's under lock-down?' I asked.

'Oh, I'm sure she'll be fine,' said the girl. 'She'll be back in a few hours.'

There was a certainty in her voice that suggested it was nothing unusual for Annie to be out late. That didn't surprise me. She was a good-looking girl. Other men obviously thought so too. I certainly wasn't the first man to have taken her to dinner. I probably wasn't even the first one this month. What bothered me, though, was the confidence the girl had that Annie would come to no harm despite what was going on in the city. Still I wasn't about to ask her where Annie was or who she might be with. Instead, I said goodnight.

The evening wasn't going quite as I'd hoped. No one, it seemed, had much time for me. I considered heading back to Lal Bazar and trying Dawson again, but I doubted there was much point. He would surely contact me when he was ready.

I turned and walked slowly back down the stairs, feeling like a child who's had his sweets stolen. Salman was surprised to see me again so soon.

'Back to guest house, *sahib*?' he enquired.

'Yes,' I said, then had a better idea. 'Wait. Take me to Tiretta Bazaar.'

The opium den didn't seem to have been affected by the rioting. The same squat Chinaman opened the door. He eyed me contemptuously before letting me in. It was still the warmest welcome I'd received that evening. I followed him down the stairs and waited until the same pretty girl from before showed me to a cot and lit my pipe. I closed my eyes and inhaled the smoke. A tableau of images soon filled my head: Annie, out somewhere in a deserted city, Sen in his cell beneath Fort William, Devi hanging lifeless from a hook in Cossipore, a massacre of innocents in a faraway city, and a white maharaja holding court in a palace upriver, entertaining American clients with Indian courtesans.

I awoke some hours later. My watch said midnight, but that meant nothing. I sat up. The place was empty. Rising unsteadily, I made my way back up the stairs and out into the alley. I inhaled deeply and looked down the street for Salman. There was no sign of him. A noise came from behind me and I turned to see two men approaching. Indians. Labourers by the look of their clothes. Tough, solid-looking individuals, not skinny like most natives. I stared at them. Both averted their eyes, trying too hard to appear nonchalant. I'd seen the look before and it never ended well.

I turned and started walking in the opposite direction. A few more yards and I'd be out of the alley and in the relative safety of the open street. Behind me I heard the men break into a run. I turned to see them rushing at me. Two against one, but I didn't mind too much. I was actually quite happy to hit someone. I got the first punch in, striking the leader with a solid right hook to the side of the head. Even with the full force of my frustrations behind it, it still felt like punching a wall. That pain, though, was soon wildly superseded as, an instant later, the other thug delivered a punch to my injured left arm. My eyes watered. It might have been a lucky punch, but it felt as though he knew exactly where to hit me. There wasn't time to consider it further on account of one of them punching me in the gut and knocking the wind out of me. I doubled over and fought for breath. Then came a blow to my head. A sharp crack and the world spun upwards to meet me. I hit the ground and tasted blood. A boot hit me in the ribs. I closed my eyes and tried to keep myself from passing out, but all I could think of was the absurdity of it all. From somewhere came the sound of bells. Small bells. Tinkling. First one, then others. Then voices. Shouts. I looked up in time to see my attackers turn and run.

———

I was dragged to my feet. Two men, my arms over their shoulders, were carrying me. Gently, they lowered me onto the ground beside a rickshaw. I looked up and recognised Salman. I tried to speak, spat blood, and wiped my mouth with the back of my sleeve. Salman pulled out a battered tin hip flask from somewhere, unscrewed it and held it to my lips. The hooch, whatever it was, tasted disgusting, like raw alcohol. I choked, almost spitting it out. It burned as it went down.

'You are all right, *sahib*?'

Salman took a sip, then helped me to my feet. Unfortunately, my legs took their time receiving the message and I almost collapsed again. He caught me and helped me up on to the seat of the rickshaw. A searing pain ran through my ribs and I closed my eyes.

The next thing I remember, the rickshaw was being pulled back through the silent streets. The roads looked familiar.

'Where are we going?' I asked.

'Hospital, *sahib*,' puffed Salman. He was moving at a fair clip.

'No,' I said, 'no hospital.' Hospitals were full of dreadful, well-meaning doctors who specialised in awkward questions. *What were you doing in Tiretta Bazaar in the middle of the night? And tonight of all nights?* I could make up some excuse, but a good doctor wouldn't believe me. It wouldn't take a genius to work out I'd been at an opium den, and then, a discreet word in the wrong ears and who knew what might happen? I wasn't sure of the Imperial Police

340

Force's policy on opium addiction, but it was unlikely to include promotion.

'Guest house?' asked Salman.

The one place worse than hospital was Mrs Tebbit's guest house. I imagined the look on her face as I bled all over her precious Persian rugs. I'd rather have taken my chances with the thugs who attacked me.

'No,' I said.

'Then where, *sahib*?'

'Anywhere.'

I closed my eyes and began to drift off again. The next thing I knew, we had stopped, and Salman was shaking me awake. I recognised the grey outline of Annie's building. A light shone on the first floor and a figure stood silhouetted in the doorway.

'Come, *sahib*,' said Salman. He helped me to my feet and supported me up the stairs.

'My God, Sam. What the hell's happened to you?' asked Annie as she gently touched my face.

'I fell off another elephant.'

'You look like the elephant fell on *you*.'

'I think it might have.'

'Let's get you inside and cleaned up.'

Her housemate, the skinny girl with the stern face, stood in the corridor with her arms folded and her lips pursed tightly together, like a young Mrs Tebbit in training. One of the rollers in her hair had come loose. It was probably trying to escape from her head. I didn't blame it.

Annie led the way to a small bathroom. She took off my shirt, accidentally brushing the wound on my arm. I winced.

She looked at me pityingly. 'Is there anywhere on you that doesn't hurt?'

'My lips?'

She smiled and poured some water from a large enamel jug into a basin, then took a cloth and began mopping the blood from my head. She left the room and returned with what looked like makeshift bandages.

'I don't think I need any,' I said.

'How about you let me do the thinking tonight, Captain Wyndham? You can remove them in the morning if you wish.'

'I can't stay here,' I said. 'I need to get back.'

'You're not going anywhere, Captain. Not without my say-so.'

Suddenly I didn't feel like arguing. She took my hand and led me to her room.

'Now do you want to tell me what *really* happened?'

'I had a slight disagreement with some people I bumped into,' I said, collapsing onto the bed. 'I'll tell you about it in the morning.'

THIRTY-THREE

Tuesday, 15 April 1919

I woke to a blinding ache behind the eyes. Beside me, Annie lay sleeping, and to be honest, the sight of her helped ease the pain somewhat.

The first light of day was falling through slats in the shuttered windows. I got up slowly, partly out of consideration for the sleeping Annie, but also to avoid hurting my bruised body. On one side of the room, atop a wooden dresser, sat a large oval mirror. I hobbled over to it and examined my injuries. I touched the dressing on my head. It was wound thick as a turban and made me look like a coolie. I removed it slowly. A dark gash was etched into the purple skin of my right temple. Over my ribs, a large boot-shaped bruise had nicely flowered. Gingerly I felt the back of my skull. A sharp pain ran through my head as I touched a lump the size of a cricket ball. I'd had better mornings. Then again, I'd also had worse. I sat back on the bed as Annie stirred beside me.

'So you made it through the night, then?'

I moved a stray hair from her face. 'Thanks to you.'

'It's not me you should be thanking but that rickshaw *wallah* friend of yours. He's the one who dragged you over here. Would you care to tell me what happened?'

'I was jumped. I remember being attacked by two men. Then it all gets a bit confusing. I know it sounds odd, but I swear I heard little bells ringing. The next thing I know, Salman and his friends are helping me onto a rickshaw.'

Annie smiled. 'Those little bells. All rickshaw *wallahs* have them. You must have seen them. They ring them to let people know they're coming, like the bell on a bicycle. Maybe they also use them to call other rickshaw *wallahs* if they're in trouble?'

'Like a policeman's whistle?'

'I suppose so. No one else would care if a rickshaw *wallah's* in trouble. I imagine they look out for each other. By the look of you, it seems Salman and his friends got to you just in time. Any idea who attacked you?'

I told her it was just some street thugs. It might even have been the truth. What with the goings-on in Amritsar, people's blood was up. Maybe I'd just been unlucky. Wrong place, wrong time. But there was a more disturbing possibility: that it hadn't been a random attack. The men had been better built than most of the locals: the bruises on my body were testimony to that. Then there were the boots. How many natives go around Calcutta in hob-nail boots? They seemed too well nourished and too well shod to be mere labourers. But if it was a targeted attack, then why and by whom?

Indian separatists, angered by Sen's arrest? My name had been splashed across the papers, after all. Or maybe it was MacAuley's murderer? Maybe he feared I was getting too close to the truth? But there was a problem with that. There was no way for anyone to have known I'd be going to the opium den that night. I didn't even know myself. It had been a spur-of-the-moment decision. Someone must have followed me, at least from when I left Mrs Tebbit's for Annie's house. I hadn't noticed anyone on my tail, certainly not a couple of natives built like dockers. Whoever it was must have had access to significant resources and there was only one organisation I could think of with the network and the manpower to have carried out such an operation: Section H.

I wasn't exactly in their good books. What if Colonel Dawson was sending me a message? The men were obviously fit enough to be military, and they also seemed to know about my wounded arm. If it was Section H, they now knew about opium habit. The information was probably already on Dawson's desk. But whoever was responsible and whatever their motive, I wasn't going to find the answers in Annie's bed. More's the pity.

The thought of Dawson jogged my memory. I needed to speak to him urgently. I stood up and pulled on my shirt as fast as I could without aggravating the pain.

Annie looked at her wrist. 'You're not going, are you? It's not even half past five yet.'

'I have to.'

'At least let me make you some breakfast before you go.'

'No time,' I said. 'But thank you.'

———

Five minutes later I hobbled down the stairs, armed with two bread rolls which Annie had insisted I take. Salman lay dozing on a mat under his rickshaw. He heard me coming, yawned, stretched and stood up. I placed a hand on his shoulder and handed him one of the rolls. He nodded, before storing it in a box under the seat of his rickshaw. From beside it he removed a glass bottle, unscrewed the cap and held it above his mouth. Careful to avoid touching the bottle with his lips, he let a stream of water fall into his mouth. He gargled, then spat it into the gutter at the side of the road. He turned and smiled.

'Where to, *sahib*?'

'Lal Bazar.'

The roads were quiet. The checkpoints were still there, manned by sleepy-looking sepoys. Lal Bazar too lacked the febrile atmosphere that had engulfed it the day before, and the building exuded the air of a quiet regional outpost rather than the centre of police operations for half a subcontinent.

There was no note waiting on my desk. Nothing to say Dawson had tried to contact me in the ten hours since I'd called his secretary. That didn't necessarily mean anything. It was still only six a.m. Still, Dawson didn't seem the type of man who went more than a few hours without being in contact with his office.

I considered what I was about to do. A lot had happened since the previous evening, not much of it good, and some of it still visible on my head and body. I suspected Dawson and his men might have been responsible for a lot of my troubles, but I was an officer of the Imperial Police and I had my duty to do, regardless of my personal feelings towards the man.

I picked up the telephone and placed another call to Fort William. A different secretary answered this time. There was a delay on the line before I was connected to Dawson, I guessed on his telephone at home.

'What can I do for you, Wyndham?' He sounded alert and betrayed no surprise at hearing my voice. Nor did he mention whether he had received my message the previous evening. Not that either of these mattered now.

'Do you have a surveillance team at your disposal?'

'Of course.'

'Then it's more of a question of what *I* can do for *you.*'

———

The call lasted about five minutes. It should have been quicker but he spent much of it asking why he should trust me after what had happened out in Kona. I might have asked him the same question. In the end we reached a compromise. He'd investigate my lead and I'd stay out of his business. He promised to give me an update on his progress but I wasn't about to hold my breath.

I hung up and went in search of Digby and Surrender-not. Digby's office was empty, so I made my way down to the pit where the junior officers sat. Few men were around this early, and other than the duty sergeant, the pit looked deserted. It was only when I passed Surrender-not's desk that I noticed the pair of skinny brown legs sticking out from under it. For an instant I feared he too had been attacked and left for dead. It was an irrational thought. No one murders a policeman in a police station and hides the body under a desk. I blamed it on the knock on the head I'd received from the two ugly sisters the previous night. Anyway, it was ridiculous to think he might be dead when he was snoring.

'Sergeant,' I called out, rather louder than necessary. He woke with a start and sat up, slamming his head against the underside of the desk. I'm not normally one for *schadenfreude*, but the thought that I wasn't the only one with a sore head that morning did cheer me up.

Surrender-not, dressed only in his khaki police shorts and a vest, crawled out from his foxhole, jumped to his feet and, after rubbing his head, finally remembered to salute. He looked shocked at the sight of my bruised face, but had the good sense to say nothing about it. I could have berated him for wandering around the office dressed like a coolie but I wasn't exactly in full dress uniform myself. Instead, I asked him what the devil he was doing under his desk.

'Sleeping, sir,' he replied.

'I can see that, but why?'

'It pertains to my intention and subsequent retreat from that—'

347

'Small words please, Sergeant.'

He started again. 'I have been forced to leave the family residence on account of my failure to resign my position.'

'Your parents threw you out?'

'In a manner of speaking.'

'And there's nowhere else you can go?'

He shook his head. 'Not that I can think of, sir.'

'What about your elder brother? Doesn't he live in Calcutta?'

'He does, sir, but we haven't spoken in several years. We don't really get on, and . . .' His voice trailed off.

'You have irreconcilable differences?'

'Oh no,' he said, 'they're reconcilable. That's part of the problem.'

'Well, you can't keep sleeping under your desk. We'll have to come up with a better solution when we have the time. Right now, though, I need to know the progress on Devi's post-mortem.'

'It's scheduled for this afternoon.'

'And Mrs Bose?'

'Transferred to the women's section last night.'

'What about Stevens' alibi? Any progress on that?'

'His wife, a maid and the *durwan* all confirm Mr Stevens was at home on the night of the murder. I can bring the maid and *durwan* in for further questioning if you wish?'

'Maybe later,' I said. 'For now, I want you to get dressed, then speak to Buchan's people in Serampore. Find out what time he's due back.'

He looked at me as though I'd just asked him to organise a tea party in the tiger enclosure at Calcutta Zoo.

'We've no choice,' I said. 'Without Devi or this man she confided in, we've no way of finding out what it was that MacAuley was so upset about the night he died. We know Buchan's involved, so we might as well try to shake him up.'

348

'Is that wise, sir?' asked Surrender-not. 'He's a very powerful man. If we were to accuse him without proof, I imagine he could make life very difficult for us.'

I failed to see how Buchan could make things much worse. 'In the space of the last few days, Sergeant, I've been attacked, shot and almost poisoned by my landlady. If Mr Buchan feels he can top that, then good luck to him.'

As Surrender-not had anticipated, the roads north were still closed, and the fastest way from Calcutta to Serampore was by boat up the Hooghly. So an hour later, after a quick stop off at Mrs Tebbit's for a change of clothes, we drove to the police jetty near the Prinsep Ghat. Surrender-not had telephoned ahead to the jetty, as well as the *thana* in Serampore, and a police launch was waiting on the pier. The vessel was commanded by a young English officer named Remnant and manned by a crew of several natives. The boat itself was a bit of a tub, but Remnant and his crew seemed to treat her like a ship of the line. Every inch of her deck was scrubbed clean and her brass bell polished to a shine.

The tide was with us and we made decent progress upriver. Remnant pointed out the Hindu burning *ghat* at Neemtollah as the smoke from a funeral pyre drifted out lazily onto the silver water. On the topmost step of the *ghat*, a priest, his chest bare but for the sacred thread, sat cross-legged, a small congregation at his feet, and solemnly intoned the cremation rites. All were dressed in white.

The city gradually melted into jungle and the journey took on the air of an expedition. This was the India I'd dreamed of. The wild, mysterious land described by Kipling and Sir Henry Cunningham. The morning mist hung low over the river and clung to the banks like a fine muslin sheet, broken only by the occasional banyan tree or native dwelling. Small wooden boats, some with a simple sail, others little more than hollowed-out canoes, drifted slowly by, their pilots steering their course with long poles.

On the east bank of the river, a great temple loomed out of the haze, a hundred feet high and utterly alien. The main temple, a large, white, double-tiered construct, was topped with a strange, dome-like structure surrounded by half a dozen or more spires. A row of shrines, twelve in all, stood facing the main temple like disciples paying homage. All shone bright in the early-morning light, their walls pristine white and roofs blood red.

'That,' said Remnant, 'is the temple of Kali, or one of them, anyway. There's quite a few of them dotted around Calcutta, but this one's my favourite.'

Offerings to the goddess floated out from the shore, a myriad marigolds, rose petals and small votive lamps carrying the prayers of devotees. Remnant pointed to a row of steps leading down to the water.

'Those are the bathing *ghats*,' he said. 'Hindus believe that a dip in these waters washes away all sins.'

'Odd,' I said. 'Yesterday, a Hindu told me that there was no forgiveness of sins. That his *karma* was unalterable.'

'That's the thing about Hinduism,' replied Remnant, 'it's so mystical, even the Hindus get confused.'

———

Some time later, several brick smokestacks appeared on the horizon, belching black smoke high into the blue sky.

'Serampore,' said Remnant, as his crew steered the boat towards the west bank. The jungle gradually cleared, revealing several large mansions. They reminded me of photographs of the cotton plantations of South Carolina, their manicured lawns stretching down to the river.

'Elegant little place,' I said.

'Isn't it just?' replied Remnant. 'It was founded by the Danes, apparently. Vikings on the Hooghly! By all accounts it was a prosperous little trading post until the East India Company throttled it by banning ships from coming upriver. In the end the Danes sold the place to us for a song. Since then it's been pretty much run by Scots.'

The launch heaved to shore and slowly docked at an old wooden jetty where stood a bear of an officer who introduced himself as Superintendent MacLean. He was a curious-looking fellow. Flame haired and built like a dreadnought, but with the ruddy pink complexion and soft features of a child, as though his face hadn't kept up with the growth of the rest of him. His uniform merely accentuated the effect and gave him the look of an overgrown schoolboy, the sort who looks like he was born to play the tuba in the school orchestra.

'Welcome tae Serampore,' he said. A Scots accent. No surprise there. If I were a betting man I'd have put quite a tidy sum on him hailing from Dundee. He shook my hand with the vigour of a long-lost friend, then proceeded to do the same to Surrender-not, almost lifting the little sergeant clean off his feet. The pleasantries concluded, he led us off towards a Sunbeam 16/20 that stood idling by the roadside.

'You're in luck, Captain,' said MacLean as we drove down a pitted dirt track, 'I believe Mr Buchan returned from Calcutta just this morning.'

'You keep track of his movements?'

'Not at all,' he laughed, 'but the pace of things in our sleepy wee town changes when he's around. There's always a lot of activity when he comes and goes.'

'The lord of the manor?'

He smiled. 'We prefer the Scottish term: *laird*.'

The car left the dirt track and joined a main road bordered by a high wall on one side and train tracks on the other. From somewhere close by came the shrill note of a steam whistle. MacLean checked his wristwatch.

'Shift change at the mills,' he said to no one in particular.

A little further on there came a break in the wall. A stream of men, both white and native, poured through a set of iron gates embossed with a large metal seal bearing the legend:

BUCHAN JUTE WORKS

DUNKELD MILL

SERAMPORE

Behind the gates stood a long brick building topped with a corrugated-metal roof, from the top of which rose a large chimney belching black smoke. Beside it were open sheds, some stacked with wooden crates and great circular reels of burlap, others piled high with coarse textiles that shone gold in the morning sun.

'Raw jute,' explained MacLean.

Minutes later the car turned off the road and between two tall stone pillars. On one sat a shield depicting three black lion heads in profile, on the other an image of a belt encircling a sun shining on a sunflower. We continued up a long driveway towards a stately baroque pile that made Government House look like a miner's cottage.

'Here we are,' said MacLean. 'We call it Buchan-ham Palace.' He smiled, pleased with his own joke.

'Is that sandstone?' I asked.

MacLean nodded. 'There's precious little of it in Bengal,' he said. 'Most of it's from the Rajput princely states, but some of it was even shipped in from the old country.'

As we approached, it became clear why the driveway was so long. It was only from a distance that the whole edifice could be taken in. Two vast wings, three storeys tall, surrounded a central core fronted by enough columns to make the Parthenon jealous.

The car pulled up beside a set of stone stairs that ran up to two large black doors, open to the heat. A couple of native footmen dressed in dark blue and gold livery ran over and opened the car doors, the sun glinting off the fans atop their stiffly starched turbans.

'Thanks for your assistance,' I said to MacLean, exiting the car.

'Oh, right,' he said, seeming rather put out. 'You don't want me to come in with you?'

He seemed a nice enough sort, but I didn't know if I could trust him. Serampore was Buchan's town and I had no idea where MacLean's loyalties lay. It was better to keep him out of it.

'There's no need. I assume Buchan has a telephone rattling around somewhere in this place. We'll telephone the police station when we're done.'

'Very good, sir,' he said, stiffening. He saluted and squeezed back into the Sunbeam.

Surrender-not and I climbed the stairs to the front entrance. Behind us the car started up and sped off back down the driveway, churning up a cloud of dust in its wake.

We were met at the top by a butler. Not a native, but a white man. In a land where native labour is cheaper than livestock, the presence of a white butler spoke volumes. He was bald, save for a band of white hair that encircled the back of his head. Dressed in a pristine morning suit, he was old and bent and had a creased face that reminded me somewhat of Ratan, Mrs Bose's decrepit manservant.

'This way please, gentlemen,' he said. 'Mr Buchan will see you shortly and apologises for your wait.'

We followed him through what I presumed was the hallway but could just as easily have been an art gallery, its walls covered with more paintings than I'd seen anywhere since a trip to the Louvre during the war.

He stopped outside a door and directed us inside. The room smelled of tobacco and appeared to be Buchan's library. It was the sort of room favoured by a certain type of self-made man: oak panelled with shelves full of books that looked like they'd never been read. Light streamed in through French windows set in the far wall.

'May I bring you some refreshment?' asked the butler.

I declined.

'And you, sir?' he said, turning to Banerjee.

'Yes please. A glass of water, thank you.'

'Very good, sir.' The butler nodded and exited.

Banerjee looked amused.

'What's so funny?' I asked.

'Nothing, sir.'

I sat down in one of several high-backed leather chairs dotted about the room while Surrender-not busied himself examining the book-lined shelves. Above us, a large *punkah* started moving on the ceiling, delivering a cooling breeze. The butler returned with a glass and a jug on a silver tray.

'Will there be anything else, sir?'

Surrender-not looked at me. I shook my head.

'No, that will be all, my good man,' he said, 'now please kindly leave us.'

A week earlier and I might have thought the sergeant was being facetious. Now, though, I wasn't so sure. In a land where everything was seen through the prism of race, his words, directed as they were to a white man, could just as easily have been a political act.

The minutes ticked by. For want of something to do, I wandered over to the French windows. They opened on to a veranda beyond which lush green lawns ran down to the languorous Hooghly. Behind me, the door suddenly opened and Buchan strode in, dressed in blue silk trousers and a white shirt, open at the neck.

'My apologies, Captain, but as you can imagine, your request to see me this morning took me a wee bit by surprise.' His tone was businesslike. 'It's a pleasure, nonetheless. I read about your arrest of that terrorist. Hell, they've been chasing him for years and you catch him like that.' He snapped his fingers and smiled. 'If you ever get tired of police work, or fancy something a wee bit more lucrative, you let me know. I could use a man like you.'

He gestured towards a couple of the leather chairs beside a small glass table. 'Please, take a seat and tell me what I can do for you.'

'It's about MacAuley's murder. I need to ask you a few more questions.'

He raised an eyebrow. 'More questions? I assumed the case had been closed.'

'We're tying up a few loose ends.'

Buchan nodded slowly. 'Very well.'

'We have it from a witness that MacAuley was seen arguing with you shortly before he left the Bengal Club on the night of his death. Could you tell me what you were arguing about?'

'I don't know where you heard that, Captain, but it's not true. We did speak afore he left but it wasn't an argument. MacAuley was asking me for money.'

'But he was well paid. What did he need money for?'

Buchan shrugged. 'He didn't tell me.'

'And you didn't think to mention it when we spoke last week?'

'It was a delicate matter, Captain, and irrelevant to your investigation. I saw no reason to sully the man's reputation.'

'Did you also think it irrelevant to tell us that MacAuley supplied you with prostitutes?'

His expression darkened. 'I don't see the relevance of *any* of this, Captain. Frankly, it's an intrusion into my private affairs.' His voice hardened. 'I should warn you, Captain, to choose your words carefully. It would be foolish to throw about accusations like that without proof or reason. Such actions can have far-reaching consequences.'

'The question is pertinent to a murder investigation.'

Exasperated, Buchan threw up his hands. 'But the investigation has been closed, Captain! The murderer has already been caught! By *you!*'

'It may not be quite so straight forward,' I said.

He gave a bitter laugh. 'So it's true, then. You don't believe Sen's guilty. I'd heard as much.'

'From whom?'

'Och, it hardly matters. You shouldn't be so naive, Captain. I know pretty much everything worth knowing in Calcutta. I dare say if your employment were to be terminated out here, I'd know about it afore you did.'

There was little point arguing the matter. The way things were going, we'd find out soon enough whether he was right. Instead, I returned to the original question.

'Was MacAuley supplying girls for you?'

The colour rose in Buchan's face. 'Very well, Captain,' he said, 'I see you won't be warned. I'll answer your question, but the consequences'll be on your own head. MacAuley did, on occasion, provide entertainment for some o' the parties I held for clients.'

'And what did you argue about on the night of his death?'

'I told you. It wasnae an argument. He asked for money and I refused.'

356

'He didn't try to blackmail you, then?'

Something flickered in Buchan's eyes. 'Not at all.'

'Here's what I think happened,' I said. 'I think you asked him to supply you with some girls for your party that night, but he confronted you and told you he wanted out and you couldn't allow that.'

'And for that, I had him killed? Answer me this, Captain – assuming MacAuley did wish to stop supplyin' these women, what does that prove? I've no shortage of fixers. I could have replaced him with a snap o' my fingers. On top of that, he was my friend. Why would I want him dead?'

'I think he tried to blackmail you. Threatened you that he'd come clean if you didn't pay up.'

Buchan laughed. 'Is that it, Captain? That's your great theory? That I was afraid of being exposed for utilisin' the services of whores? That wouldnae be news to many in Calcutta, and those that didnae know wouldnae care. Now is there anything else?'

I said nothing. Mainly because I had nothing to say.

'In that case . . .' Buchan rose from his chair. 'You've wasted your time *and* mine comin' out here, Captain. Given what's been goin' on in Calcutta these past few days, I'd have thought the Commissioner would want his men working for more productive purposes. Rest assured I'll be informing him of our wee chat today. Now if you'll excuse me, I have business to attend to. Fraser will show you out when you're ready.'

With that he turned and left the room. There was silence for some moments. I stood and stared out of the French windows.

'Well, that could have gone better,' I said drily.

'Yes,' agreed Surrender-not, 'I was hoping to ask to borrow one or two of his books. I don't suppose he'll be willing now.'

I turned and walked over to him. 'And exactly where were you planning on reading them?' I asked. 'You're homeless, remember?

Maybe you'd be better asking him for a bed for the night? It doesn't look as though he's short on space.'

I suddenly felt exhausted. The sheer size of the hole I'd just dug myself was becoming clear. It had been stupid to come and question a man as powerful as Buchan with nothing more than a salacious titbit about his predilection for prostitutes. It was an act born of desperation. I turned and dropped into one of the leather chairs.

'So where does this leave us?' asked Surrender-not.

'Who knows?' I said wearily. 'I'm convinced Buchan's involved. We just don't have the right motive. If only we knew what MacAuley was doing at the brothel the night he was killed. Devi was adamant that he hadn't been with any of the girls, even though Mrs Bose tried to make out otherwise.'

'So what do you think he was doing there?'

'I don't know, but it must be linked to whatever secret he was keeping from Reverend Gunn. That's the key to the whole thing. Though without Devi, we've no way of discovering what it was.'

'Unless we find the man she mentioned? The one she'd confided in. Or have we given up on that?'

I shrugged. 'We questioned everyone in the building. There was no one else there.'

I leaned back, put my hands behind my head and immediately lowered them again as a bolt of pain shot through my skull. I sighed. It really was the end of the road. I might as well stop off at the P&O office on the way back and book myself a ticket back to Southampton. I couldn't see any way forward. We'd hit a wall of silence. Those who might know the truth either wouldn't speak – like Buchan or Mrs Bose – or were dead – like Devi. And no one else wanted any explanation other than that of Sen's guilt. I watched as a small brown lizard appeared from behind a book on one of the shelves. It climbed quickly up the wall and on to the ceiling. There it clambered hesitantly forward, waiting patiently for the *punkah* to swing past, then darted through the gap.

That's when it hit me.

The *punkah*.

I jumped up and stared at it. It was connected to a pulley, which made it sway back and forth. I followed the pulley rope across the ceiling to where it passed through a small hole in the wall and into the corridor beyond. I ran out into the hallway and followed the rope, first along the hall and then around a corner. There sat a small native man, his foot rhythmically moving up and down on a pedal attached to the end of the rope. If he seemed surprised to see me, I was overjoyed to see him.

I turned and ran back towards the library, almost colliding with Surrender-not coming the other way.

'The *punkah wallah!*' I exclaimed.

Surrender-not looked at me as if I'd gone mad. 'What about him?'

'That first day,' I gasped. 'At the brothel. When we questioned Mrs Bose and the girls. The *punkah*. It was moving!'

The light went on in Surrender-not's head. '*Hai Ram!* There must have been a *punkah wallah*! He would have been operating it from the courtyard outside. That's why we didn't see him.'

'We need to get back to town,' I said. 'I'll head to Cossipore. I want you back at Lal Bazar. I want an update on Devi's post-mortem. And find out where Digby is.'

'What should I tell him?'

'Tell him about our little chat with Buchan, but that's all. I'll telephone you from Cossipore *thana* later.'

THIRTY-FOUR

We took the launch back to Calcutta where Surrender-not and I parted ways, he hailing a cab to Lal Bazar while I commandeered the motor car and driver and set off for Cossipore.

It was late afternoon by the time I made it to Maniktollah Lane. Adrenalin coursed through my veins and I felt that sense of exhilaration that I always did when my instincts told me I was on to something. With a sense of nervous anticipation, I rapped loudly on the door of number 47. The old man Ratan opened it far more quickly than on the previous occasions. He looked out expectantly, but his face fell when he saw me there alone.

'*Ha, sahib?*'

'I need to speak to the man who operates the *punkah*.'

The old man strained to hear.

'Eh? Pankaj? No Pankaj here, *sahib*. This Mrs Bose house.'

'I want to speak to the p*unkah wallah*,' I said, then for good measure shouted '*Punkah wallah!*' again, loud enough to wake the mongrel dogs that were asleep in the alley.

The old man's face broke into a toothless smile. 'Oh, *punkah wallah*! *Ha* yes! Come, *sahib*. Come, come.'

I followed as he led the way to the now familiar drawing room. The house seemed deserted, with no sign of the maid or the girls.

I waited while he left to fetch the man I'd come to see, the man who was my last hope to get to the bottom of things before Sen was hanged. I looked up at the *punkah* hanging limp from the ceiling. A rope ran from it along the ceiling, then disappeared through a small grate high up on the wall and out into the courtyard beyond.

The door opened and a stocky, dark-skinned native stood in the doorway, with Ratan trying to peer round from behind him. He was powerfully built and reeked of sweat in the way only a working man can. I realised I'd seen him before: outside the house when we'd removed Devi's body.

'You speak English?'

The man nodded warily.

'What's your name?'

'Das.'

'Well, Das, you're not in any trouble. I just want to ask you some questions. Understand?'

The man stood there, mute.

'The girl, Devi. She was a friend of yours?'

'Her name not "Devi", *sahib*. That only her work name. Her real name Anjali.'

'Before she died, she told me you could help me. I need to know about MacAuley, the *burra sahib* who was killed in the alley last week. Did you know him?'

'I know MacAuley *sahib*. He comes many times.'

'Why did he come here that last time? Devi . . . Anjali said that he didn't come to lay with the girls.'

Das nodded. '*Sahib* come to pay money. He come every month to pay money.'

'To pay Mrs Bose for the girls?'

He smiled and shook his head. 'No, *sahib*. For that he pays on day of use. He pays this money for family of different girl. Girl who died. She die in . . .' He struggled to find the right word. 'Operation. Operation to take out baby.'

Haltingly and through broken English, Das began to paint a picture. Some time the previous year, one of the girls had fallen pregnant. The father was some big-shot *sahib*, a most *pukka* gentleman and one of Mrs Bose's most eminent clients. Das had never seen the man. He was too important to come to the house. Instead, the girls would always go to him. MacAuley was the go-between who made all the arrangements. The pregnancy came as a shock. It wasn't supposed to happen. Mrs Bose took care to prevent girls working at that particular time in their cycle, but clients can be demanding, and mistakes happen. The girl, her name was Parvati, was special, the client's favourite. Mrs Bose had reported the news to MacAuley, who'd come back and insisted the girl have an abortion. Das had taken the girl to some back-alley surgeon near the railway lines in Chitpore, as he'd done before with another of Mrs Bose's girls. This time, though, the operation was botched. Both girl and baby died and it was MacAuley, ever the fixer, who'd disposed of the bodies. Das didn't know what he'd done with them, but since then, MacAuley had shown up, once a month, with money for the girl's family.

Suddenly everything clicked into place. The client was Buchan. MacAuley had been his trusted man for over twenty years, but the deaths of mother and child echoed his own loss many years before. Most likely he'd struggled with his conscience, the reunion with his old friend, the Reverend Gunn, no doubt adding to his compunction. Over time, something inside him snapped. He couldn't do it any more. I guessed he confronted Buchan at the Bengal Club that night, told him he wanted out and that he was going to come clean. It was one thing to consort with prostitutes, but in race-obsessed

Calcutta, I guessed siring a half-caste bastard child might be quite another. And if that was too much for his reputation, how much worse would it be if the world were to learn of his involvement in the death of the child and its mother? So MacAuley had to be silenced. But Buchan had an alibi. He'd been in the Bengal Club at the time of the murder . . .

'Did you see the man who killed MacAuley *sahib*?'

Das shook his head. 'Only Anjali saw. She told me.'

It didn't matter. My suspicions about Buchan had been right. I now finally had the motive. As for who'd carried it out, well, I had my suspicions about that too.

———

I thanked Das and all but ran out of the house and back to the car. It was five p.m. and darkness was closing in. I ordered the driver to make for Cossipore *thana*. From there I placed a telephone call to Surrender-not at Lal Bazar. The line crackled as I waited an eternity while the desk sergeant tracked him down. Eventually Surrender-not came on the line.

'What news, Sergeant?'

'The results of the post-mortem are back, sir. They confirm that death was caused by the snapping of the neck, thus severing the spinal column.'

'Where's Digby?'

'He's not here, sir, but he left a message for you. He needs to see you urgently at the safe house in Bagh Bazaar. He claims to have received information that proves Sen's innocence. He says you should come as soon as it's dark.'

'Fine,' I said, 'I'll head straight there. You join me as soon as you can. And, Surrender-not, bring a gun.'

'There's one more thing, sir,' said Surrender-not.

'Let me guess,' I said, 'Mrs Bose has been transferred to Section H.'

'How did you know?' he said. 'The paperwork came in from Government House a few hours ago.'

THIRTY-FIVE

It was dark by the time I approached the steps of the safe house. I'd had the driver drop me off near Grey Street, where I'd purchased a thick grey shawl, which Bengalis call a *chador*, and a pair of sandals from a market stall. I'd wrapped the shawl around my shoulders and head, before making the rest of the journey on foot, retracing the route we'd followed previously.

I knocked and waited. The street was deserted. Eerily quiet. The door opened a crack and a figure, features hidden in the darkness, looked out, then opened it wider.

'Come in quickly, old boy.'

I did as asked. Digby closed the door and locked and barred it with a wooden beam, then led me through to the front room. On a table, the flame from a solitary candle flickered.

'So what have you got?'

Digby looked ashen. 'I'll let Vikram tell you. He should be here soon.' He checked his watch. 'He seems to be running late.'

'I hope he's all right,' I said. 'It would be terrible if someone slit his throat . . . or broke his neck.'

His expression changed. Even in the dim light, I caught the flicker in his eyes. The unmistakable flash as he realised.

We went for our guns at the same instant. He got there first. Maybe if I hadn't had my head used for batting practice the previous night I'd have beaten him to it. I might also have been thinking clearly enough not to have gone straight there without waiting for Surrender-not, and with no plan other than confronting Digby. The truth was, though, that since my telephone call with Surrender-not, I'd had no other thought in my head besides confronting him. Call it ego, but I don't take kindly to anyone pulling the wool over my eyes, least of all a trusted subordinate. That sort of thing can make a fellow look bad, and I preferred to do that all on my own.

He gestured for me to drop my revolver, and seeing as how he had a Smith & Wesson pointed at my face, it seemed the prudent thing to do. I placed it slowly on the floor in front of me.

'That's a good fellow,' he said, smiling. 'Best not to do anything stupid. I must say, old boy, I *am* impressed. However did you work it out?'

'That you killed Devi?'

'Was that her name? I can't remember. The prostitute, at any rate.'

'The drop,' I said. 'It wasn't long enough.'

'Of course,' he said. 'That was careless. I suppose she'd have needed to fall a few feet more for her neck to break. Still, I could hardly have strangled her without some signs of a struggle. But that's hardly conclusive.'

'Of itself no,' I said. 'I thought at first it might have been Mrs Bose, but it would probably have taken a man to snap it cleanly. And there were other signs too. Our friend Buchan seemed to know far more about our inquiries than he should have, and let's not forget that it was your pal Vikram who sent us chasing up that blind alley after Sen in the first place. Finally, when I heard Mrs Bose had been taken by Section H, it confirmed my suspicions. What possible use could she be to them? None as far as I could see. No, they took her to protect her from further questions from me. And how did they come to know she was in our custody? They might have eyes and ears everywhere, but the most obvious source was you.'

'Very good, old boy. You really are a suspicious bastard, aren't you? I don't suppose there's anyone you trust.'

That was true. Sometimes not even myself.

'Why'd you do it?' I asked. 'Why kill the girl?'

'Orders, dear boy. There was a chance she might have known more than she'd told you.'

'And MacAuley? Was that *orders* too? Just how much did Buchan pay you? Enough to retire?'

Digby's face contorted with hate so that he resembled some medieval gargoyle. Then he laughed.

'Is that what you think happened? All your vaunted detection skills and *that's* the conclusion you've come to? Bloody hell, Wyndham, I've been giving you too much credit. You're supposed to be Scotland Yard's finest but you wouldn't be able to find your arse if it wasn't in your underpants. I wish Taggart could see you now. His prize monkey, so cocksure but still hasn't a clue.'

He looked pityingly at me.

'Buchan had nothing to do with it,' he said.

'That's nonsense,' I said. 'I know about the botched abortion. I know about the death of the girl, Parvati, and the effect it had on MacAuley.'

'And what else do you *know*, Captain?' he taunted.

'I know he was going to come clean. That's what he went to tell Buchan the night he was murdered. And if Buchan was scared of the scandal of a living illegitimate child, then MacAuley spreading tales of a dead one would have been too much for him. That's why he had you kill him.'

Digby laughed and shook his head. 'You really are an idiot, aren't you, Wyndham? Believe me. None of this is Buchan's doing.'

'You're lying,' I said.

'You should have stayed in England,' he sneered. 'You think you know everything, but the truth is you don't know the first thing about life out here. Buchan's got half a dozen bastard children already! One of them runs his damn jute mill, for Christ's sake! You think one more would make a difference? He's not afraid of scandal. He's too rich to care. What possible damage could this child have done him?'

'Then who?' I asked. 'Who did you do it for?'

Digby sighed, as though I were expending what patience he had left.

'Ask yourself this, old boy, who else did MacAuley work for? Who would have the most to lose if it ever came to light that he'd sired a bastard brown baby?'

The answer hit me like a punch in the gut.

He was laughing now. 'The penny finally drops!'

Even as I realised the truth, I still couldn't believe it.

'The L-G?'

'That's right, old boy. Our friend the Lieutenant Governor of Bengal has a thing for young native fillies. It wasn't even the first time he'd got one pregnant. Of course, MacAuley always took care of it. Good old dependable MacAuley. Except it turns out he wasn't that dependable after all.'

I felt sick.

Digby must have read my expression.

'Cheer up, old boy,' he said. 'You *were* right about one thing. MacAuley did tell Buchan about it on the night of his death. He told Buchan he was going to the papers and to the police. I believe Buchan tried to talk him out of it but MacAuley was adamant. After he left, Buchan telephoned the L-G in a panic and told him what

MacAuley planned to do. The L-G telephoned me and ordered me to find MacAuley and try to talk some sense into him. If he failed to see reason, I was to make sure the matter was appropriately dealt with.'

'And what was in it for you?'

'Isn't that obvious, old boy? My career put back on track. I should be a Chief Inspector by now. I guessed MacAuley would be at the brothel and confronted him when he came out. He wouldn't listen. We argued and he tried to push me out of the way. That's when I slit his throat.'

'And stabbed him.'

'Oh no. That wasn't me. After I'd cut his throat, I left him in the alley and fled. I telephoned the L-G and reported what had happened. He told me not to worry, that he'd have Section H deal with it. It was those fools who wanted to make it look like a terrorist assassination. They stabbed him and stuck that idiotic note in his mouth. Any India-hand with half a brain could have told them it was melodramatic nonsense. At the very least it should have been written in English, but you know these university types, fresh off the boat from England. A degree in oriental languages and they think they're bloody Clive of India.'

'And Sen?'

'That was their idea too. Vikram was paid to spin you that story.'

'So Section H knew where Sen was? Is that how they found him so quickly?'

'*Of course* they knew where he was. They've known for the last four years! It was they who let him escape when the rest of his comrades were killed at Balasore. They wanted to see who else he might lead them to. It was just a happy coincidence that he'd returned to Calcutta. If it hadn't been him, they'd have found someone else to take the fall. In fact, I think Section H would have preferred to have kept him at large, but sometimes you have to sacrifice a pawn to protect the king.'

369

My head was spinning. I'd never stood a chance. The L-G was the embodiment of British power in Bengal. A threat to him was a threat to the whole Raj. There was no way I could make the truth known now. The entire might of the empire would be brought down on me if the L-G required it. Not that much seemed necessary, Digby and his revolver would be more than adequate for the task.

It begged the question, did Taggart know? Why let me keep digging if he did? He might not have known but I was sure he'd suspected something. Why else would he warn me to be careful? He knew that if his suspicions were correct, even he couldn't have protected me. After all, I was expendable. Just another pawn.

'What happens now?' I asked. 'Are you going to shoot me?'

'With any luck I won't have to. Vikram will be happy to do it. The chance to kill an Englishman? He'll jump at it, especially after that massacre in the Punjab the other day. He's quite a patriot in his own way. He might do it even if I didn't pay him. You'll just be another victim of the terrible violence unleashed by that unfortunate incident.'

He poked my chest with the revolver. 'You brought this on yourself, you know. You could have just accepted that Sen was guilty. It would all have been neatly wrapped up and everyone would have been happy. But you just couldn't let it go. The vaunted Captain Wyndham and his insufferable ego. You couldn't accept it even though you knew there was no chance you'd be able to save him.'

'I like to get to the truth,' I said. 'I'm old fashioned that way.'

He was so near I could smell his sour breath. Anger had made him reckless. I had only one chance. I had to take it. Before he had a chance to move, I pivoted forward and, with as much force as I could muster, slammed my forehead into his face. A headbutt isn't exactly gentlemanly, but if you get the positioning right, it's crudely effective. I was lucky. I smashed right into his nose. He dropped his revolver and staggered back, bringing his hands up to his damaged face. Blood poured from through his fingers. He cursed and lashed out wildly, missing me and hitting the table, and knocking the candle to the floor. I dropped to my hands and knees and searched frantically for my revolver. The headbutt had reopened the wound I'd received the night before and blood was trickling into my eye. Digby was hunting for his gun. I heard metal scraping off the wooden floor. He'd beaten me to it.

I got to my feet and made a run for it. I just got out into the hall as Digby fired wildly, the bullet hitting plasterwork somewhere behind me. He'd have his bearings soon. The next time he fired I might not be so lucky. I made for the back of the house. A split-second decision. I just hoped I'd remembered the building's layout.

I reached the worm-eaten back door. Something glinted in the half-light. Since my last visit, a sturdy padlock had been bolted on to the latch. Behind me, Digby had made his way into the hall. He fired. Splinters flew as the bullet punched a hole in the thin door. It gave me an idea. I threw myself at the door. It gave way under the force of my momentum and I crashed through and landed on the ground outside, the taste of dirt and blood in my mouth. I quickly hauled myself up and raced towards the wall at the far end of the compound. The crate we had used to scale the wall previously was too far away and I had no time to retrieve it. Instead, I took a run at the wall and jumped.

My fingers reached the top and held. Pain shot up my left shoulder. With what strength I had left, I pulled myself up and over the wall, dropping down on the far side. Behind me I heard Digby jump. For a moment it seemed as though he too would make it over, but his hands slipped and he fell backwards. He cursed wildly. I figured I'd bought myself thirty seconds while he went to retrieve the crate, but I was wrong. He took another jump and this time his fingers held. He began pulling himself up as I scrambled to my feet and started running towards the house in the distance. It was the only way out. Digby was now on top of the wall. I heard him reach for his gun. A shot rang out. The bullet whizzed past my ear. I kept running. Behind me there was a thud as Digby landed on my side of the wall. In front of me, I could see a thin sliver of light. Then the door of the house in the distance flew open. Vikram stood silhouetted in the doorway, a rifle in his hands. I stopped dead. There was nowhere left to go. Slowly I raised my hands above my head. Behind me Digby got to his feet.

'About fucking time,' he shouted. The Indian remained motionless in the doorway. Digby walked over to me. His nose was a mass of bloody flesh and there was a madness in his eyes.

'You're going to pay for that, you bastard,' he said, pulling out his revolver and bringing the butt down forcefully on the side of my head. I slumped to my knees. In front of me, Vikram took a step forward. I heard a click as he cocked his rifle. I looked up at his silhouette. He seemed different from how I remembered. He raised the gun then paused. It was the legs. The skinny legs.

'Go ahead,' said Digby, 'shoot him.' Then he too noticed. 'You?' he said, frantically raising his revolver. But he was too slow. A shot rang out and Digby slumped to the ground, a neat round hole in his forehead like the red dots the native women wear.

'You took your time,' I said drily.

'Yes, sir,' said Surrender-not. 'Sorry, sir. It took a while to fill out the chits to requisition the rifle. After the riots of the last few days, the authorities are a bit skittish about allowing Indians access to weapons.'

'That's understandable,' I said. 'Look what you've done to poor Digby here.'

EPILOGUE

I was sat on a wicker chair in Lord Taggart's garden, soaking up the late-afternoon sun as a servant poured out two large measures of single malt. He placed them on the table between us as another servant helped the Commissioner light a cigar. His Lordship puffed several times, turning the cigar, ensuring it was evenly lit. Content, he gave an almost imperceptible nod and the servants retreated silently into the shade.

'I still can't quite believe it,' he said, shaking his head. 'Digby of all people. I never thought he had the balls.'

I took a sip of whisky.

'What happens now?'

'That's hard to say.'

'You're going to sweep the whole thing under the carpet?'

He took a puff of his cigar. The tip glowed red. 'What would you suggest? That we go and arrest the Lieutenant-Governor?'

'The last time I checked, murder, conspiracy and attempting to pervert the course of justice were all serious offences.'

Taggart shook his head.

'What do you think our role out here is, Sam?'

No one had ever asked me that before, probably because I was a copper, and a copper's job was pretty much universally acknowledged to be making sure the bad guys didn't get away. Surely even in India, that went without saying?

'To dispense justice?'

Taggart laughed. 'Justice is a matter for the courts, Sam, and is best left to better men than you or me. Our job is to maintain law and order within His Majesty's province of Bengal. We are here to keep the status quo. That can hardly be done if we try to arrest the man who's been put in charge of the place.'

'So it was all for nothing?'

'On the contrary, my boy. We might not be able to bring charges, but your work has given us something much more valuable. It's given us *leverage*. I doubt the L-G will be quite so keen to stick his nose in police matters in future. And he might also be a little more open to acting on our advice. Take your man Sen, for instance. The L-G has, upon my guidance, seen fit to commute his death sentence to one of deportation and incarceration on the Andaman Islands. The L-G will portray it as a gesture of British magnanimity, which, in the light of that unfortunate business in Amritsar, might help to win back some native hearts and minds. In a few years' time, once all the fuss has died down, we'll quietly bring him back to India. We can use a man like him.'

It was my turn to laugh. 'He'll never work for us.'

Taggart was unmoved. 'He doesn't have to. If he really has converted to the path of non-violence, the best thing for us is to have him back here as soon as possible, converting more of his followers to the peaceful path. After all, what would you rather have to deal with: an armed revolution or a bunch of conscientious objectors? No, this *non-violence* nonsense is the most positive thing that's happened in years.'

'So Sen will still be guilty of MacAuley's murder?'

Taggart nodded. 'I think that's a fair exchange for his life.'

'And Digby?'

'A posthumous promotion. For his sterling work on this case. It's just a shame his informant turned on him like that.'

He'd have liked that, I thought. And in a perverse way, he deserved it. If he hadn't killed MacAuley, the Darjeeling Mail would have been packed with cash the night it was attacked and the chances were we'd be looking at a full-blown terrorist campaign right now. That we weren't was as much down to Digby as it was to anything I or Section H had done subsequently. That reminded me . . .

'I have to go to see Dawson at Fort William.'

Taggart smiled. 'I hear the two of you have started playing nicely with each other.'

'I wouldn't go that far,' I said. 'I doubt he'll be sending me a Christmas card any time soon.'

The situation between us had stabilised into a wary stand-off. I knew about his involvement in the MacAuley cover-up and I guessed he knew about my little issue with the O. We both had dirt on each other, but preferred, for the time being at least, to keep our powder dry. Besides, I'd done him a favour by calling him that morning and telling him my hunch. That would hopefully make him less inclined to try to have me killed. But as with all secret policemen, you could never be totally sure.

Taggart took a puff of his cigar and looked out across the lawn. In the distance, a sentry patrolled the perimeter.

'And you, Sam? Have you decided whether to stay on with us?'

I drained my glass. The Scotch had a sharp edge to it. I swallowed it down like medicine.

'I need some time to think.'

Unbidden, the manservant came up and refreshed my glass.

Taggart smiled. 'Take all the time you need, my boy.'

375

Dawson met me outside the church at the centre of Fort William. It was an odd choice of location. I assumed I was now *persona non grata* up in Room 207. There were probably secrets up there he didn't want me to see. Or maybe he just didn't want me chatting up Miss Braithwaite.

'Have you got anything out of him yet?'

Dawson puffed on his pipe. 'Not yet. But it's only a matter of time. So far, though, he's been doing a pretty good impression of a Trappist monk.'

'I don't suppose there's much he can say.'

'Not really. Not when we caught him outside a godown full of arms and explosives with a hundred and fifty thousand rupees in his suitcase. Enough money to keep him in Guinness for a while.'

'Did you catch anyone else?' I asked.

Dawson shook his head. 'We followed him to the godown in Howrah where he met two natives. We tried to tail them but they got wind of us and ran for it. They were both shot trying to escape.'

'That's a shame,' I said. 'Taking them alive might have provided some useful information.' It might also have provided Section H with a new pawn to replace Sen, but I kept that particular thought to myself.

'We got the money and the weapons,' said Dawson. 'That's all that matters.'

'How many weapons?'

'Three crate loads: small arms, rifles and explosives. Enough to start quite a nasty little war.'

We walked down a path towards the garrison's cemetery.

'Can I see the prisoner?' I asked.

'I'm afraid that's outside your jurisdiction, Captain.'

'Your men haven't been over-zealous in their questioning, I hope.'

Dawson smiled. 'Not at all, Captain. This is India. We have certain rules that we maintain steadfastly out here. One is that we never strenuously interrogate a white man, even an Irishman. That would send an unacceptable message to our native soldiers. I admit, though, it does make things a bit complicated in this case.'

So they hadn't beaten him up, and they'd not managed to get anything useful out of him in over two days. I guessed Section H's interrogation techniques centred more on brute force than astute questioning. Take away their knuckledusters and they were left floundering.

'He might talk to me.'

Dawson puffed on his pipe and considered it.

'Very well. I suppose we might make an exception. Just this once.'

The cell block still smelled of disinfectant. I followed the sepoy down a long corridor to a cell at the far end.

'Hello, Byrne,' I said, as the sepoy unlocked the cell door.

'Captain Wyndham!' he said, startled. 'By God am I glad to see you! Maybe you can explain to these gentlemen that they've got the wrong man and get me the hell out of here.' His knuckles were white as he gripped the bars of the cell door.

I had to hand it to him, he played the innocent textile salesman pretty well. Even so, he must have known the game was up.

'Are they treating you well?'

'Not in the slightest. Sure, I've been locked up here for forty-eight hours without any explanation and no access to a lawyer.'

'You're lucky you're not Indian,' I said.

'Can you get me outta here?'

'It's going to be difficult. They tell me you had a hundred and fifty thousand rupees in cash on you when they arrested you. Did you rob a bank?'

He smiled anxiously. 'Ah, not at all, Captain. You know I was working on a large sales contract. The cash was just the payment on it.'

'A hundred and fifty thousand rupees for a textile deal? What did you do, Byrne? Sell them the Shroud of Turin?'

He was pleading now. 'I'm tellin' the truth. I swear.'

Except of course, he wasn't.

'It was me who put them on to you,' I said.

He looked genuinely confused.

'You? Why the devil would ye do that?'

It was a fair question. One I'd asked myself a few times.

'Because textiles isn't your real business. In fact, I doubt *Byrne* is even your real name.'

There was a slight stiffening of the muscles of his jaw. It was enough.

'That night when I met you on the stairs. We were talking about Sen. You said he resembled Leon Trotsky. How did you know what he looked like?'

'I . . . I must have seen his picture in the papers,' he stammered.

'I don't think you did. Our police files didn't even have a picture of him, not so much as a sketch, but you knew what he looked like. I'm guessing your friends in Ireland are supplying weapons to their fellow revolutionaries here in India and you're their man on the ground. You've probably met a whole host of Indian revolutionaries. I think you must have met Sen at some point, maybe even over the last year when you were in Assam and he was hiding out in East Bengal.'

'That's all nonsense, Captain.'

Maybe it was. Maybe he really had only seen a picture of Sen in a paper, but that didn't explain what he was doing next to a warehouse full of weapons with a hundred and fifty grand in his luggage.

'Let me give you some advice, Byrne,' I said. 'Confess quickly. Do it here. Do it before they send you back to Britain. It'll be less painful for you.'

I turned to go.

'Wyndham,' he called from behind me. 'There's a storm comin'. Both in India and in Ireland, and when it breaks, there's going to be a reckoning. Men of good conscience are going to have to stand up and be counted. You'll have to choose which side you're on.'

I should have told him to save his breath. After all I'd been through, my conscience was anything but good. And as for what side I was on, well Taggart had already told me: I was on the side of the status quo. I guessed I could live with that as long as the alternatives were bloodier.

I called for the guard to let me out and walked back down the corridor to the sound of cell doors being locked behind me.

———

I moved out of the guest house the next day. It seemed to be for the best. Mrs Tebbit's attitude towards me had cooled somewhat after I'd returned bruised and bloody the night Digby had had his head ventilated. It wasn't really my appearance she objected to, rather it was my insistence that she provide a room for Surrender-not. She'd protested quite vociferously, appealing to my common sense. Of course, she personally had no problem with a *darkie* under her roof, but what would her other guests make of it? No, it just wasn't possible. She'd only relented when I pointed out that the sergeant had a first-class law degree from Cambridge, and even then she couldn't help a parting shot.

379

'That's the problem with these natives,' she muttered as she stalked off, 'too smart for their own good.'

My trunk stood packed and upright in the downstairs hall. It contained pretty much all my worldly possessions. I'd requisitioned Salman the rickshaw *wallah* and a few of his comrades to transport it the short distance to my new lodgings in Premchand Boral Street. They were nothing fancy. The landlords of the fancier places tended to object to my choice of flatmate.

Surrender-not was at first mortified by the idea of sharing accommodation with a *sahib* senior officer, but I was quite insistent. I told him it would be good for his career and he eventually relented. I had my reasons. I felt partly responsible for his parents kicking him out. It was, after all, my fault he hadn't resigned his position. The truth, though, was that he'd saved my life twice in the space of a week, and only a fool parts with such a lucky rabbit's foot.

———

A week later I was in conversation with Surrender-not over a bottle of some local firewater. It turned out that our lodgings were cheap because they were situated above one brothel and beside another. It wasn't a problem for either of us, and I think Surrender-not secretly enjoyed it. I'd caught him staring wistfully at one particular girl who worked in the place next door. Not that he was the type to do anything other than stare. Even talking to her was beyond him. I was in the process of questioning him about it, employing the twin strategies of pulling rank and getting him hopelessly drunk.

'Come on, Surrender-not,' I said, 'faint heart never won fair lady.'

'I don't need to worry about that, sir,' he replied, shaking his head in that curious Indian manner. 'When it comes to my marriage, you can rest assured that my mother will be anything but faint of heart.

And she'll make sure it's a fair lady. It would be a social disgrace for her to have a daughter in law with dark skin.'

'So you're not even going to talk to the girl?'

'As I have explained to you several times already, sir, I find it difficult to converse with the opposite sex. It is not a problem, though. As an Indian, I never really have to talk to a woman until I am married to her. It's just one of the many ways in which my culture is superior to yours . . . sir.'

Maybe he had a point. The Indian way probably saved a lot of time and effort, not to mention heartache.

'But surely you must have been in love with a woman?' I teased, alcohol getting the better of my discretion. 'Or some nice girl's fallen in love with you?'

The young man blushed and shook his head.

'Why not?' I asked. 'A good-looking lad such as yourself, I'd have expected you to be fighting off the ladies.'

'That's not really how it works in our culture.'

'What about when you were down at Oxford?'

'Cambridge.'

'Cambridge, then. Same thing. Surely there must have been some warm-bosomed suffragette who took you to her bed? I believe taking an Indian lover is all the rage among certain classes of politically active women. It burnishes their socialist credentials, apparently.'

'I'm afraid,' he lamented, 'I've never had the pleasure of burnishing any woman's credentials, socialist or otherwise.'

There was a knock at the door.

I looked at Surrender-not. 'You expecting anyone?'

'I don't think so.'

From the hall came the sound of Sandesh opening the front door. MacAulay's old manservant was now in my employ. It seemed a good fit. He needed a job and I needed someone to iron my uniform, and so far, things were working out well.

I heard a woman's voice. The door opened and Annie walked in. I hadn't seen her since I'd left her place the morning after I'd been attacked. She looked as beautiful as she did the night we'd had dinner at the Great Eastern.

Surrender-not rose unsteadily to his feet, grinning like a chimp.

'I'm going out for a walk,' he said. 'I think the air will do me good.'

I nodded and he left at a pace that suggested his shoes might be on fire. I picked up the bottle and gestured to Annie to join me for a drink.

'What is it?' she asked.

'Buggered if I know. Some local gut-rot that Surrender-not picked up from the liquor *wallah*. It's my fault really. I should have gone myself. The boy knows precious little about alcohol.'

'And you're teaching him?'

'Something like that.'

I poured her a glass. She picked it up, knocked it back and set the tumbler down on the table. I was impressed. The stuff tasted like petrol. It had brought tears to my eyes when I first drank it and poor Surrender-not had fallen off his chair. I poured her another.

'I haven't heard from you in over a week,' she said.

That much was true. I'd been avoiding her since the night of Digby's death.

'I've been busy.'

'So I see, Sam. Nice little place you have here.'

'Yes,' I said, 'I decided to go with just the one servant. You might remember him. By the way, how did you get the address?'

'Your friend, Sergeant Banerjee,' she replied. 'I came to Lal Bazar looking for you. They told me you were on leave but that the sergeant could get a message to you. I asked him where you were staying and he was most obliging. He didn't mention he'd moved in too.'

'I like to keep my friends close.'

She took a couple of cigarettes from a silver case in her bag and offered me one. I took it and lit us both. She took a drag and exhaled.

'Do you want to tell me what I've done wrong, Sam?'

I looked into her eyes. Even now it was difficult not to be besotted by her.

I picked up my drink and walked out onto the balcony. It was easier to talk with my back to her.

'You should have told me,' I said.

'About what?'

'About Buchan.'

I expected her to lie, but she was above that sort of thing. Instead, she came and stood beside me.

'How did you find out?'

'He knew too much about the investigation. He knew I thought Sen was innocent. Someone was passing him information. At first I suspected Digby, but it wasn't him. It was you.'

She said nothing.

'The night I was attacked. It was him you were out with, wasn't it?'

'MacAuley was his friend,' she said. 'He asked me to keep him informed of your progress. I don't regret it.'

'And what did he promise you in return? Surely you didn't think he'd take you as his wife? Or were you content just being his mistress?'

She slapped me.

'He offered me money,' she shot back. 'He offered me security. That's something no one else has. Maybe you haven't noticed, Sam, but Calcutta isn't exactly a bed of roses for half-castes.

My cheek stung.

'How much money?'

'Enough to leave this place and make a fresh start.'

'And that was enough to betray me?'

She shook her head. 'I didn't betray you.'

'Did you sleep with him?'

'That's none of your business.'

I guessed she was right about that.

'Where would you go?'

She looked flustered. 'I haven't decided. I thought Bombay. Or maybe even London.'

'Not London,' I said. 'Trust me, you wouldn't like it. And as for Bombay, I've never been, but I doubt it's a patch on Calcutta. All human life is here, you know.'

She smiled, despite herself. 'Calcutta's always an option.'

'You should consider it most carefully, Miss Grant,' I said. 'You should stay here tonight and consider it. I could help you.'

She looked at me and thought about it for a moment, then lifted her hand to my reddened cheek.

'No, Sam,' she said, 'I don't think so.'

ACKNOWLEDGEMENTS

This book would never have seen the light of day without the support and encouragement of a great many people, first and foremost, Alison Hennessey, Sam Copeland, Bethan Jones, Jon Stock, and Richard Reynolds, the judges of the Telegraph Harvill Secker Crime Writing Competition. In particular, my thanks go out to Alison, who became my editor, for her expertise and guidance, and her patience in taking an accountant and turning him into a writer; to Sam my agent for his tireless encouragement, constant reassurance and good humor; and to Jon for his advice and insight into the daily travails of being an author.

Thanks also to my US publishers, Pegasus Books, especially Maia Larson and Claiborne Hancock.

I'm grateful too to my sister, Elora and to Sherrie Steyn for their good sense, keen eyes and wise words; to Alan Simon, the finest mentor and English teacher one could wish for; to Amit Roy for his comments, advice and insight into all matters Bengali and his ongoing support for the future adventures of Sam and Surrender-not; to Darren Sharma, for knowing everything about everything; to Alok, Hash and Neeraj, my partners at Houghton Street Capital for their understanding and patience; and to the good people at the Glenfarclas Distillery for their fine bottlings, especially the 25 year old, which proved invaluable to the creative process.

A special thank you to Baba and Ma for their faith and constant love; and to Bapu and Ma for letting me marry their daughter.

The biggest thank you, of course, goes to my wife, Sonal, for her patience, her unwavering support and her love, for which I give thanks every day.